THE SECOND MOTHER

TERESA DI BIASE

BLUE FORGE PRESS
Port Orchard ✸ Washington

Blue Forge Press is the print division of the volunteer-run, federal 501(c)3 nonprofit, Blue Legacy (EIN 83-4307421), founded in 1989 and dedicated to supporting artisans marginalized due to race, age, disability, economics or other factors. We strive to empower storytellers from all walks of life with our four divisions: Blue Forge Press, Blue Forge Films, Blue Forge Gaming, and Blue Forge Sound. Find out more at www.BlueForgeGroup.org

Blue Forge Press
7419 Ebbert Drive Southeast
Port Orchard, Washington 98367
blueforgepress@gmail.com
360-550-2071 ph.txt

For my husband

&

*In memory of
David Nakagawa*

Courtesy of the Archives of the Episcopal Church

THE
SECOND
MOTHER

TERESA DI BIASE

PART 1: 1910–1917
California

CHAPTER 1

October 1915, Berkeley, California

Take a snap of Hallie and me." Impulsively, Margaret Peppers led the four-year-old child onto the wooden steps of the front porch of Deaconess House and sat, pulling Hallie down beside her. The customary morning fog had burned off early, and the day promised to be perfect for their outing across the bay. There was no answering warmth from Martina, who reluctantly positioned herself to take a picture, her thin lips tightening into their trademark frown. Checking a sigh, Margaret composed a benign expression. When they first met last spring she'd hoped in vain that her sister-in-law would be different from the rest of the family. *Of all Hal's siblings, she should understand what it's like to be an outsider*, Margaret thought. How wrong she'd been.

"Smile, dear," Martina said, directing a smile of her own to the little girl. Involuntarily, Margaret lowered her eyes, like an unworthy servant.

Released from immobility by the camera's click, Ruth Hal—Hallie for short—jumped up and immediately began pulling on her mother's arm. "Come on," she demanded, hopping up and down in excitement like a ragtime dancer. Margaret willingly complied, content to be led away from her sister-in-law.

Years later, when Margaret looked at this picture, it was like witnessing a secret understanding between Hallie and her aunt. Was that the day, Margaret wondered, that she had begun to lose her daughter?

CHAPTER 2

L et's go, Hallie!" Margaret smiled. She was as eager as her daughter to start their adventure. Taking Hallie to the Panama Pacific Exposition had been a last-minute decision on Margaret's part, inspired by her own visit a few days before with classmates from St. Margaret's Deaconess Training Program. Then, the women had visited only the most edifying exhibits, depicting advances in science, technology, and social services. Of course, the exhibit sponsored by their own denomination, the Protestant Episcopal Church, had been a must. But there had been little time or encouragement to visit the so-called "Joy Zone," with its carnival attractions. That would be Hallie's and Margaret's destination today.

Best of all, Margaret would have Hallie all to herself. Even Martina acknowledged that a mother had the right to spend time alone with a daughter she saw only on weekends.

On the boat to San Francisco Hallie chattered and giggled as the wind ruffled her hair and dress. "We're taking a ferry to the fair!" Margaret exclaimed gaily, catching her daughter's excitement. "A ferry to the fair!" Hallie chanted in response, hopping from one foot to the other. An elderly couple smiled at them and Hallie, forgetting her usual shyness, beamed back.

Like tributaries of a mighty river, Margaret and Hallie were swept into the surge of fairgoers headed toward the amusement zone. Stretching for seven city blocks, the Zone teemed with enticements. To the left of the entrance was the Italianate Ghirardelli Chocolate pavilion. Margaret was glad that Hallie didn't yet read, or else she would want to go there immediately. "Let's go find Toyland," Margaret proposed, naming the attraction she had seen advertised as one sure to delight children of all ages.

Mother and daughter began to make their way down the avenue. Overhead a canopy of red ribbons fluttered in the breeze. A cacophony of voices, music, and mechanical contraptions swirled around them. They had only gone a block when Margaret spied an enormous building called "Creation." At its entrance was a huge plaster statue of a woman, at least three stories high, flanked by a pair of sculpted peacocks. Margaret had overheard someone at Deaconess House enthusiastically describe the attraction as displaying the seven days of creation in a series of scenic tableaus. With a twinge of regret, she decided to stick to attractions more in keeping with a four-year-old's tastes.

As they walked toward the giant toy soldiers flanking the entrance to the nursery rhyme attraction, Margaret's attention was diverted by a sign pointing to various "foreign villages" on display. Squeezing Hallie's hand, Margaret decided that a quick stop at one of them wouldn't hurt. *Who knows, God may call us to the mission field*, she thought.

"Come see Rosie, the Belle of the Igorots!" trumpeted a mustachioed man handing out leaflets as they neared the first village. The slightly crinkled pamphlet he thrust into Margaret's hand claimed that the Igorot women of the northern Philippines were attractive, unlike most "savages." In contrast to the "charming ways" of Rosie and her sisters, the publicity claimed that the Igorot men were fierce warriors, earning prestige by the number of heads taken in battle. While Margaret pondered if this was a suitable attraction for a child, Hallie noticed one of the tattooed Igorot men, bending over an anvil and hammering on what appeared to be an iron spearhead. "What's that funny man doing, Mommy?" Margaret let herself be dragged along and soon was watching, fascinated, while her mind flashed on the blacksmith's shop where she grew up. *I wonder if he'll use that spearhead in a battle,* she thought, before reminding herself that the Joy Zone was more carnival than real life. *Maybe he'll kill a wild animal with it, instead.*

She nudged her daughter toward three women demonstrating traditional textile arts, one pounding banana leaves into fiber, another using a spinning wheel, the third weaving with a back-strap loom. It seemed primitive to Margaret, who'd grown up buying machine-produced fabric from the general store.

A brass band playing a Sousa march paraded down the street, breaking Margaret out of her too-serious analysis of the exhibits. Toyland awaited.

By the time they arrived at the final Toyland attraction, "Captain, the Educated Horse," Margaret was glad to be able to sit for the thirty-minute show. She held Hallie on her lap as the audience marveled at the arithmetic feats of the beautiful Arabian stallion.

"Captain, count the number of ladies in the first row," commanded the trainer. At once the horse seemed to scan the length of the row and then by pawing, told the number. To the amazement of the audience, this performance was repeated several times. Then someone brought a standard containing numbers, seemingly in random order, each having an attached leather tag. When the trainer asked Captain to pull off a given numeral, the horse did as instructed for as many numerals as were requested. The finale brought down the house. By tapping a series of levers attached to chimes, Captain contrived to play the hymn, "Nearer, My God, To Thee."

During the performance, one side of Margaret's head had begun to throb, and before long there was an answering chorus on the other side. She knew she had to leave soon. Migraines—it was her own particular cross, the one she'd carried ever since adolescence.

"Come on, dear," Margaret said, dragging her protesting daughter away from Captain's tent. "Mommy isn't feeling well."

Now shivering with cold, Margaret looked for a place to rest and spied the entrance to the nearby Japanese Village. Under the peaceful gaze of an enormous golden Buddha which sat atop the trio of gates, Margaret staggered to a nearby bench and closed her eyes, willing the pounding to end.

"Mommy, are you all right?" Hallie asked in a frightened voice. She had seen her mother in pain before, but always there had been someone to lead her away from the suffering and reassure her. When no response came, Hallie sprang up and ran toward the main avenue of the Zone which they had just crossed, hoping to find help.

A moment later, Margaret opened her eyes and attempted a consoling smile for her daughter, but it was too late. Hallie was gone.

Margaret's heart constricted. She struggled to her feet, ignoring the wave of nausea that swept over her. Glancing around, she saw the artificial streets of Tokyo and Kyoto, a tea house, and several curio shops. Which way would Hallie go? Another Sousa marching band—or was it the same one as before?—seemed to be approaching, the rat-a-tat-tat of its drums mocking Margaret's panic with fierce jabs at her temples.

Margaret's stricken appearance attracted the attention of a pair of passersby, two women in their fifties, laden with purchases. One woman was tall, thin and angular. A straw hat bearing a purple, gold, and white ribbon perched on her coif of iron-gray hair. The other woman, a bit shorter and plumper, wore an identical hat at a more rakish angle, and her hair was a bit browner and frizzier than her companion's. Each woman sported a gold and purple button which proclaimed, "I'm a Voter."

The taller one spoke. "Miss, is there anything wrong?"

"My little girl is gone!" was all Margaret could manage to say. The Sousa march had given way to George M. Cohan's "You're a Grand Old Flag" but to Margaret's hypersensitive ears, it sounded like a train was about to run her over.

"Myrtle, go and find a guard while I sit with this poor woman. Now!" the tall woman commanded.

Myrtle hastened away as Margaret collapsed back onto the bench. *God please help. God please help.* Her panicked prayers matched the drum beating mercilessly in her head. With every second, it seemed that Hallie was being carried further away, like the vanishing musical notes. Just when Margaret thought she could not bear another instant, Hallie suddenly appeared, running, with a policeman puffing behind her. "Mommy!" she screamed.

Somehow Margaret managed to stand and take a few steps toward her daughter. Hallie ran to her arms as Margaret burst into tears of relief and joy.

"Ma'am, your little girl told me you were ill. How can I help?" the policeman asked.

"It's just a migraine. I haven't had one for a long time. I'll be all right if I can rest somewhere quiet and dark." The words came out jerkily, like she was speaking a foreign language.

The nearby restroom facility wasn't ideal, but at least the women's section had a cot where Margaret could rest. The policeman, who had brought a wheelchair just in case, helped Margaret into it and they headed off, accompanied by the tall woman and Hallie. Myrtle had failed to appear, but her companion didn't seem worried. En route to the restroom, she described the missing woman to the officer and dispatched him to find her.

Blessedly, the migraine began to ease almost as soon as Margaret lay down and closed her eyes. The tall woman had produced a piece of paper from her handbag and entertained Hallie by drawing pictures of animals. Slipping in and out of consciousness, Margaret could hear her daughter giggle softly.

After about twenty minutes Margaret sat up. She felt exhausted but knew they had to return home somehow. "We need to leave now, Hallie." Her voice sounded weak to her ears.

"Nonsense!" proclaimed the tall woman. "You are in no condition to go anywhere on your own. Is your husband home?"

"I'm a widow. I live with other women who are training for church work."

"Where is that?"

"Berkeley. Once we get across the Bay I can take a cab to

my sister-in-law's."

Meanwhile, Myrtle had returned with yet another guard. After a quick conference the tall woman announced the decision. "My sister and I want to take you to our home in San Francisco to spend the night. Your little girl will come too, of course."

"Oh, I couldn't inconvenience you."

"Never mind that. Does the home where you live have a telephone? If you give me the telephone number, I will make the call. Is there anyone else we should notify?"

"Yes, my sister-in-law, Mrs. Jury. She just got a phone. Hallie lives... with her." Too weak to protest or explain further, Margaret gave out the numbers, then lay down again while the tall woman went to accomplish the deed.

"Julia and I will see that you are cared for," spoke Myrtle softly. "I know what it is to have sick headaches." Whether it was from shyness, a customary deference to her resolute sister, or consideration for a fellow sufferer, Myrtle fell silent again.

Hallie, who lay curled up against her mother, had already fallen asleep. Margaret was on the brink of joining her when Julia returned. "George will meet us at the Van Ness entrance. Let's see if we can catch one of those auto trains to take us there."

When the tram let them out Margaret was surprised to see that George, who stood ready to help her into the Dodge touring car, was a chauffeur, not a family member. He also was Japanese. Until then the only Japanese she had encountered were gardeners or truck farmers excepting, of course, the "residents" of the Japanese village at today's fair. Another surprise was George's youth—he looked to be the same age as Margaret, who was just twenty-one. Though she had never met a chauffeur in her life, she had always imagined a middle-aged and dignified man, resembling her idea of an English butler. As they rode to the sisters' home, she began to wonder if he lived on the premises or in San Francisco's Japantown.

They reached the new residential neighborhood of Forest Hill by climbing a series of curved roads, lined by pines, cypress, and eucalyptus, that snaked up the hillside, finally arriving at a two-story, half-timbered house with a sweeping set of stairs leading to the front door. While the women and Hallie ascended the stairs, George put the car in the garage.

The house was bigger than it first appeared; only the living room faced the street, with the remaining rooms extending behind it. A trellis framed the large, multi-paned front window, over which a rose bush was beginning to climb. The balcony was octagonal in shape, its wooden sides pierced by a series of Gothic quatrefoils. Margaret imagined that the view from the balcony must be splendid, taking in both the city and the surrounding bay.

The living room was more rustic than she expected, with a high-peaked ceiling braced with heavy beams and lined with rough-sawn boards laid diagonally. The walls and ceiling were redwood, and at one end of the room was a tall concrete fireplace, its chimney exposed all the way to the second story ceiling. In front of the fire were two leather Morris chairs and a Navajo rug. A grand piano was positioned at the other end of the room. Around the room were bookcases and cabinets, their shelves displaying a variety of baskets, pottery, and curiously carved wooden religious figures.

"Let me take you to our guest room," Myrtle said to the weary mother and daughter, as she led them through the dining room and past a set of stairs. Margaret's eyes eagerly took in the pair of beds that promised real sleep at last. Myrtle opened a bureau drawer and took out a white cotton nightgown. "I'm sorry, but we don't have a little girl's nightie," she apologized. "Perhaps she can sleep in one of my shirtwaists. I'll go fetch it."

After cleaning up and praying, mother and daughter collapsed into bed. Margaret's dreams were populated by midgets and pagodas and a flock of peacocks that relentlessly pursued her down the labyrinthine streets of the Zone.

CHAPTER 3

Margaret woke before Hallie, and for a moment was bewildered by her surroundings until she remembered what had happened the day before. The spacious light-filled bedroom was so different from the cramped dormitory of St. Margaret's House, where the deaconesses lived and trained. As she moved her eyes around the room she took in the Japanese prints on the walls and the colorful woven textile on the dresser. Margaret remembered the unusual figurines and other crafts she had seen last evening in the sisters' living room and wondered if they had come from Gumps' department store or had been acquired as souvenirs abroad.

She bent over to kiss her daughter. Hallie woke up immediately and smiled at her mother. Feeling worn out after her migraine, Margaret would have liked just to lie there snuggling, but when she saw that it was after nine o'clock, she knew they needed to get up and go back to Berkeley. As it turned out, the ever-resourceful Julia had eased the way. Over breakfast Margaret learned that Julia had made the call to Deaconess House, explaining that Margaret had felt unwell without providing any details.

"Thank you for taking us in," Margaret said, as she buttered her piece of toast.

"No bother at all," Julia responded, looking fondly at Hallie as she uttered the words. "You were clearly in need of help and we were only too happy to be of service."

"Mommy, can we stay and play here?" pleaded Hallie, responding to the women's friendliness.

"No, dear, Mommy has to go back to school, and you need to go home to Aunt Martina," Margaret replied, her sense of duty overcoming the desire she felt to stay and become more acquainted with the sisters and their inviting, intriguing home. Regretfully, mother and daughter said their goodbyes, but not before Julia and Myrtle had invited them to return for lunch in a few weeks. "You can play with the dolly I had as a little girl," Myrtle told Hallie.

It had been arranged that George would take them to the Ferry Building downtown. Margaret paused at the front door, thanking the women once more. "I'm afraid I don't know your last names," she admitted.

"I am Miss Judson and Myrtle is Mrs. Connelly. Myrtle's husband died of malaria during the building of the Panama Canal," Julia stated matter-of-factly. Margaret had the impression that she was used to explaining this to others on her sister's behalf.

"I'm so sorry," Margaret murmured. At that moment George appeared with the car. He helped Margaret and Hallie into the back of the auto and took his position in the front seat. Last night in her exhaustion, Margaret had paid little attention to her driver apart from his age and ethnicity. But today, lacking the company of Julia and Myrtle, she didn't know whether to make conversation with George and couldn't remember what the sisters had done.

"Your employers are lovely people," Margaret finally murmured. It seemed rude not to say anything at all. "Yes, they are," George responded. "They are helping me through medical school."

Margaret was astonished. Not only did the man speak English like a native, but he seemed hardly old enough to be out of high school. Though some people would be surprised to learn that at her age, she was already a widow with a young child and training to be a deaconess.

"I didn't even know there was a medical school here," Margaret admitted. "I'm fairly new to the area."

"The University's medical branch is only two miles away, near Golden Gate Park," George remarked. "I board with Miss Judson and Mrs. Connelly during the school year."

"Where is your home?" Margaret asked.

"My family are farmers in the Santa Clara Valley. They came from Japan, but my sister and I were born in the U.S. Fortunately, my parents didn't insist their children become farmers. They were glad when I graduated from college, and now my sister is a student at the University of the Pacific."

Margaret thought of her brother-in-law, Charles, who was a physician in Los Angeles. He was a bit of a braggart and always seemed focused on getting ahead. In contrast, George's manner, even when he was acknowledging his own educational accomplishments, had none of the boastfulness she had observed in Charles. There was more pride in his voice when he mentioned his sister than when he was speaking about himself.

Their arrival at the Ferry Building put an end to further conversation. Margaret and Hallie alighted from the vehicle, bidding goodbye to George. Margaret hoped the sisters would act on their promise to invite them for a return visit. The last few years of her life had seemed but a succession of doors slamming shut. Now, at last, they were beginning to open, and she wanted to walk through every one of them—just because she could.

CHAPTER 4

I've arranged for you to be admitted to the County Hospital, Hal," Charles said, in his practiced family doctor voice. Margaret could imagine him rehearsing his delivery before a mirror, the better to inspire confidence in his patients—and in himself. He was a newly minted professional in a town which, if not exactly young chronologically, was making the awkward transition of adolescence as it changed from a sleepy Mexican village into a modern American city. Like a teenager himself, Charles Henderson Peppers seemed to alternate between personae. He wanted to project an image of the wise, experienced physician, while at heart he was a brash young entrepreneur. Thirty-six years old, his medical degree earned the previous year in Nebraska, he would do well in Los Angeles

"Technically, you need to be resident for a year to be admitted," Hal's brother continued. "But your landlady is a patient of mine and in exchange for my services, she's giving you a letter testifying that you've been her tenant since September 1912." Any qualms of conscience Margaret felt at this falsehood were obliterated by the sound of Hal's wracking cough.

Margaret trained her eyes on Charles, deliberately avoiding looking at her stricken husband. Hal did not want to be pitied, especially by his brother, and Margaret had learned it was better not to call attention to her concern but simply to do the next thing necessary for his recovery and peace of mind. It was a role she had assumed with her father, too, and it had made her older than her years. Most were surprised to learn that she was only nineteen.

Last month they had boarded the Chicago, Quincy, and Burlington train in Ottumwa, Iowa, bound for southern California, the destination of thousands of health-seekers like themselves. Margaret had never left her home state, much less ridden a train across the country. Once she would have been thrilled to embark on such a journey, but encumbered with a toddler and a tubercular husband, she dreaded the time ahead.

The first leg of the trip, twenty-one hours to Denver, was agony. It was impossible to disguise Hal's condition, and Margaret had to shut her ears to the angry mutterings of other passengers, who demanded to be seated as far away from the contagious consumptive as possible. Fortunately, a quartet of nuns had boarded the train in Ottumwa at the same time and gladly traded seats with the fearful passengers—an act of mercy if she ever saw one. They not only watched Hallie but took turns "spelling" Margaret in tending to her husband's needs. Although at home his cough could be alleviated with sips of cold water and slippery elm lozenges, the smoke from the engine, which invaded their railroad car through windows passengers had opened as it grew warmer, defeated any attempts to silence Hal's hacking. At least it was a dry cough, and Hal had little need to resort to the lard tin Margaret had brought along to catch his sputum.

At Denver she bid a grateful farewell to the nuns, and new help appeared in the form of Charles, who was at the station to accompany the Peppers party to Los Angeles. Charles made a show of displaying his doctor's bag to dispel any passenger alarm and silence the inevitable grumbling. For the rest of the trip Margaret attended to Hallie as both a distraction and a gift. Having passed a better night in Denver, Margaret was able to appreciate the scenic wonders of the Garden of the Gods, the Royal Gorge, and the Rocky Mountains. They reached Tennessee Pass at sunset and in the fading light Margaret saw what she believed was a sign of God's blessing on their enterprise: the

Mountain of the Holy Cross. High against the brow of the 14,000-foot peak a snowy cross was clearly evident, formed by two intersecting canyons. She overheard one passenger read to another from a railroad guidebook describing the sight: *"From Tennessee Pass can be seen this snow-white banner of the Christian faith. The symbol is perfect, and while gazing with wonder and awe upon this 'sign set in the heavens,' the traveler realizes that he has now reached the height 'around whose summit splendid visions rise,' as he beholds that snow white cross shining high above all the turbulence and din of earthly strife."* Margaret prayed fervently not to lose sight of this grace in the difficult days ahead.

CHAPTER 5

October 1915, Berkeley

Today many women long to be in some recognized ministry of the Church. They serve gladly and constantly, but they long for more. I doubt not that among you young women here more than one has envied her brother, that to him the Church has opened a ministry. She has thought that for her there is no ministry to fulfill her longing. But I stand before you today to assure you, there is!"

Margaret found herself leaning forward, her breath suspended, as she listened to Reverend Parsons exhort her class. Forgotten were the past weekend's excursion to the Fair, the sisters who came to her aid, even her daughter. Margaret knew that the clergyman was addressing *her*. Clearly God had been calling her, otherwise why else would she find herself here, a thousand miles from her birthplace and even farther from the circumstances in which she lived but a few years ago?

The tall, distinguished-looking clergyman continued his address. "This training school began a decade ago when one woman approached me about receiving preparation for this calling. Within a year she was joined by a few more women, and it became evident that more was needed than an informal set of classes held in our parish church. Through God's providence we now have a full-fledged school, with a curriculum, faculty, and facility.

"The interesting fact about the school is that its growth has been perfectly natural—indeed, we have been pushed forward in ways we did not intend. With each passing year the Church calls more loudly for service from her daughters. The slums call. The country districts call. From the mission field the cry is loud. In China, Japan, Alaska, the Philippines, everywhere women are wanted for the work of the ministry. Who will respond?"

Listening to Reverend Parsons speak, Margaret had no doubts about the rightness of the choices she'd made that had brought her to this place. Until a year ago, it seemed that so much of her life had just happened. At last, she was living a real life, one of her own choosing; all the events of her past had been but preparation. *And motherhood?* asked a small voice in her head. *Was that just "preparation," too? Wasn't that "real life"?* Margaret sighed. Not even this consecrated classroom offered refuge from the questions that always lurked around the edges of her mind, waiting to pounce and destroy her fragile confidence.

Suddenly she was aware that Reverend Parsons had stopped talking, and her fellow students were gathering up their things to go to lunch. Margaret shook her head imperceptibly, as if flicking the questions away like water off a dog's back. Then she rose and joined the procession out of the room.

CHAPTER 6

November 1915

When Margaret saw the envelope bearing a San Francisco postmark, she smiled, certain it must be the invitation she'd hoped for.

> *Dear Mrs. Peppers:*
>
> *We should be very pleased if you and your daughter would lunch with us on Saturday next, the thirteenth. George informs us that the ferry from Oakland arrives at noon, and he will meet you at the terminal at that time. You do remember that ours is a Dodge touring car?*
>
> *Please excuse the delay in issuing this invitation, but my sister and I have both just recovered from colds. Trusting there is no prior engagement to prevent your coming, I am*
>
> *Sincerely yours,*
> *Myrtle G. Connelly*

Saturday was the one day of the week Margaret was free to spend time with her daughter, but she didn't begrudge doing so in the company of the sisters who had treated her and Hallie so kindly. Although she had little in common with Julia and Myrtle, their interest in her appeared genuine and she suddenly realized that they seemed to her like dear maiden aunts, only far more cultured than her own relatives back home.

It had rained the night before the visit, but by morning the clouds had cleared, and it promised to be a beautiful day. Margaret decided to walk through the University campus and up to the Hillside neighborhood where her sister-in-law and Hallie lived with Dr. Mead, a physician who employed Martina as housekeeper. The recently widowed doctor had a nine-year-old boy named Jeremy whom Martina cared for along with Hallie.

Martina. *I owe this woman a lot*, Margaret reminded herself yet again, but the resentment persisted like a stubborn stain. She knew it was beyond her power financially to repay either of Hal's siblings, Martina or Charles, for everything they'd done for her or Hallie. *But haven't I sacrificed enough by loaning my daughter, my only treasure?*

It had not taken much persuasion for Martina to assume the role of Hallie's second mother. After Hal's death, just four months after their move to Los Angeles, Margaret had groped her way toward the vocation that eventually led to St. Margaret's House. The role of deaconess was one of the few ways a young widowed mother could earn a respectable living, but it required three years of dedicated training—and children were not encouraged on campus. And so Martina, aggrandizing her own "sacrifice," moved to Berkeley to care for Hallie while Margaret trained. Recently divorced after a brief, disastrous marriage, Martina lived with Charles and was at loose ends. The situation seemed perfect for everyone—including Charles, who by tapping into his professional contacts to arrange his sister's employment, was freed from his remaining sibling whose primness he often complained about. *I don't know the financial arrangements, but whatever Charles sends Martina for Hallie must be a small price for him to pay*, Margaret assured herself, as she approached Dr. Mead's two-story Foursquare.

After ringing the bell, Margaret could hear Hallie running to open the door and Martina gently reproving the child for usurping the housekeeper's prerogative. "Is that a new shirtwaist, Margaret?" Martina asked, as she swung open the Federal blue door. "It suits you. I hope I can find something like it at the Lace House today." Normally Martina's tall, spare figure was plainly clothed as befitted her position, but even she might relish the chance to shop for some finery unencumbered by a four-year-old. Margaret smiled, acknowledging the rare compliment. "I hope you do, too," she responded warmly. The day was getting off to a good start.

When Hallie and her mother arrived at the Ferry Building in San Francisco, George was there to meet them as promised. Margaret was determined to be less tongue-tied with the young chauffeur and began asking him questions about school. She wished she had known something about Charles's medical education so she could converse more intelligently. Meanwhile, Hallie sat wide-eyed, looking all around her but saying little. Like her mother, she preferred to observe before giving herself over to new people and situations.

"How did you decide to become a doctor?" Margaret asked.

George, whose face was partially visible in the rear-view mirror, looked chagrined. "My father was constantly bragging about his nephew, my cousin, who had become a lawyer. I knew I had to study something equally prestigious, so I picked medicine. I liked science a lot in school, but I couldn't see myself becoming a chemist or something like that. Besides," he added with a twinkle, "my sister wants to be a nurse, and I always want to be able to boss her around."

Margaret could see Myrtle and Julia standing in front of their house as the car approached. Myrtle was holding a basket of bright red flowers which she had apparently been cutting from the prolific fuchsia which carpeted a large section of their side garden. Even after two years in California, Margaret couldn't get over the fact that there were flowers still blooming in November.

"Oh, you caught us before we had time to make up the flower arrangements," Myrtle confessed.

"I wanna help," Hallie said, running up the path toward Myrtle.

"Of course, dear. Let's go inside." The two of them

disappeared into the kitchen while Julia led Margaret into the living room.

"Do sit down," Julia said, motioning to the settee while she positioned herself on the nearby Morris chair.

"I brought you some apple butter I made the other day." Margaret offered the jar to her hostess. "Someone gave us a bushel of apples which we decided to cook up right away." Margaret didn't add that the decision had been made after a couple of rotten apples had been discovered in the lot. People were always donating produce of questionable quality; it was as if the deaconess school were an orphanage.

"That's very kind of you," Julia responded, then added, "I didn't realize you did your own cooking. I would think with your studies and all, you wouldn't have time for it."

"Not usually. But our regular cook had the flu so we have been taking turns helping her assistant."

"I used to do quite a bit of cooking, though I can't say I really enjoyed it. But when I was in the Philippines I got spoiled, since it cost next to nothing to have help."

"When were you in the Philippines?" Margaret asked, intrigued.

"I went in '02 and stayed for eight years. I had been a principal in Oakland but the salary in the Philippines was almost double what I earned in the States. We were part of the 'civilizing vanguard.'" Margaret, who knew the phrase from missionary accounts, wondered if someday she, too, might become part of that vanguard.

She listened, fascinated, as Julia told her about her time in Cadiz, a town of twenty-five thousand located in the western Philippines. It was clear that Julia relished the adventure and independence of those days, even if the tropical climate was not so much to her liking, especially the annual typhoon season. Her enthusiasm must have rubbed off, because in 1908 her brother Warren joined her in that country as a civil engineer in Cebu, about 60 miles southeast of Cadiz. He was still in the Philippines today.

"What made you leave?"

"Two things. Myrtle became a widow, and our father died, leaving us an inheritance. Myrtle needed me, and I didn't need to work anymore."

Margaret now understood the sisters' comfortable station in life, one in which a sense of entitlement was blessedly absent. It might also explain some of the exotic decorations on display throughout their home. Before she had a chance to ask about them, Hallie stepped importantly into the room wearing a pinafore that was only slightly too large, and announced that luncheon was served.

Myrtle had made a simple meal of Spanish eggs and green salad, Parker House rolls, and jam tarts for dessert. Hallie did a creditable job of eating something of each dish to earn her sweets, but even if she hadn't, Myrtle would not have begrudged her a jam tart or two. Clearly the two of them were becoming fast friends.

"Myrtle," Julia began after the last dishes were cleared away. "Margaret has been interested in Warren's and my time in the Philippines. Shall I read her some of Warren's latest letter?"

"Of course, dear. I left it on the library table."

Julia fetched the letter and began to read aloud. From time to time, she stopped to give context to her brother's words. He had recently been married to his high school sweetheart and was working as a district engineer in San Fernando, the capital of the province of Pampanga. It was a much more rural assignment than Cebu—urban Filipinos dismissively called such places a *bundoc.*

> *We live in an old Spanish house near the plaza in the best residential area. It is two stories with an adobe-walled yard shaded by mango trees. As is the custom, the ground floor is uninhabited, being subject to flooding in the monsoon season. For earthquake protection the upper floor is supported by stout wooden posts. Perhaps if San Francisco buildings had had this protection, fewer of them*

would have fallen in '06—though of course there would have been no protection in the ensuing fire.

Our hardwood floors are shined each morning to a mirror finish by a houseboy who skates across them on a pair of coconut husk halves. I had never realized the many uses of coconut until moving to the Philippines! For instance, until I am able to devise a shower we bathe Malay fashion by ladling water from a big clay jar with half a coconut shell.

While Julia read, Hallie fidgeted in her seat. Suddenly a young, fair-haired woman appeared, anxiously apologizing for her tardiness.

"That's all right, Gretchen, we know you needed to wait until your sister could come home from work," Myrtle said reassuringly. "Gretchen helps care for a sick mother," she told Margaret.

Margaret turned to the young maid and murmured, "I hope your mother's health improves."

Gretchen stammered, "Well, ma'am, we expect the Lord to take her any day now, but thank you for saying what you did." She turned and hurried into the kitchen.

What a stupid thing for me to say. As if I don't know what it is to care for someone dying. Or even to work as a maid. Margaret's enjoyment of the afternoon had suddenly evaporated. "We mustn't wear out our welcome," she said, apologetically addressing the sisters. She turned to her daughter. "It's time to go, Hallie. Say 'thank you' to the nice ladies."

But Hallie had remembered the promise to play with Mrs. Connelly's doll and having made her desire known, happily took Myrtle's hand to seek the toy upstairs. Margaret had no choice but to return to the living room with Julia.

"Shall I show you some of the things my brother and I collected in the Orient?" Julia asked. Without waiting for a response, Julia began to point out the woven baskets and mats she'd acquired in the Philippines. "Thomas insisted I bring home this *santo*," Julia explained, taking up a small wooden figure of a naked infant holding a globe in his hand. "It's a crude copy of a very famous one of the child Jesus holding the world in his hand, but somehow its innocence speaks to me."

"Why isn't he wearing clothes?" Margaret asked. This baby looked like nothing she'd seen in a Christmas card nativity scene.

"Oh, that's because the faithful dress him in different outfits. Just like a doll."

"Just like a doll..." Margaret repeated, disapproval tinging her voice. It seemed so irreverent.

Julia quickly turned to a color woodblock print displayed nearby. "Here's something completely different. My brother brought it back from a trip to Japan." Margaret found the delicate cherry blossom scene much more to her liking.

"Well, I've talked enough," Julia said abruptly, inviting her guest to sit. "Now it's your turn. Why don't you tell me about your life in the Deaconess House."

"I'm not sure there's that much to tell," Margaret began reluctantly. "I'm a first-year student, so my courses are basic: Bible, theology, church history, and fundamentals of religious education. We have chapel in the morning and evening, and on Sundays we assist at local parishes. I live in a dormitory with three other women. Two of them are training for social work and one is preparing to be a missionary."

"And how did you decide to pursue this calling?"

She'd answered this question before on the Deaconess House application but had never spoken the words aloud. She felt she was being asked to expose something very private, like being commanded to undress at the doctor's office.

After a moment she said quietly, "I felt the Lord's hand on me during the final days of my husband's illness. He died of tuberculosis." Margaret hurried past the details. "I came to understand that even though I was no longer a wife, I still had a purpose in life." *No matter that some people would think being a mother purpose enough…*

She braced herself for the inevitable shower of pity, but the older woman merely nodded, her eyes full of unspoken sympathy.

When the clock struck three, Margaret rose. "I've had a lovely time, but I really need to fetch Hallie and return home. Your sister must be tired of entertaining my daughter."

"I doubt that," Julia chuckled. "But let's invade the nursery and attempt to carry off the child."

"The child" was not ready to be carried off, but Margaret was firm before her tearful protests. George was summoned, farewells exchanged, and another invitation extended for December.

On the way to the Ferry Building, Margaret asked George if his family had many woodblock prints like she had seen at his employers' home.

"That is for cultured people," he replied. "My family are simple farmers."

"Of course," she said. It was not so different from back home in Iowa.

When it was time to sleep that night, Margaret lay wide awake. Her mind was a relentless kaleidoscope, turning to reveal images from her childhood and youth, her early marriage and its premature end. The visit with the sisters had disturbed her more than she was willing to admit.

Chapter 7

December 1913, Los Angeles

"Your husband's a lunger, ain't he?" Whether intended or not, Margaret heard her neighbor's question as a challenge. Returning her house key to her purse, Margaret turned from locking her front door to face the elderly woman. *A busybody, my landlady called her—always poking her nose into other people's business.*

"Took one look at him and I knew," the neighbor continued, with a satisfied air. "'Course the cough also gave it away."

Margaret fought the impulse to stalk off with all the dignity a nineteen-year-old could muster. *Who knows, I may have to turn to Mrs. Morgan for help one day. Better stay on her good side.*

"Yes, while you were visiting your daughter, he went to the County hospital for the cure. My brother-in-law, the doctor, says he has an excellent chance of recovery." That was, indeed, what Charles had said, though compared to many of the patients at the hospital Hal seemed in far worse condition. Probably they had been there longer, Margaret told herself. Surely it must be testimony to the effectiveness of the treatment.

Forestalling further conversation, Margaret descended the porch steps, placed Hallie in her green Go-Cart, and turned to leave. It was only two blocks to the home of Faith Stanley, her friend from church. Faith's four-year-old daughter Louise was delighted to have a "little sister" in Hallie, who was at the time a rambunctious toddler. Margaret tried to return the babysitting favor as often as possible, but sometimes she found it hard to summon the energy to watch two children after spending hours at the hospital.

"Faith, we're here!" Hallie was already attempting to extricate herself from the Go-Cart so she could join Louise.

A clattering in the kitchen was the prelude to Faith's cheerful greeting. "Come on in. I'm just taking some cookies out of the oven."

"Mmm, they smell good!"

Fortunately, Hallie's appetite for lunch remained unspoiled as she and Louise had run out to the backyard together before they could notice the treats. Faith put a couple of molasses cookies onto a plate and poured Margaret a cup of coffee before her friend could protest.

"Now, you sit down and take a break," Faith insisted. "You look peaked. You don't want to run yourself down so you get sick and are of no use to either Hal or Hallie."

It had been Margaret's idea to incorporate her husband's name into their daughter's. Another futile attempt to ingratiate herself with Hal's family. But as soon as Hal had told his siblings it was his wife's idea, they seemed determined to call the child Ruth. *Did they ever regret their decision once he was gone?* she often wondered. For Margaret, clinging to that name changed from an act of peacemaking to a symbol of defiance, her rejection of his family's rejection of her. After Hal died, she clung to the name all the more, preferring it to her child's legal first name, just as she rarely used her own first name of Sarah. It became a badge signifying her devotion, however imperfect, to Hal.

Margaret let herself be persuaded to sit and rest. Truth to tell, the daily visits to Hal were wearing on her. Her husband said she didn't need to visit so frequently, but Margaret could see from the way he perked up at her arrival that they were important. Only on Sundays, when Charles was sure to visit him, did she take the day off.

"Listen to this," Faith read from the paper, "'Traffic Clears as if by Magic: Semaphore Replaces Whistle at Street

Crossing.' The paper says there were at least a thousand people at noon gawking at the 'wigwag' at Third and Broadway. It may soon put traffic officers and their whistles out of business."

Margaret tried to appear interested, knowing that Faith's husband worked downtown and would care about such innovations. *Perhaps Hal might enjoy the story.* Spurred by the thought, she wiped a cookie crumb from her lips and pushed her chair back. "I should be getting on," she said. "Too bad they won't let me share your delicious cookies with Hal."

Margaret caught the streetcar to the County Hospital and before long found herself at the entrance on Mission Road. The large brick Tuberculosis Building had only been completed two years ago. To reach it, she had to pass the Surgical Building and skirt the Ward for the Insane. *What if Hal were in that ward,* Margaret wondered. *Would it be easier or harder on him—on me— than what he now faces?*

As always, before Margaret went to the men's sleeping porch she checked in with the nurse to see if there had been any change in Hal overnight. She knew it was useless to ask, because the answer never seemed to vary: "Mr. Peppers is about the same." *Charles would tell me if his condition worsened. Everything I've read says it just takes time.*

Margaret saw the familiar row of twenty identical white beds, separated by small white tables. Each table held a covered cuspidor for the infectious sputum. Even though the area was open to the outdoors and the air circulated freely, the faint smell of antiseptic was pervasive. She passed six beds before she arrived at Hal's. She smiled at the men along the way, and they smiled back at her, except for one who was asleep and another who stared blankly into space. Margaret had never considered herself a beauty, and she underestimated the effect that a young woman of even average looks could have on a man's healing.

Hal was dozing when she arrived, allowing Margaret to look at him more closely than either of them was comfortable with when he was awake. Was it her imagination, or had his cheeks become more hollow, his eyes more sunken, in the last few days? He had always been as lean as a beanpole, but now he seemed more skeleton than flesh. *He's wasting away, and there's no one who can do anything about it. Except for God.*

Suddenly Hal, who was propped up with a couple of pillows, woke with an explosive cough. Margaret moved quickly to give him the cuspidor, but he shook his head. "No—need," he managed to whisper. When his hacking subsided, Hal lay back against his pillows, exhausted. "Too—hard—to—talk," Hal explained hoarsely, pausing between words to catch his breath.

Six months into their marriage, Hal had become ill with influenza. The doctor urged Margaret, who was pregnant, to leave her husband in the care of his family while she went to stay with her own relatives. She returned a month later to find Hal recovered from the acute illness, but weakened, and plagued by a cough that never seemed to improve. He began to sleep in the spare room, a situation Margaret expected to change once the baby was born and Hal got used to sleeping through their child's nighttime cries. It never did.

One day, about three months after Hallie was born, Margaret went to the general store and overheard two young women talking by the counter. She knew Hannah and Sarah had been schoolmates of Hal's years ago.

"I wonder if they will all go to Colorado and live with his uncle this time," Hannah mused. "You remember how much it improved his health."

"If my husband had consumption, I'd want to put several states between him and me—especially with a child. Margaret is a sweet woman but she's a fool if she wants to sacrifice her own health and her daughter's for Hal's sake," asserted Sarah.

That night Margaret confronted Hal with what she'd heard. He didn't try to deny it but excused himself, saying, "By the time we met, I thought I was well." He paused as another cough wracked his body, then added, "Didn't seem much point in saying anything."

"And your family knew and didn't tell me, either! I should have been told and given the chance to make up my own mind about marrying you!" Her shouting woke the baby, and Hallie started to wail.

Hal's lungs didn't allow him to shout back, but his low response struck its devastating blow with surpassing force. "Are you forgetting, Maggie? You didn't have a choice."

After that time, Margaret had been relieved they slept in separate rooms, and not just to reduce the chance of contagion. She felt betrayed, even when a part of her admitted it was possible to mistake a remission in the disease for a cure. From then on, she approached caring for her husband as she might any other relative with a claim upon her. It was her Christian duty, but only now and again did the embers of the love Margaret once felt for her husband flicker into a flame capable of really warming either of them. If she clung to resentment, she found she could ignore her feelings of despair.

Another cough rattled through the TB ward, wrenching Margaret back to the present. She shook her head imperceptibly to dispel the dark memories. She read a couple of newspaper articles aloud, pausing whenever Hal coughed, and before long he lay with his eyes closed. It was her signal to leave.

"Give—Hallie—a kiss—from me," he whispered as she quietly placed the paper on his bedside table. Margaret's lips brushed Hal's ever-warm forehead and, reminding him she would come back tomorrow, she tiptoed away.

Margaret couldn't afford a telephone, but she had given Charles and the hospital Faith Stanley's number in case of emergency. The nurse that New Year's Eve had noticed the telltale change in Hal's breathing but decided to wait until dawn to make the necessary calls. In her experience, when the death rattle made its fateful appearance, it was often twenty hours until the patient finally succumbed. But she was off by ten hours in case of thirty-year-old Hal Peppers. By the time Margaret had gotten the word and reached the room where her husband had been moved, the sheet had already been pulled over his corpse. With a tenderness that surprised her, Charles pulled it back to expose Hal's wasted face and upper torso.

Hal reminded her of Jesus on the crucifix she had once seen in the home of a Catholic playmate. At the time she hadn't been able to take her eyes off him, and her friend, noticing, told her Christ looked that way because he was carrying the sins of the whole world. Then, it was just strange and spooky. Now, as she gazed on the man who had changed her life irrevocably, she felt an overwhelming urge to confess.

"He was unconscious when I got here, Margaret, and he never woke up."

"I hope... I hope he didn't suffer." She couldn't bring herself to frame it as a question to be answered.

"No, it was very peaceful," he said. "I hope when the time comes for the good Lord to call me home, it will be like that." Later, she wondered if he had only said that to reassure her. If so, it had been a compassionate lie.

There was a knock at the door and a woman of about sixty appeared, dressed in a dark gown with a starched white color and cuffs. The band of gray hair left exposed beneath her dark veil showed she was an Episcopal deaconess, rather than a Roman Catholic nun. On her breast she wore a plain silver cross. Margaret recognized her as Deaconess Steiger, who mostly served in the women's ward but had also visited patients in the tuberculosis wing on Christmas Eve.

"I'm sorry to disturb you," the deaconess apologized. "The chaplain sent me to tell you he would be here in a short while. He is with another bereaved family just now." She took a step closer to Margaret and gently placed her hand on the young woman's forearm. "I'm so sorry," she repeated.

"Thank you," Margaret responded, not knowing what else to say. Now that the initial shock of seeing her husband dead had passed, she felt numb.

She let herself be led away to sit in the adjacent waiting room. Still the tears did not come.

"Would you like a drink of water?" the deaconess asked. Margaret shook her head. Charles was busy filling out the death certificate, so the two women sat there silently, the deaconess looking down at her hands nestled in her lap, while Margaret stared ahead at some indeterminate point as if trying to discern the future that lay ahead for her and her child.

"Mrs. Peppers?" The chaplain suddenly materialized, a tall, gaunt man in his fifties who might have doubled for the Grim Reaper in street clothes. His voice had a high, reedy quality which contrasted oddly with his somber appearance. She assented to his praying out loud from the Episcopal *Book of Common Prayer*.

"O merciful God and heavenly Father," intoned the priest, "who has taught us in thy holy Word that thou dost not willingly afflict or grieve the children of men; Look with pity, we beseech thee, upon the sorrows of thy servant Margaret for whom our prayers are desired. In wisdom thou hast seen fit to visit her with trouble and to bring distress upon her. Remember her, O Lord, in mercy; sanctify thy fatherly correction to her; endue her soul with patience under her affliction, and with resignation to thy blessed will; support her with a sense of goodness; lift up thy countenance upon her and give her peace; through Jesus Christ our Lord."

The words washed over her, scarcely penetrating, like a sudden rain shower over dry, hard earth. How long would it be before she would truly know peace?

CHAPTER 8

February 13, 1910, Bloomfield, Iowa

It had been the day before her sixteenth birthday. She knew that tomorrow, Valentine's Day, many of her female schoolmates would be receiving cards from beaux and perhaps candy or even some kind of bauble. Having no boyfriend, Margaret expected none of these, and this year she could not even look forward to the diversion of a family celebration.

That afternoon the police had taken her father away, this time maybe for good. The day before he had disappeared from the livery stable where he worked and was found trying to climb the flagpole in front of the courthouse in the middle of a snowstorm. The police held him overnight, but her mother Mary finally took the step she had threatened for so long and refused to take him home. There being no other family member willing to take him in, John William Guthrie became the twenty-eighth inmate of the Davis County Almshouse.

Years later, Matilda Owen, an old friend of her mother's, had explained Mary's point of view. "Your mother was a forgiving woman," Mrs. Owen had said, "but there came a time when even the ladies in the Baptist Sewing Circle thought she should leave the forgiving to God. When your father first began to suffer his strange spells—you would have been about ten at the time—Mary asked herself what she or you youngsters might have done to cause him to act that way. First, he'd be all riled up, like a whipped racehorse, but then he would always get into a funk. He drank then—a lot—and muttered and moaned and sobbed like a baby. Even your father, when he recovered, couldn't explain what came over him."

"Your mother finally figured out how to tell an attack was coming on. She noticed John began to stay up later and rise earlier. Your father was never one much for speechifying, but he started to bend everyone's ear, talking a mile a minute. At first Mary was happy that John got busy with chores that needed doing, but he never seemed to finish them."

Mrs. Owen's wrinkled face seemed to pucker even more with every recalled detail. "Mary began to worry about how John's behavior would affect you children. Once, when he was in one of his riled-up moods, he took little Johnny and Editha on a buggy ride and drove so reckless the trap overturned. When Mr. Beatty rescued them from the ditch, he could see that your brother and sister were terrified. Do you remember that, Maggie?"

Of course she did. Hadn't she let Editha sleep in her bed for many nights afterwards because the child suddenly became afraid of the dark? Was that when her own headaches began?

"Your mother tried not to let on how tight money became as your father got sicker and sicker and couldn't keep a job. That's why you moved when you were fourteen or fifteen—it was cheaper. By then Mary was sewing and taking in laundry to make ends meet. I guess she mostly confided in Willie, seeing as how he's the oldest son."

That fateful evening, Margaret's mother tried to carry on as though nothing was wrong. But then little Johnny raised the inevitable question: "When will we be able to see Daddy in the Almshouse?"

"Your daddy needs to be left alone for a little while, or else he won't get well," her mother replied. "We can't go to see him, but you can write him a letter." That seemed to satisfy the lad for the moment. Mary waited until Johnny and Editha were in bed asleep before approaching Margaret, who was studying at the kitchen table.

"Maggie, I want to talk with you," Mary said.

Margaret looked up from her Cicero. Though she was not a quick learner, her diligence earned the approval of her teachers, who often made her an example for lazier classmates. Such recognition did not grant her many friendships, but to her mother it was a source of pride.

Mary hesitated a moment before delivering the blow. "Your father's… sickness… has put the family in a precarious situation," she began. "Each of us needs to make some sacrifices so we can live."

Margaret stirred uneasily. "What do you mean, 'so we can live'?"

"I mean that your father has bankrupted the family. We have debts which must be paid, and the only way that can happen is if we all pitch in." Again, the hesitation. Then, speaking more forcefully, Mary forged ahead. "You and I need to find work just as your brother has done. I'll let you finish your high school year, but then you must get a job."

Margaret's dreams of attending the Normal School and becoming a schoolteacher were snatched away in an instant, and in their place was left the grim reality of becoming a maid in the Trimble House across town.

No wonder that months later, when a young man began to pay her attention, Margaret was eager to receive it.

CHAPTER 9

September 1917, Berkeley

She was nine months from graduating, and she still had no idea where or how she would be serving God. Sometimes at night, after her dormitory roommates had gone to sleep, she'd sit up in bed holding a flashlight in one hand and the St. Margaret's Deaconess Training Program catalog in the other. Then Margaret would read and reread the role of deaconesses according to the rules of the Episcopal Church. It was right there on page one: *"The duty of a Deaconess is to assist the Minister in the care of the poor and sick, the religious training of the young and others, and the work of moral reformation."* Whispering the words like a mantra, Margaret prayed that God's will for her would become clear, and soon.

Sometimes her imagination might be fired by a guest speaker. She would see herself working among the mountain folk in Appalachia or ministering in a far-off land, helping women relegated to subservience by a culture yet untouched by Western enlightenment. Or perhaps she would teach among the native peoples of the Far North—though, truth to tell, four years in California had made the Arctic a less attractive prospect. Still, she knew she could get used to anything if God equipped her. And besides, Hallie, young and amenable as she was, would adapt anywhere they went.

But there were still some areas of service she prayed God would not test her courage with. A hospital, where she'd be haunted by Hal's ghost. Or a women's shelter, where she spent her summer practicum and learned a lesson that needed no repetition.

"You'll get along famously," Julia had pronounced, when she told Margaret she'd invited Thirmuthis Brookman, founder of the House of Friendship, to join them for dinner one day last spring. "She's an Episcopalian like you, and your Reverend Parsons is on the board of her new charity. I got to know her when she oversaw the welfare of women employees of the Exposition—made sure they were cared for and not victimized by unscrupulous men."

Margaret had been inspired by Miss Brookman's vision of a refuge where women who have nowhere to turn could find sanctuary and hope. Hadn't she been in that situation when Hal had died, leaving her penniless with a two-year-old to raise? But what Margaret didn't understand, until she began to work at the House of Friendship, was that few of its residents were the kind that occupied the pews of the typical Episcopal church. Their poverty was not genteel, their circumstances far more desperate than any Margaret had faced.

Managing drunken husbands demanding to see their wives wasn't a problem—after all, she'd managed her father when he went off the rails. Pimps and prostitutes were another thing entirely. Fortunately, she didn't work at night, and never alone. She'd never forget the first time she had to phone the police, her voice cracking with fear. The operator gave up trying to understand her and guessed who Margaret intended to call.

When Delia arrived, seventeen and pregnant, Margaret saw her younger, innocent self. Delia's plans to attend college in the fall were shattered by her disgrace, and Margaret couldn't help getting involved, even though it was against the rules. *What would my life have been like if I could have become a teacher? If I hadn't been flattered by Hal and persuaded to give in? At least he had married me, even if his family wasn't happy about it. And he did love me, in his own way.*

The shelter sent its more educated single women to

stenography school, and that was Miss Brookman's plan for Delia, after her baby had been adopted. In the meantime, she would finish out her pregnancy at the St. Catherine's Catholic Home for Wayward Girls, since the House of Friendship was not a home for unwed mothers. Having heard talk about the dire conditions at St. Catherine's, Margaret was desperate to arrange a different future for Delia, even though the girl herself seemed uninterested in anything and anyone. As luck would have it, Julia and Myrtle had just left for New York, and even Reverend Parsons couldn't be reached for assistance.

One day, Delia disappeared from the shelter. A few days later, they heard she died on an abortionist's table. Margaret blamed herself for not doing more to help.

Chapter 10

October 1917

> *Humpty Dumpty sat on a wall,*
> *Humpty Dumpty had a great fall.*
> *All the king's horses and all the king's men*
> *Couldn't put Humpty together again.*

Margaret fingered the worn pages of Hallie's Mother Goose book, which her now-six-year-old was finding too childish to be of interest. She could never read the sad tale of Humpty Dumpty without thinking back to the first dark months of her widowhood. Then, it had seemed that the tragic fate of the make-believe character exactly mirrored hers and Hallie's. But what that fragile shell of illusion had failed to protect, somehow managed to survive. She and Hallie went on—as a different kind of family, to be sure—but a family, nonetheless.

Had it really been almost four years since Hal had died? Soon it would be time to donate to the local parish, St. Mark's, for flowers in his honor. She reflected sadly that since America entered the Great War, flower memorials for dead young men were becoming more and more common. Sometimes, she wondered that if Hal had recovered, might he then have died as a soldier? To have him brought back to health, only to lose him for good—*that* would have been unbearable.

She remembered how, once the numbness after his death had begun to wear off, she'd finally come to realize how much she loved her husband—and how much she had failed him. That epiphany she owed to her little girl.

A couple months into her widowhood, Margaret had been sitting dejectedly on a park bench, watching Hallie and Louise Stanley play together. "Look, Mommy," her child had called, pointing to a robin that was engaged in pulling a worm from the ground. Suddenly, in Hallie's profile, she saw Hal. The same high cheeks, the same pencil-straight nose, the same slightly receding chin. How could she have not seen it before? When Margaret first discovered Hal's tuberculosis, it felt as if she'd been whipped around to *face facts*—about her husband and about her marriage. But now she knew there had been something wrong with her orientation. She thought she had been looking truth squarely in the eye, but there was another side she failed to see. A side that was every bit as true as failed dreams and shattered hopes.

What Margaret saw that day in Hallie's profile was the preciousness of her own marriage, and how she had squandered it in bitterness and self-pity. She had almost cried aloud, right there on the park bench: *What a waste; what a terrible, terrible waste.* It was too late to beg Hal's forgiveness, but maybe, somehow, she could make it up to God.

Hallie's impatient voice yanked Margaret back to the present. "Mommy, you said you would read me another fairy tale."

"Sorry, darling." Margaret quickly closed *Mother Goose* and picked up the requested volume. Snug in Julia and Myrtle's spare bedroom, where she and Hallie had become almost weekly guests, they were working their way through the tales of the Brothers Grimm.

"Let's see… how about Hansel and Gretel?" Propping herself in bed, with Hallie nestled against her, Margaret began to read, "Once upon a time, on the edge of a great forest…" Minutes later, long before "happily ever after," her little girl was fast asleep.

Margaret gently tucked Hallie in and brushed her lips against her daughter's cheek. She wanted to capture this tender moment forever; the way the black and white letters of a book hold a story to be treasured for years to come. She was suddenly conscious of a transience that was more than the transience of childhood. She couldn't explain it, but she felt it had to do with her own motherhood.

"Margaret," Julia said the next morning, as the maid was clearing away the remains of their pancake breakfast, "you've never told us how you found your way up here, besides saying that God called you. It's Saturday, and you don't need to rush off. Tell me, and I'll share it with Myrtle. You know I can't drag her away from that girl of yours."

Margaret smiled, acknowledging the certainties of life with the Fairy Godmothers, the name she had secretly come to apply to the sisters, whose many kindnesses had sustained her during her deaconess training. Julia would, naturally, take it upon herself to enlighten her younger sister; and Myrtle would, just as naturally, find any excuse to play with Hallie. The inexplicable sense of foreboding that overcame her the night before had passed, and Margaret felt ready to respond to Julia's question.

Putting aside her usual reticence in discussing her personal circumstances—though she could not yet bring herself to talk about that day in the park, years ago—Margaret began to describe how Faith Stanley had befriended her and Hallie, even inviting them into her own home when they could no longer afford to pay the rent after Hal's death. "And when the Stanleys joined St. Paul's Episcopal Church in L. A., I went with them and came to know the Reverend William MacCormack, the rector. I was so inspired by Dr. MacCormack's sermons that I felt like I belonged in the Church, and not just as a woman sitting in the pew or teaching Sunday school.

"One day Deaconess Anita Hodgkin came to speak to the Woman's Auxiliary at church. She talked about St. Margaret's Training Program and the need for young women willing and able to dedicate their lives to God's work. And when I heard her,

I said to myself, 'maybe *I* am that woman.'"

As always, Julia didn't waste time beating around the bush. "Miss Brookman is a spinster, with no dependents. But you have Hallie. Isn't your situation unusual?"

"Yes…" Margaret admitted. "At first, Dr. MacCormack was reluctant to sponsor my application to the deaconess program. I couldn't have applied if I had still been married, with or without children, but as a widow, I fit the requirements. In the end, I think Mrs. MacCormack persuaded her husband that just because I was a mother, it didn't mean I had to stay at home. She told me once she thought the Church was behind the times in terms of what women were and weren't allowed to do. I can still hear her saying, 'Women can vote in state and local elections, but they can't even vote or serve on the lay governing bodies of the Episcopal Church. That's ridiculous!'"

"Sounds like my kind of woman," Julia agreed, smiling.

Later that evening, Margaret was back at Deaconess House, having returned Hallie to the care of her aunt until next weekend. She wished her daughter could spend the night at her dormitory, but while Miss Hodgkin had been persuaded to allow Hallie the run of St. Margaret's House on Saturdays, her generosity did not extend to sleepovers.

Time to catch up on my assignments. Margaret decided that the week's accumulation of embroidery and mending work—a small but necessary supplement to her own scholarship support, courtesy of her Fairy Godmothers and their friends—could easily wait another day.

Resolutely, Margaret opened the maroon-covered book on her desk. Called *The Burden of the City*, it had been written by Lucy Rider Meyer, a Methodist. That denomination, too, had deaconesses. In the fading light of day, Margaret read:

> *Why has the deaconess work been so successful?*
> *Why is it attracting such eager attention and expectation*
> *from those who love God and humanity? One might*
> *answer in the words of one of the wisest of our Bishops, "It*

furnished the principal meeting-place between the Church and the lapsed masses." But there is, I believe, a more profound reason. The world wants mothering. Mother-love has its part to do in winning the world for Christ as well as father-wisdom and guidance. The deaconess movement puts the mother into the Church. It supplies the feminine element so greatly needed in the Protestant Church, and thus is rooted deep in the very heart of humanity's needs.

Julia's earlier words began echoing in her head about her "situation." Unusual, she had called it. But is there anything unusual about mother-love? Could she share hers with the world without forsaking her own duty to Hallie?

Chapter 11

November 1917

In the past Martina had shown little interest in what Margaret had been studying and doing, but suddenly she wanted to hear about the kinds of positions open to graduates of the training program. "They all seem far away, and in destitute places," she observed drily after one such conversation.

"Not always," Margaret said. "There's hospital ministry, even here in California, but I'm not a trained nurse. And I don't feel called to be a hospital chaplain." *I couldn't face being reminded every day of Hal's suffering,* she added silently.

Martina dismissed that possibility with a wave of her hand. "No, I think it's best that you go where you can be of most use," she said, surprising Margaret by expressing a sentiment that she herself had come to embrace. Only later did Margaret wonder if there had been an implied suggestion that she would be as useless working in a hospital as she had been caring for her tubercular husband.

Magaret was in her next-to-last term at school, and her classes kept her busier than ever. Her time with Hallie shortened as Margaret's commitments increased. Martina, however, appeared content with the arrangement. Margaret reflected that lately her sister-in-law seemed less disapproving and more accommodating—indeed, almost friendly. While grateful, Margaret couldn't shake a feeling of unease, as if something menacing were moving beneath the placid surface.

That fall the second surviving Peppers brother, Edgar,

joined his sister Martina in the Bay area. When Margaret learned that their sister Effa would also be moving from the Midwest, completing the exodus of Hal's siblings from Iowa to California, she was more than ever determined to leave the state with Hallie after graduation. She'd long felt that only Hallie counted with the Peppers clan, never her. It would be a relief to finally escape the family's shadow of obligation and reproach.

Toward the end of October, a letter came from Charles. Hoping against hope that he, as the most prosperous of the family, had seen fit to provide some much-needed financial assistance, Margaret tore open the envelope. But even with all her forebodings, she was unprepared for the words that now swam before her eyes.

Dear Margaret,

As the time nears for your graduation from the Deaconess Training Program, you must certainly be anticipating your future in service of the Church. We pray that God will lead you to the place where you may be of most use.

It will come as reassurance to know that our family will see to Ruth's education and upbringing. We have the means, as you do not and will not, to afford her every advantage.

Understand that our care is predicated on Ruth's continuing to live with Mrs. Jury. Over the last two and one-half years the day-to-day responsibility of caring for your daughter has been cheerfully and competently assumed by her aunt, and it would be extremely detrimental to Ruth Hall's well-being to separate them now. The child warmly reciprocates the tender love she has received from Mrs. Jury. Having lost her father at a young age, what Ruth needs is stability and the assurance of constant presence, something that your duties as a deaconess at the beck and call of a bishop will not permit, however much you desire otherwise.

Should you decide to attempt the impossible task of raising Ruth Hal by yourself, know that this will occur without any assistance whatsoever from our family.

With confidence that you have Ruth's highest interests in mind, and that you will agree our proposal is the best for all concerned, I am

Sincerely yours,
Charles H. Peppers, M.D.

Margaret reread the letter several times, unconsciously mouthing each word so as not to mistake its meaning. Martina's voice resounded in the letter, even if it was Charles who had in fact penned it. The careful turn of phrase, the studious avoidance of any mention of Margaret as Hallie's mother—she could easily picture Martina dictating at her brother's elbow, grim with determination.

At last, Margaret shakily folded the devastating missive and replaced it in its envelope. Stumbling from the school parlor, she found herself outside in the bright sunshine, which beat down with mocking indifference. She began to walk, traversing the adjacent University campus, with neither purpose nor awareness.

A stone bench suddenly presented itself, and Margaret sat down. Soon a pair of pigeons approached, murmuring eagerly in anticipation of a meal. Somehow the sight and sound of them penetrated her obliviousness, making her conscious once more of her surroundings. Then she remembered an incident from her childhood. Four boys had surrounded an injured robin and were taking turns hitting it with their slingshots. Margaret had called to them to stop but they ignored her. She ran home to tell her mother, but by the time they had returned the boys were gone and the bird lay inert on the ground. Crying, she ran to cradle the creature in her hands. Its head lolled as she picked it up and she noticed that one of its eyes had been smashed.

I am that bird, she now realized.

It was Wednesday, a full three days before she was due

to see Hallie. Her first impulse was to rush to Dr. Mead's house and snatch her daughter away. And take her—where? She could not live at the Deaconess House, and Julia and Myrtle were in Portland, visiting their cousin.

She could give up and return to Iowa, but her mother had neither the means nor the health to help care for Hallie while Margaret attempted to find work. Besides, she shuddered at the thought of a life spent in drudgery as a maid, the only real wage-earning job she had ever held.

No, God had called her to become a deaconess, and a deaconess she would be. He would show her the way.

Chapter 12

"Good morning, Margaret." Was it her imagination, or did her sister-in-law avoid looking directly at her?

Margaret had rehearsed this moment ever since she had put aside the impractical notion of taking Hallie to live with her. She would hold her head high and not reveal to anyone, especially not to Martina or any of the school administration, how deeply she was wounded. She would show the Peppers clan that she was not a hysterical girl but a consecrated woman called to do the Lord's work.

As Martina motioned her to enter the house, Margaret greeted her politely, searching her face in vain for any evidence of remorse. What she saw was a mixture of unease and of resolution—as firm a resolution as Margaret herself retained.

She greeted Hallie as always with a hug and kiss, though she may have held her a little longer and tighter than usual. She was determined not to reveal anything of her turmoil to her daughter, so she merely said, "Let's go, dear" and turning to Martina, mentioned casually that Hallie would be with her until after supper. After they left the house, Margaret gave a sigh of relief, having passed the first of what she expected to be many ordeals to come.

Hallie skipped down the walk, oblivious to any tension between her caregivers. "Are we going to the park now?" she asked, reminding her mother of their customary routine.

"Yes, of course," Margaret responded. "And then we'll spend the day together at the Deaconess House. You'll even get to eat with all of us."

A mother-daughter dinner at St. Margaret's House was a rare treat, but many rules were relaxed when Deaconess Hodgkin was gone. Margaret still had schoolwork to do, as well as prepare for a Sunday School lesson she would teach at St. Mark's the next day, but she had enlisted the help of her roommate Joan to entertain her daughter.

Joan had a Sunday School class of her own to prepare for, and soon she set Hallie to work making lambs out of paper and cotton wool for a lesson on Jesus the Good Shepherd. After a time, Margaret, who was studying in the room next door, heard Joan teaching the little girl a song.

> *The Lord's my Shepherd, I'll not want.*
> *He maketh me to lie*
> *In pastures green He leadeth me,*
> *The quiet waters by.*
> *He leadeth me, He leadeth me,*
> *The quiet waters by.*

A few minutes later Hallie burst into the room with a "sheep" in hand, eager to sing her new song. Margaret listened attentively to the sweet voice of her daughter testifying to the goodness of God. When Hallie had finished, both the women applauded, but not before Margaret surreptitiously wiped away a tear. To disguise her emotion, Margaret quickly said, "I don't know this song. Where did you learn it, Joan?"

Joan explained it had come from a book her cousin had sent her from England. "It's mostly pacifist essays written at the beginning of the Great War, but there are a few songs interspersed," she replied. "It's by a Theosophist, but that doesn't mean everything he writes is wrong, does it?"

"Not if he sticks to the Twenty-third Psalm," Margaret agreed. "Just don't say too much about where you got the song if you're asked."

"Yeah, and no mention of pacifism, now that we're in the war, too. The Sunday School Superintendent is all worked up about our patriotic duty and wants us to sing 'Onward, Christian Soldiers' in the children's chapel every week."

Margaret turned back to her daughter, smiling as she fondly stroked Hallie's silky brown bob. Once it had been almost blonde, but now it was chestnut, like her own hair. "Just a few more minutes, dear, and then we'll go outside and let you run around." With a grateful glance at her roommate, she returned to her *Atlas of the Holy Land* with its bewildering succession of ancient kingdoms and settlements.

After supper Margaret and Hallie walked back to Dr. Mead's. It was chilly and foggy, and they hurried along, holding hands. Hallie kept practicing "The Lord's My Shepherd" so she could sing it for Aunt Martina when she got home.

"Enough, Hallie!" Margaret's abrupt rebuke put an end to the music. Where earlier she had taken heart from the song's message, now all she could think of was the woman who would next hear its words. They took the last block in silence as Margaret prepared to surrender her daughter to Martina for another week.

Before they reached the house, Margaret bent down so that her face was level with Hallie's and her hands rested on the child's shoulders. "Remember that no one loves you as much as Mommy does," she said solemnly and emphatically, her voice catching. Giving her daughter a hug, she gently prodded her ahead. Margaret stepped back quickly as Dr. Mead's Irish setter barked a greeting and the door creaked open. Then she disappeared into the enveloping fog.

Three days later Margaret was sitting in the cramped office of Deaconess Hodgkin. Raindrops slithered down the window as she watched the deaconess go to the file cabinet and extract what she assumed was the folder containing all her records. In making the appointment Margaret had murmured something about discussing her future, but it surprised her nonetheless that Miss Hodgkin might need this file.

"I was talking with Miss Ramp recently about the

church's provisions for educating children of missionaries, and she said it depended on the posting. As you know, I have a little girl to consider in my plans after I graduate."

"Hallie is what—six or seven?" the deaconess asked, in her clipped British accent.

"Six, now. She began the first grade this year."

"That's a bit young for boarding school, which is where many missionaries send their children. Quite frankly, I can't think of a single widow with a young child who is working in the mission field." She paused a minute, trying to recollect. "Oh, yes—I believe we do have one deaconess in China who has adopted a little girl, but the child is Chinese and goes to school at the mission where the deaconess is headmistress."

"What do other missionaries do?"

"Almost all the missionaries with children are married couples. The woman generally cares for the children until they are able to be sent away to boarding school, either in the host country or back in the home country. It really depends on the particular day school and its purpose whether or not it is suitable for a missionary's child."

Margaret tried another tack. "What if I were called to work at an Episcopal school in this country, one for white children?"

"You mean like St. Helen's Hall in Portland?" Miss Hodgkin hesitated, then flipped open the file she had retrieved. She scanned it a moment while she considered her response.

"Margaret…" The deaconess closed the file and cleared her throat, as if she were getting ready to deliver a pronouncement. "It takes a certain kind of woman to work at an Episcopal educational institution in this country. You know you lack the qualifications to teach in America, and"—she raised her hand to fend off an interruption—"even for a position such as house matron, a bishop is looking for a certain kind of experience and comportment. You have many fine qualities and will be a wonderful worker in the Lord's vineyard, but I believe your call is among children who are not privileged like the students of St.

Helen's, much less the preparatory schools of the East Coast."

You mean I'm not a fourth-generation Episcopalian with a priest or two in the family, Margaret thought rebelliously, but she kept silent.

"If I may be blunt—the lack of family entanglements is precisely what makes a deaconess so valuable to the Church. She is able to offer herself to the work without any encumbrances. Now in your case, you are fortunate to have a sister-in-law who can care for your daughter while you are at school. Is she willing and able to continue afterwards? That would certainly make everything easier."

More than willing, Margaret thought grimly. Aloud she said, "She is willing. I just want to understand what is possible for Hallie and me."

"My advice is to get settled in some work and after a year or so you will know better how to proceed. You may be in an American church where a parishioner can watch your child when she is out of school, and you are occupied on parish business. If you are in a foreign mission, it is more difficult, but perhaps your daughter can continue to live with her aunt until she is of an age to attend a boarding school in the country that caters to the expatriate community. There is a small stipend to help with those expenses, though like our salaries"—here she shrugged her shoulders apologetically—"it must be managed carefully."

"Thank you, Deaconess Hodgkin. I will consider all you have told me." Hoping she did not look as disappointed as she felt at finding no easy solution to her dilemma, Margaret rose to leave.

"Oh, and Margaret," Miss Hodgkin interjected, "next week Deaconess Hargreaves will be coming to tell us about her work in the Philippines. I believe Bishop Brent has need of someone to assist at the mission school in Bontoc. You may wish to talk with her about it."

Bontoc. The word sounded exotic, everything her life was not. Was this where she was being led to share her "mother-love"? Even if it meant—for the moment—leaving Hallie behind?

That evening after prayers Margaret stayed in the parlor to look through issues of *The Spirit of Missions* magazine to learn what she could about the Episcopal Church's mission in Bontoc. It was not an area that she had heard about from Warren Judson's letters, but she discovered it was the capital of the Mountain Province in the northern Philippines and the location of several villages of the indigenous Igorot people. Margaret recalled having visited a so-called Igorot "village" at the Panama Pacific International Exposition with Hallie. Now she wondered how accurate a portrayal it had been of Bontoc life.

Several articles she read referred to a monsoon whose fury had uprooted giant, one-hundred-year-old pine trees and demolished several buildings in the mission compound. Bishop Brent described the former site of the missionaries' residence as "now the stony bed of the river now some twelve or fifteen feet below the original land." As Margaret pored over the photographs illustrating the devastation she tried to imagine herself in that place, amid terrified schoolchildren. Her closest experience was a couple of tornadoes from her childhood. Were the Igorots as resigned to these natural disasters as her people back home? Apparently so, for a later issue revealed them repairing and rethatching their houses. One photograph, which showed a long line of young women carrying bundles of grass, bore the caption, *"Even the girls lend a hand."*

Margaret smiled as she read an article on Igorot music, in which a little boy was described as believing the sound emitted by an organ was the hum of a very large man! Though the Igorot musical instruments sounded primitive in the extreme—only gongs and a kind of reed pipe played through the nostrils—she was happy to learn they enjoyed singing, for she did too. Perhaps, she thought, she could teach children some of the hymns her Sunday School class sang. Before long she was picturing herself standing before a group of wide-eyed native boys and girls as they sang "Jesus Loves Me"—in English. That they might instead wish to sing in Igorot never occurred to her.

With this briefest of introductions to mission life in the Philippines, Margaret impatiently awaited Deaconess Hargreaves's arrival. Her first glimpse of the woman came at Sunday night chapel. She was petite—Margaret supposed about four inches shorter than her own five-and-a-half-foot height—with blonde hair beginning to be touched by silver. Whether singing a hymn or intoning a prayer, the deaconess seemed to radiate energy. *That's what a genuine call will do,* Margaret thought. *I want to be that way.*

When Mrs. Hargreaves addressed the missions class the next morning, Margaret listened eagerly. In a voice tinged with a faint Cockney accent, the deaconess began to describe her work in the mountains of Luzon among the native people.

"The Igorot are a conservative folk, maintaining the same way of life generation after generation. Their needs are simple, materially speaking, a simplicity that ignores Western notions of cleanliness and proper attire." One young woman in the room tittered but was immediately silenced by a stern look from Miss Ramp while the speaker continued. "They are a moral people, with clear notions of right and wrong, but their religion is dominated by *anitos,* or spirits of the dead, whom it is necessary to appease in various ways including, as you likely have heard, the offering of human heads, though this practice has been greatly exaggerated and is indeed dying out under the American jurisdiction." Margaret nodded, reassured by the notion that western civilization had already made inroads into ancient customs.

"When I was appointed to be the sole missionary in the village of Besao, I knew that I must teach the youth, but first I needed to win over the old men, who maintain the Igorot traditions and dictate how life is to be. It was too much to ask them to convert to a new religion and way of life, but if they would consent for their boys and girls to be educated, then there was hope."

Deaconess Hargreaves recounted how, with the help of an Igorot convert as translator and exemplar, she gained grudging acceptance by the elders and permission to undertake her work. Margaret was intrigued as she described her own "head-hunting" expeditions in search of students, fearlessly entering homes and "capturing" children for school, who would otherwise be toiling in the fields.

"This is my little 'L'," she said, referring to the shape of her mission building shown in the accompanying lantern slide—only her Cockney aspirate rendered the word more like "h-ell," much to the amusement of her American audience. This time the deaconess smiled too. With educated Igorots as teachers and Mrs. Hargreaves as "Ina"—"Mother" in the native tongue—St. James had the distinction of being the first coeducational school in the Philippines. More missionaries were desperately needed for educating the new generation. Margaret leaned forward in her chair, enthralled. *Could I be one of them?*

A group of students clustered around the deaconess after class, Margaret among them. Staying behind after the rest had finally dispersed, she ventured her own question. "Mrs. Hargreaves," she began, as she sought a diplomatic way to phrase her query, "I am a widow like yourself." As expected, the deaconess nodded. "May I ask if you know about the school for girls in Bagulo?"

"I understand it will close at the end of the year until more funds are found to support it."

"Oh," Margaret said, her heart sinking. Then she asked, hoping against hope, "Would you say it's likely the money will be found?"

"Oh yes, I'm sure it will. I think missionaries are in fact more willing to send their sons overseas for education rather than their daughters. Bishop Brent contributed his own money to found the boys' school in Baguio and if he weren't retiring, I think he'd give his attention to the girls' school. Once his successor is chosen and gets settled, and this war ends, I think you'll see the school start up again."

Margaret exhaled, releasing the breath she had unconsciously been holding as she waited for an answer. Her mind whirred as she processed this information, weighing the possibilities. *I suppose I could let Hallie live with Martina temporarily, if I go to Bontoc. The war can't last much longer.*

"Why don't we take a walk outdoors and I can tell you more about the opening in Bontoc?" Deaconess Hargreaves said.

PART 2: 1918–1928
The Philippines

Chapter 13

August 1918, Manila, Philippines

Somewhere a bell was tolling. The sound punctured her sleep, allowing her dream to escape, like air from a balloon, into the gauzy light of day. Margaret groaned as she tried in vain to hold onto the joy of running as a child on the Iowa prairie. Reluctantly opening her eyes, she wondered if she was still dreaming. She was enclosed by mosquito netting and her skin glistened with perspiration.

Margaret sat up and remembered where she was. After a three-week sea voyage, she had at last reached Manila harbor, where she had been met by the Very Reverend and Mrs. Artley Beeber Parson of the Episcopal Cathedral of St. Mary and St. John. In his late thirties and about the same height as Margaret, her Philippine host was a good decade younger than Dr. MacCormack, the man who had played such an important role in her becoming a deaconess. In contrast to her husband, who was energetic, authoritative, and outgoing, Mrs. Parson was reserved, though not unfriendly. Her face bore a certain sadness which caused Margaret to wonder if she had lost a child.

Following the Customs inspection, Mrs. Parson had accompanied Margaret off the steamer, while her husband had seen to the young missionary's trunk, which was taken by a *cargador* for delivery to the Parson home. With Father Parson at the wheel—Margaret remembered to address the priest using the "High Church" designation preferred by the Philippine clergy—the three had motored along the narrow streets of Old Manila, somehow avoiding collisions with the many other vehicles, some motorized, others drawn by horse or water buffalo, the favored beast of burden known as a *carabao*. As he drove, Father Parson had pointed out the notable sights. "The walls enclosing Old Manila were started in the sixteenth century, but they have been patched and added to up to today. They were built for protection, and here"—gesturing toward a large gray stone complex on his right—"is Fort Santiago, once the site of the ancient Spanish citadel and now the headquarters of the U.S. Army. When the Americans came, they drained the moat surrounding it and turned it into a golf course. That's what I call Yankee ingenuity!"

To Margaret's inexperienced eyes, everything had seemed as if it had been transported directly from medieval Spain—faintly reminiscent of a California mission in building style, but much grander, at least in the case of the larger churches and public buildings. She had been surprised to learn that the imposing Roman Catholic cathedral was less than fifty years old, the previous one having been destroyed by an earthquake. "Oh, earthquakes happen here a lot," Mrs. Parson had explained, "but they're mostly not very strong. Not like what you had in San Francisco a few years ago."

Leaving behind the picturesque precincts of Old Manila, they had driven to the newer commercial and residential district where the Episcopal cathedral stood. Massively built in the Spanish style, it served a primarily American congregation which, she had been told, was diminishing in size with the Filipinization of the civil service. Not far from the cathedral was the Parson home, and by the time she had settled in, eaten an American-style supper, and taken a sponge-bath, she had been more than grateful to ascend the sleeping platform. Despite its unfamiliar construction—a bamboo mat stretched across an elevated, taut expanse of rattan, which permitted more air circulation than a conventional mattress—it had been surprisingly comfortable.

Perhaps adjusting to life in the tropics won't be as difficult as

I'd feared. Still, I'm glad I'm being posted to the Mountain Province. Bontoc, the province's capital and Margaret's mission destination, was situated 3,000 feet higher than Manila, giving it a more pleasant and healthful climate. She had followed the suggestion of Dr. Wood, the Episcopal missions secretary, to prepare for a range of climatic conditions.

Choosing her lightest clothing for a day intended to acquaint her with the city's Episcopal missions, Margaret was ready when Father Parson returned from leading the Cathedral's morning service. "Don't worry, we'll make sure you do some sightseeing before Father Henningsen claims you in two days," Mrs. Parson reassured her as they set out. "Manila is such a mix of cultures: Spanish and Malay, with a dash of Chinese, Japanese, and American thrown in—it's wonderful."

The three mission sites were located near each other in the Trozo district, a slum two or three miles north of the cathedral. Leaving the lovely gardens and residences of the American section, Father Parson drove across one of the bridges spanning the Pasig River, through the city's crowded commercial district, and into the Binondo neighborhood, which he said was the oldest Chinatown in the world. This area seemed almost familiar to Margaret, having visited San Francisco's Chinatown several times when she lived in California. She tried to memorize everything she saw so she could write Hallie about it.

Hallie. In the last few weeks, the child had been her unseen companion—by day a presence to whom Margaret might address a question or comment about what she was experiencing, by night a specter that haunted her sleep, leaving her aching in the morning with loneliness and longing. The parting from her daughter had been a test of her resolve to serve the Lord in the mission field. Though she had tried to prepare for Hallie's tears and pleas, when the actual time came to say goodbye, it was more wrenching than she could have imagined. At least she didn't have to witness her sister-in-law's glee at her departure; Margaret had insisted that Julia and Myrtle take Hallie and her to the dock and drive the little girl to Martina's afterwards.

Approaching the two-story building that housed the St. Stephen's Chinese School, she thought of her daughter who would soon begin the second grade. About twenty boys and girls of kindergarten age were playing outside under the watchful eye of two Chinese women. Mrs. Hobart Studley, the head of the girls' school and wife of the rector of St. Stephen's, was with a group of older girls, one of whom was reading haltingly from a textbook.

"Is not this a buh—buh…"

"Beautiful," supplied Mrs. Studley.

"… river," the child continued. "See how clear the water is." Margaret suppressed a smile at the notion of a "beautiful livel," which is how the girl's pronunciation sounded to her ears.

At that moment the instructor looked up to see Father Parson and his party. She excused herself, telling the girl to continue reading until Miss Lee should come and call on another pupil. After summoning her assistant, Mrs. Studley took her visitors to the chapel, a small area separated from the rest of the school by fabric strung up between posts.

The headmistress was shaking her head as she sat down. "Our textbook is better suited for a different kind of pupil," she said. "It assumes everyone in the Philippines washes their clothes in a river, but many of these families have servants to do that." She must have caught a look of surprise on Margaret's face, because she added, "Oh yes, as Father and Mrs. Parson already know, after the Americans, the most prosperous people in Manila are the Chinese. They are in charge of most of the commerce in this town. You noticed all the banks when you were driving here?" Before Margaret could answer, Mrs. Studley suddenly clapped her hands together and said, "Forgive my manners. I not only failed to introduce myself, but I failed to welcome you as well. Welcome! I am Edith Studley, and you must be our new missionary, Mrs. Peppers." She smiled benevolently on the newcomer. There was something in this wiry, middle-aged woman's manner that was reminiscent of Julia.

After the pleasantries abated, Mrs. Studley rose to give

the visitors a tour of school. "As you can see, we are bursting at the seams," Mrs. Studley explained as they walked through the downstairs classrooms. "The girls' school only began last year, but the enrollment has grown beyond our wildest hopes."

"What Mrs. Studley is too modest to say," Father Parson interjected, "is that she started with eighteen pupils and now there are ten times that number."

"It's the Lord's doing," the headmistress responded, but her pleasure at the commendation was evident. "At any rate, with the boy's school upstairs and the night school, both of which are growing too, we need a new building. The Chinese will raise the necessary money, just like they did to construct this building."

"And your plans to find a principal for the girls' school?" asked Mrs. Parson.

"This month my husband's article in *The Spirit of Missions* will appear and we have every confidence that God will send us a wonderful young woman in response to his appeal."

At the sound of "wonderful young woman" Margaret's ears pricked up. So far, all the missionaries she had met were middle-aged. It would be nice to have another young missionary working in the field, even if the chances of the two women's paths crossing were slim.

It was at the House of the Holy Child, the last stop on their tour, that Margaret ceased being merely a tourist. It was past noon when the visitors entered the old massive-walled Spanish structure, and though it was sweltering outside, it was quite comfortable within. Margaret marveled at the wisdom of the Spanish builders who knew how to create cool shelter in such a torrid environment. She wondered if the California missions were like this before they fell into ruins.

A tall, thin, gray-haired woman with rather mannish features approached the group, interrupting Margaret's musings. She introduced herself as Miss Frances Bartter, the house mother.

"You must be Mrs. Peppers, the new missionary," she said, in a clipped British accent. "We are delighted to have you here. We are just sitting down to a meal—won't you all join us?"

Father Parson nodded, and Miss Bartter led them down the long vestibule towards the dining hall. Margaret saw several crucifixes hanging on the walls, along with a few bamboo hats which she recognized as being like Myrtle's back home. Noticing her interest, Miss Bartter commented, "Those are called Manila hats, but they're made in another province. Here they serve to cover up the peeling paint." She glanced ruefully at Father Parson, as if he had the power to change the situation.

As they approached the dining room they could hear the sound of childrens' voices and the clatter of dishes. Miss Bartter opened the door and three dozen pairs of curious eyes turned in sync to survey the visitors; only a few of the youngest tots ignored them. The children were seated such that an older girl alternated with a younger one. The ages of the diners ranged from four or five to eighteen years old, plus two older Filipina women.

Stacks of hymnals covered a small round table near the doors, but at the sight of Miss Bartter and her guests, the two older Filipina women immediately got up, removed the books, and returned with plates and utensils. Perceiving their headmistress was not going to address them, the children returned to their eating and chatter.

Lunch was a kind of hash called *picadillo* and a fruit that Margaret had never seen before, which her hostess called *lanzones*. Mrs. Parson showed Margaret how to peel off the hairy skin and squeeze the gel-like fruit segments to remove the tiny bitter seeds.

"Our girls may be the abandoned daughters of American fathers, but they belong to the Filipino society of their mothers. We want them to be able to fit into that society which for now has rejected them as *mestizas*. Everything we do here is to that end, including serving Filipino food," Miss Bartter explained.

"My predecessor had different ideas," she continued. "She encouraged the girls to think of themselves as Americans and aspire to becoming nurses and teachers. But this was a settlement house before it became an orphanage, and we did good work training girls and women in domestic skills that are suitable for any woman. Besides, our sewing and other industrial activities helped pay the bills. God delights in a well-sewn seam as much as in a well-administered inoculation."

Margaret looked around at the sea of young faces that bore the evidence of their mixed parentage. *Some of these girls might even pass for Americans, their skin is so light. Yet no one wants them.* She felt a mixture of righteous indignation that mothers were compelled to give up their children—for she couldn't believe the Filipinas had abandoned their daughters willingly—and thankfulness that the Church at least had accepted these *mestizas*. For a moment she wished that the Bishop had wanted her to work here rather than among the pagans of the north. Then she shook her head as she remembered her call was to the Igorots.

Interpreting her gesture as evidence of disagreement, Father Parson ventured, "You have a different opinion?"

"No… I just wish the world were different."

"Ah, St. Paul admonishes us to be *in* the world but not *of* the world. We must be realistic and accept that things are the way they are. It does no good to anyone, least of all these half-castes, to teach our girls to ape the Americans. But we must show them the love they never knew from their own parents."

Margaret wasn't so sure that their mothers did not love them, but she held her tongue.

Chapter 14

Aug. 12, 1918, Manila, P. I.

Darling Hallie,

Yesterday I saw many boys and girls your age in Manila, which is the capital of the Philippines. Their families had come from the country of China, which is very far away. They go to a special school where they learn to speak English like you and I do, and also things that you are learning in school, like reading and writing and arithmetic. They looked very happy.

There are so many things here I have never seen or heard or smelled before! The Filipinos (which is what the people of this country are called) have horses and motorcars, but they also use water buffalo, which is a kind of large cow, when they want to carry heavy packages from one place to another. Sometimes they even carry things on their head!

It is very warm here and it rains often. That makes trees and flowers grow large and beautiful.

Last night I saw a beautiful sunset. It is the same sun that shines on both you and Mommy—just like the moon and the stars are the same ones you see at night. When you say your prayers before bedtime, remember that Mommy is looking at the same sky and thinking of you.

Please ask Aunt Martina to help you write a letter to me. She knows where to send it. I want to know all about school and all the things you are doing.

Mommy loves you very much and will be very happy when you can come live with her in the Philippines.

Margaret put down her pen and sighed. She had hoped a letter from her daughter would be waiting for her when she arrived in Manila. Perhaps Martina had sent it on to Bontoc, knowing that was her eventual destination.

Tomorrow morning Father Henningsen would meet her at the cathedral to begin the first leg of the trip to Bontoc. The entire journey would last several days and involve taking two trains, an autobus, and finally a horse. She was very uneasy about the horseback ride—an occasional short ride on a docile mare in Iowa was nothing like being in the saddle for hours, maybe days, on a steep mountain trail, among head-hunters no less! The Parsons had started to say something about it over supper that evening but when they saw Margaret's worried look, they promptly changed the subject. At times like this Margaret took comfort in the Scripture verse she had first memorized as a child in Baptist Sunday School: *"And we know that all things work together for good to them that love God, to them who are called according to his purpose."* How often in the last few years she had clung to the promise of that verse like a person in danger of drowning clings to a lifebuoy?

The next morning Margaret donned the garb of a deaconess for the first time since arriving in the Philippines. She had brought three of these garments with her: two black dresses, one a light-weight woolen and the other made of cotton, and one white dress, also of cotton. All were durable, long-sleeved, and simple in design. In addition, she had several white collars and cuffs she could exchange when soiled without having to wash her dress. A short veil of matching fabric, worn so that the hair surrounding her face was clearly visible—the Church wanted no mistaking deaconesses for nuns!—and a simple silver cross completed the ensemble. Not knowing how much dirt she would encounter when traveling, Margaret decided to wear her black cotton dress and veil.

Her hands trembled as she pinned her collar into place. The reality of her calling began to assert itself with a force that took her by surprise. She, Sarah Margaret Peppers, age twenty-four, was leaving for her first assignment—to help the heathen Igorots! How well would her three years of deaconess training prepare her for what she would encounter? She paused to murmur a prayer for divine assistance before sitting down to read—what, for the tenth time?—the letter that Dr. Woods, the Board of Missions secretary, had sent her this spring about how to prepare for her new life.

> *Your duties will be teaching of a very elementary character, so far as the regular day school work is concerned. Then you will have Sunday school teaching, the Catechism, simple Bible subjects, etc. All through the week you will have the opportunity day by day of trying to form the characters of the Igorot girls who are living in the school. That will be one of the most important parts of your work but as you can see it is very hard to define it exactly. Your life among them will count for more than anything you may be likely to do.*

To have a life that counts—that is what she has wanted all these years. No longer would she be thwarted by circumstances she could not control; she had finally taken her future into her own hands. If God had sent her trials, were they not intended to strengthen her so she might ultimately overcome them?

Unfortunately, any conviction that her time of testing was over was doomed to vanish like a fugitive moment of coolness before a Manila sunrise. For Margaret had not reckoned with Thomas C. Henningsen, the priest whom Father Parson introduced later that morning as her companion on the journey to Bontoc.

He was already waiting for her when she entered the drawing room after repacking her valise. His pinched face and bald head were bathed in perspiration. The contrast between his icy blue eyes and his flushed countenance, more from anger than heat she'd discover, could not be more marked.

Not waiting to be introduced, Father Henningsen said curtly, "Mrs. Peppers, I expected you to be waiting for me, not the other way around."

"I'm so sorry. I must have mistaken the hour that Father Parson told me you would arrive," she stammered, momentarily cowed by the presence of this six-foot stranger with Teutonic coloring and manner. Even his speech bore the hint of a German accent.

"No matter, there is plenty of time before you catch the train to Dagupan," Father Parson interjected, amiably.

"One never knows what delays one may encounter en route to the station," came the stiff response. "Why, coming over here there was a terrible collision between an auto and a *carabao* that snarled things for quite some time." Turning back to Margaret, Father Henningsen asked, "Are you ready?"

"Yes—yes." Margaret bade farewell to Mrs. Parson as servants hastened to carry the luggage outside, where the rector's car was waiting. It did seem a long time before they reached the station of the Manila North Railway, owing to the discomfort Margaret felt in the presence of her disapproving companion.

At last, they boarded the train and were off. They rode in the first-class car, which consisted of a series of compartments offering two crosswise seats upholstered with khaki cloth. Margaret didn't relish the prospect of a five-hour trip with Father Henningsen, but there was no helping it. For the first hour he was busy reading the Bible and making notes, causing her to wonder if he was preparing a sermon.

Meanwhile she settled down to take in the passing sites. In theory the first-class car was located sufficiently close to the engine to avoid the inevitable soot, but cinders were sucked through their open window anyway. It was a matter of enduring grime or sweltering, and by tacit agreement the window stayed as it was. Margaret was glad she had chosen to wear her black dress and veil. Already the handkerchief she used to cover her nose was becoming soiled.

At first, they passed through mile after mile of flat plains, where rice grew in orderly green rows emerging from the muddy waters of the paddy. Occasionally they saw mango and banana plantations, as well as fields of sugar cane. Margaret pitied any field worker who had to labor outdoors; even though the sun was obscured by clouds, the heat was oppressive.

Gradually a lone mountain became visible in the east, which her companion identified as the inactive volcano Arayat. It kept them company for hours, though much of the time it was hidden by the lowering clouds. After a lunch in the dining car consisting of *paksiw na pata*—pig's feet served with rice and bananas, which Margaret found surprisingly delicious—she returned to her compartment and dozed in her seat.

She awoke with a start when the train's piercing whistle signaled their arrival at Bautista station. The colorful clothing of the men and women who thronged the place entranced her, and she especially delighted in the billowy sleeves that graced the female costumes—*baro't saya* in Tagalog.

By five p.m. they had arrived at Dagupan, a community of some 22,000 people located on the coast. As they approached the town Margaret saw coconut groves and some kind of palm growing in swamp plantations. Father Henningsen told her it was *nipa*, and that it was used to build houses and roofs, as well as woven into hats for export.

The pouring rain of the last fifty miles of their journey had tapered off, but still it was miserably hot when, 30 minutes later, they arrived at the San Fabian terminus and headed to their hotel, which bore the grand name of El Presidente but was merely a modest rooming house made of nipa, run by a Chinese entrepreneur. From her sparsely furnished second-floor room Margaret could glimpse Lingayan Gulf to the west, and she told herself the beautiful sunset would compensate for any discomfort she might experience because of the heat. At least the place seemed clean.

She and Father Henningsen being the only guests, they ate their evening meal together at one end of a long table that took up most of the space in the dining room. Over a dish of broiled fish and rice, Margaret tried to make small talk, and she learned that the priest was married and had no children. At first Margaret said nothing about Hallie, fearing criticism by Father

Henningsen about forsaking her daughter. But when he asked her directly about having children, she told the truth and was surprised at his response.

"That's good," he said. "One must be completely dedicated to the Church and her mission here. Besides, it is not good for white children to grow up among savages. They are so impressionable."

"Do you mean the white children or the Igorots, Father?"

"I'm referring to the children of missionaries, of course." He frowned at her as if she were an obtuse pupil in one of his catechism classes.

"But isn't that the point of a mission school, to influence the Igorot children for good? Aren't they impressionable, too?" Margaret asked, trying not to sound argumentative. But there was something about Father Henningsen that made her want to challenge every statement he made.

"Think for a moment, Mrs. Peppers," Father Henningsen said, assuming an air of patience which seemed as unnatural as a circus bear attired in a tutu. "As adults we have the power to mold children, whether it be ours or a foreign culture's. We need not fear contamination from childish ways, nor from savagery. But the same is not true of even the most well-brought-up child. Surely, as a mother yourself, you must agree." It was clear no response was expected, agreement being presumed.

Will all missionaries at Bontoc be this way? Margaret wondered apprehensively.

That night, closing the door to her room, she was overcome with exhaustion. She had planned to begin a letter to Hallie but instead Margaret quickly washed her face, undressed, and climbed onto the elevated bamboo mat, being careful to draw the protective netting close around her. The last sound she remembered was the high whine of a mosquito as she drifted off to sleep reciting the Lord's Prayer.

Chapter 15

When Margaret met Father Henningsen for breakfast, she noticed he had already finished his boiled egg and was halfway through his toast. Glancing at the clock nearby, she saw she was exactly on time. She offered no apology. After a curt "Good morning," they ate in silence until Margaret ventured a question about the next leg of their journey.

"When does the spur train from San Fabian leave?"

The priest fixed his ice-blue eyes on her, clearly astonished at her ignorance. "The train doesn't run in the wet season," he said. "They take up the tracks each May before the nearby river floods. That's why I thought it was very foolish to have you come in August, but Miss Whitcombe is overdue for her furlough and wanted no more delays in bringing in an assistant. She prevailed, of course." Disapproval etched his voice.

As if intuiting her question, the priest launched into a description of their alternative transportation. "The natives often walk the section from San Fabian to Camp One, but we will go by horseback. Unless you want me to hire some Igorots to carry you in a sedan chair while I ride." He paused, and Margaret wondered if he was being sincere or sarcastic.

"How good a rider *are* you, Mrs. Peppers?"

Perceiving a challenge in the priest's question, Margaret decided that honesty was the best policy. "I haven't ridden very much at all, I'm afraid. I'm counting on having a horse that is familiar with the territory. And on your expertise, too," she quickly added.

During this interchange Father Henningsen's face had

displayed the swift variability of a sky in a passing storm, going from cloudy to sunny as he perceived Margaret's inexperience to be an opportunity for him to display knowledge and mastery.

"The San Fabian spur is a gentle, four-mile ride, and our only challenge will be wading through the water. On the other hand, the riding trail from Baguio to Bontoc is narrow and steep, with the mountain on one side and a chasm on the other." He concluded more encouragingly, "Still, with the Lord's help, we will make it through."

Rather than easing Margaret's worries, this news only intensified them. She told herself that all the missionaries before her had managed it, even the Bishop himself, so there was nothing to fear. *Yea, though I walk through the valley of the shadow of death, I shall fear no evil....*

When the time came for them to leave, Father Henningsen decided that all the available horses were too spirited for a novice, so he grumbled an order for a litter for his companion. Soon Margaret found herself being hoisted up into the air on a rattan chair balanced on two bamboo poles. Her two carriers were barefoot men clad in light-colored, short trousers and loose-fitting, long-sleeved shirts. Each wore a colorful band of cloth tied around his forehead. Embarrassed, Margaret felt like a princess being carried by her subjects.

The luggage was carried in a cart drawn by a *carabao*, attended by a third man. Twice during the two-hour journey, they halted because the cart got stuck in the mud. Father Henningsen had to dismount to help extricate the vehicle while Margaret and her carriers continued on, there being no place to put down the litter before their destination. She pitied them all—the natives who slogged uncomplainingly through the muck, the plodding horse and water buffalo, even her prickly priest companion who arrived at Camp One with boots and pants caked in mud. At least it had not rained that morning.

On the drive to Baguio, she experienced an unnerving introduction to the reality of travel in the mountains. The Kennon Road, completed in 1905, had been hailed an engineering marvel by the Americans and derided as an expensive boondoggle by Filipino skeptics. As the Benguet Motor Bus zig-zagged its way up the 3,600-foot incline, the grind of its gears mingled with the sound of the rushing waters of the Bued River, which had carved the steep gorge along which they now traveled. Pelting rain obscured not only the canyon walls but much of the road as well. The driver seemed to enjoy the challenge of motoring along a ledge only slightly wider than his vehicle, and to Margaret's alarm he began to pick up speed as they neared their destination, like a horse quickening into a run as it approaches its corral. All she could do was to pray with a fervency that was every bit equal to the best of Father Henningsen's capabilities.

Finally, the three-hour ordeal ended, and after passing a military road leading to the U.S. Army Camp John Hay, they reached Baguio, a settlement like no other in the Philippines. The Americans had established it in 1900 as their summer capital, and it had all the amenities of a city in the United States. Laid out by a noted American city planner and architect, it possessed gravel-paved roads, a public water system, and septic tanks. Much of it was electrified, and a telegraph and daily mail service linked the city to Manila. There were also two Episcopal schools: Baguio School for American boys and Easter School for Igorot children.

"How beautiful this is!" Margaret exclaimed as she stepped off the motor bus, instantly forgetting her fright as she surveyed with delight the pine-clad hills sheltering the settlement. A pleasant breeze ruffled her hair as a sandy-haired young man wearing a clerical collar moved quickly to greet her and Father Henningsen.

"Welcome to the City of Pines!" smiled the good-looking stranger, who introduced himself as Clarence Wagner.

Before Margaret could say a word, Father Henningsen said, "You must be the new missionary I heard about. Teaching at Baguio School, aren't you?"

"Yes, and in a couple of months I'll step in as headmaster." He turned to focus on Margaret.

"So nice to meet you, Father Wagner. I am Deaconess

Peppers," she said, rejecting the usual "Mrs." For some reason Margaret preferred he think of her that way than by her married title.

"I won't be a priest for a few months yet, so just 'Mr.' is fine." I must have arrived on the ship ahead of you, since I've only been here for two weeks. Too bad we didn't take the same steamer—it would have been nice to have had a companion."

Margaret found herself blushing. To cover her embarrassment, she said, "I wouldn't have been that good a companion, since I was seasick for several days."

Mr. Wagner opened his mouth to reply, but Father Henningsen interrupted impatiently, "I assume there is Evening Prayer at the Church of the Resurrection? If we hurry, we can make it."

Later that night, at the Baguio mission compound where she would sleep, Margaret told herself it was only the journey that was making her feel excited. Meeting Clarence Wagner was simply getting to know someone her own age. Perhaps, when he became headmaster, he might even have a part to play in launching a girls' school at Baguio—Hallie's school, God willing.

The thought of Hallie banished, for the moment, the memory of the brief encounter which, in the days and months ahead, Margaret would relive again and again in her mind. For now, she would let her longing take her to the child who was growing up in the California sunshine—without her.

My sweet little girl,

Do you remember when we rode on a train to Los Angeles? Well, I have ridden a train and a motor bus to get to the place where I am now staying. It is in a beautiful land of mountains and pine trees, but oh my! the road to get here zigged and zagged like a snake, higher and higher until we reached the town called Baguio. It is the most important city in all this part of the Philippine Islands.

Tonight, I am staying with teachers in the Easter School. Isn't that a lovely name for a school? You might expect there to be bunnies and little chicks around, but it is called that to remind the students that Jesus always lives in our hearts.

The students are little boys and girls called Igorots. They come to school here to learn about Jesus and also to learn many useful things that will help them all their lives.

The girls weave beautiful skirts and other clothes using something called a loom. They have to sit down in front of a tree to do this weaving. The boys are learning to build things.

There are four children who live in the house where I am staying. Their names are Muriel, Arthur, Howie, and Bobby. Howie is seven years old, like you.

Tomorrow I will ride a horse to where I will live and work, the town of Bontoc. It will take four days to get there. I hope I will find a letter from you when I arrive.

Mommy loves you very much and blows lots of kisses to you across the sea to America.

At that moment, the sea separating herself from Hallie seemed a million miles wide.

Chapter 16

Sept. 10, 1918, Bontoc, P.I.

Dear Myrtle and Julia,
I want to write you now while I have time, because once I finish my apprenticeship and am fully in charge of the girls' school and dormitory at Bontoc, Heaven knows when I will have another opportunity.

It seems so very long ago that I used to sit in your home and listen to letters from the Philippines written by your brother Warren. Never could I have imagined that I would one day have adventures such as I've experienced these last few days as I've made my way from Manila to Bontoc, the capital of the Mountain Province.

Margaret paused to swat away a fly before launching into her account of the four-day trip by rail, litter, motor bus, and horse which had brought her to the mission. She was glad she could be honest with her friends about how anxious and inept she'd felt much of that time.

You read me something Warren wrote once about the Kennon Road, but I was still not prepared for the zigs and zags and the steepness. I had to close my eyes sometimes when it looked like the motor bus was going to go over the edge. But that was nothing compared to the Mountain Trail.

An Igorot young man who is a student at the

University of the Philippines was visiting the Baguio mission, and he loaned me his horse, which he said had once belonged to Bishop Brent. The animal was sweet but veered toward the outer edge of the trail—and those edges overlooked canyons of a thousand feet or more! I was afraid to look but I was also afraid to close my eyes, so I repeated to myself Psalm 121, especially the line, "He shall not suffer thy foot to be moved."

As we got closer to Bontoc, we began to see the rice terraces made by the Igorots. Father Henningsen, who likes to explain things, told me how they are made, with stone walls and mud barriers and irrigation ditches. They seem quite ingenious, unlike the primitive Igorot houses which are really just grass shacks.

After four days we reached Bontoc, elevation 3,500 feet. Since it is the capital of the Mountain Province, there are some Lowlanders as well as Igorots. They live in separate areas, and the Episcopal mission, called All Saints, operates in the Igorot area. The Lowlanders are Catholic, by and large, and we are careful not to interfere with that flock. Across the Rio Chico is Bontoc's twin community, Samoki, a much smaller Igorot village we also serve. In the dry season I'm told the river is easily fordable.

There are four of us at Bontoc, two priests— Father Sibley, who is in charge, and Father Frost, his assistant—Miss Whitcombe, and myself. We divide duties at the schools, but of course, the services are led by the priests. I like them all except for Father Henningsen; fortunately, he is at an outstation, so I won't see him every day. A couple more deaconesses are at other outstations, but I haven't met them yet.

The Igorot people do everything their elders tell them. It took a long time to persuade them to accept a Christian school and even now, we have a problem with children running away to their homes and the parents refusing to make them return to school. Still, if these people are to advance and not get exploited in dealings with the Lowlanders or the white people, their best hope is to embrace the new life and learning we offer them. Of course we also want them to know the one true God, but as Father Sibley likes to say, "True Christianity is caught, not taught."

Dusk had deepened into darkness, causing Margaret to pause to light the kerosene lamp. Its pungent odor made her think of growing up in Iowa.

This letter has been all about me and my concerns and nothing about you. Do write and let me know what you are doing. I am a little worried about the Spanish influenza outbreak that was affecting the troops when I left. I couldn't bear to think that you or my dear Hallie might be taken ill.

I still haven't received any letters from Hallie, and I don't know what to make of it.

Tomorrow, I help Miss Whitcombe teach Sunday School—my first Igorot class!

May the Lord bless you and keep you,
Margaret

CHAPTER 17

"Missus Teacher, why you wear this?" The young girl at All Saints School tugged on the long sleeve of Margaret's white dress.

Smiling down at Udao, the deaconess answered, "Because I am God's helper." She said the words slowly, not being sure how much English the youngster knew.

"Too hot!" Udao responded with a frown, either not understanding, or else ignoring, the reason given.

Margaret regarded her little inquisitor, unsure what next to say. Because Udao was a mission child she wore a loose white short-sleeved blouse along with the customary woven wrap-around skirt, called a *lufid,* striped like a red and white candy cane. If she were in her village, she would have been naked to the waist, and perhaps only wear a *tapis,* or sash.

"Missus Teacher" looked helplessly at Agnes, one of the several Igorot assistants who taught at the school, hoping she could offer an explanation in the Bontoc tongue. "Tell her I don't mind because I am doing God's work," Margaret said, though in fact she sometimes wished she could wear clothes more suitable for the climate. Agnes said something to Udao which seemed to satisfy her, and the child trotted off to rejoin her friends. *I wonder if I will ever be able to communicate with these people.* Agnes herself had been a student at the girls' school only a few years before, though when she entered, she was known by her Igorot name of Kanayu. All the pupils at All Saints were given Christian names at the time of their baptism, which they used ever afterwards in

Christian settings.

Margaret wished she had Lizzie Whitcombe to talk things over with. Her co-worker had previously taught kindergarten in Chicago and had even worked with Jane Addams at Hull House. But Lizzie was on four months' furlough, and now Margaret only had Father Sibley to turn to, or occasionally, Deaconess Routledge or Deaconess Diggs when they came to Bontoc from the mission outstations. To her dismay, kind Father Frost had recently been sent to another mountain mission, Sagada, and Father Henningsen had come in his place. It was impossible not to have dealings with that insufferable priest, but she certainly wasn't going to confide in him. Nor did she care for his wife, who liked to gossip and had an acid tongue.

There were many things about the Igorots that made her uncomfortable. Head-hunting among enemy tribes had mostly disappeared, though Deaconess Routledge had told her how last year a Christian boy was directed by his village elders to avenge a murder and decapitated a fellow student at the Tukukan outstation school. "There was feasting and dancing in the avenging village," the deaconess recalled, "but I told them I would withhold all Christmas gifts, and they were very sorry and accepted their punishment as just."

Of all the Igorot tribes, the Bontoc were the most traditional. Father Sibley told her how the people lived in fear of the *anito*, the ancestor spirits, and that this held them back. She was especially indignant at the way the women were made to do so much work while the men took their ease. And when it came time to harvest the sweet potatoes that, along with rice, made up much of their diet, the village tried to conscript the mission girls! The girls would have given in, if she hadn't put her foot down.

Four months into her missionary service, a letter finally arrived from Hallie.

> *Dear Mama,*
>
> *I am fine. Aunt Martina is taking good care of me. I like my school and my teacher. Her name is Miss*

Schultz. We study many things such as arithmetic and reading. I am also taking piano lessons. Jeremy takes lessons too but he doesn't like to practice. Mrs. Murphy gives me a gold star when I play a piece perfectly.

Are there many little girls where you are teaching? Do they take piano lessons?

Tomorrow I am going to a birthday party for my friend Eileen. She says we will get to ride a pony and eat cake and ice cream. I can hardly wait.

That's all for now.

Love,

Ruth Hal

P.S. Aunt Martina says that my real first name is Ruth and that I should use it. Because Ruth was a very important person in the Bible.

After rereading it twice, Margaret folded the letter and carefully placed it next to the snapshot of Hallie that had been taken last Easter. The brief communication left Margaret feeling bereft. Did Hallie even miss her, or had Martina made sure no longing could be voiced? Why did she think she could ever be a foreign missionary and live apart from her daughter? *It's only temporary,* she reminded herself, for the umpteenth time.

In October, Margaret experienced her first typhoon. At the time she had told herself it was like a Midwest tornado or even a Santa Ana wind in Los Angeles, but with the added excitement of torrential rain. Neither her fellow missionaries nor the children had seemed particularly alarmed, and afterwards Lizzie had said it was mild in comparison to the 1916 typhoon, which completely destroyed the girls' dormitory. Landslides, it seemed, were the most fearsome effect of typhoons in the mountains, often obliterating roads and sometimes even whole villages.

This year no landslide prevented the delivery of Christmas packages for the All Saints boys and girls. From the

States the Woman's Auxiliary and the Girls' Friendly Society could be counted on for gifts ranging from cloth for sewing clothing to beads, whistles, combs, and simple toys. As the holiday grew near, the children's excitement quickened, and the exclamation *"Kaat nan Kolismas?"* ("How long before Christmas?") began to resound like a drum accompanying an Igorot dance.

But suddenly, and ominously, the dance of anticipation faltered, as first one child and then another were stricken by the dreaded Spanish influenza. Classes, Christmas pageant rehearsals, even some chapel services were suspended as more pupils fell ill. Of the missionaries, only Father Henningsen became sick, and his wife attended him. Margaret found herself caring for two dozen girls at one time, assisted by Rose Fontek, one of the first Bontoc converts and head of the school's primary department.   The stricken children were separated from their supposedly healthy peers, some of whom made for home at the first opportunity. This action, though understandable, was strongly discouraged by the mission, and it unfortunately spread the disease in the native villages. Meanwhile the influenza raged in town among the Lowlanders and Americans. Some Igorots justifiably blamed them for the calamity. The more traditional tribesmen made animal sacrifices to the *anitos*.

As Margaret went from sickbed to sickbed, administering aspirin and cold compresses, her worst fears were coming true. Not only was she reliving Hal's final days, but she saw in each girl's feverish face her own daughter. *What if she has fallen ill?* She tried to remind herself that Hallie lived in a doctor's home and would receive excellent care. Still, worry dogged her day and night, and guilt that she was tending to other people's daughters rather than her own.

She decided to send a telegram to Martina, asking for assurance that Hallie was well. Not trusting her sister-in-law to answer by telegram, she sent another one to her friend Julia, whom she knew would find out the situation and respond with alacrity. *What if Julia is sick!* Margaret thought, as another worry seized her. With a determination born from experience in the TB ward, she did her best to set aside her fears. *All I can do is wait—and pray.*

The first answer came two days later. RUTH FINE NOW, wired Martina. That meant Hallie must have been sick, but blessedly she was better. Margaret resolved to write her daughter a letter that very night, and one to her sister-in-law too, thanking her for the care she must have given Hallie.

No response came from Julia and Myrtle for several days, and when it did, the news was somber. George, their one-time chauffeur who had become a doctor, had succumbed to the virus, like so many young adults in the influenza's second wave. Margaret's telegram had arrived the day he had died, and since then the sisters had been assisting his parents in any way they could. All public funerals were banned in San Francisco. Margaret wondered if his Buddhist parents were permitted some kind of ritual in the rural area where they lived. She hoped they would be allowed at least that small comfort.

In the end, even the All Saints Mission was not spared death's visitation. Ten-year-old Mary sank under the fever as if she were a stone in her father's rice paddy. Her five-year-old sister Anna, to whom Mary was more like a mother after their own mother died the previous year, was inconsolable.

A voice inside kept whispering, *Do something!*—and for one crazy moment Margaret considered adopting Anna herself. After all, Deaconess Diggs had adopted the little Igorot boy James after his mother had died giving birth to him. She could ease little Anna's loneliness and raise her to be a good Christian, an exemplar for the other Igorot girls. And Anna could be Hallie's little sister. But the notion was worse than impractical; it felt like a violation of the mother-daughter bond that she and Hallie shared. Margaret was ashamed for having entertained it, even for an instant.

The Great War had been over for a month, but no bishop had been elected to replace Bishop Brent, whose health had prevented him from returning to the Philippines. It was anyone's guess when his successor might be chosen. In the meantime, nothing was happening to revive the missionary girls' school in Baguio. Margaret was beginning to fear her reunion with Hallie might never come.

Chapter 18

By February, the Spanish influenza had run its course and life returned to a routine that was by now becoming familiar to Margaret. She was kept busy from early morning to late at night, especially with Lizzie Whitcombe gone. She missed her comrade and missed her counsel. There was that matter of the *olag*, for instance.

One morning Margaret had wakened early and decided to get up for a walk before accompanying the girls to morning chapel. After descending the stairs from the women's missionary quarters, she paused to look in on the older girls' dormitory located on the ground level. To her horror, on opening the door to their sleeping quarters she saw several teenage boys making a hasty exit through the windows.

Immediately she ran outside to apprehend the boys, but they were too fast for her and had disappeared into the trees. Returning with the intent to confront the girls, Margaret changed her mind, deciding it was better to enlist the help of one of the Igorot teachers.

"Martha, come here, please," she said to the young woman readying the classroom for the day. "Something's happened, and I need you to translate."

Martha looked uncomfortable as the deaconess explained the situation. "Mrs. Peppers," the woman started to say, but Margaret ignored her and practically dragged her to the dormitory.

"I want to know why this happened and who was involved," Margaret demanded of her assistant. Anger and shame that this had occurred on her watch made her unusually brusque. Grimly, she watched as Martha calmly determined the facts. She did not seem to share Margaret's sense of outrage.

Once the miscreant girls had been identified, Margaret left them and the others in the care of Martha while hastening to inform Father Sibley and ask his advice. To her astonishment he did not display anger so much as resignation and embarrassment.

"These lapses occur from time to time," he said. "Did Miss Whitcombe not tell you about the *olag*?"

"What's an *olag*?"

"The Igorots have a system of—ah—trial marriage. You know that by the time a child is five or six they sleep in a boys' or girls' house away from their parents. The girls' house is called an *olag*, and when they reach puberty they will entertain a young man or two of their choosing there overnight. Becoming—ah—pregnant is a sign that the couple involved should get married. And usually they do. It's all part of their culture, I'm afraid."

"What should we do?"

"Well, I know more now than when this first happened to Miss Whitcombe two years ago. Then I sent her to Governor Kane, thinking he would punish the boys for violating the girls."

"And what happened?"

"The governor called in the local headman, who explained that the boys were merely behaving as they were expected to. It was decided not to intervene officially, but to leave any punishment up to us."

"You mean the boys were from the mission? I couldn't get a good view of which boys were involved this time, but I asked Martha to find out."

"In Miss Whitcombe's case, some but not all of the boys were ours. We gave everyone a good talking to and have tried to keep a closer eye on the dormitories since then. Two girls ended up pregnant and got married—in the church." He watched as Margaret silently pondered this piece of intelligence.

"Do you know what one of the mission boys said when I

told him it was a great sin to sleep with a girl you are not married to?" Father Sibley said, as Margaret prepared to leave. "'I'm sorry, *Apo*. We thought you had a nice new *olag* built so we Christians would not have to go to the dirty *olags* at home to sleep.'" Shaking his head, the priest added, "The headman told me this: 'Igorot boy good Christian when got coat on. Take off coat, go to bed, he good Igorot again.'"

"That," Father Sibley concluded, "is how it is."

Thankfully, Lizzie returned right after Easter, in time for a grand fiesta held every April in Bontoc, which the whole mission attended. It was a day dedicated to dancing and sports competition among the Igorots. The Governor of the Mountain Province presided, and even a few governmental officials from Baguio had come.

The children at All Saints had been excited all week, and a couple of scuffles had broken out between boys from different villages, each claiming that theirs would emerge triumphant. For her part, Margaret was looking forward not only to the spectacle but also to the chance to be with her fellow deaconesses from Tukukan and Alab, Margaret Routledge and Eveline Diggs. Even Father Henningsen and his wife seemed to be in a good mood as the entire mission walked the mile to the event.

As they approached the festivities the rhythmic "dong, dong" of the *gansa* could be heard above the noise of the crowd. The sound of this ubiquitous Igorot instrument, a hand-held brass gong, had taken some getting used to, but she had begun to wonder if it might not be as fitting an accompaniment to the chapel hymns as the pump organ which Mrs. Henningsen played on Sundays. She smiled at her heresy.

"You seem in a happy mood, Margaret," observed Lizzie, who herself seemed more relaxed since her return from furlough.

"It feels a bit like a holiday, doesn't it?"

They arrived in the middle of a dance performed by the village men. Each held a *gansa* which he beat in an ever-increasing tempo with a skin-covered drumstick.

The dancers were arrayed in a circle and advanced counterclockwise, semi-crouched, in a line. While continuing to beat their *gansas*, one after another began to spring toward the center of the circle as if attacking a foe, then return to his place in line. Spring—pause—retire, spring—pause—retire: the steps were performed with perfect timing and grace.

This dance was followed by several others executed by neighboring villagers, usually male, though one dance involved only women. Throwing their blankets about them, the women danced in a circle, clutching tobacco leaves in each extended hand, which were collected by an old man who passed among them. They danced less vigorously than the men, their bare feet scarcely leaving the ground, though a few of the older women made a pawing kind of movement that sent dust and gravel flying behind them, to the discomfort of the nearest onlookers.

All this time the mission children moved their feet to the rhythm of the gongs. Some tried to imitate the adult dancers.

I wish Hallie could be here, Margaret thought wistfully, recalling the little girl's captivation with the Igorot "village" at the Exposition. All of a sudden, she remembered her own grade-school teacher intoning, in a slightly nasal voice, Rudyard Kipling's imperialistic couplet: "Oh, East is East and West is West, and never the twain shall meet." It was a pronouncement Margaret had once believed—but did she still? Was the gulf between the world she left behind—Hallie's world—and the world Margaret lived in now, unbridgeable?

CHAPTER 19

1920

"Here's a Bontoc riddle for you, Margaret. There are two brothers, and they turn their backs on each other. Who are they?" Lizzie stopped brushing her ginger curls to fix an eye on her roommate, who was sitting in a rocking chair, staring into space.

"I give up," Margaret answered after a moment's puzzling. She had never been good at riddles.

"Ears!" Lizzie responded, grasping her own and wiggling them for good measure. Margaret smiled despite herself. *Thank goodness for Lizzie—she keeps me from getting glum.* She asked, "Did one of the children tell you this?"

"In fact, it was one of the village elders," Lizzie answered before adding mischievously, "Do you think I should try this on Henny Penny?" Henny Penny was the name the women missionaries had started calling Father Henningsen behind his back. It perfectly suited the pessimistic priest who reminded them of the chicken in the fable who went around shouting, "The sky is falling! The sky is falling!"

It was common knowledge that Father Henningsen had been transferred to Bontoc after alienating everyone at Sagada. Deaconess Anne Hargreaves, who taught at the Sagada mission's Besao School, had warned her Bontoc comrades to expect the worst. "You can't imagine the havoc that man managed to create," she said, then began to recite one transgression after another. "I don't know which was worse: his walking into my school—*my school!*—and removing children without a by-your-leave, or the fact that he'd been making a personal profit from selling horses to the mission. Father Staunton was a saint to tolerate him!"

Things only got worse when Father Sibley, who somehow managed to keep his troublesome subordinate in check, went on furlough in late 1919 and Father Henningsen was left in charge at Bontoc. Each day, petty annoyances reflecting Father Henningsen's need to be in control—such as forbidding the singing of hymns at the outstations if they were not accompanied by the mission's portable organ—mounted. So did the women missionaries' resentment of the autocrat.

For some reason Eveline Diggs, a prim but innocuous soul who had arrived the year after Margaret, particularly incited his ire. It may have started when she took objection to his slandering of Father Staunton in front of the other missionaries. From that point on Father Henningsen seemed to view her every action as a personal affront and did not hesitate to berate her before others, even the Igorot students and teachers. Margaret, who remembered how he had once accused her of incompetence in front of her own class, was indignant.

Early in 1920, after a particularly extreme response to Deaconess Diggs being five minutes late to Mass, the women considered using their only possible ally—Mrs. Henningsen—to try to moderate her husband's behavior. Margaret proposed using Lizzie to persuade her: she herself was out of favor with Mrs. Henningsen, who'd scolded her for venturing a mild complaint at the end of a trying day.

Despite her misgivings, Lizzie's efforts bore fruit: after shunning Deaconess Diggs and her Alab outstation for ten weeks, Father Henningsen suddenly reappeared. He offered no explanation for resuming his ecclesiastical duties there but deliberately disregarded the deaconess, instead working exclusively through the native teacher and commanding the villagers to do likewise. As if his pointed ignoring of Deaconess Diggs were not sufficient evidence of his continued belligerence, the events of the following month fairly bellowed his antipathy.

It began innocuously enough with Christmas carols. For as long as there had been an outstation at Alab, the children had sung Christmas carols at the festal Mass. Despite Father Henningsen's prohibition of hymns not accompanied by the organ, Eveline Diggs assumed an exception would be made in this case. She taught the children two hymns: "Oh Come All ye Faithful" to begin the service, and "Silent Night" for its conclusion. Even though the words were in English, the children enjoyed singing the hymns and became more proficient with each rehearsal. The deaconess was certain Father Henningsen would be favorably impressed.

On Christmas Eve the children enthusiastically began the first hymn as Father Henningsen entered the chapel. Instead of the usual Igorot gong, Eveline's own school bell was rung as accompaniment by a solemn eight-year-old boy. It was hard to see the priest's reaction at first since he stood facing the altar, with his back to the congregation, while the carolers sang. But when he wheeled to face the hundred or so adults and children in attendance, there was no mistaking the fury in his eyes. He waited until the end of his homily to drop his bombshell: "After long and careful prayer, I have concluded that there is one among us who is not worthy to take Holy Communion on this high feast day. Miss Diggs is nevertheless welcome to approach the altar rail to pray for a change of heart."

Margaret turned to Evaline, who was sitting beside her in the front pew, in dismay and disbelief. Did Father Henningsen really think that Deaconess Diggs maliciously disobeyed his decree that hymns should be played "properly, with an organ" — however ridiculous that decree might be? The priest then announced there would be no further hymns that night. The only consolation that could be salvaged from the evening's wreckage was that Margaret would not be called on to display her rudimentary skills at the organ, which would doubtless have incited further wrath.

But Deaconess Diggs's torments were not yet over. The

next Saturday she had the misfortune to enter the church in Bontoc to arrange the altar flowers while Father Henningsen was hearing confessions. Realizing her inadvertent intrusion, she immediately left, but he sought her out afterwards, threatening to excommunicate her for violating the sanctity of the confessional.

"Excommunication is for notorious sins, and you are innocent!" Margaret could scarcely believe her ears when Evaline told her. "Besides, I've never heard of an Episcopal priest doing this—have you, Lizzie?"

Lizzie shook her head. "That man is crazy. We *must* write to the Bishop." Evaline shrank from taking up the pen to defend herself, but the other two deaconesses agreed they would each write a letter within the week.

The next morning the three of them sat together in church, Margaret and Lizzie flanking their comrade in solidarity. Margaret's mood was one of defiance. *How dare he treat Eveline this way? Thank the Lord Father Sibley is returning in two weeks. It won't be soon enough!*

She tried to concentrate on the Scripture readings, so she could meditate on them while Father Henningsen preached his sermon. With only half an ear she heard the priest solemnly invoke the Holy Trinity as he began his homily. His next words, spoken in a tone of exaggerated regret, made her sit up with astonishment and fury.

"On Christmas Eve I had the sad duty to deprive someone of Communion owing to continued willful sinning. Alas, since that day her actions reveal the repentance she expressed to be false. It is a grave matter to be separated from the body of Christ, but the articles of our religion are clear on what must be done."

Taking up the *Book of Common Prayer* from the lectern, Henningsen read the Thirty-third Article of Religion in a ringing voice: *"That person which by open denunciation of the Church is rightly cut off from the unity of the Church, and excommunicated, ought to be taken of the whole multitude of the faithful, as an Heathen and Publican…"*

Quickly Margaret glanced around the congregation, and judging from the blank expressions on the childrens' faces, they had no idea what was being said.

"Let us now kneel down and pray to our merciful Father to change her heart, that she might be restored to fellowship with our Lord and His holy Church."

Margaret and Lizzie looked at one another and without a word, rose, pulling the denounced deaconess up with them. "We're leaving," Margaret whispered fiercely to her companion. "I refuse to listen to one more word from that demon!"

With heads held high, she and Lizzie stalked out. Deaconess Diggs shambled after them, barely able to see the bowed heads of the congregation through her tears. About fifty feet from the chapel she collapsed sobbing in Lizzie's arms.

For the next hour they tried to comfort the distraught woman, to little avail. Finally, Lizzie suggested it would be best if she return to Alab, where she and her boy James could wait things out until Father Sibley returned. Lizzie offered to walk her back.

"But Father Henningsen said he would write the Bishop to have me recalled," Eveline wailed.

"Never mind that," Margaret said. "I'm sitting down and writing him a letter right now, and so will Lizzie when she gets back."

Later than night, as Lizzie extinguished the kerosene lamp, she muttered to Margaret, "You know, when Henny Penny told everyone to kneel and pray that Eveline repent, I half-expected to see the door to the tabernacle where we keep the reserved sacrament open as a sign that God would not allow such blasphemy to go unpunished. That man better watch out."

Her utterance proved to be prophetic. After Father Sibley returned two weeks later, Father Henningsen took a few days' leave on his superior's advice. He and Mrs. Henningsen decided to visit a beautiful lake they had heard some men in Alab describe. It was in a remote location, but a Christian Igorot who attended the Episcopal chapel in Alab offered to guide them. Days later, the guide was seen tending his rice paddy but neither the priest nor his wife had returned. The Igorot Constabulary was alerted, and when they questioned the guide, they were told the priest had insisted he could find his way back to Bontoc without his help.

It was another two weeks before Father and Mrs. Henningsen were finally located. They were alive but weak, their ample food supplies having run out after a few days. Their efforts at fishing had only met with limited success, so they subsisted on the relatively scarce wild banana and pineapple. According to a Constabulary report, they were in "serious mental and physical condition." Someone privy to the report later informed Father Sibley that the pair had apparently spent their time "sitting on the bank of the river crying."

In a matter of days, the Henningsens left the mission for Canada, never to return to the Philippines. The mood among the deaconesses was jubilant.

CHAPTER 20

Aug. 7, 1920, Tukukan, P.I.

Dear Myrtle and Julia,

Here I am in my little wooden house on the hill overlooking the village of Tukukan, with its terraced rice fields that seem to me a real engineering marvel—and such a contrast with the primitive huts that the Igorots call their homes. My cottage consists of a bed-sitting room and a little kitchen, and there is a porch large enough for outdoor sleeping if I choose. Deaconess Routledge liked to put the Victrola—yes, I even have a Victrola!—on the porch and play music, much to the amazement and delight of the Igorots. I've continued that tradition, as well as her honorific of "Ina"—"Mother." If priests are called "Father," does it not seem fitting for a woman missionary to be called "Mother," especially since the natives here are so child-like?

It's hard to believe it's been five months since Deaconess Routledge went on furlough. I've been so busy that I don't have time to think much about being the only white woman in this village of 800 souls. Between supervising two primary schools, tending the sick, giving religious instruction, and generally being available for anyone who happens by, I haven't had the chance to master the dialect like I'd hoped. Thank goodness for my Igorot helpers, Francis and Dorothy, who can translate when needed.

Miss Routledge had told me to expect frequent visitors during the daylight hours—the Igorots rarely venture out at night—and she was right. The main trail in this area passes my door and then branches off in different directions to the rice fields. Everyone works in the fields, but especially the women and—unfortunately—the girls. Some always stop by my house on the way to the fields, perhaps to have a flesh wound dressed, or to trade camotes *or bananas for calico or beads. At the end of the day, they return from the fields and like to sit down and rest on my porch, the men smoking their pipes while the women watch me shyly.*

You asked in your last letter about Igorot child-rearing. It's funny, really—on the one hand the children are spoiled, yet on the other they are forced into adulthood very early, especially the girls. Parents let their children run free at an early age, which makes it very hard to get the youngsters to go to school and stay in school. But when they do come to school, if they are girls, often it's with an infant strapped to their back or a younger child in tow. Perhaps that's why I have never seen an Igorot girl with a doll—who needs to play at being a mother when she is already fulfilling that role?

You also wondered if I liked my work among the Igorots well enough to stay for a long time. Now that the Henningsens are gone there is no one I can't get along with, but I must say that I am happiest when I am on my own, like here. If one of the women in charge of an outstation were to leave, I would be the first to volunteer. But that doesn't look likely, and the Church doesn't have the money to open new outstations, though they are desperately needed. So, after Miss Routledge returns in three months, I will go back to Bontoc and see what the Lord has in mind for my future.

Margaret put down her pen as she considered the possibilities. She was beginning her third year in the Philippines, and there was a new bishop. Either event could indicate a change was in the offing for her. Would she have a choice in where she went next?

She scribbled a few more lines to her Fairy Godmothers before starting her weekly letter to her daughter. A response from Hallie every six months was the best she could hope for, but still she persisted. Even the rare epistle from Martina bore the fragrance of home, and Margaret found herself anticipating these perfunctory communications more eagerly than she could ever have imagined.

Outside, the *bee-AHWEE* of a nightjar was signaling the day's end. Margaret pushed back from her desk, finally succumbing to her weariness. Time enough to write tomorrow.

Chapter 21

April 1921, Baguio, Philippines

> *Jesus Christ is risen today, Alleluia!*
> *Our triumphant holy day, Alleluia!*

The Church of the Resurrection's one-hundred-member congregation that Sunday, the largest of the year because it was Easter Day, sang the familiar hymn with enthusiasm. Mostly Americans with a smattering of Filipinos, they were joined by two dozen young visitors to Baguio, orphan girls from the House of the Holy Child, Manila. Margaret stood proudly among the children, her alto complementing the light soprano tones of her charges. She had every reason to rejoice: not only was it the most sacred festival of the Christian year, but God had seen fit to place her in charge of the very orphanage which had called to her on her first day in Manila, back in 1918.

She had taken up her new position only weeks before, and her first task had been to get the children ready for their annual two-month vacation in the Mountain Province, trading Manila's sweltering summer heat for Bagiuo's more comfortable climate. Fortunately, she had the help of two teachers from the orphanage, one American and one Filipino, and Mrs. Alice Massey, the temporary supervisor whom she was replacing.

Founded in 1909, the outgrowth of a broader Episcopal mission to Manila's poor, the House of the Holy Child had struggled under a series of house mothers since Margaret first visited it, and there had been talk of inviting a group of

Episcopal nuns to take over. Instead, the new bishop, Governeur Frank Mosher, had decided to put Margaret in charge.

"It's good to have a deaconess at the helm again," Alice Massey had said as she bade farewell to Margaret and the children two weeks before. "I was only a temporary stop-gap to hold things together after Miss Bartter returned to her regular post in Zamboanga. I have grown quite fond of the girls here in the last four months, and I know you will grow to love them too. Poor little waifs!"

Margaret already had all sorts of plans, including resurrecting the mission's embroidery program, which had taught useful skills and through the sale of goods, provided income for the orphanage. Her first responsibility, though, was the well-being of the girls in her care. She was just beginning to get to know them, and she hoped that the relaxed atmosphere of Baguio would give her ample opportunity to deepen her understanding and sympathy.

> *Sing we to our God above, Alleluia!*
> *Praise eternal as His love, Alleluia!*
> *Praise him all ye heavenly host, Alleluia!*
> *Father, Son, and Holy Ghost, Alleluia!*

The hymn marked the end of the Easter service. Since they had sat in the front two rows, Margaret and the children were the last to file out and greet the priest.

"Good morning, Deaconess Peppers," Clarence Wagner smiled, his deep brown eyes coming to rest on the young woman's face. Nodding toward the cluster of chattering and giggling girls, he added, "They may try to be solemn as befits their white veils, but you can't expect them to keep it up. And how are you faring? We haven't had a chance to talk much since you came to Baguio."

"Very well, Father." Her words sounded stilted in her ears. Ever since learning that Father Wagner was married, Margaret had felt awkward and ashamed in his presence. All those daydreams of serving alongside a man as consecrated as she—but as a missionary wife, not a deaconess! Margaret used her girls' impatience as an excuse to break away. If she lingered a moment longer under this man's gaze, she was sure he could see right through her.

The trek back to the school was two miles over the hilly terrain of north Baguio, but unlike the area around Bontoc, here the roads were paved and easily travelled. They passed the large public market, but fortunately it was closed owing to the holiday, else the girls would have pleaded to visit.

The place where they were staying was a large, two-story wooden building, constructed a few years before. Two dormitory wings flanked a middle section devoted to classrooms. The entrance was off a large front porch that doubled as the school chapel. The structure sat atop a raised foundation typical of buildings constructed by the Americans in Baguio, a word meaning "typhoon" in Tagalog. Though the town's record downpours justified its name, the months of January through April were relatively dry. By May the wet season would begin, and then the children—and the tourists—would return to Manila.

Arriving in her temporary quarters, Margaret felt a new disquiet. She took a moment before adjusting her white deaconess veil to examine her visage in the mirror. The twenty-eight-year-old woman who stared back at her that morning looked solemn, her unruly dark curls framing a too-high forehead and face more rectangular than oval. Her nose, though nicely shaped, was too big. At least her large, blue-grey eyes were nothing to be ashamed of—hadn't her husband wooed her by calling them "deep pools of fascination?" Her lips, too, were well-formed and proportionate, albeit less ready to smile as others might like. Even now she could hear her grade-school teacher admonishing her, "You are far too serious, Maggie!"

It had been eight years or more since any man had kissed those lips. Did she even remember what it was like to be desired?

I am here on the Lord's business. I don't have time for such nonsense.

The solution was work, and more work. If the House of the Holy Child offered anything to her, it was the chance to forget.

Chapter 22

Miss Marguerite Wolfson of the American Guardian Association is here, Deaconess Peppers."

"Thank you, Amparo. Please tell her I will be with her shortly." Margaret dismissed the young woman, a former resident of the House of the Holy Child, who was helping with administrative matters while studying at the Metropolitan Business College. After alerting her sewing class assistant Miss Dawes that she would be absent for thirty minutes or so, the deaconess hurried to meet the visitor.

A dark-haired woman in her mid-thirties waited in the sitting room, tapping her foot impatiently on the wooden floor. Margaret immediately perceived that her visitor was a force to be reckoned with—an impression confirmed by the conversation that ensued.

"Mrs. Peppers, I am delighted to meet you," Miss Wolfson said, holding out her hand before the deaconess had a chance to utter own her greeting. "Or do you prefer to be called Deaconess Peppers?"

"Deaconess Peppers would be fine," Margaret said, wishing to establish some authority of her own to counter that exuded by her visitor. "Welcome to the House of the Holy Child, Miss Wolfson. The Bishop has told me a little of you and your role with the American Guardian Association, but I would be happy if you would tell me more yourself."

"That's precisely why I am here," Miss Wolfson assured

her, with an air of one accustomed to enlightening others on a variety of subjects. "I have the honor of chairing the Woman's Advisory Committee of the Association. As our committee has the crucial responsibility of recommending which orphans will receive direct support from the AGA, you will understand why we must acquaint ourselves with the institutions that are available to house them."

Now that she was face to face with the superintendent of the orphanage, Miss Wolfson no longer seemed in a hurry. Margaret felt that she was under inspection and hoped that she would not be found wanting. She was certain her bishop would hear if anything, including herself, was not up to Miss Wolfson's standards.

"I understand there was a succession of women in charge of the orphanage before you came. I hope that the Bishop's appointment of a deaconess means there will be more continuity."

"I have every intention of remaining, Miss Wolfson."

Leaning forward as if to emphasize the importance of what she was about to convey, Miss Wolfson said, "The American Guardian Association has estimated there are 18,000 mestizos—I don't like the pejorative expression 'half-breed'—in the Philippines. Think of it! Police reports show that at least 8,000 of these are in a sad plight. These are children whose American fathers have abandoned them, and their Filipina mothers are left destitute. Many of the women were not of good character in the first place, and if the child is a girl, she will likely follow her mother's 'profession' when she is older. But you must know this already," she conceded, returning to her former position in the chair.

Instead of nodding sagely, Margaret shivered, suddenly remembering Delia at the House of Friendship, and her determination never to go to a home for "wayward girls." *Even women who are "not of good character" want a better life for themselves and for their children.*

Miss Wolfson continued with scarcely a pause. "These are

citizens of our country, and the American Guardian Association intends to arouse public sentiment in the United States to take responsibility for educating the next generation of leaders and their wives in the Philippines. Their intelligent, enterprising American blood—I won't say 'Yankee blood,' for you may notice my Southern accent—will win out if given half a chance. It will be many years before the native Philippine population will be ready for true self-government, but the process can be accelerated if we care for such orphans as inhabit the House of the Holy Child now."

"You must receive so many applications. How do you decide?" Margaret asked.

"We depend on partners such as the churches and the schools to bring the most needy and deserving to our attention. We could do so much more," she shook her head, "with more money."

Margaret nodded her agreement.

"The expatriate community here is quite generous, you know. Why, when I was last in Baguio, I tackled a number of the wives in the Country Club and you should have seen the husbands' wallets open!" She chuckled at the memory.

Abruptly changing the subject, the AGA representative asked, "Now tell me about yourself. What did you do before you came to the House of the Holy Child?"

Margaret briefly described her three years in Bontoc and her prior experience with social service while training in Berkeley. "It's quite a change from the Igorots, but I feel I belong here," she concluded. Before her visitor could probe further, she asked, "Shall we take a tour of the facility now?"

Together they toured the facility, which hadn't changed a great deal since Margaret first visited three years before, except for some new desks and added beds to accommodate the growing numbers.

"We have thirty-two girls now," Margaret explained. "Like you, we could do more if we had more funding." She opened the door to a classroom, where an American teacher was quizzing a group of eight- to ten-year-olds on geography. "Yolanda is one of the AGA children," she whispered, pointing out a bobbed-hair *mestiza* sitting in the back.

"I want you to have her and the other AGA wards summoned," Miss Wolfson said, in a voice that brooked no dissent. "I have something I want to give to each of them."

Margaret frowned. "We try to keep all the girls on an equal footing…"

Now it was Miss Wolfson's turn to frown. "It is a mere trifle, but we feel it's important for our girls to remember who they are and to inspire them to succeed." She paused, waiting for a response from Margaret, who remained silent. "Perhaps the young lady who first greeted me will do this…"

It was obvious that the Association representative would not leave until she had her way, so Margaret gave Amparo the names of the girls the visitor wanted to see. As they waited in the sitting room, Miss Wolfson began conversationally, "I met your Bishop Brent when we were both in France during the war. He was chaplain to the American Expeditionary Force, and I led a Red Cross ambulance unit. He was a fine man."

A vision of a formidable woman in a white uniform dispatching drivers to the front immediately presented itself. "I wish I had met Bishop Brent. Even though he'd appointed me as a missionary, by the time I arrived in this country, he was already gone. Everyone speaks so highly of him."

A moment later Amparo appeared with five girls, ranging in age from four to twelve. Some bore more obvious evidence of their American parentage than others—one even had blue eyes and freckles. The younger children had bobbed hair and wore cotton frocks of various colors and styles, betraying their missionary box origin. The two older girls, each with a long braid, were clothed in identical blue drop waist dresses which they had sewn in their Domestic Science class.

"Children, this is Miss Wolfson from the American Guardian Association. She is one of the nice ladies and gentlemen who are helping us take care of you," Margaret said, putting her arm around the youngest tot. She and the other girls stood wide-eyed before the visitor, unsure what to say or do.

"My dears," Miss Wolfson began, as she proceeded to tell the youngsters how fortunate they were to be at the House of the Holy Child. After asking each girl her name and age, she told the little assemblage they might call her Aunt Marguerite. As their American aunt, she had a special little gift for each one—a pin bearing the image of both the American and Philippine flags. Turning to the youngest girl, Miss Wolfson made a show of holding up the pin as if displaying a rare diamond, before affixing it solemnly to the child's dress. This procedure was repeated until every child had been invested with the insignia of her dual heritage.

"Say thank you, girls," Margaret said, trying not to show her displeasure at the impromptu ceremony of which she had no part.

Acknowledging the chorus of gratitude, Miss Wolfson smiled and then made a little speech about how they should never forget they were specially chosen by the American Guardian Association and that they should always behave in a manner that credits the United States of America, which God had made the teacher of the Filipinos until they were ready to join the family of nations. Margaret worried that the phrase "specially chosen" would linger in their memories, bringing disruption to the harmony of the orphanage in the days to come.

Miss Wolfson concluded by kissing each child on the forehead and then dismissed them to the care of Amparo, who had been watching impassively from the sidelines. Satisfied, she turned to Margaret and said, "I will be coming from time to time to check on the progress of my protégés, Deaconess Peppers. Thank you for making me feel so welcome."

Margaret wondered if this last remark was a veiled barb revealing Miss Wolfson's perception of insufficient hospitality or even downright opposition to her aims. Not until her Cadillac disappeared down the road did Margaret turn back toward her duties with a sigh.

Chapter 23

Margaret's concerns about the repercussions of the visit of "Aunt Marguerite" were not unfounded. During her short tenure at the House of the Holy Child, she had seen many children, aware of their tenuous place as "half breeds" on the social ladder—a hierarchy Margaret personally rejected, but felt powerless to overcome, so pervasive was its acceptance—seize on any distinction that might elevate them above their fellows. Even when a girl was not inclined to lord it over others, she might be the victim of a kind of preemptive retaliation, as happened a few weeks later, though it had no connection with Miss Wolfson's visit.

Despite being called an orphanage, for the most part the House of the Holy Child sheltered girls with two living parents, with the father almost always an American who had refused responsibility for the care of his daughter and her mother. Contrary to Miss Wolfson's insinuation, not all the mothers were of deplorable character, and as Margaret knew only too well, the decision to give their children up to another's care was a painful one, often made only as a last resort. Usually poverty dictated the mother's choice to give up her child, but in the case of seven-year-old Josefina there were other reasons.

Both of Josefina's parents had been born to Filipino families. Her mother was of higher social class than her father, and when the pair eloped, her mother's family disowned her. A few years after Josefina was born, her father died, leaving her mother nearly destitute. Owing to her beauty and family background, Josefina's mother didn't lack for suitors. Sadly, the man she chose to wed resented Josefina and treated her harshly. He eventually demanded that the child be given up—if not to his wife's family, then to an orphanage. As her family remained intransigent, Josefina's mother had no choice but to bring her daughter to the House of the Holy Child. At least the stepfather had agreed to pay the costs of raising the child at the group home.

The other girls resented Josefina for her light skin, her quick intelligence, and, most of all, the fact that she had a mother who sent her letters even if the orphanage rules forbade her visiting or sending gifts. Josefina had one prized possession—a pearl rosary her mother had pressed into her hand on the day she had delivered her into the care of the Episcopal Church. Margaret had often seen her fingering the lustrous beads at chapel, and the little girl insisted on holding them when she knelt to say her prayers every night before bedtime. Saying the rosary was a Catholic practice, but the deaconess allowed Josefina this reminder of her mother's love.

One morning before breakfast Winifred Mann, a young woman about Margaret's age who had recently joined the mission, led a sobbing and distraught Josefina to Margaret's office.

"What's the matter?" Margaret asked, directing the question to her assistant, as she pulled the child into her arms.

"Josefina has lost her rosary," Miss Mann replied. "She had it last night when she went to bed, but now it's missing. We looked under the bed and in the covers, but it's not there. Someone must have played a prank and hidden it."

Compassion for the bereft little girl congealed into anger. "It's not a prank, it's theft," Margaret responded grimly.

Softening her tone, she looked down at Josefina's tear-streaked face and said, "There, there, dear. Let's wipe those tears. We'll find your rosary." She gently dabbed the child's face, gave her a kiss, and returned her to Miss Mann.

"It's almost time for chapel. I will address the children afterwards at breakfast. We'll get to the bottom of this," Margaret said tersely to her assistant.

Before the cacophony of voices could erupt over the breakfast table, Margaret said an abbreviated grace, immediately following it with a sober announcement.

"Children, I am sorry to report that there has been a theft. Someone has stolen the rosary belonging to Josefina. This was a gift from her mother and is precious to her. Who can tell me what 'precious' means?" Several hands shot up.

Margaret called on nine-year-old María. "Precious is something very, very important to you," came the prompt reply.

"That's exactly right, María. Whoever has done this has taken something very, very important to Josefina. How would you like someone to take something that is important to you?"

Were the uneasy glances she witnessed ones of actual guilt or only disturbance at the idea of losing something precious? *We shall see,* Margaret thought.

"Who can tell me what the Eighth Commandment is?"

"Thou shalt not steal," the girls said in unison.

"Yes. Someone has stolen, and that is a very wrong thing to do. I expect the thief to see me in my office before classes start and bring the rosary with her." Margaret paused, before adding dramatically, "If no one comes forward, there will be no lunch for anyone—except for Josefina. That is all." She sat down and began to eat her breakfast in silence. It took a few minutes before the customary mealtime hubbub arose, and even so it seemed diminished over the usual.

No one had arrived by eleven-thirty, leaving her to face the imposition of her threatened punishment. *I hate to have the whole group suffer for one guilty member, but if I don't follow through, justice won't be done.*

Margaret resolved to use the time that would have been given over to lunch to search each child and her belongings, meager though they were. Nothing was found, except for a few forbidden sweets.

She considered her options. To continue withholding food was cruel. Keeping the children indoors during the first dry respite in several days punished not only the children, but the teachers as well, as recent experience had shown. In the last two weeks of nearly constant rain tempers had frayed, Margaret's most of all, as she had sought with limited success to restrain the energy of her confined charges. She remembered the disapproving look she had received from Winifred Mann when she lost her temper and spanked two girls who had defied her.

She decided to try sending the children to bed early. This punishment was likewise ineffectual, even after several nights, so Margaret finally gave up. Perhaps in the next big storm it would emerge from a secret burial spot on the orphanage grounds.

That left the problem of whether to replace the rosary. Margaret was torn between allowing Josefina's mother to send her daughter another one—possibly to suffer the same fate as the first—or to find some other means of assuaging the girl's heartbreak. In the end she decided to write Josefina's mother and explain the situation, suggesting that she give the child another, less valuable rosary, which Margaret would keep and give to Josefina whenever she wanted to use it. In the meantime, Margaret would keep her eyes open.

The weeks slid by in a routine punctuated by small crises, such as the partial collapse of one of the dormitory ceilings because of termites. There were happier events as well. Margaret had organized a branch of the Girls' Friendly Society, inviting older orphanage girls and young nursing students at the nearby hospital, some of whom Margaret had known at All Saints School. At the induction ceremony when Margaret placed a crown of white Cadena de Amor ("Chain of Love") flowers on each girl's glossy dark hair, she thought of the chain of love that linked herself with her former students at Bontoc. And what of the chain of love extending across the miles to Hallie? Would she be welcoming her own daughter into the Girls' Friendly Society someday, right here in Manila? If things went as hoped on next year's furlough, the answer would be yes.

Chapter 24

August 1922, the Pacific Northwest

Gleaming ivory in the late summer sun, the thirty-five floor Smith Tower, the tallest skyscraper west of Chicago, proclaimed to the passengers of the *President Grant* that their long voyage across the Pacific had finally ended. To Margaret's disappointment, Seattle's more spectacular landmark, Mount Rainier, was mostly obscured, its snowy summit barely distinguishable from the white clouds that swaddled the peak like an enwrapped Christ child in a Nativity scene.

"Our mountain makes its own weather," commented another passenger, as if he had read her thoughts. "But stick around a few days and I'm sure you'll see it. Better yet, pay it a visit."

Margaret was hoping to do just that, once she was settled in Seattle. She would be staying with another deaconess, Myrtle Nosler, for a few days until they both traveled to Portland for the Triennial meeting of the Woman's Auxiliary of the Episcopal Church.

The smiling face of the deaconess, easily identifiable by her white veil, greeted Margaret after she cleared U.S. Customs. A small, angular lady in her mid-forties, her dark hair flecked with gray, Miss Nosler resembled one of those pigmy woodpeckers so common in the Philippines, down to the woman's pointed, beak-like nose.

"Welcome back to America!" Deaconess Nosler said,

reaching for the battered satchel the traveler carried. Moments later she was supervising the loading of Margaret's belongings into a taxi—again Margaret smiled, remembering the dictum of her own training program, "A deaconess discharges her duties with efficiency"—and instructing the driver to take the pair to her apartment a couple of miles away. Once there, Margaret was suddenly overcome by exhaustion, barely managing to stay awake for dinner. Sleep came immediately after she lay down on one of the twin beds in her hostess's bedroom.

Miss Nosler, Margaret learned the next day, was a westerner born and bred, the daughter of early pioneers in eastern Washington. She had taught grade school in Spokane and now served the Diocese of Olympia–headquartered in Seattle—by coordinating its work with children. She also helped with parish visitation at the nearby Episcopal Church.

In the presence of this friendly woman, Margaret was already feeling lighter and able to disregard temporarily the duties that loomed, especially the circuit of meetings with women's groups to enlist support for the Philippine mission. She even slackened her tight hold on the concern that had increasingly haunted her, the nearer her furlough had approached. Soon enough it would be time to rekindle her relationship with Hallie and try to persuade her to return with her mother to the Philippines.

That was the outcome the Board of Missions, in the person of its Executive Secretary Dr. Wood, had been pressing for, ever since she had been accepted to go overseas. With almost every communication he had managed to insinuate that it was unnatural for a mother and her young daughter to be separated in this way. He had also expressed his disapproval by stonewalling Margaret's requests for the customary educational allowance for a missionary's child, pointing out that her original explanation for leaving Hallie in her aunt's care was the Peppers family's insistence on educating the girl.

She resolved not to worry about the future and instead concentrate on enjoying herself during this brief period when she had no immediate responsibilities to anyone but herself. It took little to convince her to go on an outing to Mt. Rainier, even though she had never camped before in a tent. *It can't be any more primitive than living at Tukukan or even Bontoc.*

Myrtle—for by then they were on first-name basis—made all the arrangements. They caught the excursion car one morning at the train station in Seattle, watching the landscape give way to wooded prairies and forests, occasionally marred by clear-cuts. As the terrain became hillier, Margaret thought of the pine-clad surroundings of Baguio. The air felt cool on her face and she wondered if she would be chilled camping at the national park's much higher elevation. On Myrtle's advice she had brought the warmest clothes she had packed, but she had been preparing for a fall and winter in Southern California, not anything colder.

By noon they had reached Longmire Springs, a few miles inside the park. They drove along the rim of canyon of the turbulent Nisqually River, the mountain road climbing ever higher with switchbacks reminiscent of the Baguio motorway, except instead of pines and rice paddies, there were dense stands of fir and hemlock. Reaching the Nisqually Glacier, source of the waterway they had been following, Margaret was awestruck by the sight of her first mighty river of ice. It was nothing like the frozen streams she had known in Iowa.

After ten more winding miles of breathtaking beauty, they arrived at last at Paradise, so named because of the sublime combination of meadows, bejewelled with wildflowers like so many gemstones of the Heavenly City, and the towering mountain fastness of Rainier, gleaming white in the sun like the veritable throne of God. Ever after when Margaret heard the words of the psalm, "I will lift mine eyes unto the hills, from whence cometh my help," she remembered that day when she first stepped onto the flanks of what the locals simply called, The Mountain.

Even a night spent shivering in a tent listening to Myrtle's muffled snores didn't dim her delight. She knew that if she were ever to leave the mission field, Washington State would be the place she'd like to live.

Three days later she and Myrtle boarded the train for Portland, Oregon, site of the Episcopal Church's triennial General Convention. As only male clergy and laity could be delegates and transact official church business, the Woman's Auxiliary had for many years run a concurrent meeting, focusing on the domestic and foreign missionary endeavors it supported financially with the United Thank Offering, or U.T.O. Margaret being one of the missionaries funded completely by the U.T.O., her presence at the women's meeting was assumed.

"How lovely to see you again, Deaconess!" gushed Fanny Mosher, wife of the Bishop of the Philippines, at the opening session of the Women's Triennial. The stubby fifty-year-old, her brown eyes capped by bushy brows and underscored with dark circles, reminded Margaret of a raccoon, with an inquisitive nature to match. Soon after the Moshers had come to the Philippines, she'd spent the day with the Bishop's wife, who had wanted to know everything about the House of the Holy Child and its new superintendent. It was apparent that Mrs. Mosher served as a second set of eyes and ears for her busy husband, and Margaret was always a bit wary around her.

Margaret was grateful she was not expected to speak formally at any of the sessions; she'd rather clean latrines than address a group of strangers any day. She consoled herself by remembering that in scarcely two weeks, she would be arriving at the MacCormacks' in Los Angeles, where she would be welcome to stay as long as she wanted. How long would depend in part on Hallie—and Martina.

Chapter 25

September 1922, Los Angeles

Four years, two months, and two days of separation stretched between mother and daughter like a yawning gap, defying traverse. More than the vastness of an ocean, it was the vastness of time that had sundered them.

A handful of letters and three school photographs had been the only clues to Hallie's growth and development in the time Margaret had been in the Philippines. These, and fond maternal imaginings, were what had sustained her until this very day. But now, with her daughter standing before her on the MacCormacks' doorstep, the reality of Hallie made Margaret gasp with astonishment, joy—and fear.

Gone was the little dancing elf and in her place stood a solemn, neatly attired girl shifting from one gangly leg to the other, her blue eyes magnified by round, tortoiseshell glasses. Hallie was eleven years old now, and she was a stranger.

Margaret had visualized this scene countless times. Hallie rushing to her, crying "Mama, Mama," with a smile that seemed too big for such a small face to contain.

Instead, Hallie was glancing uncertainly back at her aunt, who sat in the car with the engine running, having deposited her charge at Dr. and Mrs. MacCormack's house precisely at 10 a.m. *Of course she would be a little skittish,* Margaret told herself, brushing aside the awareness that Hallie was seeking her aunt's approval. *In a little while she'll remember me and everything will be fine.*

Margaret forced herself to smile and wave at Martina, who drove slowly away. Hallie's eyes followed her aunt, but at least they held no tears. "Hallie, darling, how good it is to see you," Margaret said, opening her arms wide and taking a step toward her daughter. "Let Mommy give you a hug."

She could feel the reluctance in Hallie's body, and to her horror she was suddenly back in the TB ward of the County Hospital, tending to Hal. The same inner protest which she had struggled to mask, knowing it was her duty to love and care for this member of her intimate family. Just as Hallie knew it was her duty to submit to Margaret's embrace. *She is her mother's daughter, after all.*

"My name is Ruth," her daughter insisted within minutes of their first embrace, before retreating to an inner place where her mother dared not follow. Hallie was like a wary animal; like the wild deer the Igorot men used to hunt in the forest surrounding the mission. Margaret realized that she must become the one who coaxes and lures, if she was to reclaim the relationship of mother and daughter she once took for granted. She'd never had to do this before, and she didn't know if she could do it now. But she had to try. Everything was at stake.

"I thought we'd visit the house where we lived when you were a baby," Margaret said one Saturday morning in October. "And then we've been invited to see Mrs. Stanley and her daughter Louise. Do you remember playing with Louise?"

Hallie's bored expression, which had often been evident since she had begun to stay at the MacCormacks' on weekends with her mother, brightened. "Sure I do! Louise had a tricycle that I used to beg her to let me ride. Once her mother made her share with me, and Louise threw a fit."

Relieved at the reception of her plan, Margaret said, "Which dress do you want to wear—the blue striped one or the yellow flowered one?"

"I want to wear my pink one," Hallie said, with a toss of her head.

"Don't you remember, we noticed it's missing a button?" Seeing the glower beginning to form on the girl's face, Margaret said, "All right, I'll try pinning it." It was best to keep on her daughter's good side. *Who knows what Martina has been telling her about me?*

Putting aside her desire for Hallie to look perfect for meeting the Stanleys, Margaret quickly fixed the dress, then said, "We need to hurry if we want to catch the trolley." Although Margaret knew how to drive, the now-unfamiliar streets of Los Angeles intimidated her.

Fortunately, the trolley system hadn't changed very much since she had moved away, and they made it to the Highland Park suburb without difficulty. Not much was different in the old neighborhood, either, except a few new bungalows had cropped up in formerly vacant lots.

Hallie looked around with interest as they walked toward their old house. Margaret could see her daughter was trying to summon up memories of the neighborhood, to no avail.

They arrived at the bungalow on Elder Street she and Hal had once rented. Whoever lived there now had painted it yellow—it had been white before—and there were many more flowers in the garden. She glanced at the neighbor's house before climbing the porch steps with Hallie, wondering if nosy old Mrs. Morgan still lived there. At her knock the door opened, and a Japanese man of about thirty-five answered. Margaret introduced herself and her daughter, explaining they had lived in the house about ten years ago.

The man nodded, as a woman his age hovered in the background. "My name is Dr. Keitoku Watanabe," he said in only slightly accented English. "And this is my wife Tomiko. Please come in."

Some of the furniture was left from when she and Hal rented the house. Gone were the framed prints of flowers and a desert landscape that had adorned the cream-colored walls. In their place were scrolls with delicate, indecipherable writing, and black ink brush images of mountains and pine trees. It reminded

Margaret of pieces she'd seen in Julia and Myrtle's home.

She had decided not to impose by asking to see the rooms in the house, but Dr. Watanabe took the initiative, offering to show them the kitchen, dining area and small study, and the garden out back. "This was your baby nursery," she whispered to Hallie when they entered the study. She noticed that among the Japanese books lining the walls there were a number of English language texts on dentistry. Her host explained, before she could venture a question, that he had a practice in Little Tokyo.

Hallie broke into a smile at the sight of the kumquat tree in the garden, green with unripened fruit. "I remember this!" she said, delighted at the memory. "I used to grab at the fruit, didn't I, and pop them in my mouth?"

"You sure did," her mother responded, "but only once or twice because they're so sour."

Margaret recognized several of the bushes in the back yard, but there were also a few innovations, including an arrangement of stones mimicking the flow of a river. The garden felt much more serene than when it had been hers.

Not wanting to overstay their welcome, Margaret motioned to her daughter that it was time to leave. Then Mrs. Watanabe shyly produced a crimson origami crane and offered it to Hallie, who took it with a murmured "thank you." With bows and smiles all around, the present and past residents of the Elder Street bungalow bid each other farewell. "They were nice," Hallie remarked as mother and daughter descended the porch steps.

Their pleasant visit, though, was spoiled by the appearance of Mrs. Morgan, who called out to them when they had reached the sidewalk. Hurrying over to the pair, the woman made a point of exclaiming over Hallie and how she had grown. "You look just like your poor father," she said with mock commiseration. Margaret turned away angrily, not even bothering to feign politeness. Dragging Hallie along with her, she heard Mrs. Morgan mutter something about "them Japs" as they retreated quickly in the direction of the Stanleys' house. Suddenly, Margaret remembered the unfortunate young George Yamamoto, in some ways a younger version of Dr. Watanabe. *George had more intelligence and character in his little finger than you ever had or ever will have, Mrs. Morgan,* she thought. *And that's a fact.*

Chapter 26

November, 1922

Margaret toyed with her chicken à la king as she listened to the effusive introduction being given her in the stifling church hall. "Mother to half-caste girls no one wants… join me in welcoming one of St. Paul's own…" To the sound of three dozen pairs of clapping hands, Margaret got up and walked to the podium, flashing a nervous smile to Lillian MacCormack and Faith Stanley as she passed their seats.

She had left nothing to chance, writing out her entire talk by hand, although having spoken to similar groups twice before, she had begun to memorize her remarks. *Besides, I'm among friends here,* she reminded herself. Margaret knew that once she got beyond describing in general terms the three principal areas of Episcopal work—Manila, the Mountain Province in the north, and Zamboanga in the south—she could speak more or less extemporaneously about her own experiences. It was the Igorots that seemed to hold the women's attention, and as she showed the slides of Bontoc she was interrupted several times with questions.

Predictably, one woman asked, "Weren't you afraid of being killed by headhunters?"—a question that would be repeated, Margaret learned, at nearly every venue where she spoke. She hoped to counteract the popular image of the Igorots offered up by carnivals and expositions, like the one she and Hallie had visited a decade ago. After three years in the Mountain Province, Margaret knew this fearsome stereotype captured neither the reality of Bontoc life, nor what the Igorots were capable of achieving, if given a decent education. To make her point, she told the story of Pit-a-pit, the early Igorot convert who had himself once been hired to populate a world's fair "village," and who was now a medical doctor in the Philippines, using his adopted name of Hilary Clapp.

"Do you think Dr. Clapp might come to the U.S. and speak to our Indians?" was one surprising suggestion from the audience. "It would be so inspiring if he could visit the reservation schools and show there are no limits to what a savage can accomplish." Cringing at the use of "savage"—a term also favored by Father Henningsen, she remembered—Margaret mumbled something noncommittal in response. When, exactly, had the savages of her imagination become for her simply... people? She couldn't say, but for the first time she realized that that her time at the Bontoc mission had changed not only the Igorots she worked among, but herself as well.

The House of the Holy Child was far less compelling to her audience than the exotic mountain people. Margaret noticed their restlessness and figured she had spoken long enough, so she ended quickly with an invitation to purchase one of the handmade items from the Philippines she had brought with her. The ladies crowded around the table in front, where embroidered lace from the Tukukan mission, colorful woven scarves from the Moro Settlement House in Zamboanga, and *piña* fiber hats from Manila were on display. Sales were brisk, especially of the lace. One woman considering a Manila hat asked if the purchase would help the House of the Holy Child. "I suppose the children are deserving," she mused, "if they can be educated to lead lives different from their mothers. My son was in the Philippines, and he said the women who fraternize with soldiers are no better than they have to be."

"Some women are, but certainly not everyone," Margaret said, stung to respond. Glaring at the deaconess, the woman put down the hat and stalked away. Almost immediately, Margaret became aware of a dull pain in her abdomen. She dismissed it as nerves from speechifying, or more likely a reaction to the ignorant, judgmental woman she had just addressed. *And what's the soldier's excuse?* she thought. *Isn't he "no better than he has to be?"*

"Excellent talk, my girl!" Faith enthused, as she helped Margaret gather up the unsold items, placing them in boxes to take to the next presentation. "I overheard you contradict Mrs. Jenner about the morals of the Filipina mothers. Don't mind her—she thinks the sun rises and sets on her son, not to mention she dislikes anyone who might dare to disagree with her."

"It's so unfair," Margaret said. "Why is it always the woman's fault? "

"I wish there were more interest in the *mestizas*," she added, putting away the last of her wares. "After all, they are American citizens."

"Shouldn't the U.S. government provide for them, then?"

"The excuse the politicians give is that there's no money. I think the real reason is that people don't want to believe these things actually happen. Ignore it, and it goes away—that's the idea."

Faith glanced at her friend, surprised at the note of bitterness in her response. "Let's get back to my house and we can have a cup of tea. I want to show you what I've been embroidering lately," she said.

"Maybe tea will settle my stomach," Margaret said. "Just now it began to hurt. I hope it wasn't something I ate."

They walked to Faith's Model T. Getting in, she said, "I was so glad when John bought us the new model with an automatic starter. He always had to crank the engine in our old 'Tin Lizzie' because I never could do it."

As she drove them back to Highland Park, Faith asked her companion about Hallie. "She seems more grown up than Louise, somehow. Does it seem that the little girl you knew has gone, or have you been able to adjust to the changes? As her mother, you must see the same Hallie underneath the older child you're getting acquainted with."

Margaret hesitated a long time before answering—so long, that Faith glanced over and murmured, "Sorry; I can tell you're not feeling up to snuff."

Margaret wanted to unburden herself to her friend; to have someone share the load of worry and dread that had weighed her down ever since returning to the States. But how could she say to Faith, *I don't know my daughter anymore, and I may never know her.* How could she say, *The orphans at the House of the Holy Child love me more than my own flesh and blood?*

Instead, Margaret responded lightly, "Oh, Hallie's the same, once you dig a little beneath the surface. It just takes time and patience. I wish I could have her with me all the time now, but since I have to travel around during my furlough, I must content myself with weekends only. I can't take her out of school—yet. But come April, when I go back to Manila..."

"Can she go to school at the House of the Holy Child?"

It wasn't the perfect solution—for all Margaret's sympathy toward the *mestizas*, some were hardly her choice of companions for Hallie—but she hoped that by having her daughter living with her at the orphanage, her influence would prevail, at least until adolescence. Surely by the time Hallie was fourteen or fifteen, the Episcopal girls' boarding school in Baguio would finally reopen.

All the while they were conversing Margaret's stomach pains had grown sharper. Something was definitely wrong. Suddenly engulfed by a wave of nausea, she managed to gasp, "Pull over—I think I'm going to be sick," just in time. Margaret retched into the street, frightening two little girls who were skipping along the sidewalk. "I'm so sorry," she said weakly to the rapidly retreating pair as Faith hurried to her friend.

"Are you all right?" Faith asked, anxiously.

"I—I haven't been sick like this since I ate something bad in Tukukan. If I could have a drink of water when we get to your house..." Margaret's mouth tasted vile.

"Why, you've broken out into a sweat!" her friend said.

Faith helped her into the car and drove home as fast as she dared.

"Louise will be home from school any minute now, but don't you worry about her. Let's get you onto the davenport." Margaret collapsed on the sofa, groaning. She pressed her hand to her right side in a futile attempt to ease the pain.

As Faith hurried to bring her friend a glass of water, Margaret could hear thirteen-year-old Louise announce her arrival as she entered the kitchen through the back door. The giggling voice of another girl joined Louise's, immediately followed by a "shush" from Faith. In a minute Faith reappeared with the two teenagers following behind her, their faces solemn as owls.

"I'm sorry you're not feeling well, Aunt Margaret," Louise said quietly, while her young companion averted her eyes.

"I'll be all right," Margaret managed to say with a weak smile. "You don't have to go tiptoeing around." Faith, however, had felt Margaret's forehead and with a worried expression, confirmed that her friend had a fever.

"Shall I call the doctor?" she asked.

"No, I'm sure this will pass," Margaret replied, but the pain and chills seemed to be getting worse rather than better.

Thank goodness it's Wednesday, and I have two days to recover before Hallie comes, she thought. *But I have to give another talk tomorrow afternoon. Let's hope this will clear up by the morning.*

It didn't. At Lillian MacCormack's insistence, their doctor was called, a ruddy Scotsman whom Margaret thought she recognized from the St. Paul's congregation. His jovial countenance soon took on a graver cast after examining his patient. What Margaret thought was food poisoning was in fact appendicitis. She needed to go to the hospital and have surgery—immediately.

"Please let me call my brother-in-law," Margaret managed to gasp. "He is Dr. Charles Peppers. I want him to attend me." Whatever his failings—including not taking her side in the test of wills over who would raise Hallie—he was a competent doctor, and Margaret was sure he would not charge her for his services. She didn't know how much of her medical expenses the Woman's Auxiliary, the organization that paid her salary, would agree to cover. On top of that, she had cancel her speaking engagements and day with Hallie.

Within twenty-four hours of her falling ill, Margaret lay on the operating table at the County Hospital. Her last thought before succumbing to ether-induced oblivion was of Hallie. *Will Martina let her visit me in the hospital?*

Chapter 27

Dear Mrs. Peppers,

I hope this letter finds you well and enjoying being back in the States with family and friends. I'm sure you are kept busy but I also know you have not forgotten us at the House of the Holy Child. We have certainly not forgotten about you, and we pray for you every day.

Two new girls have joined us since you left—María Elena, a two-year-old tot, and Hortencia, a child of five. María Elena had been in the Infant Jesus Orphanage but when the father's family learned it was a Catholic institution they insisted that she be removed and placed elsewhere. Hortencia is a dear child who unfortunately lost her mother to TB—the father in this case <u>had</u> done the honest thing and married the mother, but now that he is a widower, his matrimonial attentions are focused on an American girl here, who has no desire to raise another woman's daughter. At least he is providing for Hortencia at H.H.C.

The rains, of course, have begun to abate and we are enjoying the chance to go on walks and engage in other outdoor activities without the risk of being drowned! We will begin roof repairs soon—unfortunately, the damage the white ants have done to our northwest wall is not so easily dealt with.

You will be proud of our three girls who are studying at the Business College, as reports of their progress are very favorable. Dorotea and Alicia have *distinguished themselves in their secondary school studies, and the other ones at the high school are all earning passing grades.*

As you will see, the children have prepared little missives for you according to their ability. I think you will find some of the drawings quite charming.

Father and Mrs. Bartter join me and the children in sending our best wishes to you.

Faithfully,

Winifred Mann

Margaret carefully folded up the letter from her colleague and turned her attention to the sheaf of notes and drawings Winnie Mann had enclosed. She smiled as she perused the carefully penned—albeit sometimes creatively spelled—sentiments. Of course, no one at the orphanage knew of her recent surgery, and neither did the Missions Office. Gingerly shifting her position in her bed at the MacCormacks', she decided to write the Missions Secretary.

Dear Dr. Wood,

By this time I expect you feel quite sure that I am a very good liar, rather than a missionary dealing in truths—but—I have but one excuse and am afraid it could not be helped.

I came home Tuesday from the Hospital to which I was taken on short notice for an appendectomy and am even now unable to sit up but a few minutes at a time.

I shall however be able to take up my work again by December the first—and as my next engagement is the fifth, I shall be safe.

If it would not be too much of an inconvenience, I should like you to send my salary up until Jan. 1st, as I have the extra expense of the Hospital bill—and it was necessary also to have two special nurses. My bill will be almost $200 in all. I am not asking for any part of this to *be paid by the Board of Missions, but have told you only to explain where I would use my advance funds*

It is a great inconvenience to have to pay this as there are so very many things I need and that I need also for my daughter as I expect to take her back to Manila with me. If the Woman's Auxiliary feel they can help with these extra expenses I should be very pleased and will try in every possible way to do everything in my power to repay them even though it may not be in actual money.

These are all my wants at present—except to go quickly back to Manila and get warm again. People may talk about the climate of warm and sunny California, but I nearly freeze.

Very sincerely yours,
Mrs. Margaret Peppers
Deaconess

Her incision throbbing, Margaret eased herself into a prone position, ticking off in her mind the things she needed to get before she and Hallie set sail across the Pacific. She fell asleep imagining the joy of shopping with her daughter to start their new life together.

Hallie spent Christmas Eve with her mother at the MacCormacks', an arrangement that suited Margaret because she'd be first to give her daughter her presents, undiminished by any comparison with gifts from Martina or other family members.

Margaret chose the time when Lillian MacCormack was busy with dinner preparations, and her husband his sermon, to have Hallie fetch her two presents from under the Christmas tree. "Open that one first," she said, directing her daughter to the smaller gift. *Pablo and Paz, a Story of Two Little Filipinos* had seemed like a good choice at the time, but now Margaret fretted that the book was too childish for an eleven-year-old. Apparently, Hallie thought so too, because she gave it only a cursory glance before turning her attention to the other gift.

"Go gently, that's banana fiber paper," Margaret admonished when Hallie tore upon the package, then immediately regretted both her chastisement and choice of gift wrap. *I should have chosen something an American girl would expect, like red and green paper*

"Oooh," Hallie exclaimed, holding up the pale gold dress Margaret had lavished hours sewing, its collar and cuffs ornamented with ivory lace from Tukukan. Turning excitedly towards her mother, she asked, "Can I wear it tonight?"

Her face crinkling into a smile, Margaret let out the breath she'd been holding all through the gift's unwrapping. "Of course you can," she answered, her doubts about the dress's size momentarily eclipsed by Hallie's enthusiasm. It did fit—barely— but it didn't matter that the dress would soon be too small, or that Martina would probably give Hallie another new dress tomorrow. *Someday she'll appreciate all the work that went into it and want it for her daughter.*

Later that night, as they lay in the dark on the twin beds in the MacCormacks' spare room, Margaret reminded Hallie that she would be going away for a few weeks to complete her speaking tour, which had been put on hold for her health. "I know we haven't spent much time together since I got sick, but when I get back, I promise we'll do something jolly," she said, secretly hoping that Hallie would protest her mother's departure. But all that greeted her announcement was silence. Her daughter had fallen asleep.

Chapter 28

February, 1923

"Mrs. Peppers, your talk on the Igorots was so fascinating. To think that people still live like this in the twentieth century! How brave you missionaries must be." The round-faced matron sitting beside Margaret at the luncheon table fluttered her hands as if to emphasize the sincerity of her comments.

The deaconess gave an involuntary sigh. In her presentation today at St. John's Church, Stockton, she had also spoken about the *mestizas* at the House of the Holy Child, but as usual, the audience craved the most exotic. *Let's see what these ladies have to say about the Filipinos closer to home*, Margaret thought. On her way up California's rich agricultural Central Valley, she had been surprised to see Filipino field workers, and in the riverfront district of Stockton itself, a "Little Manila" sandwiched among the buildings and businesses with Japanese and Chinese names.

"I notice you have Filipinos living in Stockton. Does St. John's have any kind of mission to them?"

An older woman sitting across the table, the widow of a prominent banker and lay church officer, spoke up. "They're all Catholics, aren't they? St. Mary's can take care of them."

"My sister-in-law helps at the Lighthouse Mission. She's a Methodist, and she told me there are quite a few Filipino Protestants," said a woman about Margaret's age, a note of hesitation in her voice. Apparently the "pillar of the church" who had just spoken was not used to being contradicted, least of all by a young whippersnapper.

"Well, all *I* know is that they are a shiftless lot, whatever they call themselves. We should send them all back to the Islands," opined Mrs. Know-It-All, glancing around the table with satisfaction as several heads nodded in agreement.

So the Episcopal Church can take care of them there? Margaret wanted to say but held her tongue. She was tired of being pleasant, tired of making allowances for willful ignorance, even downright malice. *Thank God I am going back to L.A. tomorrow.*

It was Margaret's good fortune that she was staying with the young woman who had dared to contradict Mrs. Know-It-All. Jenny Martin was her name, and she lived with her husband, an accountant, and their son not far from the church.

"I wish St. John's would join the Methodists and Presbyterians at the Lighthouse Mission," Mrs. Martin said without preamble over dinner, evoking a puzzled expression on the face of her husband, who had not been party to the earlier conversation. "They do a lot of good there, I'm told."

As much as Margaret favored improving the lot of immigrants, she felt the Episcopalians should have their own mission, where they could offer dignified Anglican worship and sound religious teaching, and not some kind of watered-down Protestant mishmash. When she said as much, Mr. Martin suddenly jumped into the conversation. He explained that he had been raised a Congregationalist but had fallen away from organized religion, partly from disgust at the denominational in-fighting he had witnessed.

"If the Methodists and Presbyterians can cooperate, more power to them," he said. "Maybe when Christian churches start to demonstrate that they actually love one another, pagans will listen to them. I know I will."

Mrs. Martin cast Margaret a rueful glance. Apparently, this was a familiar refrain in her household. The deaconess remembered Father Henningsen, who had attacked anyone who did not see eye to eye with him. How many Igorots had refused to join the Church because of him?

As she lay down that night, tired from the long day, her thoughts turned from advancing the Episcopal mission in the Philippines to advancing her cause with Hallie, whom she would see in a couple of days. She had rehearsed various approaches in her mind, but none had revealed itself as the obvious choice. *Help me*, she prayed to God for the umpteenth time. *Make me as persuasive as St. Peter preaching to the crowds in Jerusalem. I don't need three thousand converts. Only one.*

In her dream she was back at the House of the Holy Child teaching the younger girls how to hem a handkerchief. A couple of the more adept ones were helping others with the task, and everyone seemed absorbed in their work. Margaret walked among the children, looking at their progress, occasionally stopping to praise and encourage. She smiled in satisfaction, thinking how pleased the Bishop would be when he came to visit.

Suddenly the door to the classroom burst open, and to her astonishment, Father Henningsen and Marguerite Wolfson appeared. "We're married now," Marguerite announced, causing her to wonder what had become of the first Mrs. Henningsen.

It clearly hasn't improved his disposition any, Margaret thought, as she saw the priest looking about with disdain. He started to open his mouth to deliver what she was sure would be a cutting remark when his wife spoke up.

"We've come to assume control of the orphanage," Marguerite said. "The Board of Missions has decided that unless Hallie comes to live with you here, you must go home to America."

"But she *is* coming to live with me," Margaret responded. "Julia is bringing her on the steamer."

"You have twenty-nine minutes to produce her, and if not, we're taking over." She crossed her arms and began tapping her foot impatiently.

Margaret rushed out of the room and began running to the dock. Everything seemed to impede her. Suddenly there was one of the cloudbursts that brings life to a halt in Manila, forcing everyone to run for cover. Margaret needed to cross the Pasig River, but the waters were rising rapidly. Soon it would flood, and then how would she get to the dock? *I only have a few minutes left,* she thought despairingly.

Sure enough, the river topped its banks as easily as a child jumps over a stick. All manner of things floated her way—a man's hat, produce from the market, even a pig and a chicken. Then Margaret spied a black and yellow sea snake swimming directly towards her, its flattened tail rhythmically moving back and forth like a rudder. As it neared, it grew larger and larger, until its head was the size of a human's and its body a foot in diameter. She watched in horror as the snake slithered right up to her feet, its head beginning to rise like a cobra's. "Go away! Go away!" she yelled, but the snake paid no heed.

Slowly its head began to change into the likeness of a human's. Not just any human—there were the narrow blue eyes of her sister-in-law, the snub nose, the thin lips. Then the lips began to speak.

"I have your daughter," the creature Margaret recognized as Martina said.

"She needs to come with me right away!" Margaret cried.

"If you want her, you must have me," came the throaty response. "Look!"

And as the snake stretched out before her, Margaret saw for the first time a bulge distending the otherwise cylindrical body. Panic seized her as she realized Martina had swallowed Hallie alive.

Margaret awoke, drenched as if having indeed been in a downpour, her hands clenching the corner of her sheet. She sobbed uncontrollably as she twisted the wad of fabric tighter and tighter.

It was Wednesday, February 14, 1923, her twenty-ninth birthday.

That weekend at the MacCormacks', after opening the box of airmail stationery Hallie had brought her as a birthday present,

Margaret spoke to her daughter of the gift she most longed to take back with her to the Philippines. "I miss you, dearest, and I want us to live together," Margaret said, simply, abandoning any further efforts at persuasion.

Hallie turned away. No words were needed, but a minute later, the child spoke.

"No," she said, her young voice etched with a terrible finality. "I won't go."

CHAPTER 29

May 1924, Manila

"No! I won't go!"

Margaret clutched her skirt, her fingers tightening around the black gabardine as if Bishop Mosher, who sat calmly across from her at his desk, had ordered her to stand up and strip naked.

"I beg your pardon, Mrs. Peppers. Surely, I must have misheard you. You didn't say you refuse you leave the House of the Holy Child, did you?"

"The work is mine—*mine.* I'm their mother. They trust me. I have a ministry there that God *is* blessing, so there's no reason to make me leave! I can't abandon the girls… I *won't* !"

"Mrs. Peppers, I wish you could hear how hysterical you sound. You are supposed to be setting a Christian example for these children, and that includes how to accept the inevitable disappointments in life."

"Of course, I–"

"You know, you once wrote the Missions Office that you'd like to do pioneering work in Mindinao, in the south. The new work I have in mind for you and Miss Whitcombe in the north is every bit as pioneering. The Balbalasan people of the Kalinga province are eager to advance. They built their own school when the government ignored them, and now they have turned to us for a clinic. By establishing this clinic, you would be establishing a toehold for the Church. They want a clinic, but even more, they want the Gospel. Yet who knows when we will be able to send priests there? You must be the presence of God in their midst."

The Bishop picked up his pen and began to fiddle with it, causing its gold nib to glint in the sun like a shiny bauble.

Margaret took a deep breath and made the effort to fold her hands in her lap. Her skirt now looked like the crinkled mountainside of Bontoc.

"But Bishop—I no longer have the health to live in the mountains. Ever since my surgery, when I am at higher altitudes I get tired at the slightest exertion. And I suffer sleepless nights afterwards. I noticed this when I was with the children at Baguio for our last two months' stay." Even to her ears Margaret's protest sounded hollow, but she persisted. "Miss Whitcombe's and my training is for institutional work, not for running a dispensary. We are teachers, but as you just said, there's already a school right next door to where the Mission would locate. Besides… neither of us knows the dialect and I for one am hopeless when it comes to learning languages."

Without any reply, Bishop Mosher suddenly stood up and approached her, his pen still poised between his long, aristocratic fingers. Dropping it on the corner of the desk, he placed his other hand on her shoulder and said, "We'll let the matter rest for a week. You and I will meet to discuss this after the Ascension Day service. In the meantime, let us both pray that Our Lord's will be done."

In the months since returning to Manila, after Hallie's rejection, Margaret had plunged herself even more deeply into helping "those less fortunate ones" at the House of the Holy Child. At night her mind swam with "what-ifs" and "why-didn't-I's." *If only I'd* insisted *that Hallie come back with me. And now Bishop Mosher wants to take even the House of the Holy Child away from me!* With the reproving tones of her ecclesiastical superior still echoing in her mind, Margaret wasted no time in writing a letter to the Secretary of the Missions Board. She would not lose this fight to protect and preserve her vow to provide mother's love.

My dear Dr. Wood,

I am again taking advantage of your request to write to you when we meet with troubling perplexities. This time the results may be serious for I am going to refuse to obey the Bishop's request that I go to Balbalasang with Miss Whitcombe.

I think that the change in Bontoc is one of the most cruel, unjust things that has ever been done in these Islands. Miss Whitcombe has built up the work there from nothing—she is the only person who knows the language well—the Bontocs all like her well and trust her—she has done good work, and it is not as if it were at a standstill for it is not. Her attitude toward the whole thing is wonderful, for notwithstanding the heartaches at leaving the work for which she has spent sixteen of the best years of her life.

Although I should not criticize my superiors, I believe firmly that the whole arrangement is wrong. Let the work center around the Church and the Services, not a clinic. They are only pagans—they must see in order to believe. How else can they know that it is the Christ Spirit which underlies the lives of the Christians and that we receive our help from the Sacraments of the Church?

As for leaving the House of the Holy Child, I have worked hard the past three years and am just beginning to get things in shape and the children trained as we want them that they may be able to care for themselves outside. I have not institutionalized the school but have cared for them as if they were a large family and no one could have cared for them or taken a greater interest in them individually than I have.

The school is to be in charge of Miss Mann after June the first. It may be better in many ways. No more legal wards but a school for Mestiza and Filipino girls who can pay. There will be no more rescue or preventative work as in past years. There are so many who need our help still. There are now two other schools but there are hundreds of children who need our help and who cannot be cared for because there is no money.

I shall not say more to the Bishop for I think he quite understands my feelings in the matter. I shall refuse to go to Balbalasan even though it may mean that I will be sent back to the United States. There is no other place in the Philippines except the House of the Holy Child where I feel I can give my best. There is also the uncertainty of things at home.

Margaret paused to consider the best way to describe her family situation. It was important that Dr. Wood understand the futility of urging her and her daughter to be reunited. Even if every word she wrote battered her heart.

I have no home now. Ruth Hal made her choice before I left California, preferring to stay with her aunt. In justice to the child, I could not take her away no matter how I felt personally. She has been with her aunt since she was two years old, and it would have been cruel to separate them now. I can endure such things better than to cause so many others to suffer.

I have always done my best in the Mission field and while I can see where I might have done better in some cases, I leave no regrets except that I might have been able to do more.

With sincere regrets for the trouble all this will cause and grateful thanks for all that has been done in the past I am

> *Faithfully yours,*
> *Margaret Peppers*

Margaret did prevail, at least in part, over her bishop. She got to stay in Manila—but not at the House of the Holy Child. In the summer of 1924 she was transferred to St. Stephens Chinese Girls School, where she gave lessons in music and art, besides teaching ecclesiastical embroidery, superintending the Sunday School, and assisting the principal. Bishop Mosher told Margaret not to get too settled, for he had several things for her under consideration. One year stretched to two, then three—until in 1928 she found herself again on furlough in the States. This time, determined to find a more congenial bishop and posting away from the Philippines, she decided not to return.

Part 3: 1929–1941
Washington State

Chapter 30

1929, Washington State

The acrid smell of Longview's paper and pulp mills assaulted Margaret's nostrils even before she spied the sign on Highway 99 announcing the approaching town. When she first imagined life as a rural missionary, the odors that had come to mind were those of a barnyard, not a chemical vat.

Oh, she had visited farms all right. Mostly dairy farms, but also some truck farms and even a few homesteads intended more for self-sufficiency than a livelihood, because the husband had outside employment. In some ways it was familiar—after all, she had grown up in a farming community, if not on a farm—but it was also different.

She smiled as she remembered the summer day a year ago when she'd first visited the Holton family out on the Olympic Peninsula. Like today, it had been overcast with the threat of rain. Margaret had made sure to carry her Sunday School lessons in her waterproof leather satchel. Mrs. Holton, a broad-hipped woman in her forties with an ample bosom, must have noticed the dust-cloud of Margaret's car as it made its way to the house, for she'd opened the door even before her visitor had a chance to knock. Her eyebrow cocked quizzically as she took in the unfamiliar garb of a deaconess, the farm woman suddenly clapped her hand to her forehead in recognition. "You're the one who sent us a postcard," she said apologetically. "Do come in."

"Amy," she said, addressing her twelve-year-old

daughter who hovered in the background, "go fetch the boys. There's a lady from the church come for a visit, an' she'll want to meet you all."

Margaret had scarcely introduced herself when Mrs. Holton interrupted, "Mind if I finish shellin' my peas? It won't take but a moment. You can follow me to the kitchen, if you like—no need to stand on ceremony, is there? Too much to do."

Margaret obeyed as her hostess, chattering all the while, led her into a large sunny room. Mrs. Holton motioned for her to sit down at the kitchen table and taking up the grey enamel pot on the wood stove, poured her a cup of coffee. Then she disappeared into the adjoining service porch. Suddenly the kitchen was filled with rapid popping sounds—or were they *plopping* sounds? After a few minutes Margaret's curiosity got the better of her and she went to the service porch to investigate. To her astonishment she witnessed Mrs. Bolton, her head and torso covered by a large white sheet, hard at work at a machine which was likewise covered by the same sheet. She guessed it to be a wringer washer, noting that the agitator had been removed and lay nearby on the floor. A hose vented the gasoline fumes out the window into the back yard.

"What is your mother doing?" Margaret asked young Amy above the noise. "Shelling peas," answered the girl, who had returned with her three younger brothers.

Remembering the purpose of her visit, Margaret led the children back to the front room and began to chat with them about God and the Bible. Unlike some she had visited, they were not ignorant of Christian teachings. Probably they'd attended a Sunday school somewhere before.

A few minutes later Mrs. Holton emerged, patting her dark hair into place. "I heard you ask my daughter what I was doin'," she said. "I learned to shell peas this way from my neighbor. First you put a bucket of peas in a flour sack, throw 'em into boiling water for a couple of minutes, then take 'em out and dip 'em in a tub of cold water. Pour the pods through the wringer an' let 'er rip. The minute the pods hit the wringer, they pop an' the peas fall back into the machine. Not a squished pea among 'em!"

Mrs. Holton—God bless her! Margaret thought, savoring the memory. She liked the resourcefulness of these farm women, even though Margaret herself had no wish to return to the rural life she had known in Iowa. When she wasn't out in the countryside, staying with church families on occasions requiring overnight trips, she lived in a Seattle apartment. The combination of city and country life seemed ideal, mimicking in some ways Margaret's ten years in the Philippines, divided between urban Manila and the remote Mountain Province. Maybe snobbish Bishop Mosher was right when he'd told her she didn't really belong on the Atlantic Seaboard. She'd been tempted to seek an Eastern position just to prove him wrong, but in the end she chose the West to be nearer to Hallie—just in case.

The thought of the bishop who had forced her to leave her beloved orphanage snapped Margaret out of her reverie, and she was dismayed to see she had driven right past the road headed to Cathlamet, where she was going to lead a vacation church school. If she hurried, she could retrace her steps and still arrive in time. The village was located near a bend of the Columbia River as it turned from north to west in its final, inexorable journey to the Pacific Ocean. Its economy depended on the timber industry, although cucumber farming and dairying in the tidelands reclaimed by dikes also played a part. Farther down the river were several salmon canneries which employed some of the women Margaret wanted to reach with her "church by mail" material. Although she could not visit the canneries, she hoped these publications would find their way to their intended audience through family members she might meet.

By the time Margaret arrived in Cathlamet, the drizzle that had been her constant companion for the last thirty miles had stopped. She knew better than to expect the usual dry Puget Sound summer here in southwest Washington, and she'd dressed accordingly, wearing the raincoat Julia and Myrtle had given her when she returned to the States. One hundred inches of rain a year fell in the area, she'd been told—more than twice Manila's annual precipitation. And in wintertime when it was the rainiest, it was also very cold. How did people stand it?

The dozen giggling children, ages four to eleven, who filed into the schoolhouse—there being no church available— seemed oblivious to any discomfort. Several of them, Margaret noticed, had fingers stained purple. When she mentioned this to Mrs. Barker, the school superintendent who had opened the building, the woman explained it was from picking berries. "The girls do it every summer to earn money for school clothes." Mrs. Barker seemed anxious to leave, remaining only long enough to introduce the deaconess and to remind her she would return in two hours to lock up. Margaret wondered if she had no religion or if she belonged to a church that disapproved of Episcopalians.

"Who can tell me something about Jesus Christ?" Margaret asked the little group, and several hands shot up. The answers varied. One response she had come to expect was offered by a seven-year-old boy who said, "He's mad a lot."

"What makes you say that, dear?" she asked sweetly, though she knew from past experience the substance of his answer.

"'Cause my pa is always mad when he says his name."

Margaret cut short the titters by pulling out her pictures from the life of Christ and asking for a volunteer to hold each one while she talked about it. Tomorrow she would bring her Futterer's Eye-o-graphic Slides which portrayed various stories from the Bible. They were always a big hit.

Children are children the world over, Margaret thought, reminding herself that no child could be expected to sit meekly for two hours. Experience had taught her to vary her instruction with songs and art activities. The time passed quickly, and she was surprised when the blond head of Mrs. Barker appeared in the window, still wearing the vaguely anxious expression Margaret had noticed earlier. This time she was accompanied by a sullen girl of about fifteen.

When the last child had left, Margaret introduced herself

to the young stranger, who was darker complexioned than Mrs. Barker. "This is Mary Ann," Mrs. Barker said, before the girl had a chance to respond. "She's my stepdaughter."

There's a story there, Margaret thought. The girl was clothed in a well-made blue gingham dress that looked new, and her hair was a lustrous brown. She seemed well cared for materially, but what about her spirit?

"Mary Ann, you're welcome to join us tomorrow."

"I can't," was the muttered response. It was hard to know if the invitation was being met with scorn or resignation.

"Mary Ann is on her way to Kelso to work for the mayor's family," Mrs. Barker interjected. "We need to leave right now, so if you don't mind…"

"Yes, I understand," Margaret said, stepping aside as the superintendent locked the door. "I wish you all the best, Mary Ann." Her sentiment was genuine. In her mind's eye she saw the girl she had once been, the girl who'd had her dreams of schooling cut short to work as a maid in the local hotel. She wondered how the story would end for Mary Ann.

After putting away her teaching materials, Margaret decided to eat the lunch she had packed before setting out on foot to visit the two Episcopalian families who did not have children in the vacation church school. As she ate her sandwich, her thoughts strayed from Mary Ann to another stepchild, a boy she had met in Whatcom County. When she'd sought out the lad, whose behavior had earned him a reputation at school, she discovered a boy no older than Mary Ann living in a shack alone, with only a dog for company. After his father had died, his stepmother had left him to fend for himself while she returned to her hometown—the boy didn't know where, nor did he care— with her two children, the boy's half-sisters. Margaret hadn't known what to do except take the boy to the Episcopal priest twenty miles away and report the situation to the local sheriff. From the lawman she'd learned that such situations were, tragically, not all that rare.

Her heart went out to these waifs, but she was also

moved by the plight of some of the women she had encountered during her brief time as a rural missionary. Prohibition had been enacted to eliminate the temptation of alcohol and its devastating effects on families, but between the liquor smuggled in from Canada and the moonshine manufactured in backwoods stills, there was plenty of supply to satisfy the cravings of loggers and fishermen. Once she had noticed bruises on the face of a woman she had visited, but there was nothing she could do with her suspicions, since her solicitous inquiry had been immediately rebuffed. She remembered her father's drinking and was thankful that at least he had never laid a hand on her mother or any of the children.

She had also seen faces whose expression reminded her of her father's dark despair, though none quite as hopeless as his when he was in the grip of his illness. But she recognized the listlessness and apathy that enveloped some women like the gloom of a Northwest forest. Marooned on a homestead, often with a passel of children to care for, not every woman was able to transcend loneliness by dint of hard work.

As her mother had done. As she herself had done—as she was doing even now.

CHAPTER 31

When the envelope arrived, the left-leaning cursive that spelled out her address made Margaret's pulse quicken.

The fact that Hallie's hand had touched the card made even this impersonal gesture—only the 1929 holiday message from Los Angeles—exciting. She ripped it open, nearly decapitating the white-bearded Wise Man depicted inside, seated next to his red and yellow striped tent. Some distance away a shepherd could be seen gesturing to the other two Magi. Except for the shepherd, all eyes were focused on the luminous Nativity star in the distance. Inside the card was a printed greeting which read, "This little card comes to you with my best wishes and compliments of the Season." It was hand signed, "With love, Martina and Ruth."

Ever since Martina had won legal recognition as her niece's guardian, she had been punctilious in sending annual holiday greetings, always accompanied by a letter informing her sister-in-law of Hallie's growth and development. These were as colorless as the bland commercial sentiment expressed in the Christmas card Margaret had just opened, but since they were the only link she had to her daughter, she devoured them eagerly. Nevertheless, she entertained no illusions about the sincerity of these professions of regard. Once, Hallie might have loved her, but Martina never had.

This time, not one, but two letters were enclosed. She turned first to her sister-in-law's single-page note, scanning it quickly.

Amid the usual unremarkable information about home,

work, and weather, Martina described her increasing involvement in the local Episcopal Church, which included being selected to lead its Woman's Auxiliary chapter. "I have convinced the members to donate an additional ten dollars to support rural ministry in your diocese," she wrote. Margaret wondered at Martina's sudden generosity, but decided instead to concentrate on what Hallie had to say.

> *Dear Mother,*
>
> *I hope this letter finds you well. I wanted to tell you that I will be starting Business College in January. I will be living with Uncle Charles and his wife in L.A. while I attend school there. Aunt Martina is very happy being back in Southern California but Redlands is too pokey a town for me. After we moved there I worked as a salesclerk at Kress's but I didn't enjoy it one bit. I think being a stenographer is more my style.*
>
> *Have you seen the movie "Where East Is East"? I thought of you because it is set in the Orient. I've become so used to talkies that I found it a little boring, though.*
>
> *I'll be attending the Christmas services at the Cathedral downtown. Didn't we once go there? Aunt Martina and I will be staying with Uncle Claude over the holidays, then I will move in with Uncle Charles.*
>
> *I hope you have a Merry Christmas and a Happy New Year in chilly Seattle!*
>
> *Love, Ruth*

Margaret was grateful that communication, however dutiful, had resumed on her daughter's side. For so many years Martina had served as the lone conduit of information. Never receiving a reply to her letters, Margaret had long since stopped writing to Hallie except at Christmas and her birthday, which fell on the Fourth of July.

She recalled that the first sign of change had come on Margaret's own birthday last February 14th. With a thumping heart she had opened the envelope with Martina and Hallie's return address written in a hand that was not her sister-in-law's. A Valentine's card fell out, bearing the image of a little girl in a pink dress, wearing an enormous bonnet and clutching a bouquet of red roses. "A Joyous Valentine" read the printed inscription, to which Hallie had added the words, *And a happy Birthday, Ruth Hal.* Four words and a signature, and Margaret felt she'd been given the best gift of her life.

Two months later, another card arrived. It was her daughter's high school graduation announcement, but it might as well have been Cinderella's invitation to the ball, for all it set Margaret's imagination and hopes soaring. One day she was convinced she would attend the event, but the next day, as if uttered by the evil stepsisters in the fairy tale, mocking voices within demolished her assurance.

In the end, she had gone, enduring the suffocating heat and jovial welcome of the Peppers clan—*How good to see you, Margaret! It's been far too long!*—just so she could witness this milestone in her daughter's life. And also because there would be memories Margaret could treasure for years to come. Memories of Hallie crossing the stage, tall and slender, her white mortarboard slightly askew on top of her straight bobbed hair, which was chestnut like her mother's. Memories of Hallie pausing to scan the audience before resuming her seat, a slight frown on her face, until—Margaret was sure of it—she spied the one person among the Peppers party to whom she owed her very life. The smile that suddenly lit Hallie's otherwise serious face could only have been for her.

On that graduation visit they had spent less than twelve hours together, over a period of two days, before it was time to return to Seattle. As for the chance to be alone with Hallie, Margaret counted at most four hours. Those hours had begun with lunch at the Tam O'Shanter roadhouse, chosen by Hallie for being favored by the Hollywood crowd. Within its faux Tudor half-timbered walls, between bites of Welsh rarebit and sips of malted milk, Hallie chattered about her favorite movies, occasionally glancing expectantly around in the vain hope of recognizing a film star.

Once, Margaret interrupted to ask a few questions about Hallie's high school experience. What had been her favorite subjects? Had she been in any clubs or sports activities? Margaret had ventured the same questions before in her letters, but Hallie had mostly overlooked them.

"I guess I liked music and drama the best. You know I played Josephine in *H.M.S. Pinafore.*"

Margaret did not know. Swallowing the reproof she was tempted to utter, she congratulated Hallie, then added, "You probably don't remember me singing to you when you were a little girl, do you?"

Hallie looked thoughtful. "I remember one time when you took me to a Sunday school class in Chinatown, and we all sang 'Jesus Loves Me,'" she said. "The children wore such funny clothes. I hadn't seen any Chinks before then."

"They're called *Chinese*, Hallie, not 'Chinks'," Margaret said.

"Everybody here calls them Chinks. So what do they call the Japs and Greasers up your way?"

"Only ignorant people use those names. I'm surprised your Aunt Martina allows you to call them that."

"You should hear Uncle Claude. He's the worst of all," Hallie sniffed.

Margaret decided to change the subject. "I'm so glad I was able to come to your graduation, my dear. You don't know how sorry I was to miss your confirmation a few years ago."

Hallie fiddled with the straw in her drink, then took a long sip. "Well, I guess you had all those other confirmations to attend, being a deaconess and all," she muttered, and began cutting up her Welsh rarebit into small pieces.

Nearby, a woman could be heard berating a waiter. Her shrill tones shredded the silence that had begun to envelop their table like a shroud. "You don't understand–" Margaret started to say. Just then their waiter came to ask if they needed anything more. Shaking her head, she turned back to Hallie, who seemed intent on her food.

Margaret was glad she'd suggested visiting Hal's grave at Forest Lawn Cemetery after lunch. In that place silence would be natural. Anyone observing them with their bouquets would think they were honoring a loved one's memory, not taking refuge in unspoken thoughts they dared not share.

The scent of lilies still permeated the car when Margaret drove back to Martina's. "Perhaps you could come up to Seattle," Margaret ventured.

"I don't know, Mama. Uncle Charles has said he will take me to Catalina Island. And then I need to get a job."

"Well, it will work out sometime, I'm sure," Margaret said, trying to keep the disappointment out of her voice as she pulled up to the house. "Listen, dear, I'm late getting back to Dr. MacCormack's. I think I'll just give you a kiss right now and let you go on inside without me." Assuming a cheerful countenance, she leaned over to embrace her daughter.

"Good-bye, sweetheart. I love you."

"Bye-bye, Mama," Hallie responded, bestowing a quick kiss before sliding out of the car. Pausing for a moment on the sidewalk, she glanced in Margaret's direction.

"Have a safe trip home," Hallie said. Then she walked into the house, disappearing like an unfinished thought.

Chapter 32

August, 1930

In Paul Seikichi Shigaya, M.D.—known familiarly as "Dr. Paul"—was the unusual combination of a physician's mature assurance and the disarming enthusiasm of a man much younger than his forty years. Margaret had taken to him immediately.

They were on their way to Sunday service at the Taylor Japanese mission in the White River Valley, where Margaret was to meet the parents of Keiko Kohama. If all went as planned, baby Keiko—Americanized as Kay—would become Margaret's first American godchild, joining the scores of godchildren she had in the Philippines.

The hour-long drive was familiar to her from the daily trips she had made during the Vacation Church School she'd run last month at the mission. Since that had been a weekday event, she had not then had a chance to meet Dr. Paul, who she'd learned was the head of the Sunday School program and mainstay of the church. Dr. Arney, who oversaw the mission as well as his own mostly white congregation, St. James in nearby Kent, had asked Dr. Paul to be baby Kay's other godparent.

Cruising along in his new, top-of-the-line Buick, Margaret and Dr. Paul conversed easily as the miles passed by. Margaret had been surprised at her companion's excellent English, since she knew he was an immigrant. *What a contrast,* she thought, *with the Japanese mothers at my church school,* as she remembered the challenges of communication. She asked him how long he had been in this country.

"Oh, I've lived here for over twenty years. I attended Kent High School and graduated, if you can believe it, at the ripe old age of twenty-four. By then I was pretty good with English, and by the time I graduated from university and medical school, I was even better. Of course, my medical practice is in *Nihonmachi*—you'd call it Japantown—so I still converse mostly in Japanese with my patients."

"Did you come from a Christian family in Japan?"

"No, in fact, my grandfather was a Buddhist priest. I worked as a houseboy for several years in Seattle, and then I moved to Kent and started working for Mrs. Murbach. She attends St. James and invited me to come with her. It seemed like the polite thing to do, so I did, but I kept meeting with my Buddhist group too."

"What made you join the Church?"

He paused a moment as he negotiated a left turn onto the highway. "Dr. Arney and people at St. James were kind to me— the first white people who saw me as more than cheap labor. I listened to the Gospels every Sunday when I went to church, and the first thing I noticed was that Jesus and his disciples were healers. It started to make sense to me, more than the Buddhist belief that suffering is inevitable. I decided to become a doctor because I also wanted to be a healer. I prayed to Jesus to help me—and he did. I was baptized and now I help others get baptized."

After a moment he added, glancing over at Margaret, "Just like you do, Mrs. Peppers."

"That's kind of you to say," she murmured. She felt a sense of solidarity which surprised and pleased her.

That summer day it seemed as if God had spread a green blanket over the entire White River district, from the village of Orillia in the north down past the town of Auburn in the south. Like velvety ribs of corduroy, row upon row of lettuce stretched as far as the eye could see. In some fields brown-skinned men and women, their bent forms evoking memories of Igorots in their rice paddies, were busily harvesting the crop while children scampered to and fro. Their calls and laughter, accompanied by the *clunk* of crated produce being loaded onto trucks parked in the field, were a counterpoint to their parents' silent labor.

"Are all these workers Japanese?" she asked. "I thought I saw some Filipinos loading up the trucks."

"The Japanese—we call ourselves Nikkei, by the way—often hire Filipinos. They're not always as reliable or hardworking as we are, but they do a good job if we keep after them." Even had Dr. Paul's English not been excellent, there was no mistaking his tone of superiority.

Margaret raised an eyebrow but kept her thoughts to herself. In the Philippines the governing class—both American and European—had admired the Chinese and Japanese for their industry and looked down on the Filipino peasants as being lazy and happy-go-lucky. Yet ask the humblest mixed-race Filipino about the Igorots, and he would dismiss them as "savages." It seemed that no matter where you were in the world, someone was looking down on someone else.

As she was still pondering this law of human behavior, they pulled up to a long, one-story wooden building topped by an attic with a dormer. "It was a public schoolhouse, once," Dr. Paul explained, as they got out of the car. "The Issei raised $1,000 to buy this building and the acre it sits on, so we could have a language school for our children."

"Who are the Issei?" Margaret asked.

"Issei are the first generation in this country—the immigrants. Their children are called Nisei—literally, 'Number Two Generation.'

"We had some cleaning up to do, because it had most recently been used as a stable, but we were very grateful to have it. It officially belongs to St. James, since Japanese aliens cannot own property in this state. Did you see our chapel when you were here before?" he continued, pointing to the small attic.

Margaret shook her head, so he led her up the rickety stairs to a room seating forty adults at most. Today there were more people crammed into the space because a large proportion were children. Dr. Paul explained, "The older boys and girls come to the chapel for the beginning of the service. Since many of their parents are Buddhists and decline to attend, they are supervised by Issei members of the congregation. At the time of the sermon, these children go downstairs and are joined by younger ones who are coming just for Sunday School."

They had just chosen seats near the back when Margaret's companion spied a man in his thirties entering the chapel. Dr. Paul excused himself and greeted the newcomer with a bow. A minute later he returned and introduced the man as Mr. Kohama.

It was a service of Morning Prayer, translated into Japanese from the American *Book of Common Prayer*—that much Margaret knew. She recognized the basic outline of the service, which was the same throughout the world, and one of the hymn tunes. She tried to pray silently in English while the ordained minister in charge, Reverend Ito, and his congregation prayed in Japanese, but she found it hard to ignore the voices of those around her.

After saying "thank you" with the only Japanese word she knew—*Arigato*—and exchanging bows with Reverend Ito, Margaret turned her attention to the little boys and girls who had approached her shyly, their parents smiling and bowing from a discreet distance. The children were all familiar to her from Vacation Church School, and she remembered most of their names. Meanwhile, Mr. Kohama hovered nearby, an expectant look on his sunburned face, but his English was not good enough to engage in conversation with her. Dr. Paul had excused himself briefly to attend to some church matter. After a while he returned and waited patiently while Margaret finished her greetings.

"They all seem to know and like you, Mrs. Peppers," he said.

"Yes, they are dears," she answered, but her face suddenly clouded as she thought of Mrs. Kohama and baby Kay. "We should probably be on our way, but I wonder if everything is all right with Mr. Kohama's wife and child? I expected to see them at church."

"Oh, no problem there," Dr. Paul said, without hesitation. "In traditional Japanese society, new mothers are confined for one hundred days with their babies. Mrs. Kohama's confinement will only be a few weeks, because she must help her husband on the farm, but she is eager to meet you at her home. Shall we go there now?"

Dr. Paul and Margaret followed Mr. Kohama in the car, down a dirt road bordered by rows of blackberries and raspberries, their canes neatly espaliered and heavy with fruit. After about a mile they reached the farmhouse which the couple shared with Mrs. Kohama's elder brother and sister-in-law, Mr. and Mrs. Roku, and their two children, aged five and eight. The house could have been plucked from an Iowa farm of the late nineteenth century: one-and-a-half stories, with a front porch made for sitting outside to shell peas or watch fireflies in the evening. Only in this part of the country there were no fireflies, and the house, with its sagging porch and peeling paint, had an unmistakable air of neglect—at least on the outside. But after Mrs. Roku welcomed the visitors with a bow, she stepped aside to reveal a spare but immaculate parlor, with a fir floor that gleamed. Speaking in Japanese and motioning with her hands, she invited them to sit on a worn green davenport.

Glancing into the adjoining dining room, Margaret's eyes were immediately drawn to a wooden cabinet, about two feet wide and three feet long, painted black with gold trim and set on a table in the corner. Its pair of doors were open, revealing two shelves. On the top shelf sat a small, gilded Buddha statue, beside which was a simple ceramic vase holding a single white rose. A votive candle stood on the other side. The second shelf held several wooden objects resembling signs or placards of some sort; they were oriented vertically and painted with Japanese calligraphy. Below these, on the table holding the cabinet, were photographs of a couple and of a child, a bowl of flowers, and a small bowl of rice.

Dr. Paul, noticing the focus of Margaret's attention, murmured, "It's a *butsudan*—a Buddhist home altar."

Immediately Margaret averted her eyes and pretended to study the threadbare floral carpet at her feet. Suddenly her work with the children of the Taylor Mission took on a deeper significance. *I'm saving them from this,* she thought.

Just then Mrs. Kohama entered the room holding an infant cocooned in a white blanket. She smiled shyly at Margaret and Dr. Paul, while her husband stood at her side, proud and protective. Meanwhile, Mrs. Roku had disappeared into the kitchen, reappearing a few minutes later with a tray holding a pot of tea and cups for the guests.

"What a darling baby!" Margaret exclaimed, admiring the infant's tiny nose, black button eyes, and porcelain skin, so different from the suntanned faces of her parents and aunt. She was determined now to become the godmother. She could help counteract any anti-Christian influence the child might experience growing up.

Three weeks later Margaret stood in the gothic-style sanctuary of St. James Church, ready to utter her solemn promises as godmother to Keiko "Kay" Kohama, who at that moment was being cradled on one arm of Dr. Arney, the baptizer. Little did she know that, as she mentally rehearsed her vow on the child's behalf to "obediently keep God's holy commandments, and walk in the same," her own walk with the Japanese American community was just beginning.

Chapter 33

1939, Seattle

"I will be a square shooter in my home, in school, on the playgrounds, wherever I may be. I will be truthful and strive, always, to make myself a better and more useful citizen."

With the same tones of solemn conviction they used to recite the Pledge of Allegiance, five hundred children began to intone the creed of the Mickey Mouse Club, the first order of business every Saturday afternoon when the club met at the Madrona Garden Theatre. Smiling benignly at the youthful spectacle were a few dozen mothers who were chaperoning the youngest club members, mostly children four or five years of age who were not tagging along with an older sibling.

Sitting in the crowded theater, Margaret was an exception, not being related to ten-year-old Mary, who had been pleading with her for several weeks to come. It was part of the girl's campaign to convince her parents of the suitability of the entertainment. Though not yet a club member, Mary proudly recited along with the others. Learning the pledge, like memorizing the names of the books of the Bible, had come easily to the child.

"I will respect my elders and help the aged, the helpless and children smaller than myself. In short, I will be a good American."

Creed recited, for the briefest of moments the theater was silent before the assembly suddenly erupted into loud cheers and applause. As the plush red curtains opened, several boys and girls appeared onstage, each sporting the requisite set of Mickey

Mouse ears, identical to what all the audience—excepting the adults and a few children like Mary—were wearing. Then one gangly redhaired lad of eight or nine stepped forward, clutching a baton. When he raised it, the hubbub ceased as if by magic and the collective intake of breath was audible. Responding on cue to the baton's downward sweep, the children launched into a rousing rendition of "Hail, Hail, the Gang's All Here," followed by several other songs and Mickey Mouse yells.

The day's contest was introduced by the Chief Minnie Mouse, a self-assured preadolescent named Loretta. Even if she had not been trained from the cradle to shun any appearance of putting herself forward, Mary would never have joined the parade of boys and girls eagerly ascending the stage. For in a contest to decide who had the most freckles, a Japanese American girl had no place.

When the Bishop called her into his downtown Seattle office one autumn day in 1930 to discuss "new ministry opportunities," Margaret had been intrigued, but also a little worried. She was ready for a change from her life of bad roads, company towns, and grange halls with peeling paint. At the same time, it didn't take supernatural insight to realize that the country was in a bad way, economically and socially, and that no institution, including the Church, would be spared the impact of the Depression, as people were starting to call the crisis. One had only to look at the nearby St. Mark's Episcopal Cathedral. The grand Gothic edifice, begun during the late 1920's boom, had been reduced by the stock market crash to a simple, almost ignominious, cube, its roof the rough timber beams once used in the building's concrete formwork.

Margaret was relieved to learn that the Bishop wanted her to reduce the time she spent on widely dispersed rural ministry and focus instead on two Japanese American congregations: the White River Valley's Taylor Mission, now known as St. Paul's, and an urban mission, called St. Peter's.

"Tell me everything I should know about St. Peter's,"

Margaret had asked Dr. Paul shortly after her fateful meeting with Bishop Huston. "And about the Japanese in Seattle. I want to be ready to start right away."

A few days after their conversation, Dr. Paul had offered to take her on a tour of *Nihonmachi*. Until then, she had never even visited the two-square mile section of town that was home to the Japanese community, as well as smaller numbers of Chinese and Filipinos. The neighborhood reminded her of the Japanese merchant section of Manila, which she visited sometimes when she'd worked at St. Stephen's Chinese mission. Seattle's *Nihonmachi* was much larger, though, and it bustled with activity and purpose. She was not, like one of her shocked acquaintances who warned her against taking the job, afraid of being accosted by ne'er-do-wells on "skid road" (which, in fact, was the waterfront area beyond Japantown.) "We Issei have worked hard and made a good life here," Dr. Paul said, as he pulled up next to his office on Sixth Avenue. "We don't let the fact that we aren't allowed to become citizens or own property keep us from operating businesses or organizing *kenjinkai*—that's a kind of mutual aid society—or publishing our own newspapers. Several, actually."

"Or running a successful medical practice," Margaret added.

"Yes, the Lord has blessed me."

She thought of her brother-in-law. These men had the same profession and training, but just because Charles was born in the United States and a citizen, he enjoyed a privilege and respect that someone from Japan, who would always be an alien, would never receive.

Dr. Paul continued, "Most Issei have no need or desire to venture beyond this neighborhood. But their children—they are part of a different world. They speak English. They are learning in school what it means to be an American citizen. They are growing and adapting in ways that their parents cannot. The Nisei are our future."

As they strolled down the sidewalk, the smells of *soba*

broth and *shoyu* sauce wafted through the air. The clanging of trolleys on nearby Jackson Street, the main thoroughfare, punctuated the Japanese and English conversations on the street. Everywhere Margaret looked there were people, young and old, hurrying in and out of shops whose purpose she could often guess—here a barber shop, there a laundry, over there a bookstore—even when the signs were not in English.

"On weekends there are more people in town because the farmers and laborers drive in from outside the city. You might even see someone from the Valley you recognize, Deaconess."

There was no St. Peter's church building to visit that day in 1930—prayer meetings and Sunday school classes were still being held in a couple of bungalows in the neighborhood. But the mission's longtime Vicar, Gennosuke Shoji, and his congregation had a dream. Somehow, in the middle of the Depression, they would scrape together enough money to buy property and construct a "real" church. It was dedicated in 1932, one year after Margaret's new assignment had begun.

Now, almost a decade since her introduction to St. Peter's, Margaret sometimes felt no closer to understanding the world of the Issei than she had in her early days of ignorance. In her first few months at the church, she had tried to seek advice from Father Shoji, but he always put her off, quoting the Japanese proverb, *"Narau yori narau yo"*—"Better than being taught is gaining experience." She had even conceived the idea of visiting the Japanese Language School which many Nisei children attended so she might learn more about their culture. "Oh, you don't want to do that," several boys had told her, clearly horrified. "It's boring and besides, they'd keep us late for days just so they could show us off to you when the time came."

She confided from time to time in Dr. Paul, but since he was an Issei himself, though more Americanized than most, she kept many of her judgments to herself. *The Issei may dress like Americans, but they act more like the Chinese I knew in Manila,* she was tempted to say. *They wear a mask of politeness and agreeableness, at least in front of me, but I want to know what's underneath. What are they really thinking and feeling?*

One afternoon Margaret walked by the Japanese Pentecostal Church a few blocks from St. Peter's. Some kind of service was going on—but such shrieking and shouting! Nothing like the sedate worship she loved, and nothing like any Japanese person she knew. It only emphasized how much she had to learn about the Nikkei.

Chapter 34

January 1940, Seattle

Who can tell me the two principal ways that Christians have understood the sacrament of Holy Communion?" Margaret scanned the circle of adolescents, willing one of them to respond and break the silence that had settled over the room like a muffling blanket of snow. Some sat with downcast eyes, others fixed their gaze in the distance, as if awaiting the Lord Himself to arrive with the answer. Were these boys and girls from one of her former classes on the Olympic Peninsula, she would have assumed they had not done their homework, but among her Nisei, the opposite was more likely true. Except for Henry fidgeting at the back, she knew that any one of them would be ready with the answer if she called their name.

"Jenny, would you tell us please?"

Raising her face and adjusting her glasses, the youngest confirmand recited, "Transubstantiation, meaning the bread the wine are literally the Body and Blood of Christ, or commemoration, meaning the Holy Communion is just a reminder or memorial."

"Exactly right. And what is the belief of the Episcopal Church—Ben?"

Again the answer came without hesitation. "The Episcopal Church believes that Christ is truly present in the sacrament of Holy Communion. The Bread and Wine are the outward and visible sign of the inward and spiritual grace of Christ's Body and Blood."

"Yes, that's very good." There was a silence as Margaret fumbled through her notes. She must have left a page back at her apartment. Suddenly a masculine voice interrupted, "I beg your pardon, Mrs. Peppers. Kindly allow me to ask a question. Now, who can give an everyday example of 'an outward and visible sign of an inward and spiritual grace'?"

All eyes turned to the doorway where the new young clergyman, Daisuke Kitigawa—or Father Dai, as he preferred to be called—was standing. The children's blank expressions turned from diffidence to puzzlement.

"When you write letter to Grandfather in Japan, ink and paper are real, yes?"

Heads nodded cautiously.

"But why is Grandfather happy to receive letter? Ink and paper are not rare and valuable. It is because *you*, your thoughts and hopes, are carried across sea to Grandfather, by ink and paper, yes? Like you are there, talking with Grandfather, at end of day. He sleeps happily on *tatami* that night."

He paused, looking about him, to see if his hearers understood. Judging from the youths' expressions, a few had caught on, but others remained perplexed. Margaret guessed it had more to do with the concept Father Dai was trying to convey than the expression.

"Think about Grandfather's letter, and next week we discuss it." Before anyone could leave, Father Dai held up his hand and said, "Mrs. Peppers may have other things to say." Then he added with an apologetic smile and a slight bow, "Thank you for allowing me to address the class, Deaconess."

It was no use continuing after such an interruption. "I think that's enough for today," she said to the confirmands. "Next week's topic is the Creed. Please come prepared to recite the Nicene Creed. You'll find it on page 71 of the *Book of Common Prayer*." Suddenly the hushed room was filled with movement and sound as the young people rose to leave, chattering like a flock of geese preparing for takeoff.

Margaret stuffed her prayer book and notes into her

satchel, heedless of everything except her boiling resentment. She couldn't leave the stuffy room fast enough.

"I sincerely apologize, Mrs. Peppers," Father Dai said as he hurried to meet his departing assistant. Not yet thirty and newly ordained, Bishop Huston had appointed him to lead the Valley mission and to work with the St. Peter's Nisei while Father Shoji ministered to the Issei. *But two years studying in a New York City seminary hardly qualifies him as an expert on American life,* Margaret had fumed when learning that someone might come and interfere with her work.

"You might have asked me in advance," she muttered. She would never have talked to Paul Shigaya or Father Shoji that way, given their comparative age and experience. Besides, Dr. Paul was genuinely happy to share his workload in the Valley mission, and if Father Shoji seemed less cognizant of her work, it was because only the Issei congregation seemed to matter to him.

"This morning, I read *The Episcopal Church: Its Faith and Order,*" he said, holding up the standard text that was used by many clergy—and Margaret herself—to teach confirmation classes. "It had such excellent manner of explaining sacraments that when I observed you teaching, I was moved to present it immediately. I am deeply sorry if I offend you."

His English is surprisingly good, one part of her brain noted, even as another part fanned the flames of resentment. Still, she managed to stammer an acceptance of his genuine apology. Then she remembered his having said something to the class about a discussion next week and decided to listen to her wiser self.

"Father Dai, do you want to help me teach the confirmation class?" she ventured as a peace offering. "This is one of my responsibilities, but if you want to better acquaint yourself with the Nisei at St. Peter's, I am happy to work with you." She tried to sound gracious even as she asserted her authority.

"Yes, that would be wonderful," he said eagerly. "If you would kindly meet with me in the morning at 9 o'clock—you are here tomorrow, yes?—we can discuss how best to proceed."

"I will meet you then," she answered. In the meantime, she would pray about how to manage her new young priest.

They were about to leave the church when Margaret happened to notice a message that Miss Kogita, the part-time church secretary, had left on Father Dai's desk. "Call Dr. Shigaya about fire ASAP!!!!" she'd written in large letters, as if to emphasize their urgency.

Immediately concerned, Margaret pointed out the note and explained the meaning of "ASAP." She decided to wait while Father Dai made his call, so she could learn what it was all about. Surely, it couldn't be that something was amiss at St. Paul's? Neither Father Dai nor she had been there all day.

After a few words in English, Father Dai began speaking in rapid Japanese and jotting down some notes. An occasional *hai*—"yes"—was all Margaret understood. After a few minutes the priest hung up and turned to her.

"Is everything all right at the mission?" she blurted out.

"Yes, yes. Dr. Paul says there was fire at the"—he paused a moment to consult his notes—"Iseri Western Packing House. It burned almost everything."

"Was it an accident?"

"No. Police are there studying it. I will go home and watch over St. Paul's," Father Dai said, as he put on his coat. The vicarage was right next to the mission.

"Oh, do get one or two of our young men to stay with you. They can watch too, so you don't have to stay awake all night."

"Yes, I will ask. Do not worry, Mrs. Peppers. Just pray a little."

Margaret did pray as she drove the short distance to the Star Apartments where she lived, not only for the Iseri family, but for anyone else in the Valley who might need protection. As she thought of Father Dai's willingness to drop everything and help, she felt a little ashamed at how unwelcoming she'd been towards him. After all, it hadn't been that long ago that she'd been a newcomer herself. *Forgive me, Lord,* she prayed, resolving to do better.

"'Evening, Mrs. Peppers," a raspy voice sounded behind her as she was fishing through her purse for the key to her building's entrance.

"Let me get that for you." Mr. Jenkins, the elderly tenant who lived directly above her, shuffled up to Margaret, produced his own key, and opened the door with a flourish.

"Thank you," Margaret said, rewarding him a smile. "And how is Percival today?" Percival was the parakeet whom Mr. Jenkins had once described as his next of kin. In the summer, when everyone kept their windows open, Margaret could hear her neighbor and Percival conversing animatedly, or so it seemed. Now, in wintertime, Margaret missed the familiar sounds.

"He tells me he wishes he were in Havana doing the rumba, instead of shivering in Seattle, Mrs. Peppers."

"Well, I hope he gets a chance to go there, soon." Margaret smiled again before turning to her mailbox. Tucked between a telephone bill and the latest issue of *The Living Church* were two letters, one from Lizzie Whitcombe and the other from Hallie. There was no doubt which she would open first.

Dear Mama,

I hope you had a wonderful Christmas. Thank you for the cunning little embroidered collars. Did you do them yourself or were these done by the Oriental women at your mission? (See, I've trained myself not to say "Jap," which you object to!)

Christmas was especially busy at church this year. I joined the choir so there were extra services to participate in. A group of us women also sang at the nearby orphanage and old folks' home. It was heart-warming to see their grateful faces.

Speaking of orphanages, did you happen to see the comedy "Bachelor Mother" with Ginger Rogers and

David Niven? If you didn't, the story is about a young bachelorette who finds an abandoned baby, cares for it, and is mistaken for its mother. I laughed a lot, but afterwards I couldn't get that kid out of my mind, like he was a real person. I kept hoping he'd never find out he'd had another mother, but she'd abandoned him. Silly to get so worked up about a movie, isn't it?

Well, I'm writing this on my lunch break, and I need to get back to work at Uncle Charles's office. It seems like everyone has started 1940 by resolving to see the doctor!

Happy New Year,
Ruth

P.S. Last week at Daughters of the King we had an interesting young man as a speaker, Albert John Bauer. He is an evangelist with the Church Army (not the same as the Salvation Army—it's Episcopal.) John—he goes by his middle name—has been asked by Bishop Stevens to help start a church in the Palmdale area. We're going to sponsor him, which means raising money for his work and helping in other ways.

Funny about Hallie and the movie, Margaret thought. *I would have guessed "Gone With the Wind" was more her style, not a comedy about an abandoned baby.* Something about the word "abandoned" made Margaret frown. She put Hallie's letter down and picked up Lizzie's, hoping to be entertained by the latest news from the Mountain Province.

Chapter 35

Every time Margaret went to the Pike Place Market downtown it was as if, for a moment, she was back at the City Public Market in Baguio, with its conglomeration of stalls, smells, and people. Only at the Seattle public market there were no vendors selling dogs to be slaughtered for a feast, thank heavens!

Usually, her destination was the produce stalls, two thirds of which were Nikkei, but today she headed to the Three Girls Bakery. This afternoon the Altar Guilds of both her congregations would be cleaning and decorating their respective churches for tomorrow's Easter services. Though she could not be present to help in Seattle, she'd ordered a chocolate sponge cake which she planned to drop off on her way to the Valley as a "thank you" to the hard-working women of St. Peter's.

It was too bad, she thought later as she motored through the Valley farmland in her old but reliable Model A, that the weather was so rainy, even if it was a mild 55 degrees. Once she passed a Nikkei man harvesting a golden row of daffodils by hand as his wife tied up the stems into bundles. She noticed the man was wearing a type of woven vest known in the old country as a "rice shield," only here the enterprising wife had substituted local reeds for rice straw to protect her husband from the rain.

Most of the daffodil fields had already been stripped of their glory. On her first Easter with the Japanese she had expected to see the churches filled with daffodils, but instead the women of both congregations had fashioned arrangements of flowering plum branches that seemed spare and unfinished to

Margaret's eyes. Daffodils, she learned, were for white people; in their homeland, the Japanese celebrated *Ume Matsuri*, festivals which honored the virtues of endurance, devotion, and pureness of heart associated with the plum tree, the first to flower and the longest lived of all that bore fruit.

"The *ume* is like Our Lord," Mrs. Sato, Altar Guild Directress at St. Peter's, had explained. "He is first to rise from dead, so we like to use *ume* at Easter."

According to her, many famous Japanese poems had been written about plum blossoms, and even now the *Ume Matsuri* were occasions for composing the three-line *haiku*. Mrs. Sato herself frequently composed *haiku* as well as the longer *tanka* on various occasions, a fact she had been too modest to disclose to Margaret, who had learned about it much later from Father Dai.

Margaret remembered her pang of disappointment when the young clergyman had shared this piece of information. It underscored that she was still on the outside looking in, as far as the Issei world was concerned.

Since that confirmation class when Father Dai had interrupted her teaching, they'd agreed that he could visit any of her classes as an observer, and that in the final fifteen minutes he would be given the chance to speak and ask his own questions. She had to hand it to him, he didn't try to correct or upstage her. For the most part, he concentrated on the Issei of St. Paul's and the older Nisei, especially the boys, of both congregations, while she worked more with the younger children and older girls, both in the Valley mission and in Seattle. Father Shoji, meanwhile, clung tenaciously to his role as pastor of the Issei of St. Peter's, politely but firmly rejecting any innovations his young assistant might propose. Margaret sympathized with Father Dai, who couldn't exercise any real responsibility in the Seattle congregation.

It was raining by the time she arrived at St. Paul's, but provision had already been made for inclement weather by locating the Easter egg hunt indoors. The Young People's

Fellowship were hiding the last few goodies while a flock of young children impatiently awaited entry outside the building's front door, which was guarded by an adolescent boy with a mock-ferocious expression.

"Hello, Matt. Do you mind letting me by?"

"Sure thing, Mrs. Peppers. Mrs. Kubo is already inside, if you're looking for her."

Fumiko Kubo headed the Woman's Auxiliary and was in charge of the reception after the egg hunt. Like most Japanese women in the Valley, she helped her husband in the family business, a grocery store, but as her children were almost grown, she could rely on them to pitch in when she had church obligations. It was even rarer for an Issei man to share any responsibility for childcare, cooking, or cleaning than for an American husband. But Mrs. Kubo never complained, unlike some of her Issei sisters who bemoaned having married patriarchal "Meiji men." She reminded Margaret of her own self-sacrificing mother.

"I brought some cupcakes for the party, Mrs. Kubo," she said, sliding the dessert across the table at the far end of the room. She was not expected to observe the traditional protocol which required the giver to denigrate the gift. The first time she had witnessed this behavior was at her inaugural Sunday school picnic at St. Peter's. She had been given a plate of fried chicken by Mrs. Kumojima, who'd said with downcast eyes, "Please accept this tasteless piece of food." Margaret had assumed Mrs. Kumojima's English was at fault, rather than her chicken. She became puzzled after this scene was repeated several times with other Issei women until Mabel Shigaya finally enlightened her.

"Mrs. Peppers, would you like a candy?" fifteen-year-old Janet Ogawa asked, her white pajamas and pipe cleaner ears identifying her as the Easter Bunny.

"No, thank you, I've given up sweets for Lent. You hop along now and attend to the children. But don't forget we have Altar Guild in a half-hour."

"Jeepers! I left the purificators at home." Her happy face

suddenly clouded over as she remembered the Communion linen which had needed a bit of rehemming.

"Don't worry. Since it's Easter we're using the new linen. You can bring yours when you come to church tomorrow. Hippity hop!"

It was nearing the dinner hour before she was ready to leave. Even though she had trained the Altar Guild, and trained them well, she felt obliged to look over the chapel one last time to make sure everything was in order. Mounting the stairs to the building's attic which served as the worship space, Margaret heard the sound of hammering. It was Father Dai, finishing the small wooden cruciform structure that would hold the children's offerings tomorrow— little cardboard "mite boxes" intended to hold coins put aside for the denomination's missionary activity. Father Dai's innovation would be an enhancement, she had to admit. But why leave its construction to the last moment?

As if reading her mind, Father Dai explained. "The sermons came first," referring to the fact that he would be expected to preach in English at both Japanese churches, and in Japanese at St. Paul's. "Do you remember my first Sunday when I preached only in Japanese, thinking everyone would understand?"

Margaret chuckled at the recollection. "The Issei were nodding their heads and smiling, but the Nisei only smiled. They hadn't understood a word."

"I was so green—is that the expression? But between you and Pastor Shoji, I shall do no wrong," he said, looking mischievous. She was beginning to like Father Dai.

Chapter 36

August 1940, Portland

Mrs. Peppers?" inquired the pleasant-faced woman who had hurried up to Margaret after the deaconess deboarded at the cavernous Portland Union Station.

"Oh, Miss Chase. Thank you for meeting me. I'm sorry the train was delayed."

"Well, if you are to stay with me, you must call me Jane. And don't mind about the delay—I've learned to call ahead to find out if the train is on schedule. It hardly ever is."

Jane was in her mid-forties, like Margaret, dark-haired, and generously built. The two had met briefly a few years before at a conference on rural ministry, Jane holding a position in the Oregon Episcopal Diocese akin to hers at the time. Now, Jane was involved in the Japanese mission in downtown Portland. Margaret was looking forward to comparing notes with her colleague.

But professional interest was not the main reason for her trip. One month before Margaret had received a letter from Hallie with a surprising request.

> *John will be traveling to eastern Oregon in a few weeks on behalf of the Church Army. The bishop there wants help in starting up a couple of missions in the rangelands, and John is to report back to his superiors with recommendations.*
>
> *We thought this would be a good chance for the*

two of you to meet. If he drives over to Portland, can you arrange to come down? Please say yes—I will take the train from L.A. and meet you both.

The prospect of seeing her daughter would have been enticement enough to make the journey, but clearly the young man in question had become more than "just a friend" to Hallie. Margaret decided it was important to meet this John and form her own opinion. Overcoming her reluctance to impose on a colleague, she wrote to Jane and explained the situation. Jane immediately wrote back that Margaret was more than welcome to come; not only that, she wanted to know Hallie's address so she could invite her to stay as well.

"After all, you two live far apart," Jane acknowledged, "and I'm sure you'd like to spend as much time together as you can."

Hallie had a different idea. She was planning to stay with a school friend who had moved to Portland and suggested instead that John stay at Jane's: "On the davenport is fine."

Margaret felt embarrassed and angry when she learned of the switch to which Jane graciously agreed. *If I had been allowed to raise my own child,* she had thought, remembering how hard she had worked to instill good manners into the orphans at the House of the Holy Child.

"When did you say your daughter and her beau will be arriving?"

"Hallie's train gets in at 4 p.m. tomorrow and John is supposed to arrive sometime in the evening." She added apologetically, "Hallie hinted it might be rather late because he's driving in from somewhere around Bend."

"Don't worry about that. If it gets too late, I'll just go to bed and leave the hospitality duties to you." Already Margaret found herself resenting this stranger whom she half-expected would descend upon them in the dead of night.

The next morning Margaret woke to the tantalizing aroma of percolating coffee and the sounds of Jane bustling in the kitchen. Quickly she rose and dressed, putting on a pastel blue summer dress she had packed at the last moment, having recalled that Portland in August was several degrees warmer than Seattle. On one lapel of her white collar she pinned the small gold cross denoting her status as a deaconess. She rarely wore her official black and white garb any longer, except when she was sponsoring a child in baptism or attending a diocesan function.

"Good morning, Margaret. Did you sleep well?"

"Fine, thank you," she fibbed. There had been sirens during the night, but she was not bothered by these urban noises. Instead, she had lain awake for some time pondering what might lie ahead for Hallie if she married. Would it be a happier union than her own, or her mother's?

She sat down at the small white kitchen table while Jane ladled out two steaming bowls of Cream of Wheat.

"Friday is Father Nakajo's day to work on his sermon, but I knew he would want to meet you so I made an appointment for us to see him at 9:30. We needn't trouble him for long, then we can go on to Gresham to see the Japanese truck farms. Is that all right?"

Margaret readily agreed. She had assumed the Japanese priest would be similar in age and demeanor to Father Shoji, but within minutes of being ushered into the man's tiny office by his equally diminutive wife, the deaconess sensed he was even more traditional than the vicar of St. Peter's, though he was actually a few years younger. Having soon exhausted her very limited Japanese and Father Nakajo his equally limited English, the remainder of the brief visit passed with Jane uttering a few Japanese phrases as everyone smiled at one another. Finally, Jane murmured toward the sheet of paper, half covered with Japanese characters, lying on the priest's desk. This apparent reference to Father Nakajo's sermon was the signal it was time for the women to leave, which they did, after bowing once again as custom required.

As soon as they were back in Jane's car, Margaret turned

to her. "Why are Father Nakajo's fingernails so long? Are they diseased?" The nails of the priest's little fingers had been at least an inch longer than his others. Margaret couldn't imagine shaking the man's hands even if Japanese decorum prescribed it.

"Something to do with being a scholar, I understand," Jane responded. "Father Nakajo is a wonderful man, but he does have a few peculiarities. The Nisei have trouble relating to him, since they are so Americanized."

They drove on to Gresham to view the Japanese truck farms, stopping at a roadside diner along the way for lunch. Even so, they arrived twenty minutes ahead of the train. Jane busied herself with knitting she'd brought, while Margaret chided herself for not bringing some embroidery work.

"Tell me about your daughter," Jane asked, conversationally.

"She's twenty-nine and has an apartment in Los Angeles," Margaret answered, her eyes straying from her friend's face to the empty track outside. "She works as a receptionist and general office manager at my brother-in-law's medical practice in the city."

"What's she like as a person?"

"I suppose you'd say she's on the shy side, though she can certainly talk once you get to know her. She's mad about the movies. I know she's active in her parish." Margaret hoped her answer sounded like she really knew who her daughter was as a person.

Partly to avoid further questions, and partly to give herself something to do, she got up, excused herself, and began to pace around the waiting room. The crackling sound of the public address system suddenly interrupted her thoughts as the announcer proclaimed the arrival of the train from L.A.

Hallie was one of the first to deboard. Clutching a small suitcase, she scanned the faces of the people clustered near the waiting room entrance. It didn't take long for her to locate her mother, who was standing a little back from the crowd. Quickly she walked toward the familiar presence.

"Hello, Mother." Margaret caught her breath at the sight of the beautiful, grown-up woman that Hallie had become.

"It's so good to see you, dear," Margaret murmured, hoping to infuse those few words with the pleasure and pride her own sudden awkwardness made it hard to express. *Hallie doesn't like being fussed over*, she told herself, limiting her public display of affection to a quick hug and kiss. Then she led the young woman over to the bench where Jane was placidly knitting away.

Introductions made, the threesome departed to take Jane back to the apartment. She had given Margaret use of her car so mother and daughter could go out for dinner together. "I'm sure you have a lot to catch up on," she declared.

On Jane's advice they ate at a restaurant known for its ample portions and consistent good cooking. "Now tell me about this young man," Margaret launched in after pleasantries, assuming what she hoped was an encouraging smile. "I know you met him when he came to your church, but how did you get to really know him if he is working in the—where did you say?"

"Antelope Valley. Well, we started writing to each other after John came to our church. I volunteered to write him on behalf of our Daughters of the King chapter to let him know we were praying for him and his work. John sent back general reports which I shared with the other ladies, but then he started to enclose a separate letter just for me. I did the same. That was four months ago. He drove down a couple of times just to see me and once he took me to see his little congregation and where he lives. My car isn't good enough to drive over to visit him but he has a truck, as you'll see."

"Does he have family here?"

"His family lives in Vermont. He hasn't seen them all that much since he became an evangelist with the Church Army. Before he came here, he was working in the Midwest in a big city among the poor. I can't remember the name of the city but you can be sure it's not anything like where he's working now. You know, he's a little like you, Mama."

Torn between feeling affirmed by this apparent

recognition of Margaret's missionary calling and at the same time, suspicious that this might be simply a ploy to curry favor with her, she merely observed, "You're serious about him, aren't you?" Meanwhile, she tried to ignore the voice which whispered, *Hallie never wanted to come on any missionary journey with* you, *but for this man, she's happy to!*

Her daughter paused a moment, her tanned face flushing ever so slightly. "Well, he's asked me to marry him. He needs a partner to help him in his work and he says I'm the one."

Margaret wanted to ask Hallie if she had accepted John's proposal but checked herself. Better to let Hallie volunteer the information than to pry it out of her. There was an awkward silence as if each were waiting for the other to make a move.

The arrival of the check resolved the issue for the moment. "I'll take that," Margaret said hurriedly, sliding the bill her way. Hallie began to talk animatedly about the latest movie she'd seen, a tragic romance called *'Til We Meet Again.*

"I should be getting on to Marie's," she said, as they got up to leave a few moments later. "Thanks for dinner, Mama."

Reluctantly, she drove her daughter to the destination, a Spanish revival bungalow court in the southwest part of the city. A rare feature in Portland, it reminded Margaret of the ubiquitous clustered bungalows of southern California.

"Just like home, right?" Hallie said, as she placed her fingers on the car door handle, preparing to exit.

"Just like home."

Just before midnight she was awakened by a loud knock. Struggling to her feet, she made for the door as the rapping became more insistent.

Through the peephole, Margaret saw a short young man in an ill-fitting suit holding a valise. It had to be John. With one hand she opened the door while with the other she motioned him to enter, after first making a shushing sign with her finger.

"Miss Chase?" the stranger whispered, as he stepped inside. Margaret could smell the pomade on his slicked back hair.

It was a style that looked good on Cary Grant, but John's outsized ears, perched below his carrot-colored hair, spoiled the effect.

"No, I'm Mrs. Peppers. Miss Chase has gone to bed." Despite being uttered *sotto voce,* the emphasis on the last three words was unmistakable.

"I apologize for the lateness of the hour, Mrs. Peppers," he said a little louder, as if to underscore his sincerity. Then, matching Margaret's low tone, he continued, "I stopped by to see Ruthie and her friend on my way here and they insisted on feeding me dinner." He paused before stating the obvious: "I forgot to introduce myself. I'm John Bauer."

Irritation had brought her fully awake, but she decided to postpone any substantive conversation until the morning in deference to her sleeping hostess. Instead, she shook John's proferred hand with a pasted-on smile and quickly showed him where he could wash up.

"My daughter said you wouldn't mind sleeping on the davenport. Here's a blanket and pillow for you. Will you be needing anything else?"

"No, I'm used to all kinds of accommodations. Often I sleep outside in the summer. It's cooler that way."

He makes it sound like he's doing us a favor to sleep on the sofa, Margaret thought. Then immediately chided herself for her uncharitableness. Resolving to give the visitor—who perhaps might become her son-in-law—the benefit of the doubt, she wished him a good night and turned down the hall to the guest room.

CHAPTER 37

Jane was her usual chatty self in the morning, and Margaret was content to let her colleague carry on most of the conversation with John while she listened and watched attentively. Her daughter's future was at stake.

Her hostess had made pancakes and sausage for breakfast and seemed delighted when John devoured more than the two women combined. Margaret had forgotten how much a young man could eat.

"You're a great cook, Miss Chase," John said, as he helped himself to his fourth sausage. "You should give Ruth some lessons. She can't even boil water."

Margaret bristled at the criticism, not only on her daughter's behalf, but also because of its implications concerning her own failures as a mother and role model. In the next breath, as if reading her thoughts, he hastened to add that he meant no criticism of Mrs. Peppers, since he knew she had lived far away from Ruth for most of the girl's life.

"I'd love to hear about your work, Mr. Bauer," said Jane, sitting down to eat now that her guests had been given their fill. "I must say I know very little about the Church Army."

"We're a bit like the Salvation Army, except without the band and uniforms," he responded, smiling. "Some of us take the Gospel to the slums, but others work in rural areas. Me, I've done both, but I have to say that I much prefer fresh air to the stench of the city."

"The poor would probably agree with you," Margaret said. She was remembering the times she had made a visit to a

Manila slum dwelling on behalf of the American Guardian Association and the House of the Holy Child. She'd heard some Americans overseas say that the poor were accustomed to their abysmal living conditions, but if that were true, why had so many mothers tried to get their children into her orphanage?

Ignoring the comment, John proceeded to tell the women about his work in the Southern California desert. As his explanation closely paralleled what Hallie had already told her, Margaret listened with only half an ear. Her mind was puzzling over what her daughter saw in this brash stranger. *He's skinny as a rail and not much taller than Hallie. No wonder he's cocky — the short ones often are.*

"What you need to do is start a day nursery," she heard John telling Jane. "Somewhere the women can park their children while they work on the farm."

"Oh, but the Methodists already have one," Jane was explaining. "It would look like we were trying to horn in on their work."

"That's their problem," John asserted. "Besides, I bet there are enough kids to go around."

"Well, it's something to think about," Jane said. "Now I'm afraid you two must excuse me, for I have a meeting with my bishop. I envy you your trip to Timberline today." Marie had offered to drive Hallie, John, and Margaret to visit the two-year-old Timberline Lodge, a Works Progress Administration masterpiece nestled beneath Mount Hood. At first Margaret had declined, not wishing to intrude on the young people's outing, but surprisingly, it was Hallie who had insisted her mother come along.

"Mr. Bauer, it was a pleasure to meet you. Next time I hope you'll stay longer," Jane said to the young man. Turning to her other guest she added, "Margaret, I'll see you this evening." Dismissing the pair with a smile and a wave, Jane turned and disappeared inside her apartment.

The day was sunny and warm, perfect for a motor jaunt up to the mountains. Trying to ignore John's slightly nasal voice holding forth on economics in the back seat, Margaret turned to the petite blond at the wheel. "My daughter tells me you work at Portland City Hall. What do you do?"

"Oh, nothing too exciting. I work in a steno pool. Last month I hopped between the Building Department and the Parks Department." Marie directed her voice toward the back. "John, I think you're right that we've turned the corner on this old Depression. At least that's what they say where I work—the number of building permits have been increasing every month, it seems."

Margaret felt like a fifth wheel. Why had Hallie wanted her to come?

As they drove along the Mount Hood Highway she couldn't help noticing the number of clear-cuts, further testimony to the improved economic conditions. Their ugliness was softened by the swaths of magenta fireweed that encircled the stumps, gulping up the sunshine that once had been unable to penetrate the thick forest. Ribbons of pearly everlasting, their small clusters of white blossoms bobbing in the breeze, lined the sides of the road.

The young people chatted on, apparently oblivious to their surroundings—and to Margaret. In two hours they reached the impressive lodge, which had been described as America's version of the alpine chalet. Asymmetrical in design, with a massive hexagonal central unit flanked by two wings of unequal size, the stone and timber structure was capable of withstanding the most severe winter storms, its steeply pitched roofs deflecting much of the heavy snow. To Margaret it seemed part fortress, part enchanted castle.

Even Hallie and Marie paid attention when they entered through the large wooden front door, decorated with the carved head of an Indian chief, that led into a soaring lounge with hand-hewn timber trusses supported by a massive six-sided chimney with large fireplaces. While the women wandered about, gawking at the wrought iron grilles, the whimsically carved lintels and newel posts representing beavers and other forest animals, and the Northwest-themed relief carvings and paintings adorning the walls, Margaret witnessed Hallie pulling a reluctant John to his feet and overheard his grumbled response.

"I thought we were going to have the day to ourselves, Ruthie. Not have two chaperones."

Hallie whispered something that must have mollified him, for his glum expression was replaced with a smile as he rejoined the party. He made appreciative sounds as he inspected various features of the rustic lodge, until Hallie announced that she and John were going to take a walk outside to view the scenery and wildflowers. They would return at 3 p.m., she said, the departure time that had already been agreed upon.

"Well, I guess we're not welcome, eh?" said Marie smilingly to Margaret. "Shall we find ourselves a bite to eat?"

They exchanged pleasantries over bowls of chili. Margaret insisted on paying before shooing Marie away. "I don't want to keep you from visiting the gift shop or strolling wherever you wish. I'll just have a seat here and enjoy the view." She wanted time to reflect on her own.

Margaret did not share in the jolly mood that prevailed on the ride home. It was almost a relief when the time came to say goodbye to Hallie and her companions. She would be seeing her daughter off in the morning.

"You seem very quiet," Jane observed as she cleared the last of the dinner dishes. "Are you tired from your outing?"

What can I say? Margaret thought. *That I disapprove of my daughter's boyfriend? That I'm worried sick that someday, she'll regret she ever married him?*

She did not want to engage further in gossip or ill-will, but there was something about Jane that invited confidences. Drying the dishes that Jane washed, Margaret found herself pouring out her fears. "Hallie's going to spend her life being dragged along who-knows-where by a man who only thinks of himself," was her concluding lament, after detailing John's shortcomings for the better part of half an hour.

"How do you plan to bring this up with Hallie?"

Jane asked.

"I don't know, but I must say something while she's still here. I don't want to leave this to a letter."

All night, Margaret rehearsed various ways of approaching the subject with her daughter. Her imaginings were punctuated by fervent prayers for wisdom in expressing her concerns to this young woman whom she knew could be stubborn and difficult to persuade.

All her practiced speeches seemed to die on her lips the moment Margaret laid eyes on Hallie sitting with her luggage near the entrance to Union Station. "How was your date?" Margaret asked, after they had both checked their suitcases and settled into seats at the station coffee shop. She felt it prudent to begin on a positive note.

"We had dinner at a restaurant named Huber's. It's the oldest restaurant in Portland, John said, and so beautiful. It had the most gorgeous stained-glass ceilings—it almost felt like being in church. The food was good, too." A pause, then: "How was your evening?"

"Oh, fine. Hallie—"

But her daughter was already saying, "We stayed at the table for *three hours*. Lucky it wasn't the weekend, or we would have been kicked out." Another pause.

"I've accepted his proposal."

"No!" Margaret blurted, before she could stop herself.

"What do you mean, 'No'?" Hallie's voice was at once brittle and challenging.

I need to reason with her. "I mean," Margaret began, "let's think about this…"

"There's no 'us' involved, except for John and me! We love each other, and we're going to get married. That's it!"

"Hallie, listen to me for a minute. John may be a fine Christian man, but he's not right for you. He's egotistical, he sulks when he doesn't get his own way–"

"He *never* sulks–"

"Look what happened yesterday. He really wasn't

interested in the Timberline Lodge, so rather than join us he sat down all by himself until you came and jollied him along."

"He has more important things to think about. He's an Evangelist with the Church Army, commissioned by the Bishop to start a church where there hasn't been a church before. Not many people could do that. Neither you nor your Miss Chase could do that!" With each declaration, Hallie's voice got louder. People at nearby tables were starting to stare.

"You know nothing about what we can and cannot do! Let him try running an outstation among headhunters and then you can talk!" Margaret managed, barely, to keep her voice lower than her daughter's but there was no mistaking the anger drenching her words.

I must keep calm, she reminded herself. *Arguing will achieve nothing.*

Taking a deep breath, she tried a different tack. "You're used to living in the city, Hallie, going to movies, having outings at the beach—how will you like living in the kinds of places John will be sent?"

"As long as I'm with John, I'll be happy. And I can get out once in a while. Antelope Valley isn't all that far from L.A. Besides, as these places grow, they'll have movie theaters and other things, just like in the cities."

"Hallie, you may think the love you have now will solve all your problems. But believe me–"

"Yes, I know, Aunt Martina has told me—you stopped loving Daddy, if you ever *did* love him. She said–"

"Quiet now!" Margaret snapped. "You don't know anything about my husband!"

Hallie recoiled, as if she had been slapped in the face.

"All aboard for Los Angeles!" blared the station's loudspeaker, bringing a sudden, if inconclusive, end to their argument.

"I'll pay," Hallie said grimly, throwing down a one-dollar bill.

"No, you hurry and catch your train," Margaret

responded in a softer tone, pressing the money back into her daughter's hand as she attempted to give her a conciliatory farewell kiss. Already she was regretting her outburst.

Hallie pulled back, avoiding her mother's embrace. "I *am* going to marry John, whether you like it or not!" Turning on her heel, she fled onto the platform and into the womb of the train.

Chapter 38

October 1940, Seattle

Mr. and Mrs. Albert Bauer of Hartland announce the wedding of their son Albert John Bauer to Miss Ruth Hal Peppers of Los Angeles on October 3, 1940. The marriage was solemnized at the Windsor Baptist Church, the Rev. Cecil Petrie officiating. After a brief honeymoon the bride and groom will take up residence in Detroit, Michigan.

Margaret fingered the clipping from the *Vermont Journal* that Martina had sent her. Could this really be her daughter? It seemed like a dream—or a nightmare. Martina had been apprised of the impending nuptials only a few days before Hallie was due to leave for the East, joining her fiancé who had already departed for his home in Vermont. Reading between the lines of her sister-in-law's short epistle, Margaret concluded that Martina herself was of two minds concerning the marriage. Of Charles Peppers' views there was no doubt: in a postscript Martina said he thought that at age twenty-nine it was high time Ruth got married, lest she become a hopeless old maid.

Nothing was said about why the couple would move to Detroit. Perhaps Hallie had heeded her mother's warnings and insisted that they live somewhere more civilized than the California desert. Margaret could only speculate about the kind of church work John might be engaged in. She had trouble imagining Hallie laboring beside her husband in the Negro slums.

It being Saturday, she would usually do housework, but

her arthritis was acting up today. Besides, propriety demanded that she buy a wedding present for Hallie and John. As she made the short drive from her apartment to the downtown business district, Margaret pondered the possibilities.

Hallie always loved flowers, so perhaps a lovely vase? Or something more practical, like a nice set of towels? It wasn't until she was standing under the iron marquee at the entrance to Frederick and Nelson's that Margaret remembered the lace she still had from her Bontoc days. If she bought some fine pillowcases, she knew she could embellish them with the lace to make a truly unique gift.

How ironic that it was a Japanese woman who used to teach lace making at Bontoc. Now it is I who am working among the Japanese.

Margaret smiled wistfully as she thought how little interest her girls at St. Peter's and St. Paul's would have in an intricate skill like lace making. They would much rather be learning the latest dance step or hit parade song. Nevertheless, there was a handful of Junior Altar Guild girls who diligently repaired and even embroidered some of the altar linens when necessary. Their mothers, she was certain, had at least as high standards as she did—perhaps even higher.

Completing her purchase, Margaret decided to treat herself to the store's signature Frango frozen dessert in the elegant tea room. She could afford a twenty-cent splurge. Entering the elevator to ascend to the fifth floor, she was greeted by fifteen-year-old Keiko Nakashima and her mother Suma. Keiko was one of her favorites at St. Peter's—bubbly and full of life, yet she could be serious and devout as well.

"Good afternoon, Mrs. Nakashima," she said, making a slight bow in response to the Issei's deeper one, though each woman was hampered by the presence of other elevator occupants. "Hello, Keiko. What a nice surprise!"

Keiko, however, didn't seem her usual ebullient self. *Did Mrs. Nakashima say 'no' to something Keiko wanted to buy?* Margaret wondered. Perhaps she would be given the opportunity to find out, because before the smartly dressed elevator operator—a young woman no older than Keiko—could open the doors to the fifth floor, Margaret had been invited to join the pair at the restaurant. It would be rude not to accept.

Mrs. Nakashima's English was not good, so Keiko acted as interpreter. Detecting no tension between mother and daughter, Margaret presumed Keiko's downcast manner had another cause. Mrs. Nakashima didn't seem disturbed, so it couldn't be family illness or trouble.

"Mama is bringing me here because tomorrow is my birthday," Keiko explained, after pleasantries between the elders had been exchanged. "I'll be sweet sixteen."

"Congratulations, my dear. You're getting to be quite the lady."

"Did you see the elevator girl just now? She's in my history class at Franklin High. What I wouldn't give to have her job!"

"Well, once you are sixteen you can apply if there's an opening, can't you?" She stopped herself and looked at Mrs. Nakashima, who was placidly observing the conversation. "Or do your parents want you to stay at home?" Many of the teenagers at St. Peter's were helping in their parents' business or taking care of younger siblings, but Keiko was an only child and her father worked as a dentist.

"That's not it." Keiko responded. "Muriel Sato applied and never heard back from them. Even though everyone knows Frederick and Nelson's only hires brunettes as elevator girls. Why, there's a blond at our school who dyed her hair just to get a job there." Before Keiko could say anything more, she was interrupted by the arrival of their food.

"Mrs. Peppers, will you pray?" asked Mrs. Nakashima.

Margaret murmured, "For what we are about to receive, may the Lord make us truly thankful." Then she added, "And please bless Keiko on her special birthday."

They ate for a few moments in silence, Margaret savoring the cool creaminess of her Orange Frango, not without a pang of guilt. What could she say that would take away the pain of a girl's rejection because of the shape of her eyes and her parents' native country?

"It's because we're Japanese," Keiko said, suddenly resuming her heated account. "Why are people so mean?"

"*Shikata na gai,*" Mrs. Nakashima said quietly.

Father Dai had explained this saying to Margaret once before: *It cannot be helped.* Keiko's mother must have heard the bitterness in her daughter's voice and known its cause.

"Our Lord tells us we must love those who treat us badly," Margaret said. "And pray for a change of their hearts."

"That's what Papa says, too," Keiko acknowledged. "But he's a better Christian than I am."

"Someday," Margaret said, "things will change. You will see it in your lifetime, I'm sure. People will judge you for who you are, not how you look or where your parents were born. Don't lose heart."

Don't lose heart. All at once she could hear her mother saying those very words, when everything was so dark for their family. *Don't lose heart, Maggie.*

CHAPTER 39

In November Franklin Roosevelt was re-elected President by a landslide, promising voters that "your boys are not going to be sent into any foreign wars." Margaret joined the millions who cast their ballots to send F.D.R. to the White House for an unprecedented third term. Now that Hallie was married, the arguments for keeping America neutral had taken on more personal importance than ever before. Whatever she thought of her son-in-law, Margaret didn't want him sent abroad to fight somebody else's war. Nor, for that matter, did she want any of the Nisei lads at St. Peter's or St. Paul's to be drafted.

On New Year's Eve Margaret finally heard from Hallie, in the form of a Christmas card which contained no acknowledgement of the wedding gift but did mention that John had so far escaped the draft. John was apparently working in a shoe store downtown while receiving further training with the Church Army. Hallie said nothing about what and where his next assignment would be, nor did the brief, perfunctory note give any information about her own activities. The note was signed simply, "Ruth and John."

In the same day's post, a letter arrived from Lizzie Whitcombe.

You may have heard that Bishop Mosher resigned in October due to poor health. In the Providence of God the Rt. Rev. Norman Binsted, Bishop of the Diocese of Tohoku, who, along with the other foreign missionary bishops, had been forced to leave Japan by the government, was ready and able to take charge. I like him very much, and I think you would too.

> *Events in Japan are quite alarming for the Church. The government accuses missionaries of being spies for Britain or the U.S., and there are frequent demonstrations, fomented by the government, calling for the ousting of all foreigners from the country. It won't be long before all foreign church workers will have to leave, Bishop Binsted thinks. Interestingly—and it will come as no surprise to you as a deaconess—the Japanese government seems to have overlooked the women workers. They are not considered sufficiently important to merit official attention—at least for the moment.*

As she read her friend's account Margaret reflected, not for the first time, that in the Philippines Lizzie had found her life's work.

Have I finally found my life's work? Margaret thought, as she put down her former colleague's pages. She tried to imagine herself back in the Philippines working under a new and more sympathetic bishop, but the prospect did not really tempt her. She was no longer the energetic young missionary eager to bring Christianity to a primitive race overseas. When she'd accepted the call to become a rural minister in Washington state, constantly on the move, it seemed to fit the person she'd become: someone destined never to put down roots, whose home and work were always temporary, always provisional. Perhaps God was finally declaring: *Here is your life's work, among a people who are transplants like you. Your home is with the Nikkei.*

She remembered what Bishop Huston had said the other day, when he introduced a new priest to her at a diocesan meeting. "Deaconess Peppers is a 'second mother' to the daughters of Japanese immigrants," the Bishop had explained, in a tone warm with approval. "The adolescent Nisei girls look to her for guidance when their own mothers don't understand

American ways."

The mere memory of the conversation was like water penetrating thirsty soil. Margaret hoped it was also a sign.

In February Father Dai's brother arrived from Japan and settled in with his older sibling at the St. Paul's vicarage. Instinctively, Margaret began to question her nascent sense of security. Mitsuo—or Joe, as he preferred to be called—was preparing to become a priest like his brother. His English, too, was excellent like Father Dai's, if similarly accented. How long would her own position be viable with more priests being added? *I need to trust God more*, Margaret decided, and set about memorizing the verses of the Sermon on the Mount about the futility of worry.

Still, Margaret found herself breathing a sigh of relief once Joe was on his way—St. Paul's was merely his first stop on a sightseeing tour—though he seemed to be a likable enough fellow. But the young women in the congregation—and their Issei mothers—had had their matrimonial ambitions excited by the arrival of another eligible bachelor, and they were disappointed to see him go

Apart from this novel interlude, life at St. Paul's and St. Peter's followed its predictable spring pattern. Joining the appointed round of holy days—Ash Wednesday, Lent, Easter— was the Japanese holiday known as Doll's Festival Day or Girls' Day, traditionally a time when dolls representing the Japanese Imperial Court were exhibited on a multi-tiered stand. It was one holiday that did not have overt Buddhist or Shinto associations, so Christian Nikkei girls or women could celebrate it with a clear conscience. And none enjoyed the day more than the Shojis' severely disabled daughter Florence, whose exuberant delight in the church's display of family heirlooms belonging to St. Peter's womenfolk brought joy to all who witnessed it. *It's like watching a big yellow rose suddenly burst into bloom*, thought Margaret, who was not usually given to such flights of fancy. Once, she glanced across the room and saw Father Shoji observing his daughter with a rapt tenderness. It was a look Margaret had never seen before on the priest's face and she quickly averted her eyes, feeling as if she had intruded upon something both intimate and sacred.

One Sunday afternoon in May, Margaret was walking away from St. Peter's, having just finished teaching a confirmation class. She had declined the offer of a ride home from Father Dai, her usually reliable car being in the shop, and intended instead to catch the streetcar uptown to do some marketing. Her route took her by the Japanese Pentecostal Church, where she could hear a ruckus as usual.

It was an unusually warm day, and the front door of the humble bungalow was flung open, allowing the worshippers' shouts and cries to spill out freely, as if a handful of firecrackers had been tossed into the street. Margaret glanced disdainfully toward the commotion and was preparing to cross the road when an ancient Japanese lady suddenly appeared by her side, motioning for assistance in mounting the building's front steps. As a Christian she could hardly refuse, so Margaret took her arm and led her slowly to the threshold of the church, while trying to ignore the sounds within.

Arigato, said the grandmother, bowing, but before joining the service she waved a bony hand at her companion and said, "*Musume*—daughter—sad."

Does she mean me? Margaret wondered, starting in surprise.

"Holy Ghost say, 'You *musume* sad. You pray.'" Then the woman turned away and hobbled inside.

Margaret stared after the aged messenger for a moment before retreating. The encounter had left her feeling spiritually wobbly. She hesitated—should she return to St. Peter's, to seek Father Dai's, or even Father Shoji's, reassurance and blessing? Instead, she hurried to catch the streetcar and let the normalcy of a Sunday afternoon in the city wash over her.

It was three days later in a letter from Martina that she

came to learn of her son-in-law's illness.

> *Ruth wrote Charles that John had come down with the flu in April which he seemed unable to shake. After a few weeks he began to have trouble wiggling his fingers and toes, then started to lose mobility. Their doctor referred him to a specialist, who diagnosed something called "Landry's Paralysis." It may get worse, involving all John's body, including his ability to breathe, or he may recover on his own. Apparently there is no treatment. Ruth wanted to confirm this diagnosis with her uncle. Charles said he can't be sure without examining John himself, but it sounds right.*

"Oh, Hallie!" Margaret's spontaneous cry resounded within her small apartment. Suddenly, she began to shiver uncontrollably, as she recalled her recent meeting with the wizened female prophet.

Hallie's situation was even worse than what she herself had faced with Hal so long ago. Then, until they'd moved to Los Angeles, Margaret at least had her own family to support her. Of course, she had been pregnant, which had made matters worse in a different way.

Should she take the train to Detroit to be with her daughter? Surely Hallie would welcome her mother and let bygones be bygones.

Taking up the letter once more, she continued:

> *Because John can't work, they've decided to move back to his parents in Vermont. I wish they would come down here where Charles could doctor him, but that's their choice. I'm sending you their new address because I know you'll want to write.*

Traveling to Vermont was out of the question. There was

only one choice: she must sit down and immediately write Hallie a letter which, she prayed, would surmount the emotional distance between them, a distance more formidable than any length of miles that might be separating them.

Chapter 40

"Mama?" spoke the tremulous voice out of the pre-dawn gloom.

Margaret, instantly awake, gripped the telephone receiver. She clutched the front of her nightgown and thought, *It must be bad news for her to call.*

"John's—he's—" Hallie broke down, sobbing.

Outside a robin was heralding the beginning of a new day. "Oh my dear, my dear…" Margaret murmured, her voice an anguished counterpoint to the bird's relentlessly cheerful warbling.

"It was awful… he couldn't breathe… they made me leave the room… I wanted to be there at the end…"

"Yes, I know, I know…" *Dear God, comfort her.*

"Why did he have to die? He was only twenty-five—"

Lord, give me the right words to say. "We can't always understand the Lord's ways, Hallie, but you can be sure John is in heaven, waiting for you to join him someday. He's in a better place…" Never had her assurances sounded so trite to her ears, so utterly inadequate.

"But what do I do now?" Hallie wailed.

Margaret eagerly seized on the chance to focus on practical matters. "I suppose his family wants to have the funeral there. But afterwards, would you want to come to Seattle and stay with me for a bit?"

A pause. "I'll think about it. Mama, I need to get off the phone now. It's costing a bundle."

"Do you want to call back and reverse the charges?"

"No, that's okay. I need to go send some telegrams." Margaret winced at the desolation she heard beneath the resolve in Hallie's voice.

"All right, dear. Send me a postcard and let me know your plans. And remember—call me collect anytime."

"I will. Bye, Mama."

Margaret started to say goodbye, when a sudden idea came to mind. "Hallie, dear—do you want me at the funeral? I should be able to arrange things here so I can go."

There was a brief pause on the other end of the line. "No, that's okay. It will be his family, mostly. Mama, I'll talk later—bye now."

She hung up before her mother could offer a heartfelt "I love you." Slowly, Margaret put down the receiver, her mind echoing with a cacophony of thoughts of what it would finally be like to have her daughter in her home. But better not to get her hopes up too soon.

She glanced at the kitchen clock. *5 a.m. No point in going back to bed. Might as well get ready for Vacation Church School at St. Paul's.* It was hard to believe that summer was already upon them.

Driving through the bucolic communities that supplied Seattle's produce, she began to think more deeply about what John's death must have been like. She remembered the dreadful days when she'd sat beside Hal's bed, watching helplessly while he wasted away. She had been only nineteen, a decade younger than her daughter was now. Did that make it easier—or harder? She, too, had not been present for her husband's final moments, but she'd been assured they were peaceful, unlike her son-in-law's apparently gruesome death by asphyxiation. *It's better that Hallie didn't see John's life end that way, so she won't carry that memory to her grave.* When she pulled onto the property of St. Paul's, Margaret had been remembering how she herself had had little time to grieve, given that she was suddenly responsible for raising a little girl on her own. *That's an experience I wouldn't wish on anyone.*

As she lay down after her prayers, she began to recall her earlier glib assurance that John would be waiting for his bride when God saw fit to call her to heaven. *Will Hal be waiting for me?* Margaret wondered. *What will he say?* Only when she finally fell asleep did the image of Hal's fever-flushed countenance cease confronting her like an accusation.

One evening in mid-July, Hallie arrived in Seattle on the *Empire Builder*. She disembarked the train with only two suitcases and a trunk, which was far less than Margaret expected.

"I got rid of all my winter clothes," Hallie said, in response to her mother's query. "I don't want to live in a cold climate ever again. I'm having a few household things shipped to L.A., but really, I just want to start over. I didn't even keep all my wedding presents."

Margaret checked her impulse to reiterate her invitation to move to Seattle. Hallie had neither said nor written anything in response to her mother's earlier overture, and Margaret knew better than to press her at this time. Hallie intended to travel to L.A. in three days, but that didn't mean she had to stay there. If she wanted to begin a new life in a place that held no memories of her marriage, why not Seattle?

"Mama, I hope you don't mind, but all I want to do is to crawl into bed. I didn't sleep very well on the train."

"Of course, dear." Hallie did look pale, and Margaret guessed she had not slept well for quite some time.

The days of sleeping any old place had long been only a memory for Margaret, and she passed an uncomfortable night on her davenport. On the other hand, her wakefulness afforded her the opportunity to consider how best to persuade Hallie to move to Seattle. She decided only to drop a hint now and then until she had conferred with Charles about whether he'd be willing to help his niece find work in Seattle.

Margaret had finished her toast and coffee and was halfway through her daily Bible reading—ironically, a chapter from the Book of Ruth in which the eponymous heroine pledges always to remain by the side of the woman who was like a mother to her—when Hallie, looking paler than ever, appeared.

"Shall I scramble some eggs for you?" Margaret asked.

"Not now, thanks, maybe later," Hallie replied, sitting down at the kitchen table. "Just a cup of coffee will be fine." She fingered the red-checked tablecloth nervously, as if she were unsure what else to say.

"Don't you have to be at church or something?"

"I've been allowed to take a couple of days off, under the circumstances. Maybe later we can stop by St. Peter's so I can show you around," Margaret said, as she placed a steaming cup of coffee before her daughter. After a delicate pause, she waded in to try to learn more about the last few weeks. "How are John's parents?"

"His mother is broken up, of course. It's hard to tell with his dad. I think they blame me somehow, though they've never said anything directly."

"I remember when your father got so sick," Margaret started to say, but Hallie continued after a moment's pause, apparently absorbed in expressing her thoughts.

"Excuse me, Mama, I need to go to the bathroom." Surprised, Margaret followed her daughter down the hall with her eyes. Something *was* wrong.

The apartment was too small to obscure the retching sounds coming from the bathroom. In a little while Hallie reappeared, asking for a glass of water.

"You're sick. Shouldn't you lie down? Is there anything I can do?" Margaret asked anxiously.

"No—nobody can–" said Hallie, dabbing furiously at her eyes with the handkerchief she'd produced from a pocket in her blue seersucker dress. Margaret quickly moved towards her daughter, arms outstretched. For once Hallie did not evade her mother's embrace.

"I'm sick because I'm pregnant!" she sobbed.

Sweet Jesus. It's happening again.

"How far along are you?" Margaret asked over Hallie's

shoulder, which was still pressed against her own.

"About three months. I went to a doctor in Detroit before I came here. I'd missed two periods, but I thought it was because I was so upset over John's illness. But then I started to get sick every morning. Thank goodness the funeral was in the afternoon, or else I might have had to run out like I did with you just now."

Margaret did a quick calculation. Hallie must have got pregnant a couple of weeks before John became ill.

"Now you see why I must return to L.A.," Hallie answered, sniffling as she pulled back from her mother's embrace. "I'm sure I can work for Uncle Charles again, and when the time comes, he can take care of me. After that—well, I suppose he and Aunt Martina can figure something out together."

"Do they know about this?" Margaret hoped against hope that this could be kept a secret a little longer, until she had time to figure out what to do.

"Not yet, but if they can't guess I plan to tell them. You know Aunt Martina has moved back to L.A. from Redlands, to keep house for Uncle Claude and Aunt Effa. I doubt they'll have room for me and the baby, but maybe we could all live in one big mansion next to Uncle Charles in Beverly Hills."

Margaret ignored her daughter's attempt at humor. She must not let the Peppers clan get their clutches into Hallie again.

"You don't need to rush into anything. I'm sure I could work something out here, so we could be together. After all, I am the child's grandmother." Seeing Hallie stiffen, she quickly added, "I mean, it's natural I should want to help."

At that moment the telephone rang. It was an apologetic Father Dai asking Margaret if she would mind coming down to St. Peter's and letting him in. He had left his keys in another jacket and rushed out of the vicarage this morning without them.

"That man would forget his head if it wasn't screwed on," Margaret muttered, but she was grateful to bring the awkward conversation she'd been having with her daughter to a close. "Hallie, do you feel up to coming with me to the church?

I'd like to show you around."

"I think I should stay around here until my stomach settles," she responded. "You go ahead—and if there are some things you need to do, I'll be all right here. I'll just take a look at the paper, maybe rest a bit."

A couple of hours later Margaret returned to find her daughter still sitting at the kitchen table, staring out the window at nothing in particular.

"I stopped by the Queen Anne Bakery across the street— they make the best krullers. Won't you try one?"

With a half-stifled sigh, Hallie took the proffered pastry and began to consume it under her mother's watchful eye. Margaret selected a kruller herself and between bites, proposed a plan for the afternoon.

"I thought we might go to the fabric store and look at patterns for maternity dresses. I'm happy to run up a couple for you on the sewing machine and send them off to you when I've finished."

Hallie agreed, though without much enthusiasm. Selecting a pattern and fabric seemed to dispel her lethargy, at least for the moment. Before long she was even complaining of hunger.

The last day Hallie was in town Margaret took her to St. Peter's. Having worked for years among the urban Japanese, she accepted without thought the crowded conditions in much of *Nihonmachi*—after all, hadn't it been that way in San Francisco's Chinatown, or even in Manila? But as they drove down bustling Jackson Street, past long-established businesses such as Yoshitomi Honest Grocery, Uyeki Shoe Store, and the Iwana Star Laundry, Hallie gazed about with an expression that seemed to hover between interest and disdain.

"Why do the Jap—Orientals—always keep together and not even try to learn English? At least they dress like us and don't wear those silly pigtails like they did in Chinatown when I was growing up. Do the women wear their long dresses to church?"

"You mean *kimonos*. No, only for special occasions, and usually only the older ladies do that. I guess when the men and women first came from Japan, they were so busy earning a living they didn't have time to learn English, and now that they're older it's too hard. But the boys and girls I work with speak English just like you or me."

"I saw some Colored people down the street. Do they come to your church, too?" Hallie wondered.

"No, they have their own churches," Margaret replied. "Wasn't it that way in Detroit?"

"You bet. It seems like every other storefront in the slums is a church."

Just then they pulled up at St. Peter's. Margaret parked behind the church and said, "Well, here we are. It's pretty quiet now because the children are in school and their parents are working, but this afternoon and evening, there'll be Scout troops and choir practice and Daughters of the King, just like at any Episcopal Church. I do hope we can catch Father Dai."

They walked up the gravel driveway and entered the tiny church office, where a young woman was busily typing. At the sight of the deaconess accompanied by a stranger, Miss Kogita immediately stopped her work and gave a welcoming smile.

Introductions made, Margaret showed her daughter the tiny cubicle that was her office. It was crammed with papers and books on Christian education, which sat in piles on her small desk and on the floor.

"I'm getting a new file cabinet next week—you can see the place where it will go," she apologized hastily, pointing to a bare corner by the window. "Our secretary really needed one more than I do, so I gave her mine."

Hallie teased, "If you worked for Uncle Charles, you wouldn't last a day. He insists on everything being just so."

At least there was no need to apologize for the church itself, which looked like any number of small Episcopal churches across the country, except for a few distinctive touches, such as Japanese language prayer books and Bibles. The congregation couldn't afford stained glass windows, but maybe it was better that way. Even among the brown people of the Manila, the stained glass windows had featured a white Jesus surrounded by white disciples.

Before long, Father Dai appeared in the doorway of the church. The three of them chatted for a few moments before Father Dai excused himself. "I am sorry, but I must prepare for a Bishop's Committee meeting. Mrs. Bauer, I hope you will visit us again. Perhaps you will see your mother at Christmas? Mrs. Peppers directs the pageant and it is—what do you say?—a spectacle. And the church is so beautiful then."

"That would be nice," Hallie murmured.

A lot is going to happen between now and Christmas, Margaret thought, then immediately offered up a silent prayer that by that time her daughter would have joined her for good.

Chapter 41

As summer turned to autumn, she watched her hopes of Hallie's moving north wither in the face of bland disregard. Hallie had never been a good letter writer, but her mother had expected some kind of response given the circumstances. By October the silence had become too much, causing her to sit down one rainy evening and pen a letter to Martina.

Taking care to use the name the Peppers family preferred, she wrote:

> *Ruth tells me you're now keeping house for both your brother Claude and sister Effa. Knowing how much you enjoyed living in Redlands and how active you were in your church, I admire your sacrifice in returning to L.A. to come to their aid. I, too, wish to do my duty by my family—to be for Ruth and her baby what you have been and done all these years. Now that your own responsibilities have increased, this might be a way to help you as I am helping them.*

I'm laying it on a bit thick, Margaret thought. Martina probably wouldn't be persuaded of the sincerity of her sister-in-law's admiration, but at least the idea of someone else sharing her load of family responsibilities might strike a responsive chord.

Before the month was over, Margaret had finally heard from Hallie, who mentioned having seen the letter her mother had written Martina. *That's good news—it means my sister-in-law wants her to consider my proposal*, was Margaret's initial reaction. But her hopes faded as she quickly read on.

> *I'm sorry but I need to stay here. Uncle Charles says a move now is out of the question. He told me I should rest as much as possible, or else I may give birth prematurely. For the time being I'm staying with him and his wife—remember my joke about living in Beverly Hills?—so he can keep an eye on me. He's always working so it's really Irene who is watching me. She was a practical nurse so even though she's never had children she knows what to do.*

Alarmed, Margaret sent her brother-in-law a telegram to find out how precarious was Hallie's pregnancy. The answer, which came a few days later, was reassuring: *No need to worry. Everything fine. Expect normal delivery.*

She would bide her time, Margaret decided, until after her grandchild was born.

At noon on December 7, 1941, after eighteen hours of labor, Hallie gave birth to a daughter. Little Patricia Ann seemed determined to shoulder her way into the world like a Rose Bowl quarterback—at least that was how the obstetrician, an avid college football fan, later described it to Charles. In the end, the baby could not prevail over the kinked umbilical cord that had cut off her oxygen supply, and she was pronounced dead at birth.

Three hours later, before Charles had a chance to telegraph the news to his sister-in-law, Margaret and Father Dai were finishing a meal at the home of Dr. and Mrs. Shigaya in Seattle. An announcement interrupted the New York Philharmonic program they were enjoying on the radio. Pearl Harbor had been attacked by the Empire of Japan.

PART 4: 1941–1942
Washington State

Chapter 42

December 9, 1941

The line at the Western Union office in the King Street train station was longer than Margaret ever remembered. That morning the paper had carried an article urging people to put off long-distance calls for several days, to keep lines open for vital communications. With a sigh, Margaret joined the shuffling queue, resigning herself to a long wait.

Yesterday's announcement about the imposition of a dusk to dawn blackout had repeated itself *ad nauseum* until Margaret was finally driven to turn off the radio. She wished she had been able to turn off the other images and sounds that kept surfacing in her mind. The urgent voice of CBS Radio reporter John Daly describing the attack was overlaid with the incredulous cries of the Shigayas, "It can't be!" President Roosevelt's reassuring pronouncement, "No matter how long it may take… the American people in their righteous might will win through to absolute victory" vied in her memory with the panicked phone call she'd received from a Nisei parishioner whose father had been taken away by FBI agents in the night.

Then there was her brother-in-law's telegram which had arrived late yesterday—he, too, must have had trouble communicating on the heels of the attack—and her fruitless attempts to call Hallie at the hospital. She'd read and reread the telegram so often, not wanting to believe its contents, that it was seared in her memory: *Baby girl dead at birth. Ruth recovering.*

What could she say in a telegram that would express her

feelings? As she stood in line Margaret pondered her message, trying to block out the anxious conversations that swirled around her: "I was sure last night I heard the sound of planes flying overhead." "My grandson's in the Army—what will become of his wife and little boy?" One word, uttered again and again, was impossible to ignore: *JAP*.

Much as she wanted to believe that the fear and loathing were directed only at the foreign invaders, Margaret was sure that some, at least, made no distinction between the Japanese abroad and those who had made Puget Sound their home for decades. And what about the Nisei—young men and women, boys and girls, who talked and acted like any other American-born citizen, but whose Asian features branded them as enemies in the sight of their hysterical neighbors?

The line shuffled forward until finally she came eye to eye with the bald-headed telegraph operator, who regarded her with weary impatience. Displaying a resoluteness she did not feel, Margaret handed over her message, imperfect as it was. *So very sorry about Baby. Wish I could come to L.A. Love, Mother.* She hoped Hallie would understand why she couldn't be there right now. Father Dai needed her. The people of St. Paul's and St. Peter's needed her. Now, more than ever.

She had just returned to St. Peter's when the phone rang. She answered it in the absence of the church secretary, who had left a note explaining that there had been a "family emergency." Pushing aside for the moment any worries about what the emergency might be, Margaret answered, "St. Peter's Episcopal Church, Deaconess Peppers speaking, may I help you?"

"Dr. Shigaya here," came the familiar voice, though its anxious note was new. "Mrs. Peppers, may I please speak with Father Dai?"

"He's not here at the moment, Doctor Paul, and I don't know when he'll return."

"If you see him today, will you please ask him to call me? Mr. Saito has been arrested and taken away. I'm trying to find out where he is."

"It can't be!" Margaret sat down at Miss Kogita's desk, trying to absorb the news. E. K. Saito was a prominent Issei businessman and member of St. James Church in Kent. Besides being a Christian, he was married to a white woman. How could he be under suspicion? "I doubt that Father Dai is at home, but you might try calling him there," she suggested.

"Yes, I'll try that. Thank you, Mrs. Peppers." Before she could respond, the doctor had hung up.

Her first impulse was to leave immediately and make the rounds of her parishioners, both to reassure them and to offer her services. Yet she knew she needed to stay in case someone else called the church for help. As if on cue, the telephone sounded again.

This time it was Father Dai himself. Margaret relayed the message from Dr. Paul and also mentioned the situation with the church secretary.

"I imagine Miss Kogita left to pick up her sister's little boy after school," the priest said. "Her brother-in-law was arrested last night, so her sister has to run the grocery store all by herself."

"Father, don't you think we should call everyone on the parish list to see how they are and what they need? We could divide up the congregation between Father Shoji, you and me. Father Shoji could take the Issei he knows best and—" Suddenly she remembered she knew nothing of the Shoji family. Had Father Shoji been taken away too?

"That's a good plan; I will phone Father Shoji and talk to him."

"Do you know—are they all right?"

"Dazed—is that the word? They are dazed like all of us, but fine." He continued, thinking out loud. "I must talk also with our lay leaders... we should cancel all the evening services, choir practice..."

Interrupting Father Dai for the second time she said, "Look, let me start with St. Paul's and call all the households where the children are in our junior high or high school program, but the parents don't come to church." This was a common situation with Issei Buddhists who wanted their children to integrate into American society. "If the parents only speak *nihongo* I'll ask for their son or daughter and find out what's what. I'll also pass along the message about the suspension of all evening activities. I'll let you know if there's something you should be aware of."

"Thank you, Mrs. Peppers. That's one less thing for me to do. We will talk on the phone this evening."

"Oh, and Mrs. Peppers—I have faith in the people of this country. Fairness and justice will win out, I am sure."

Father Dai was right. Just this morning she'd read in the paper that the Seattle Council of Churches had urged fairness toward the local Japanese, a message she was sure any right-minded person would embrace. Once the authorities had seen and heard for themselves the loyalty of the Issei, they would be released. And the Nisei—they were American citizens, so nothing could happen to them.

This was the message Margaret took to the youngsters of St. Paul's, asking them to convey her reassurance to their distraught parents. It didn't help that Rev. Tatsuya, the local Buddhist priest, was under custody. *How would our church members feel if Father Dai or Father Shoji were arrested?* she wondered. She hoped there would be no need to find out.

At the Girls' Friendly Society meeting later that week, the atmosphere was somber. When the time came to offer prayers out loud, one girl asked God to protect her brother in the Army reserves. Another asked help for her sister, who was suddenly being bullied.

Stopping by the church office afterwards, Margaret saw Father Dai was in and reading the newspaper. He looked up with a quizzical expression. "Mrs. Peppers, will you please explain 'fifth columnist' to me?" Pushing across his desk the front section of the latest *Kent News-Journal*, the weekly's first issue since Pearl Harbor, he indicated the opening paragraph of the lead article which proclaimed, "Kent Mobilized, Unified In Preparation For Any War-Time Emergency."

"A part of a great nation now at war," Margaret read aloud, "Kent today stands on an emergency war-time footing, mobilized to meet any emergency whether it comes by air, land or by 'fifth columnists.'" *What an odd coincidence*, she thought.

Last evening the syndicated horoscope in the *Seattle Times* had something about a likely increase in fifth column activity. She didn't want to mention it to Father Dai—what would he think of her foolish reading habit? Besides, the horoscope prediction had to do with spies in high places, certainly not with the Issei farmers of White River. Yet here was the Valley's own paper insinuating disloyalty among a group of people who had lived and worked there for years.

Quickly pushing the paper back to Father Dai she answered, "A fifth columnist is someone who pretends to be loyal but actually is working for the enemy."

The young priest looked troubled. Quietly he said, "Let us hope no one believes the Japanese here are capable of such—"

"Treachery," Margaret said, supplying the word she was sure Father Dai was seeking.

That night Margaret lay wide-eyed, staring into the dark, unable to quell her mind nor soothe her anguished heart. How puny the words she'd written to Hallie in comparison with the vastness of pain her daughter must be feeling! And how inadequate her efforts at consoling the fearful Nikkei of St. Peter's and St. Paul's! Once again, she teetered between her competing calls as mother and deaconess. President Roosevelt had spoken of "absolute victory," but in the war of compassion being waged in her divided heart, which duty would prove victorious, and at what cost?

Chapter 43

For the Japanese community, January 1st was always a red-letter day, a time to celebrate the passage of another year and begin afresh with a clean slate. Even the Christians adorned their fresh-scrubbed homes with the traditional *Kadomatsu* and *shime-kazari* decorations which derived from Shinto beliefs, and everyone, except those mourning the loss of a loved one, enjoyed visiting family and friends and partaking of a feast which put the traditional American Thanksgiving to shame. But among the Nikkei, the dawning of 1942 brought no joy. With every Issei arrest the cloud of fear thickened around them, as rumors spread to fill the void created by authorities whose vague reassurances of "protective custody" only heightened the people's anxiety.

Father Dai and Margaret did their best to reassure their flock, even as the measures imposed against the Nikkei multiplied, soon embracing not only the Issei—now officially "enemy aliens"—but the American-born Nisei as well. Four days after New Year's, the Nisei selective service registrants were reclassified as "enemy aliens." Several parishioners had sons or nephews already in the military: what would become of them? Father Dai, wanting to respond publicly in a way that would affirm the loyalty of the Nikkei and underscore their usefulness to the war effort, decided to write a letter to the editor of the *Kent News-Journal*. He asked Margaret to proofread, and she made several grammatical suggestions.

I cannot help expressing the sentiment of appreciation and gratitude on the part of the local Japanese

> *for the friendly attitude, sympathy, and understanding of the American public toward them, as well as the fair treatment. With this sentiment of thankfulness the local Japanese will, I'm sure, do their best for the defense of this country by raising food supplies if not privileged to take up arms.*

Unfortunately, it was a month before this letter was published, and by then its conciliatory message had been drowned out by other voices. Some were savage, like the syndicated columnist Henry McLemore, who delighted in stirring up racial animosity masquerading as patriotism. Margaret shuddered each time she read one of his tirades in the *Seattle Times*. His January 30th column had topped them all:

> *Herd 'em up, pack 'em off and give 'em the inside room in the badlands. Let 'em be pinched, hurt, hungry, and dead up against it.... If making one million innocent Japanese uncomfortable would prevent one scheming Japanese from costing the life of one American boy, then let the million innocents suffer.... Personally I hate the Japanese. And that goes for all of them.*

She was pleased when several letters to the editor appeared afterwards denouncing such bigotry. But even in the Valley, where hysteria had yet to take hold, some were emboldened by the voices of McLemore and others like him. One night a truckload of men swept down on the nearby Thomas Grade School and chopped down the dozen cherry trees that had been given to the school by the Nikkei community ten years earlier. "It was just a few ignorant men," was all Father Dai said, when Margaret was bemoaning the vandalism. But his face became clouded, and he sighed as he returned to writing the Sunday sermon.

On February 20, below the front-page headlines that

screamed the Japanese invasion of Bali, was a two-inch item titled, "President Gives Army Power to Move Aliens." The article reported that Roosevelt had directed the Secretary of War to set up military areas in the country from which any person, alien or citizen, might be barred or removed. No specific areas were mentioned, but Margaret read that "it is no secret that this action was directed toward citizens of Japanese extraction whose presence at certain strategic points might be deemed inimicable to the war effort." It was only a step short of martial law, according to the report.

In Japantown and the White River Valley, the Nikkei felt the noose tightening around them.

Early in February, Margaret received a letter from Hallie which made her forget for a moment the escalating problems facing the local Japanese. Hallie was planning a train trip to the Portland area in a few weeks. Would her mother be able to travel south to meet her?

Of course! Margaret's relief at this evidence of Hallie's recovery mingled with another, equally potent, kind of relief—from the nagging voice which whispered late at night that she should have done more to care for her daughter in her time of need. Not that Hallie had asked for her mother to come and be with her; indeed, she had repeated several times—even emphatically—that it was not necessary. But if there was something in her power that Margaret *could* do to make things better between them, she wanted to do it.

Unfortunately, the news was not all good. Hallie wrote:

> *Remember Louise Stanley, the little girl I used to play with growing up in L.A.? I didn't really remember her since I was so young when we moved to Berkeley, but when I came back to L.A. as an adult and started going to the Cathedral, there she was. Two weeks ago she found out that her husband, who was in the Army in the Philippines, was killed by the Japs. She's pretty broken up, of course,*

*and I came up with the idea of taking her on a trip to get
her mind off things.*

Poor Louise, Margaret thought, as she folded up the note
and placed it in the wooden box where she kept all Hallie's
letters. How many more widows would there be before this war
was over?

When she asked Father Dai if she could have some time
off to see her daughter, he didn't hesitate to say yes. "Of course
you should see her. These days, family is more important than
ever."

CHAPTER 44

A week later Margaret was ensconced in Jane Chase's Portland apartment. "You know, you really should come with me to the Congressional hearing tomorrow," her hostess had insisted over dinner. "The Tolan Committee will be in Seattle in a few days and your vicar will want to know the kinds of questions they're asking. Azalia Peet apparently is the only one testifying from the religious community, though the Portland Council of Churches has sent a letter."

Margaret swallowed a bite of her leathery pork chop and asked, "Who is Azalia Peet? Is she an Episcopalian?" In truth, the last thing she wanted to do was to sit all day in a stuffy room listening to people drone on, regardless of their religious beliefs. Especially if it meant forgoing time she could spend with Hallie.

"No, Miss Peet was a Methodist missionary in Japan for many years. Now she's involved in rural ministry around Gresham," Jane responded. "I have to say it's hard for me to imagine her going before an official body to plead for the Japanese. She's got her convictions, but her voice quavers like an old woman's. I hope people don't dismiss her as just another do-gooder. Anyway, you can come and see for yourself."

Margaret attempted a graceful refusal. "Thanks, but I probably better not. I think I should stay close to the phone, in case Hallie wants to do something."

"Whatever's best." Jane got up to clear the dishes. "How about some coffee?" she said, over her shoulder. Margaret trailed her into the kitchen.

"I suppose I could go for a while in the afternoon, unless

Hallie calls with other plans. Do you know when Miss Peet is scheduled to testify?"

"No," Jane said, taking down a pair of cobalt blue Fiestaware cups and saucers from the cupboard, "but I can probably find out tomorrow morning when I go down there. I can give you a call—but Margaret, don't go just to please me."

"I won't," Margaret said. Maybe it would help her congregations in the long run.

That night, after saying her prayers, Margaret lay wakeful in bed, her mind replaying scenes of the day just past. Was Jane disappointed by her lack of enthusiasm for attending the hearing? *Jane knows this trip was for Hallie,* she reassured herself. Margaret's stomach began to growl, and she wished she had something to snack on. Jane cooked better breakfasts than dinners, and Margaret had eaten sparingly that evening. Now she was hungry.

Her hunger went deeper than that, though. The morning's reunion with Hallie had left her feeling cheated. *The problem was Louise,* Margaret decided. The young woman and Hallie had been inseparable. Margaret understood why her daughter wanted to take care of her newly widowed friend, but still…

She pictured herself once again walking into the Portland Hotel lobby and seeing Hallie, almost dwarfed by the armchair whose dark leather perfectly matched the color of her daughter's hair. It was Louise, seated nearby in a matching chair, who first greeted her, and for a moment Margaret felt ignored by her own flesh and blood. How Louise recognized her was a mystery, unless Hallie had shown her last year's Christmas card with its photo of the deaconess at St. Peter's. The thought that her daughter might have kept this memento overcame the sting of her perceived slight.

"Mama." With that simple word, any doubts of being welcome evaporated. As mother and daughter embraced, Margaret noticed that Hallie was thinner than she'd remembered. *Almost flesh and bones,* she thought. *Sorrow will do that.*

"How was your trip up?" she asked, reluctantly releasing her daughter, who smelled faintly of gardenias.

"We started out two hours late and it got later as we headed north 'cause we had to yield to troop trains. It's good you didn't try to meet us at the station yesterday—we didn't get in until nearly midnight."

There was an empty seat across from the two young women, and Margaret took it. Turning to the blonde next to Hallie, she remarked, "Louise Stanley—I wouldn't have known you if you hadn't been with my daughter."

"Her name is Louise Adams now," Hallie interjected.

"Oh yes, of course," Margaret said hastily. "And I want to say how sorry I am for your loss."

"Thank you, Mrs. Peppers. Ruth was very kind to invite me to come away with her. It's hard to be home right now." She twisted her wedding ring as she spoke, her voice catching.

Margaret glanced at her daughter, wondering how fragile she, too, felt at this moment. Meanwhile Hallie had taken her friend's hand and was patting it gently.

"What do you think of our hotel, Mama? When I told Uncle Charles of my idea to take this trip, he told me about this place and insisted on paying for it. Said he'd been here before for conventions and liked it a lot. Marie's place is really small, so this is better for everyone."

"It seems so luxurious. How kind of your uncle to do this."

"We even had room service, just like in the movies. I could get used to this!" She gave an exaggerated sigh, then winked at her friend.

Margaret silently applauded her daughter for trying to lighten the mood. Then she decided to ask about their plans for the day.

"Marie's taking the afternoon off to spend with us, and we'll probably go shopping or something," Hallie answered. "But in the meantime, why don't we have a cup of coffee?" She gestured toward the dining room behind her.

Louise insisted on paying. As they were sipping their beverages Margaret asked about her parents.

"They're fine. Daddy is working hard as usual. Mother's busy with the Red Cross. I'll probably do some of that too when I get home—I'm living with them now, you know." There was no need to explain why.

Margaret had been on the verge of saying that the Japanese women of St. Paul's had been the first to organize a Red Cross unit in the Valley after war had been declared, but she caught herself just in time. Instead, she reminisced about Louise and Hallie when they were small and what good friends Louise's parents had been to her.

From time to time, she'd steal a glance at her daughter, trying to see behind the mask that Hallie so frequently assumed when they were together. *A cipher, just like her aunt*, she thought.

Jane called as Margaret, bleary-eyed, was buttering her morning toast. "Miss Peet will testify in the afternoon. What have you decided?"

"I can make it, just let me know where." She tried not to sound disappointed.

Three hours later, Margaret found herself staring at the coffered ceiling in the largest of the sixth-floor courtrooms of Portland's Federal Courthouse, waiting for the hearing to resume in the matter of evacuating the west coast Japanese. Margaret knew she should be excited to witness history in the making, with three Congressmen taking testimony from Oregon's leading government officials as well as from spokesmen for the American Legion and other organizations. More to the point, the questions posed by the House Select Committee Chairman John Tolan and his colleagues would doubtless be repeated at the next set of hearings in Seattle, and the answers they received had the potential to change the lives of "her people" forever. Yet as she impatiently drummed her gloved fingers on the purse she held in her lap, what was foremost in Margaret's mind was the slipping away of an opportunity to try once again to convince her daughter to move to Seattle.

Marie had invited her to join the young women for a "spaghetti feed" at her apartment. *They're just being polite*, she thought, but it was better than nothing. Still, she would have to find a way soon to have her daughter all to herself, since in two days Hallie and Louise would be boarding the train for L.A.

"It looks like Miss Peet is the last to testify," said Jane over the hum of spectator voices. "There she is in the front row, in the navy polka dot dress."

Azalia Peet was chatting with a man next to her, her gray-haired head inclined slightly upward toward her much taller neighbor. Their conversation was soon interrupted by the entrance of the Committee members, who assumed their places in the dark upholstered chairs facing the rest of the courtroom, along with several aides who sat nearby. The short, bespeckled sixtyish man in the Congressional trio turned out to be Representative John Tolan of California, the Committee Chair. In an authoritative voice accustomed to being heeded, he called the room to order.

The first men to testify were three Nikkei, two of whom represented the Japanese American Citizens' League, commonly known as the JACL, while the third was a grower from eastern Oregon. Margaret didn't pay much attention to the beginning of their testimony, which was largely facts and figures about Japanese occupations, crops and real estate. For years the Issei had been forbidden by law to own land, requiring them to lease from others or acquire property in the name of their Nisei children.

When the topic of evacuation came up, Margaret listened more carefully. One of the JACL leaders offered his opinion that to counter the rising public hysteria, those in the Japanese community who were not farming should be temporarily "scattered" away from the coast. Crop production, he felt, should continue under military supervision. The other JACL leader concurred, saying that the nation would be better served if the

Nisei farmers remained here to work under armed guards, if necessary. Then, reading from a piece of paper, he spoke about the Issei.

> *But as far as our alien parents are concerned, they are willing to go wherever the United States Government wants them. As far as ourselves are concerned, as citizens, we have our homes here, and like other American citizens, we like to have the opportunity of defending them. However, for the best interests of the Nation, we are willing to sacrifice our homes, our money, and our lives, if necessary, in order that the United States might win this war, and **will** win this war.*

A murmur of approval floated up from the audience, and Margaret could see several heads nodding, both Nikkei and white. She expected that many Nisei at St. Paul's would feel similarly.

As the afternoon went on, she heard testimony from the editor of *The Oregonian* newspaper, who emphasized the need to evacuate both the Issei and Nisei inland to protect the state's vast timber stands and other vital wartime industries from sabotage, as well as for the protection of the Japanese themselves from possible violence. A Farm Security Administration official discussed converting some Civilian Conservation Corps camps to farm labor camps in Eastern Oregon, Washington, and Idaho. Dr. William Everson, a Baptist clergyman chairing the Oregon Alien Hearing Board, talked about reviewing the cases of incarcerated aliens to determine their loyalty to America and decide whether they might be returned to their community. When he mentioned the internment camp at Fort Missoula, Margaret pricked up her ears, remembering that Mr. Saito was imprisoned there, along with other local Issei leaders. She was dismayed to hear Dr. Everson say that one-third of the families whom the arrests had deprived of their main breadwinner were dependent on charity—"not a large percentage," he asserted. Miss Peet must have been dismayed, too, for when Margaret happened to glance her way, she saw the older woman shake her head.

Then a series of statements by Oregon labor and farming associations were read into the record. All advocated for removal of the Japanese, and one even contended that the "nonaliens"— American born, Nisei citizens—were even more problematic than the aliens—though it was hardly a compliment to the aliens. "It appears to be our unanimous opinion," stated the Multnomah County Labor Association, "that there is more danger with a nonalien than there is with the alien, and the percentage of nonaliens who are trustworthy is almost nil."

"That's absurd!" said Margaret to her companion, forgetting to whisper. Several people nearby stared disapprovingly at her.

"Let's see what Miss Peet has to say," muttered Jane. As if on cue, Congressman Tolan invited the short, grandmotherly woman to speak. She walked to the microphone, her head held high.

If the audience expected a bashful apologist for the Nikkei, they were in for a surprise. Without a moment's hesitation, the Methodist missionary demanded to know, "If need for complete evacuation of Japanese is so apparent, what evidence is there to show that they have done wrong, wrong that would justify such heavy expense on the part of the Government? If it is merely fear of war hysteria, may we stop and think a minute?"

Not pausing for an instant herself, Miss Peet continued to press her case, her voice surprisingly strong. "These are law-abiding, upright people of our community," she asserted. "To put 126,000 Japanese into concentration camps, 85,000 of whom are American citizens, educated in the democratic schools of America, would deprive Caucasians in this area of much-needed food for the defense program. It will put the burden of their support on the already overtaxed and overburdened taxpayers. It will cause a serious social problem, to say nothing of taking from 85,000 American citizens their civil liberties. All this, besides causing untold suffering among our Japanese neighbors."

Judging from the stony expressions of the Committee, Miss Peet's moral appeal seemed to fall on deaf ears. When Congressman Arnold asked her if she wanted an answer to her questions, her affirmative response drew only a condescending reply from the Chairman Tolan.

"You see, Miss Peet, we are here in Oregon to get the facts from the people themselves. We haven't the answer to all the problems of evacuation or war. We are going to attempt, when we go back to Washington, to give our recommendations to Congress."

"Of course," he continued, "you make a point that there is no evidence so far of sabotage on the west coast. So far, there are no cases of sabotage; that is, generally speaking. Well, there weren't any in Pearl Harbor, either, were there, until the attack came?"

Tolan had practiced law before entering Congress. His final question was worthy of a cross-examining lawyer. "In other words, Miss Peet, if the Pacific coast is attacked, that is when the sabotage would come, with the attack and not prior, wouldn't it?"

Ignoring the appreciative murmurs from the audience, she merely replied, "Perhaps." Her tone was far from conciliatory.

With the conclusion of Azalia Peet's testimony the Portland hearing was adjourned. Margaret looked at her watch. It was 4:30. In an hour she needed to be at Marie's.

"Miss Peet, you were magnificent!" exclaimed Jane, stepping into the aisle as the older woman approached.

"It's all just a land grab!" Miss Peet fumed. "The Caucasian farmers are jealous of the Japanese, so they fabricate excuses. If you asked them, they would all swear they follow the Ten Commandments. What about, 'Thou shall not covet"?

Jane interrupted to introduce her companion. Margaret felt a bit awed in the presence of this woman whom she had assumed would be another mild-mannered church worker. All she could think to say after "How do you do?" was to compliment her on her presence of mind before an unsympathetic audience.

Azalia Peet turned a fiery eye on Margaret. "I do hope that the religious people of Seattle will stand up for what is right."

"I'm sure there will be many who will stand up for the Japanese Americans," Margaret said. "Some of the Japanese churches in Seattle have white ministers—I think one of them is even a Methodist, like you. They won't just stand by silently."

By now they'd reached the front steps of the courthouse. Ever hospitable, Jane invited Miss Peet back to her apartment for supper, but she declined because of a prayer meeting that evening. As the women parted, Jane promised to keep in touch.

"I hope we will meet again under happier circumstances," said Miss Peet to Margaret, smiling. She seemed to have calmed down, resembling more the grandmotherly figure the deaconess had first imagined.

By prearrangement, Margaret dropped Jane off at home and then drove east across the Hawthorne Bridge to the Montavilla neighborhood where Hallie's friend lived.

It had started to mist, a phenomenon which Jane had once told her was called "dry rain" by the citizens of Portland. No matter what it was called, it could still make a person wet and miserable, and Margaret pulled her wool coat closer as she walked from her parked car to Marie's three-story brick building.

The strains of Glenn Miller's orchestra greeted her as Hallie opened the door. "Hi, Mama," her daughter said, giving her a peck on the cheek. "Come on in. I hope you brought your appetite."

Surrendering her coat to Louise's outstretched hands, Margaret laughed, "I see Marie has put you two to work." At the mention of her name their hostess popped her head out of the kitchen.

"Hello, Mrs. Peppers," Marie said, wiping her hands on

her apron. "We're about ready to eat. Would you like some coffee or tea with dinner?"

"Coffee, please, if it's no trouble." Her offer of help declined, Margaret sat down in an armchair to focus on Hallie and Louise.

"Ruth's been keeping me very busy—how about you?" Louise ventured.

"You know, this and that," Margaret answered. "I spent the afternoon downtown. Portland has some very lovely parks." *That's not a lie, even if I didn't visit any parks today.*

"Brrr—you're hardier than me! I guess I've been living in L.A. too long." Louise's admiration made Margaret feel even guiltier for her little deception.

During dinner, Margaret was content to listen to the young women's conversation, occasionally interjecting a question or comment to show her interest. She had been rehearsing what she would say if the topic of Hallie's plans for tomorrow came up. If it didn't, she was going to introduce the point herself.

Despite Margaret's determination not to discuss the Tolan hearing she'd just attended, the dinner table conversation took an unexpected turn that caused her to reveal where she had spent the afternoon. It began innocently enough, with Hallie commenting how glad she was that she'd not been in L. A. during the air raid the night before. "I'm not ashamed to say, I would not have been watching the night sky for Jap planes but hiding under the table. Uncle Charles telegraphed to say it was a false alarm, and that's what I read in the paper this morning, but still..."

"*I* would have been watching," Louise said fiercely. "I'd want to see each and every Jap plane shot down and would have cheered when it happened."

"This just proves that the Japs need to be moved out of California," opined Hallie. "There's no way you can tell who's loyal and who's plotting behind our backs. The whole defense industry could be destroyed by a few bad apples."

"I think that's a little extreme—" Margaret began.

"*I* don't think so, Mrs. Peppers," Louise interjected.

"Listen, I spend my days with the Japanese. They love this country—especially the generation born here. All they want is to be American."

"If they want so much to be American, why don't they become citizens?" Hallie demanded.

Margaret tried to be patient as she explained what she thought should have been common knowledge. "They don't because they can't—that is, the ones born in Japan. They aren't allowed to by law. The ones born in this country are American citizens, of course."

"Well, as I said before, there's no way to tell the good from the bad," Hallie muttered. Then to her friends, she said apologetically, "My mother helps Japanese church people. She doesn't understand what the rest are like."

"And you do?" Margaret flared. "Today I heard someone from the Japanese American Citizens League say the Japanese community here is willing to make whatever sacrifices are necessary so America can win the war." Choosing to ignore Hallie's surprised look, she continued, "They're already making sacrifices—fathers imprisoned just because they worked for a Japanese bank, or taught in a Japanese language school, or visited their elderly parents back home a few years ago. Why, even my vicar was arrested just for trying to help a drunk driver one night."

Marie was glancing helplessly from one speaker to the next as everyone's spaghetti lay untouched on the dinner plates. Finally, she said, "We each see a part of the picture, right? I'm sure the government will do the right thing—that's why they're having these hearings. Let's just leave this to them and in the meantime, finish our dinner before it gets cold. We have spumoni ice cream for dessert."

No one would dream of arresting someone for eating Italian food, but Japanese food is another matter, Margaret thought rebelliously. But she kept her thoughts to herself.

Chapter 45

Margaret awoke to pale sunshine feebly caressing her upturned face. It took a minute before she realized that Jane was knocking on her bedroom door far less gently. How could she have forgotten to set her alarm, today of all days!

"Margaret, dear, your coffee and toast are almost ready," Jane called. "Will you be long?"

"I'll be right there," she answered, tossing aside her covers. Ignoring her stiff joints, Margaret hastened to throw on a robe and run a comb through her tangled hair before presenting herself at the kitchen table.

The percolator's diminishing sputters signaled that breakfast was indeed at hand. "Would you like some scrambled eggs?" Jane asked.

"If it's not too much trouble," Margaret said. Though by now she considered Jane more of a friend than an acquaintance, she was not yet ready to abandon all social niceties. She knew Jane's culinary skills rose with the morning light. "It's so late—shouldn't you be at work?"

"Bishop Dagwell gave me permission to work from home this morning," Jane said, cracking eggs with one hand into a ceramic bowl. "I need to finish an article I'm writing on college ministry."

"If the Japanese Americans in college have to leave the west coast, how will they finish their schooling?" Margaret wondered aloud.

"I really don't know," said Jane. "Perhaps arrangements can be made for other schools to accept them. With so many young men enlisting or being drafted, there should be plenty of vacancies."

They talked some more about yesterday's hearing before Jane asked about her friend's plans for the day.

"I was hoping you could suggest somewhere we could go and have a good talk," Margaret said. "I'm sure Hallie would be just as happy to go to the movies with me and then get a bite to eat, but I'd like to go someplace that's quiet and not too crowded."

"You're always welcome here, of course," Jane answered. "I'll be going back to the office in the afternoon. But since it looks to be a nice day, you might want to take her to the Grotto."

"Is that a restaurant?" Margaret asked.

"No," she answered, smiling. "It's an outdoor Catholic retreat on the outskirts of town, and they really have lovely gardens. Very peaceful. Normally, I wouldn't suggest going there in the winter, but often in February we get a few days' break from the cold and wet, and today's one of them."

"I like your idea. Do you mind if a borrow a jacket from you in case Hallie gets cold?"

"I don't mind at all. When do you propose to go?"

Just as Margaret opened her mouth to say she needed to check with her daughter, the phone rang. It was Hallie.

"Good morning, Hallie," Margaret said, and cutting short her daughter's greeting, began to lay out her plans. "And don't worry about being cold for our picnic," she concluded, "because I'll bring along extra clothing."

"All right, Mama," said Hallie. After arranging to come by later in the morning in Jane's car, Margaret bid a cheerful goodbye to her daughter. She knew it would be a good day. Jane's scrambled eggs hadn't been half-bad, either.

"Welcome to the National Sanctuary of our Sorrowful Mother," read Hallie as they reached their destination. "Are you sure this is a place we can have a picnic?" They pulled into the gravel parking lot and parked.

Margaret peered through the windshield, uncertain. There was no sign of the gardens Jane had recommended, only a hundred-foot-high basalt cliff crowned by a bronze statue glinting in the morning sun. A cave had been hewn from the rock, half as tall as the cliff itself, its walls daubed green with moss and ferns. Rows of wooden benches were situated perhaps twenty or thirty feet in front of the cave. It was hard to tell any more without getting out of the car and walking to the site.

"Let's go and see," she said. "We can leave the food in the car for now."

They crunched down the gravel path leading to the cave. Despite the sunshine, the air felt moist with the lush undergrowth of sword ferns, salal and ivy.

A few people were scattered among the benches facing the grotto, some sitting and some praying on the wooden kneelers. The seats were elevated a few steps above the ground on a stone and concrete platform, and in front of them was another platform of about a dozen steps leading to an altar rail, behind which was the sanctuary itself, nestled in the cliffside. Above the large stone altar was a white replica of Michelangelo's *Pieta*. On either side of it a bronze angel held aloft a glass globe which Margaret presumed was illuminated at night—except perhaps not in these days of blackouts.

Suddenly she was moved by the desire to kneel and pray. She had never imagined praying like a Catholic to a statue before, but there was something about the expression on the Virgin's face that made Margaret want to bow her head in silence. At last, she whispered, "Help me, please," and struggled up from her knees to return to her daughter.

Hallie was looking at a brochure she'd picked up nearby. "There's an elevator over there that will take us to the gardens up above," she said, pointing to the pamphlet's small map. "Let's get our picnic hamper."

As they ascended slowly, they could see northeast Portland stretched out below like a green and gray checkerboard. "Marie really likes it here, but I don't think I could take all the rain. Still, it *is* very beautiful."

"Oh, you get used to it, after a while," Margaret responded, her attention divided between Hallie and the surprising awareness of how she herself had just prayed. "Compared to the Philippines, the Pacific Northwest is a desert."

Hallie didn't respond. "Here we are," she said briskly as the elevator slowed to a halt. They exited behind two women who immediately headed toward a small wooden chapel. Margaret and her daughter paused to take in the panorama. To the north, partly shrouded in clouds, loomed Mount St. Helen, and to the east were the snowy Cascades. Jane was right: they *had* been fortunate in the weather today, for such a clear view was unusual in the wintertime.

Presiding over the gardens was a Romanesque-style structure. In the sun its sandstone façade reminded Margaret of the color of wheat on her uncle's farm. According to Hallie's brochure, the building housed a handful of Servite friars responsible for the shrine's care. One of them could be seen pruning the roses, the sleeves of his black habit rolled up to avoid being snagged by thorns.

"Let's wander over here," Margaret said, indicating a path to the right which led away from the monastery. She wanted to find a more secluded place where they could eat—and talk—without interruption. They found a bench near one of several large rhododendrons. *In a few months this garden will be full of blooms,* she thought.

"Thanks for bringing the sandwiches," Margaret smiled. She unpacked the basket's contents, laying out carrot sticks and gherkins, and a few chocolate chip cookies Jane had insisted on providing. Margaret opened a thermos of coffee and poured a cup for her daughter. She knew Hallie drank it black.

They ate for a time in silence, the only sounds a child's voice, echoing in the distance. Hallie was the first to speak.

"What was I like as a baby?" she asked, her voice low.

Margaret was surprised by the question. She thought for a moment, trying to pull aside enough of the curtain that she'd drawn over those early, painful years to glimpse the baby daughter that had given her so much joy. "You looked like an angel when you slept. "

"They wouldn't let me see my baby," Hallie said, dully. "Even when I begged. They said it was for the better."

"Hallie, I–"

"You know, I used to dream that John was still alive—still do, sometimes," she continued, looking at a spot somewhere in the distance over Margaret's left shoulder. "But I never dream about Patricia Ann except as a little blue corpse. It didn't make any difference that the nurses wouldn't show her to me; I know what she looked like." Tears began to well up in her eyes, as she turned to look directly at her mother. "Will I ever dream about her as a little girl?"

Again, Margaret started to answer, but her daughter cut her short. "Did you ever dream about *me* as a little girl, when you left me behind?"

"Of course, dear." She leaned forward and took Hallie's hand, ignoring the inner voice that warned, *Stop now.* "You understand, don't you, that when your father died, we had no money, and I had no skills to earn a living? The Church trained me to do something worthwhile, to help others less fortunate than even ourselves. It was more than just a job; it was—it is—my calling."

"Yes, well, that's all very noble. Maybe someday I'll be as selfless as you, but right now all I know is that my one chance at happiness has been stolen from me. Louise understands. She's like the sister I never had." Hallie snatched her hand away and grabbed a handkerchief.

"I do understand, Hallie. Really, I do." The words seemed so inadequate to Margaret's ears. *Come back with me, and I'll show you,* she wanted to say, but her throat choked up and nothing came out.

She never had been able to express what was in her heart. She tried again. "Hallie, I owe my life to the Church."

It was the wrong thing to say.

"Maybe *you* do, but I owe *my* life to Aunt Martina and Uncle Charles," Hallie retorted. "They provided for me and took care of me when you were gone... helping the savages." Her voice, which had been quivering with grief, was now overflowing with anger. "And you're still helping the savages!"

Hallie hurried to pack away the remnants of the meal. Margaret felt like it was their relationship that was being wrapped up and stowed away until the next time—whenever that might be.

"Do you mind if I take some cookies back to Louise?" Hallie said, resuming a conversational tone. "I'm not very hungry right now and I'm sure she would enjoy them. And speaking of Louise, I probably should get back now and see what she's up to. I really don't like to leave her alone for too long, she's so fragile."

"As you wish," Margaret said, resigned. There was no use pleading any further.

Returning to the car, Margaret cast one more glance at the grotto and the statue of the Sorrowful Mother. *She was as helpless as I am,* she thought, surprised at her feeling of kinship with a woman she had scarcely considered apart from Christmas.

If a look of understanding shone from the Virgin's face, Margaret was too far away to see it.

Chapter 46

"ARMY ORDERS EVENTUAL OUSTER OF ALL COAST JAPANESE." The front-page *Seattle Times* headline left no doubt that the Nikkei's worst fears had come to pass. With shaking hands, Margaret put down the paper and gazed out her living room window. A Smith Brothers Dairy truck drove by, clinking with empty milk bottles from its completed morning delivery. Soon it would be returning to the family farm in the White River Valley. She wondered if the dairy's owners were dismayed on behalf of their Japanese American neighbors or if they were rejoicing at the prospect of reduced competition. Perhaps Father Dai knew—he seemed to be well informed about Valley affairs.

Father Dai had attended the public session of the Tolan Committee in Seattle yesterday, and according to him, several members of the religious community had spoken out against mass removal, including the president of the Seattle Council of Churches. *What good had it done*, she thought. *The Government's mind was already made up.* She had never before doubted the veracity of her country's leadership, but now the Tolan hearings seemed only an elaborate sham.

Margaret returned to reading the *Times* article, which explained that by an unspecified date all Japanese, "including those who are American born," would need to move elsewhere if they lived in the newly designated Military Area 1. This area, proclaimed General DeWitt of the Western Defense Command, included all western Washington, Oregon, and California, and part of Arizona.

The implication was clear: Move now while you have a choice where to live. But where would the Nikkei move? Margaret knew of none who had family or connections in eastern Washington, let alone points further inland. Could the Church do something to help? She needed to talk with Father Dai.

Her eyes fell on the pair of beautifully dressed dolls, a man and a woman in elaborate Japanese court costume, accorded pride of place on the small Sears dropleaf table under her front window. Two weeks ago, Mrs. Unoura had surrendereded them to Margaret for safekeeping. The deaconess had seen enough Girls' Day displays to know that they represented the Emperor and Empress. *Last year, who would have thought that innocent dolls might be considered subversive, something to be gotten rid of before the American authorities found them?* Then Margaret realized that today, March 3rd, was in fact Girls' Day. She knew that among the Nikkei, there would be no celebrations.

If Easter seemed far off it wasn't so much because that festive holiday was still four weeks away. It had more to do with Margaret's sense that the Lenten hymns that Sunday at St. Paul's sounded more melancholy than ever. Looking around the congregation during Father Dai's sermon, which he gave in both English and Japanese, she could see the men and women straining forward to catch every word of comfort he could offer.

Later that evening, she tuned in gratefully to Jack Benny, hoping for a few laughs to break the gloom. She could not face Edward R. Murrow's *News from Europe* this evening—in fact, ever since she'd heard that the famous journalist had questioned the loyalty of University of Washington Nikkei she had found reasons not to listen to him. (A graduate of Washington State College across the Cascades, Murrow was just making a joke at the expense of his cross-state rival, someone suggested, but if so, Margaret thought the joke was in very poor taste.) Jack was in the middle of explaining how he couldn't afford to donate his decrepit old Maxwell car to the local scrap drive when the phone rang. It was Father Dai.

"Mrs. Peppers, I'm afraid something bad has happened. The FBI came and arrested my brother."

The news shouldn't have come as a complete shock, given what was happening to the Nikkei community, but Margaret had assumed that a seminary student would be considered a low security risk. Apparently, Father Dai did, too, for his voice sounded pinched with anxiety.

"Do you know where he is?" she asked.

"Joe's in the immigration jail in San Francisco. There'll be a hearing soon to decide if he can be released or not."

"What happens if he's not released? Where will he go?"

"Nobody knows right now. Maybe Fort Missoula, like Mr. Saito, maybe somewhere else."

"Can't the Bishop do something?"

"Bishop Huston told me he'll do all he can. The church authorities down in San Francisco, too. We'll just have to wait and see—and pray."

Praying didn't seem like enough, these days. "Can I write him? Do you have his address?" she asked, reaching for a pencil.

"The Bishop gave it to me," he said, and dictated the address. "I presume the letter will be forwarded if Joe gets sent elsewhere."

"I'll do it right away," she assured him. "It's the least I can do."

Margaret immediately sat down, pen in hand. She decided to keep the note brief; after all, the important thing was to let the young man know that people cared about him and were praying for him.

The morning after learning of Joe Kitagawa's arrest, Father Dai seemed more weighed down than ever with the cares of his flock. And he was angry. Entering the tiny room that served as the cramped office of St. Paul's, he grimly acknowledged the deaconess. After sitting down at the desk opposite Margaret's, he opened his leather satchel and drew out a copy of the *Seattle Post-Intelligencer.* He flipped through several pages before he found what he wanted to share with her and silently pushed the folded paper across his desk.

One article had been circled; the headline read, "Jap Adoptions Proposed Here." A University of Washington faculty member was suggesting that Seattle families be permitted to adopt "trustworthy and loyal" Nisei children "for the duration" so they could avoid the suffering of evacuation. "I hate to see these young people oppressed with the feeling that there is no way to separate the good from the bad," the professor said. "Of course, those offering homes for these children should be reputable and dependable citizens. Also, parents should be permitted to make their own selection from children whose loyalty is unquestioned; the children should not be assigned to homes arbitrarily." The article concluded with the acknowledgement that careful investigation of proposed adoptive homes would be necessary to avoid some families using the children as household servants. "But I believe the effort would be well worth while."

Margaret could hardly believe what she was reading. "When the article talks about 'parents making their selection,' it can't mean adoptive parents, can it? It's talking about the real parents, right?"

"At first, I thought it was a problem with my English, but I've read it and reread it, and it's clear Professor Dakan means that the white people who 'adopt' get their choice, not the Issei. It's like our children are cans of beans on a grocery shelf! It's bad enough that fathers are being taken from their families, but this is too much!" By now the vicar was pacing back and forth, one hand gripping the other behind his back.

"Why do people always look in from the outside and think they know it all? I hate it!" Margaret responded with such passion that Father Dai stopped his pacing and looked at her intently.

"Well, I think in his mind he's being compassionate," Father Dai said, more gently. Margaret's outburst seemed to have calmed him down. He added, "He just doesn't see the larger picture." With a sigh, the priest sat down again, holding out his hand for the paper. Margaret quickly handed it back as if it were a rancid piece of meat.

Later, after Miss Kogita and Father Dai had left for the day, she sat down at the office typewriter, pulled out a sheet of St. Peter's letterhead, and vented her feelings:

> *To the Editor:*
>
> *Professor Dakan's suggestion that Seattle families be given the opportunity to pick and choose among "trustworthy and loyal" Nisei children to adopt for the duration of this war may be well-intentioned, but it is cruel, nevertheless. Who among us would willingly give up a daughter or son to be raised by another? Is a Japanese mother's feelings any different in this respect from Mrs. Jones's or Mrs. Smith's? As a Deaconess who has spent a decade each with two Japanese mission congregations, I can assure you that the love of Japanese parents toward their children is every bit as deep as the love of the most "true-blue" American parents.*
>
> *Sincerely,*
> *Sarah Margaret Peppers, Deaconess*
> *Episcopal Diocese of Olympia*

A few days passed, and then word came from Bishop Huston: Joe was being transferred for an indeterminate period to an FBI camp in Santa Fe, New Mexico. It was a bitter blow.

Chapter 47

Two weeks later, as if to underscore that nothing—neither Christian ordination, nor marriage to a white person, nor long residence in the States—could prevent imprisonment as a Japanese spy, the *Seattle Times* carried an article titled, "Jap Preacher Is Seized, Accused As Enemy Agent." The piece reported the arrest of a 55-year-old Congregational minister, the only Issei in Vermont, a family man who had been married for over two decades to a white teacher whom he'd met while speaking on the Chautauqua circuit. *Just like Mr. Saito*, thought Margaret, *with a ministerial calling like Joe's thrown in for good measure.*

Even more troubling was the news buried several pages further in the paper about the failure of a plan by the Bainbridge Island Japanese American Citizens' League to establish a farm colony east of the Cascade mountains. The opposition of residents of Eastern Washington and Idaho had been vociferous. Bowing to the protests, on March 22 General DeWitt had ordered Bainbridge Nikkei to prepare for evacuation to California's Manzanar concentration camp scarcely a week later, even though it was still under construction. It was clear that before long the people of St. Paul's and St. Peter's would also be forced to leave their homes and livelihoods. Where would they be sent?

Margaret and Father Dai had reassured their parishioners that everything possible was being done to help them. Bishop Huston, she'd learned in strict confidence, had been trying to find cultivable tracts of land owned by inland Episcopalians; he'd also been exploring the possibility of Nikkei occupying abandoned Civilian Conservation Corps camps. Could the Bishop succeed in finding a humane alternative to this looming catastrophe when others had tried and failed?

The answer came soon. On March 27, it was announced that "voluntary removal" would end in two days. After that, only the Army decided when and where the Nikkei would move. A slew of harsh new restrictions were also imposed. Nisei were forbidden to have cameras, firearms, short-wave radios and other items that had already been declared as Issei contraband. The entire Japanese American community was immediately subject to an 8 p.m. to 6 a.m. curfew, without exception, even for reasons of employment. Finally, no Nikkei was allowed to be more than five miles from home.

"What are you going to do?" Margaret anxiously asked Father Dai when she heard of the new orders. "How are you going to travel to St. Peter's?"

The priest's shoulders lifted noticeably as he sighed, a movement that was becoming more common with each passing day. "I spoke with the Bishop and he'll apply for a pass so I can get there and back. I may need you to drive me, just in case I get pulled over. And except for doing the service on Sunday mornings, I'm going to have to stay here in the Valley. That will mean more work for you, I'm afraid."

Holy Week was almost upon them. It was the busiest time of the year for church people, even busier than Christmas. Normally, there were services every day of the week, beginning with Palm Sunday and culminating with Easter. As a woman, Margaret was only allowed to lead children's services, which meant that there would be no special English language services at St. Peter's during the week unless someone bilingual like Dr. Paul read from the Episcopal *Book of Common Prayer*.

If ever there was a time when gathering for prayer was needed, it's now, Margaret thought. But she could help St. Peter's in other ways, too. There were parishioners to visit and reassure, errands to perform, hospital calls to make. Several parents had arranged for their children to have their tonsils removed "just in case," and there were also two adult Nisei at Harborview Hospital, Jenny Murata who had recently given birth to a baby boy, and Martin Namaguchi who was recovering from appendicitis.

Hours later, she was driving up Yesler Way from St. Peter's, toward the fifteen-story Art Deco brick structure at the apex of First Hill, the city's so-called medical "beacon of light," Harborview Hospital. Along the way she passed the once-dense neighborhood that had been cleared for Yesler Terrace, Seattle's first public housing project. Even before Pearl Harbor, local authorities had decided that the many Issei forced out of the neighborhood could not return; only married American citizens would be allowed to move to the project. Now, thanks to the federal government, wherever the displaced Issei had ended up, they would soon have to leave there, too.

Clutching two bunches of daffodils intended for the adults, she decided to visit Mr. Namaguchi first, then Mrs. Murata, and lastly the children. Mr. Namaguchi was fast asleep on his cot. Margaret quietly arranged one bouquet in a glass vase the nurse gave her, taking care to prop her "get well card" against it before she left to find Mrs. Murata.

Her nose prickling from the pervasive odor of antiseptic, Margaret stopped at the maternity ward nurses' station to borrow another vase and be directed to her parishioner. "You're in luck," said the young red-headed woman at the station. "Mr. Murata has just arrived and they've arranged for a special viewing of the baby. Better hurry along."

"Deaconess Peppers, how nice that you've come!" Jenny Murata smiled. John Murata paused in helping his wife into a wheelchair to greet the newcomer. Margaret noticed his smile was not quite as broad as Jenny's. She hoped nothing was wrong—besides the fact that he didn't know where his family would be living, a month from now.

As they made their way down the corridor, they passed an older couple apparently on their way to visit a patient. Margaret immediately recognized them as being from Chinatown, but not everyone would be as discerning. As a precaution, the couple were wearing handmade badges that proclaimed, "I am Chinese." John Murata appeared not to notice, but it seemed to Margaret that he began to push his wife's wheelchair a little faster.

Like carefully wrapped treasures in a box of Christmas ornaments, rows of swaddled infants appeared on the other side of the large viewing window of the nursery. Two nurses were in attendance, and when John displayed a card with the name Murata, one of them picked up a sleeping bundle and approached the window, holding up the baby for everyone to admire. "He's beautiful!" Margaret exclaimed truthfully, as Jenny made cooing sounds. "What's his name?"

"John Peter," responded the new mother. "John after his father and Peter after our church. We thought about giving him the middle name of Daisuke, but John convinced me he should only have American names."

After a few minutes of "oohing and ahing" Margaret made her excuse to leave, mentioning other children she needed to visit. "I'll walk you to the elevator, Mrs. Peppers," John said. "I'm sure Jenny won't disappear while I'm away." He flashed a smile toward the enraptured face of his wife.

"It's quite a world we're bringing Johnny into, Deaconess," he said, when they were out of earshot. "I can't help worrying about how everything will be once we get him home. When we have to evacuate, how arc we going to take everything we need for ourselves—and now a baby? "

"I'm sure the authorities understand all this," she said, hoping she sounded more convinced than she actually felt. "Army officers have families, too. Try to focus on what needs doing each day and that will be enough. As Jesus told his disciples, 'Sufficient unto the day is the evil thereof.'"

"Speaking of evil," he added, ignoring her well-meant advice. "Did you hear what happened to that Nikkei couple down by South Park? The woman was about to give birth but was afraid to leave the house at night because of the curfew. They didn't call their Issei midwife for the same reason. Turns out there was trouble with the birth—the mother bled to death, and the baby died, too."

"Oh, John," she began. "They should have called Dr. Paul's answering service, and they would have found a white doctor to go to her house. But people don't always think clearly in these circumstances."

"At least when Jenny went into labor, it was 10 in the morning. What if it had been 10 at night?" John turned and punched the elevator call button savagely.

Margaret had no answer. Her delight at seeing Jenny so happy with her newborn had faded like the transient cherry blossoms. With a heavy heart, she said goodbye to John and entered the elevator, hoping she'd be able to fool her next little patients with the guise of cheerfulness.

CHAPTER 48

For the first time, it seemed that attendance after Easter was as high as on the holiday itself. Everyone was seeking divine assurance of better days beyond this harsh reality.

Many priests took some time off after Easter to recuperate, but Father Dai continued working from dawn to dusk, helping church members—and others who did not belong to the church—prepare for the coming evacuation. Margaret knew that at night he had been writing an article for *The Living Church* magazine which would present the Japanese American perspective on mass relocation. She'd offered to proofread his draft and had made a few suggestions to improve the syntax, but most of the writing she left alone. Who wouldn't be moved by his plea to "let America be the America of Abraham Lincoln who lifted up humanity above race and color,"—a country that excluded no one from sharing in the sacred struggle of defending democracy? When she read Father Dai's concluding words—"I cannot help weeping, not so much for the misery of the Japanese, but for the future generations of America"—Margaret could feel hot tears stinging her own eyes.

Now, as she sat in one of St. Peter's well-worn pews waiting for the service to begin, she thought back to the Sunday before, when Bishop Huston had joined them for an Easter fellowship luncheon and confirmation service. The mood had been festive and sad at the same time. Mr. Aoki from the governing board presented the bishop with a check for $125, the mission's share of the annual diocesan assessment. The bishop appeared surprised, telling the assembly they had gone far beyond what was expected under the circumstances. But what seemed to touch him the most were two other events. Three young men, Army inductees before the military had reclassified Nisei as ineligible for the draft, had asked to receive the sacrament of confirmation before reporting for duty. The sight of Jim, Stephen, and Robert kneeling beside the twelve boys and girls whom Margaret had prepared for confirmation was one she'd never forget.

Then there was the canary. Mrs. Kato had brought her beloved songbird and presented him to the bishop for safe-keeping, as no one was allowed to bring pets to the camps. "Kinshijaku" chirped happily in his bamboo cage throughout the luncheon, unaware that he, like his mistress, was about to be relocated.

The memory of the canary's song faded as Mrs. Kodaira began to play the opening hymn on the old pump organ, "Come Ye Faithful, Raise the Strain." As the adults sang, the children filed in with their Sunday School teachers and placed their missionary "mite boxes" in the cruciform structure Father Dai had built. The jingling of the coins made a lively contrast to the statelier sounds of the organ.

> *Come ye faithful, raise the strain of triumphant gladness;*
> *God has brought his Israel into joy from sadness;*
> *Loosed from Pharoah's bitter yoke Jacob's sons and daughters;*
> *Led them with unmoistened foot through the Red Sea waters.*

Afterwards the children joined their parents in the pews, unlike most Sundays when they were sequestered with Deaconess Peppers for Junior Church. It made for a noisier congregation than usual, but even the most querulous tot was not a problem today, for every adult, from the oldest Issei to the most Americanized Nisei, was determined to listen to Father Dai.

"This morning, we sang about a miraculous journey," Father Dai began. "It is the journey of the children of Israel fleeing bondage in Egypt. I know all of us have another journey on our minds. We don't know when we will leave, but we know it will be soon. We don't know where we will be going, except that it will not be a place of our own choosing."

He waited a moment for a mother to quiet her fussy infant and then continued. "This week I received in the mail a copy of the sermon that my fellow priest John Yamazaki, Vicar of St. Mary's Japanese Church in Los Angeles, preached just last week, on Easter Sunday. It was the last sermon his parishioners heard before they left for the Santa Anita Assembly Center. Although it is not my custom to read another's sermon, I would like to read you portions of this one because Father Yamazaki has said, far better than I could, what we must never forget."

Here we stand at the threshold of 'evacuation.' From Genesis to the Gospels, it is full of stories, which I may term, without exaggeration, stories of 'evacuation.' Abraham leaving his home in Terah and going out 'without knowing where he goes,' taking it as God's call, is the forerunner, but in Exodus we come to the great stories of Biblical mass evacuation in which four hundred thousand Hebrew people left Egypt, wandered around the Arabian Desert for forty years under the leadership of the great Moses, and finally reached the Promised Land.

Many failed in the wilderness. With murmurs and disbelief, they could not endure the test. There we see also many who emerged from it triumphantly with strong faith, passing the test of desert and river. They entered into the New Land. Why not accept this evacuation as a test and a great opportunity to prove our faith in Christ and loyalty to our country? By proving yourselves faithful now, you will build a future not only for yourselves but for your children. That glory cannot be compared with the sufferings and sacrifices you will undergo at the present time.

May we go out from here with an aim for the future, trusting Him and His providence. Let us go courageously in St. Paul's spirit of 'fellowship in suffering,' bearing the Cross of Jesus wherever we go, and let us come through victoriously in His faith.

In a sense, this is our Calvary, and we must be willing to say: 'Father, forgive them, they know not what they do.' We must also try, with Him, to say: 'Into Thy hands I commit my spirit.' But that is not all. As Jesus the Christ had His resurrection from the dark tomb, so may it be with us. We shall have our Easter and be triumphant.

Tears blurring her vision, Margaret fished through her purse for a handkerchief. Though by the standards of white society the congregation displayed little emotion, she was sure there were none who remained unmoved by the message they had just heard.

Father Yamazaki's view that the mass removal was an opportunity for Japanese Americans to prove their loyalty was shared by the Japanese American Citizens' League, which urged local Nisei to sign the JACL Oath of Allegiance and Affadavit. The signers promised to defend the Constitution against all enemies and to "forswear and repudiate any other allegiance which I knowingly or unknowingly may have held heretofore." Many of the older Nisei at St. Peter's and St. Paul's missions were members of the League and willingly stepped forward to sign, but one or two complained to Father Dai that second generation German and Italian Americans weren't expected to do the same. "After all, we're American citizens, too," said Joey Zakoji one day, in Margaret's hearing. Before Father Dai could respond, Joey's Issei mother, who was working in the St. Peter's office, said firmly, *"Shikata ga nai*—It cannot be helped."

"I hear that all the time!" he stormed, stalking out. Mrs. Zakoji looked embarrassed and quickly apologized for her son, explaining he was angry at not being able to join the Army like other students at the University.

"He does have a point," Father Dai said to Margaret later.

"I didn't read the congregation the part of Father Yamazaki's sermon where he talks about the Nisei needing to prove themselves worthy of the 'priceless gift of American citizenship.' Why should they have to prove that when others do not?"

Some of Margaret's former Sunday School children, now young men and women enrolled at the University of Washington, were learning that the doors of academia could be shut as firmly to any honor student Nisei as to the most brainless high school dropout. Marion and her brother Jimmy were two of a half-dozen St. Peter's youth whose transfers had been arranged by a sympathetic UW administration seeking placement for its Nisei students away from the forbidden west coast. The University of Idaho, in the town of Moscow close to the Washington state border, had agreed to admit them—or so they'd been informed by the Army, which also had to approve the transfer.

But one day Margaret received a disturbing letter from Marion which told a different story. It was written from the Moscow jail.

Dear Deaconess Peppers,

Don't worry—I have not forgotten your good training. I am not a criminal, though some people in this town think otherwise.

As you know, I got fired from Miller's Easter Sunday, but the following week I heard that the UW got places for six of us at the University of Idaho, so things were starting to look up. Somehow the Episcopal student club at the UW had worked things out with their UI counterpart, so each of us would have a place to stay while we went to school in Moscow. I was supposed to live on a farm outside town and do some chores to earn my room and board.

All was okay—if leaving the place and people I love can ever be "okay"—until we arrived in Moscow. Some of the townspeople were up in arms for our coming and they threatened mob violence. My brother, who was staying at another farm, had to hide in a ditch one night because word had gotten out where he was. Our hosts even got threatening letters.

My friend Yuri and I asked to stay at the jail until this blew over. Who knows what might have happened to us?

The sanitary conditions here are awful. They gave us pillows but no pillowcases. The jailer gave us blankets for the bunks, but I'm scared to use them, since I found a bug on my clothes already.

I feel very young and lost for once in my life. Please pray for me and Jimmy, and all our St. Peter's group.

Your friend,
Marion

Shuddering, Margaret tried to imagine the vivacious Marion cowering in fear in a jail cell far from home. Some church people she knew said that evacuating the Japanese Americans was for their own protection. It seemed that nothing had changed in 1,900 years, when a mob clamored for the death of an innocent man on a cross. In her mind's eye, she could still see Father Dai standing behind the pulpit on Good Friday, crying "Crucify him!" in his most dramatic voice as he mimicked the bloodthirsty crowd.

And then, in a low tone, he had repeated Pilate's words: "Why, what evil hath he committed?"

Without realizing it, now she uttered her own paraphrase out loud:

Why, what evil have they done?
Why? Why?

CHAPTER 49

Margaret sat clutching the steering wheel of her idling car, momentarily mesmerized by the movement of the windshield wipers as they swished back and forth in the pouring rain. The blare of a horn yanked her back to the present. *I must pay attention*, she admonished herself, as she shifted into gear and drove through the downtown intersection. *People are depending on me.*

Today she would be driving St. Peter's parishioners and the few belongings they could carry to a designated departure point in *Nihonmachi*. There, the exodus of the Nikkei from their homes and livelihoods, schools and neighborhoods, and everything that was familiar and sustaining, would begin. For now, all they knew was that the first stop on this journey would be an "Assembly Center" that had hastily been built at the state fairgrounds in Puyallup, about thirty-five miles south of Seattle.

It was the last day of April, but the weather was cool and dismal, as if the very elements were conspiring to express their dismay over the scene at hand. Only a few days before, Charles Reifsnider, the bishop newly appointed to oversee ministry to the American Episcopal Nikkei, had preached at the last service St. Peter's would have before its congregation was sent away. He had spoken about his own experience of being recently forced by the Japanese government to leave the country where he had been a missionary for many years. Many of his hearers had nodded empathetically; this man understood what it was like to be exiled unjustly.

Since that service the church had become piled high with

furniture and other belongings the Nikkei were prohibited from taking with them, or which didn't make the cut when deciding what to fit into the two suitcases each evacuee was allowed. Their things would be housed there "for the duration," but no one could say how long that might be.

The rain had diminished to a drizzle by the time Margaret pulled in front of the brown bungalow where Mr. and Mrs. Morita and their four children lived. It would be a tight squeeze with all seven of them, but she'd brought plenty of rope to tie luggage to the top of the car and tarps to protect it. A white couple she didn't recognize—perhaps the landlords?—were at the house. The woman, who appeared to be about Margaret's age, was trying to extricate a Yorkshire terrier from the unyielding grasp of the youngest Morita child, four-year-old Sally.

"Honey, Toto is going to stay with us for a while. Just until you come back. Now please give him to me," she wheedled.

"No!" wailed the child. Margaret quickly walked up to the crying girl and crouched down to talk to her.

"Sally, dear, remember how we talked about how our pets couldn't go to our new home? But this kind lady is going to take very good care of your Toto and play with him every day. I'll tell you what. You give Toto a hug and kiss and then give him to me, and then *I'll* give him a hug too before I give him to this kind lady. What do you say to that?" That finally did the trick, for Sally reluctantly bid her dog goodbye, as tears streamed down her face.

Mr. Morita paused in his labors just long enough to greet Margaret politely. His face revealed little beyond determination; only the man's eyes, as he scanned his surroundings for forgotten items, attested to his pain. Seeing him, Margaret couldn't help thinking of the Gospel passage which described Jesus as he prepared to go to his death, his face "steadfastly set to go to Jerusalem."

It was another half-hour before they were on their way to the assembly point. All the baggage, and every passenger, bore a white pasteboard tag with the unique number assigned to the family when Mr. Morita had registered a few days earlier at the Civil Control Station on Rainier Avenue. As instructed, the Moritas wore their tags on their coats. Margaret knew that everyone had several layers of clothes on beneath their outerwear, so as not to waste precious space in their luggage. Already the children were complaining of being hot, despite the chilly dampness which was making her joints ache with rheumatism.

As they neared the gathering point at Eighth and Lane, they joined a caravan of vehicles snaking its way inexorably forward. One by one, the cars pulled up at the rendezvous and discharged their passengers, who took their place amid the swelling throng of soon-to-be exiles. After what seemed like an hour, but was actually only a few minutes, it was Margaret's turn to pull up, stop, and help her friends with their belongings. From the curb a couple of young Nikkei stepped up to assist the Moritas with unstrapping their bags from the top of the car.

Hundreds of people had turned out to witness the exodus. A few jeerers were sprinkled among a larger throng of silent curiosity-seekers. Most of the onlookers, though, seemed to be sympathetic acquaintances of the unfortunates. They included Nikkei whose turn to leave had not yet come, as well as white friends displaying brave smiles of encouragement, even as some dabbed their glistening eyes with handkerchiefs. Among the crowd Margaret spotted several clerical collars, though Father Dai's was not among them, since he was prohibited from leaving the Valley.

"*Arigato*, Deaconess-*san*. Please—pray for us." After bowing gravely, she turned to take the hands of her youngest two children, while her husband finished unloading the car. Then he, too, exchanged a final solemn bow with Margaret.

"God be with you, Deaconess-*san*." He repeated his wife's plea for prayer before joining his family.

"God be with you, Morita-*san*. Remember—our Lord will not desert you." Margaret hoped that Mr. Morita's English, which was better than his wife's, was good enough for him to understand what she was saying.

Margaret had one more pickup to make before the charter buses arrived at 10:00, but since it was a pair of childless couples—one Nisei and one Issei—she expected things to go faster. By the time she returned with the Yamashitas and Mimakis, five sleek black and silver North Coast buses had arrived to transport the evacuees, and boarding was underway. A young Nisei man with a clipboard was yelling out names of families to board the first bus.

"Ronald, help everyone get their things and I'll ask if your family or the Mimakis have already been called," Margaret said, addressing the young Nisei beside her. She parked quickly and hurried to find out.

As she approached the buses, she couldn't help noticing how each was guarded by a soldier holding a rifle. None looked older than twenty-five, and Margaret wondered if, like the captives they oversaw, they assumed stolid expressions to mask their bewilderment at the circumstances that had brought them here.

"Excuse me, sir, have you called the names of the Yamashita or Mimaki families yet?"

Looking mildly irritated at the interruption, the short Nisei scanned his list and shook his head. Then he turned away from Margaret and resumed his recital: "The Okuda family, please. Mr. and Mrs. Okuda...."

"Smile, kids, you're going to have a grand adventure!" A grizzled news photographer was coaxing three elementary schoolboys in the line to appear more enthusiastic about their impending ride. They readily complied, but Margaret noticed that the grownups around them did not smile in return. The only time the adult evacuees seemed to smile was when they were responding to the greeting of a loved one among the bystanders.

Margaret had to let her actions speak love to Issei parishioners like the Mimakis—that, and the comforting Japanese language Bible verse cards she pressed into their hands before bidding them farewell. To the Yamashitas, she repeated what she she'd told the other Nisei, "I'll come out to see you just as soon as I'm able. If Father Dai is allowed, he will come along with me."

"The Yamashita family!" yelled the Nisei dispatcher, immediately halting any further conversation. The young couple hurried on, the pasteboard tags displaying their family number flapping on their coats like miniature flags on a staff. In a few minutes they were climbing aboard the bus. Marjorie gave one final wave goodbye before she was swallowed up into the belly of the North Coast whale. Overcome by the scene she had just witnessed, Margaret turned away quickly, scarcely able to breathe.

That night she fell asleep as soon as she lay down, exhausted from the day's trauma as if she had been the one torn away from her home, her life. But in less than an hour, the drone of a plane overhead roused her, and propeller-like, her thoughts began to whir as she vainly tried to sink back into unconsciousness. Though it had been a year since she had moved to a rented house in the Beacon Hill neighborhood nearer to St. Peter's, she had never become accustomed to living near Boeing Field, the city's airport. Now the frequent sound of planes reminded her of Pearl Harbor—and the inexorable advance of the Japanese Empire thoughout Asia and the Pacific. As she tossed and turned, one question after another detonated like bombs: *Will the Japanese overrun the Philippines? What will happen to Lizzie Whitcombe and the other women? And the House of the Holy Child? The children must be terrified…*

Before long the faces of imagined little *mestizas* began to give way to the very real Nisei boys and girls she had seen that morning. She remembered her indignant report to Father Dai after returning from the scene: "It was a cattle round up! Only instead of brands, they wore pasteboard tags."

Then Margaret recalled the unbelievable report in the afternoon's *Seattle Times*, which described "laughing and shouting and cheerful farewells" preceding the departure "like the start of an excursion party." Finally giving up on the possibility of sleep, she sat up, muttering, "I'd like to send that reporter on such an excursion party!" She turned on her bedside lamp. To calm herself, Margaret decided to get out her photo album from under the bed and leaf through it.

The album was covered in royal blue silk with sprays of orange chrysanthemums on one panel and yellow ones on the other. The two panels unfolded to reveal the pages beneath. It had been a gift from the St. Peter's Sunday School on her first anniversary among them.

Slowly she turned the pages, staring at the images as if that act could summon the photographer's subjects back from captivity. Here was her first confirmation class. Nine twelve-year-olds gazed solemnly ahead, trying to look pious, while a much younger Margaret was smiling slightly, anxious (she remembered) not to appear unduly proud of her achievement. *That Kenji was an imp, but he could assume the most angelic expression.* Little boys in black and white vestments carrying crucifixes, brides swathed in white satin, matrons young and old displaying their wares at the annual St. Peter's bazaar—all paraded before her eyes, moist with remembrance.

Seeing herself at Rosie Ito's christening party gave Margaret pause. *How many times have I been a godmother over the years?* Somewhere she'd kept a list of all her godchildren, whom she knew now numbered over a hundred. She may have failed at motherhood with Hallie, but surely these children must count for something in the heavenly reckoning?

All at once she knew what she must do. She must petition her bishop, and whoever else needed to approve, to be allowed to stay with her flock. She hoped the people of St. Peter's and St. Paul's would be kept together, if not at Puyallup, then at least at the relocation camp in the interior, wherever it might be. If not— then she would ask to be sent where she was needed most.

Finally, Margaret slept.

Chapter 50

The forced removal of Seattle's Nikkei took nearly two weeks, and Margaret was there every time someone from St. Peter's left for Puyallup. Meanwhile, St. Paul's members and the other Japanese of the northern White River Valley were ordered to prepare for evacuation beginning Sunday, May 10. Wanting to be available in case of emergency or mishap, Father Dai had decided to go with the final group leaving May 11.

Most St. Peter's folk had been among the first Seattle evacuees, and Father Dai was eager to see them before he himself had to leave. One wet day in early May Margaret picked him up at the tiny brown cottage next to St. Paul's that served as the vicarage. He had been given special permission to visit Camp Harmony, as the Army had euphemistically dubbed the Puyallup Assembly Center. Margaret had already been there twice to ferry a few forgotten belongings, but at the time she could only meet briefly with the intended recipients in a small enclosure just inside the gate—it being fortunate that the owners happened to live in the same area of the camp, for there were four areas, each surrounded by barbed wire and accessed separately. Limited as her knowledge of the camp was, she tried to prepare her priest for what he would see.

"The camp looks like a prison from the outside—guard towers and barbed wire fences," she said, making no attempt to keep the indignation from her voice. "And when you get inside, it looks like rows of chicken coops or rabbit hutches. You should have heard Molly Umita describe her family's room—just iron cots and a pot-bellied stove. No furniture unless the Nikkei build it themselves from scrounged wood. And already the roof leaks!"

On behalf of its membership, the Seattle Council of Churches had made overtures to camp authorities concerning religious, social, and educational programs at the Assembly Center. As it turned out, the price of such cooperation was that there would be no public criticism of the way the camp was being run. Before paying their visit, Margaret and Father Dai had to sign a paper agreeing to the government's rules, such as not using religious services as a "vehicle to propagandize or incite members of the center." As a white worker, Margaret could assist at the camp only if she had been expressly invited by Japanese congregants, and she could not live on the premises. The invitation had been made and was awaiting official approval. In the meantime, she would have to content herself with brief visits such as today's.

It was raining when she and Father Dai arrived at the Assembly Center. Seeing the large wooden roller coaster in the middle of the camp, it was hard to imagine a time when the sun shone on fairgoers queued up for a thrilling ride. Today it resembled nothing more than a mud wallow.

Unlike at some California assembly centers, most Washington Nikkei were spared the indignity of being housed in actual animal stalls, though this was the fate of a few unfortunates with communicable diseases who were sent to a makeshift isolation ward in the fairgrounds proper. Slapdash buildings thrown up in a few days formed the bulk of Camp Harmony's housing. Single men lived in windowless rooms that were like a closet with an electric bulb; families were crowded cheek by jowl into long barracks, none of which Margaret had permission to visit.

Most of St. Peter's folk lived in Area A, the camp's largest unit, located in a former parking lot. Margaret and Father Dai had to park in an adjoining residential neighborhood and walk to the Area A gate on Meridian Street, a major thoroughfare. Usually, prearranged visits took place in a small lattice enclosure just inside the gate, but because this was the one and only time the St. Peter's vicar would be able to pay a call, he received permission to meet a group of parishioners in one of the six Area A mess halls.

The first time Margaret had visited, she was amazed at the hundreds of people lined up along the barbed wire fence surrounding the compound. Many were friends and associates of inmates, judging by the conversations she'd witnessed, but other visitors were merely gawkers, whose only aim was to satisfy their curiosity. Perhaps because of the rain, today the number of idle onlookers was small. As they neared the gate, they noticed a group of school children with their teacher talking excitedly with some similarly aged youngsters on the inside. Margaret wondered if they had been classmates just a few days before.

"Look! The teacher is throwing a few baseballs over the fence! And there go a couple of bats!" Father Dai said, stopping for a moment to take in the gleeful scene.

A red-headed sentry who looked no older than twenty checked their passes and searched them for contraband before directing them to the row of mess halls behind him. It was unnerving to see someone so young with a rifle, and it didn't help when Father Dai pointed out that the guard in the tower had a Tommy gun.

Area A had twenty-three rows of barracks, each consisting of four barracks running north to south. The barracks were about twenty feet wide by 125 feet long and housed seven families apiece. Privacy didn't exist, since the walls dividing each "apartment" stopped several feet shy of the ceiling. "The couples on both sides of us *snore*," Jane Hayami had complained on Margaret's first visit. "If I give you some money, could you buy Joe and me some earplugs?" the young matron pleaded. Margaret had scoured the drug stores in Seattle to help her and many others.

They slogged along what appeared to be Area A's main street as they sought Mess Hall 3, their feet sinking into the gumbo. She was glad she'd worn her overshoes. Father Dai, unfortunately, had not. His Oxfords were covered in mud, and his trouser cuffs were spattered as well.

"Why didn't I wear my *geta*?" he lamented, referring to the wooden sandals traditionally worn in Japan. Just then an elderly Issei man padded by, the soles of his sandals elevated above the mud by a pair of platform "teeth." The advantage of his footwear was clear to see.

It was easy to tell which was the desired mess hall by the cluster of St. Peter's children gathered in front, impatiently awaiting the visitors. "There they are!" cried the youngest Teruda boy, who started to run toward them. In his eagerness he slipped and fell into the mire, allowing several other boys to outpace him. Undeterred, the child picked himself up and when he reached Father Dai, grabbed his pantleg with his muddy hands.

Laughing, the vicar said, "Whoa, Benny! They may not let us into that mess hall if we're too dirty." Seeing Benny's crestfallen look, Father Dai immediately fished out a handkerchief and solemnly wiped off the lad's hands. "There now. What do you say we both get ourselves to the latrine? Is there one nearby?"

"Eeee-oooo!" said little Alice Umita. "You don't want to go there, Father. It's not very nice." Several boys shot her a scornful look and led the priest away to a small building nearby.

Margaret had an idea what she meant, having heard that both the showers and the latrines were strictly communal. "It's just a long wooden plank with a row of holes where we sit," one of her Junior Altar Guild members had whispered to her in shocked tones. "And so stinky!" Margaret felt guilty that her status as a white religious worker meant she must use the Administration's bathrooms, which had private stalls. Knowing the meticulous habits of the Nikkei, she could only imagine how mortifying it must be to have to endure such conditions.

The reunion was a joyous one, and Margaret later reflected that an outsider ignorant of the circumstances would have been amazed to learn what this congregation had experienced in the last few weeks, and what lay ahead for their pastor. She feared, though she said nothing about it to Father Dai, that the conditions facing the White River Nikkei, wherever they might be sent, were unlikely to be any improvement over life at Camp Harmony.

All too soon a young Nisei man, apparently part of the "self-government" touted by the authorities, came to tell the visitors it was time to leave. It was then that a few of the women began to cry, for who could say when would be the next time they would see their beloved vicar?

"One minute, please," Father Dai requested, his voice full of emotion. "I'd like my congregation to sing one final hymn together." Addressing Margaret he said, "Deaconess Peppers, would you mind leading us in the hymn, 'God Be With You Till We Meet Again?'"

For once Margaret's usually strong alto faltered, but one by one, the people of St. Peter's began to sing, their voices supporting hers. All the Issei, and many of the Nisei, knew the words by heart.

God be with you till we meet again;
By his counsels guide, uphold you;
With his sheep securely fold you.
God be with you till we meet again.

Till we meet, till we meet,
Till we meet at Jesus' feet.
Till we meet, till we meet,
God be with you till we meet again.

Ten days later Father Dai, along with the last remnant of the Nikkei in the White River Valley, boarded a train for an unknown destination. When next Margaret heard from her priest, he was writing from an assembly center at Pinedale, California.

Meanwhile, she waited for word from the authorities concerning her own future destination.

Part 5: 1942–1947
Idaho and California

Chapter 51

September 1942

W elcome to the Garden of Eden, Mrs. Peppers!" The wife of the esteemed "Dr. Paul" was not given to sarcasm, but under the circumstances, there was no other interpretation possible for Mabel Shigaya's words. Searching the woman's face, Margaret looked for a clue to her true feelings. Bitterness? Resignation? Determination? In her short time at the Minidoka Relocation Center, Margaret had encountered all these reactions, and more.

Being a Nisei, Mabel had no trouble meeting her deaconess's gaze. She may have been wed to her much older Issei husband through the offices of a traditional Japanese matchmaker, but at thirty years old, she was more Americanized than many of her age group, which included a mixture of Issei, Nisei, and Kibei—the latter describing Japanese Americans who had been sent back to Japan for their schooling. Margaret had learned that despite their United States citizenship, the Kibei were as suspect as Japanese aliens in the eyes of American authorities.

Eden. Magic Valley. The names the white settlers had given to this patch of high desert scrubland could at best be described as aspirational; at worst, they smacked of mockery and bitter disappointment. Whoever bestowed the name Minidoka on a nearby county, a designation which the government had appropriated for its newly created settlement, had also been among the dreamers or deriders, if the story was true that it was a Sioux word meaning "a fountain or spring of water." Another account said Minidoka meant "broad expanse" in the local Shoshone language. That made more sense to Margaret when she surveyed the flat, desolate landscape surrounding this new "colony"—one of the preferred official euphemisms—which already had nearly 10,000 inhabitants. Then again, many people both inside and outside the camp preferred to use the postal designation, which was "Hunt." Who or what that name referred to, Margaret never learned.

Returning her attention to Mabel Shigaya, Margaret decided that she exemplified, in the best sense, the meaning of the Japanese saying, *Shikata ga nai*—"It can't be helped." It was both an acceptance of the situation and a determination to make the best of it. Just as at Camp Harmony, Mabel was not one to sit on her hands, bemoaning her fate. While her husband was toiling in the new hospital under less-than-ideal conditions—like the rest of the camp, the medical center had not been finished by the time the first inmates began to arrive in mid-August—Mabel had been busying herself making their "apartment" habitable. Now she led the way to show her deaconess the results of her efforts.

It was not Margaret's first day at Minidoka. That had been several days before, when she and others who were associated with the ecumenical Protestant ministry—known as the Federated Church—had met with George Townsend, Assistant Project Director for Community Services, the man responsible for everything from internal security to education, welfare, recreation, and religious observance. A tall, affable Quaker in his early forties, he had come to the project from a temporary assignment at the Tule Lake Relocation Center. When Margaret had introduced herself as an Episcopal religious worker, Townsend surprised her by saying he'd met Father Dai, who with the rest of the White River Nikkei had been transferred to Tule Lake in late July.

"He is well respected by both Issei and Nisei—clearly a leader," Townsend said. "We're fortunate to have him."

Margaret noted approvingly the use of "we." Here was a

man who wouldn't assume superior airs and alienate the Nikkei.

"How did he seem to you?" she asked, trying not to sound anxious. From the Pinedale Assembly Center, Father Dai's letters had always been positive, but Margaret suspected he was glossing over the true situation for the benefit of his readers.

"He wasn't ill or discouraged, if that's what you mean. Once he and I sat together on a hill just outside the gate—it was allowed by then, of course—and you could see Mount Shasta in all her glory from that spot. At the same moment we both spoke the words from the psalm, 'I lift my eyes unto the hills, from whence cometh my help. My help cometh from the Lord, which made heaven and earth.' Father Dai turned to me and said, 'You know, it's really a question, not a statement—that part about where does our help come from. The answer is that our help comes from our Creator, not from a mountain like Shasta. But whenever I look up and see this mountain, I am reminded of Mount Fuji back home. And then I think of the journey that brought me here, to this place, and how God has been with me all the time. He won't abandon me now, and he won't abandon the people he brought me to serve.'"

Margaret brushed a hand across her moist eyes. "Thank you, Mr. Townsend. I will share that story with my parishioners." Things at Minidoka might be all right if every administrator was like George Townsend.

Now, as she followed Mabel Shigaya past the tarpapered building that served as the camp hospital to the similarly tarpapered barracks beyond, Margaret struggled to regain that earlier sense of reassurance. Everywhere she looked spoke of banishment. It was a colony all right—*a penal colony*, she thought—set down in the most desolate spot imaginable. Clouds of dust, fine as talcum, coated her shoes as she walked, her steps sinking into the powder like thumbprints in a plate of confectioners' sugar. Today, there was only a slight breeze, but she'd been warned of sudden dust storms that could choke and blind anyone with the misfortune to be caught outside. The Army had created a new city in a matter of days, stripping the land of any anchoring vegetation, and this was the result.

As they approached the block where the Shigayas lived, the faint, yet unmistakable, odor of human waste signaled the presence of outdoor latrines. George Townsend had said the government was having trouble getting all the pipes needed for community-wide indoor plumbing; for now, only the staff quarters had this amenity.

The thought of cold weather made her suddenly aware of how hot it had become. *It must be nearly a hundred*, she decided, as she dabbed at her forehead with a handkerchief. She felt sorry for the men, a mixture of local workers and Nikkei inmates, who were laboring in the sun to complete the hospital barracks. Elsewhere, she knew, buildings were being readied for occupation, including for use as schools.

When they met with George Townsend, the religious workers had been briefed on the layout of the camp. Past the Military Police headquarters, the only stone building on site and the first to greet new arrivals, was an administrative area which included housing for employees of the War Relocation Authority, known to all as the WRA, the federal agency created to implement the removal of the Nikkei from the western exclusion zone. With one exception, only WRA staff were allowed to live at Minidoka with the internees, that exception being Father Leopold Tibesar, a Maryknoll missionary from Seattle. He lived in a barrack, just like members of his church. The other non-Nikkei religious workers lived in one of the two nearest towns, either Jerome or Twin Falls, each about twenty miles away in differing directions. Margaret lived in Jerome.

Beyond the administrative area were the barracks, arranged in blocks that roughly followed an arc stretching three miles from end to end. Each block had two rows of barracks, in the middle of which were three buildings: a structure housing a laundry and communal showers—and eventually, indoor toilets; a large mess hall; and a third building planned for recreation. Townsend had explained that religious services would need to be held in recreational halls in several locations throughout the camp because of the walking distances involved for church members. At some point the WRA authorities hoped to have a bus that would travel from one side of the camp to another, but it was not yet available.

A small piece of wood tacked next to the door identified the home as belonging to the Shigayas. Margaret noticed each of the doors had a label with the occupants' name, and she thought she recognized Mabel's neat lettering for all of them. "Don't worry about tracking dust in," Mabel said, anticipating Margaret's concern. "It seeps in through the cracks, and there's really no way to keep it out, except to use rags. Some of the ladies have tried wiping wet newspapers on the floor, and maybe that cleans it up for fifteen minutes. One of the first things I did when the camp post office opened was order some sheer curtains from Sears. They'll help trap the dust when the windows are open—and how can we keep the windows closed in this heat?"

Margaret looked about her, willing herself not to betray her dismay. To call the twenty by twenty-foot room "spartan" would be implying too much. The only furniture were two cots and a couple of small, crudely built tables, probably gleaned from the piles of scrap lumber that dotted the camp in the construction zones. Nails hammered into the timber framing took the place of closets; suitcases shoved under the cots substituted for chests of drawers. A single bulb hanging from the ceiling provided the only artificial light.

"One of my husband's patients in *Nihonmachi* has offered to put up wallboard for me as payment for the medical care he received in the spring. And when I can get my sewing machine from storage, then I can sew all sorts of things—curtains, bedspreads, pillow covers. With some real furniture from Sears or Monkey Wards, this will look a lot more homey." Despite her friend's cheerful air, Margaret noticed that Mabel was no longer looking her in the eye.

Seizing on the mention of a sewing machine, Margaret said, "Reverend Andrews, the Baptist minister from Seattle, has moved to Twin Falls and is planning to drive his church's bus back to get items stored in the Japanese Baptist Church basement. If I go with him, I can get things from St. Peter's like your sewing machine. I'm sure he won't mind the company."

"That would be wonderful! But you must be very busy now, setting up the Protestant Church and all..."

"Nonsense!" Margaret replied. "If Reverend Andrews can get away for a couple of days, then so can I. Is there anything else I can get besides the sewing machine? What about fabric?"

"I can order that by catalog. I've also heard that soon we can get passes into town for shopping if we have a chaperone. Let me think a little more, and I'll let you know. Are you going to get in touch with the other families that have things in storage at St. Peter's?"

"Yes, I will," she said, and immediately began to turn over in her mind the best way to proceed. At the moment, there was no separate Episcopal Church service where this plan could be announced. She could put something into the Federated Church newsletter, and of course, there was always word of mouth. In the meantime, she would start her planned visitation of all St. Peter's members with the families who had things in storage at the church.

She left Mabel sitting on a cot, flanked by the Sears catalog on one side and on the other, a copy of *The Pacific Citizen*, a newspaper published by and for the Nisei community. The paper was folded to reveal an article which, as soon as she saw its title, Margaret knew was meant for the Mabels, not only of Minidoka, but of all the so-called relocation camps scattered throughout the West and South: "Design for Center Living— Ideas for a Barrack Apartment." She wanted to say to her friend, *I'm sorry, so very sorry*, but instead she turned and walked out the door. What was needed now were actions, not words. It was time to get to work.

Chapter 52

Emery Andrews's "Blue Box" pulled up into the driveway of Margaret's duplex with a chug and a cough. She heard the vehicle door slam, followed momentarily by a knock at her own front door. There was hardly time for her nascent misgivings to grow into a full-blown reconsideration of the wisdom of traveling 1,200 miles in a rattletrap.

"Good morning, Deaconess," the reverend said cheerfully, as Margaret opened the door to reveal a thin, balding man of middling height, who looked to be about her age—a couple years shy of fifty. Behind him the eastern sky glowed like molten copper. "Are we ready to go?"

Maybe I should just follow him in my car, she thought quickly. *Then at least if his bus breaks down, I can give him a ride and we can both get home. But I'm not sure I have enough gas ration cards...*

Welcoming the Baptist minister inside, Margaret stalled for time. "Do have a seat for a minute. Say, I wonder, Reverend Andrews..."

"Everyone calls me Reverend Andy," he interrupted. "I also answer to just plain Andy, if you prefer. And you—??"

"Why, I suppose if we're travelling a distance together, you can call me Margaret. Speaking of traveling a distance, I–er—couldn't help noticing that your vehicle is fairly–"

"Noisy? Sure, but don't mistake that for a sign of decrepitude. My Blue Box is a mongrel—a Chevy bus mounted onto a Ford chassis—but like most mongrels, she's more robust than many purebreds. I had her looked over before I came to

Twin Falls, and the mechanic assured me she has many miles left in her." He slapped his hands noisily on his thighs, then leaned forward and got up. "Well, Margaret, we'd best be on our way. We've got 'miles to go before we sleep,' as the poet said."

Uttering a silent blessing on the Blue Box, Margaret decided to risk the trip. They'd figured it would be a thirteen-hour drive to Seattle, plus time for necessary stops—a longer trip than it would have been before the war, because of the new nationwide "Victory Speed" limit of 35 miles per hour. Still, she'd heard that the rail trip from Puyallup to the camp had lasted even longer, owing to the antiquated trains used as well as frequent delays due to freight traffic. Rather than spend the night en route, they agreed to drive until they reached their destination. Reverend Andy would do most of the driving, with Margaret spelling him as necessary.

The first order of business was a quick driving lesson. "Have you ever driven a truck or bus before?" asked Reverend Andy.

"No, but I got used to driving long distances on not very good roads when I was a rural worker"

"Well, you should have no trouble then," he said heartily, and proceeded to demonstrate the features and foibles of the Blue Box. They took a turn through the neighborhood, Margaret at the wheel, and once she got used to maneuvering a larger, heavier vehicle, she was fine.

"Too bad we don't have time to stop at the farm labor camp in Nyssa," Reverend Andy said several hours later, as they sat down at a coffee shop in the eastern Oregon farming community of Ontario. I hear a couple hundred Japanese are living at the old CCC camp there, topping beets and doing other work in the fields. There's a woman missionary who's started a ministry in the area—Everett told me about her after our last Federated Church meeting."

Everett Thompson was the Methodist minister overseeing the Protestant church work at Minidoka. Margaret wondered if the missionary could be Azalia Peet, but Reverend Andy didn't know her name.

Between bites of his burger, Margaret's companion told her how he had been raised on a farm in California. "My father wasn't like some of the whites around there," Reverend Andy said. "He admired the Japanese for their work ethic. I've thought about that many times as I've seen how successful they've been on Bainbridge Island growing strawberries." It turned out that for over a decade Reverend Andy, like Margaret, had served a Japanese congregation in Seattle and at a nearby rural mission.

After lunch Margaret drove deeper into Oregon, leaving the Snake River behind as she and Reverend Andy headed up the Baker Valley. When at last they reached the Blue Mountains, the sight of wildflowers and pine trees blotted out all her worries and weariness. By then Reverend Andy had taken over the wheel, and even the Blue Box seemed to gain a new lease on life.

All too soon they plunged into the Minidoka-like desert of southeastern Washington. Margaret struggled to stay awake as mile succeeded monotonous mile. Reverend Andy began to hum a gospel song that she recognized from her youth.

"Let's sing it," she suggested.

An hour and many hymns later, they reached the orchards of Yakima. They stopped to buy some peaches and ate a quick meal at a local cafe. In another hour the sun would be setting. Margaret wished they wouldn't be crossing the Cascade Mountains in the dark, but there was no helping it. At least US-10 was a well-traveled highway, and the weather was good.

It was past ten o'clock when Margaret finally arrived at the large Tudor home of Bishop Huston and his family, located in a well-to-do neighborhood on Seattle's Capitol Hill. She allowed herself to be led by Mrs. Huston to the guest room. For now, all she wanted was to sleep and not wake up for a very long time. Still, she conscientiously set her alarm clock to forestall that very possibility. It would not do to oversleep at her bishop's house.

In the morning, Margaret dressed quickly and joined the Hustons for breakfast. The faint aroma of the bishop's aftershave mingled with the fragrance of yellow roses on the table. A servant, flitting between the dining room sideboard and the kitchen, brought plates of toast, fried eggs, and bacon.

"I hope you don't mind the informality," Mrs. Huston said, as if her guest were used to being waited on by servants every day. "It seemed easiest to let everyone choose whatever they want to eat."

"Coffee and toast are usually all I have for breakfast," Margaret replied, smiling. "Bacon is a real treat these days." She helped herself to bacon and one egg and a slice of toast.

"We've learned to eat our toast without butter," Bishop Huston said. "I'd recommend Dorothea's apple butter over margarine any day."

"Apple butter is lovely," Margaret said. "My mother used to make it all the time when I was growing up in Iowa."

"What's the food like at Minidoka?" the bishop asked, after saying grace. "I've heard a rumor that the Japanese can have as much sugar and meat as they want, but I doubt that's true, is it?"

"I haven't yet eaten with our parishioners, because we're supposed to eat in the staff mess hall and not in the barracks. We certainly haven't had lots of sugar and meat, and we're eating mostly canned fruits and vegetables. Even the children are getting tired of Vienna sausages, I'm told. It's hard on the old people, having no rice or other foods they're used to. One barracks kitchen made Japanese pickles, but they did something wrong, and hundreds of people got sick. At least there *is* food, and there's milk for the children."

Mrs. Huston shook her head. "I'll be sure to set anyone straight who tries to tell me the Japanese are being coddled. Some people have nothing better to do than wag their tongues, it seems."

After breakfast Margaret told the bishop how things were faring with the people of St. Peter's. She had visited as many as she could in their barracks, when she wasn't doing work for the Federated Church. "It will be good when they get the schools up and running, and the recreation programs, too. Right now everyone has too much time on their hands," she said. "And our people really miss not having regular Episcopal services. Father Shoji can serve the Issei, but you know he really isn't the one the Nisei want as their spiritual leader. When do you think Father Joe will be released to Minidoka?"

"I wish I knew," sighed the bishop. "It's up to the FBI. The fact that Father Joe spent time in the Imperial Army isn't in his favor, even though he had no choice in the matter."

"Aren't you going to be seeing him soon?" Margaret asked.

"Yes, next week I leave for Santa Fe where he's being held in a Department of Justice Camp. The Bishop of the Diocese of California and I have provided character references, which we hope will get Father Joe released eventually. In the meantime, I will be ordaining him to the priesthood right there in prison. Sounds like something from the annals of the early church, doesn't it?"

Dr. Paul had left his new De Soto in the bishop's safekeeping for the duration of his confinement, giving Margaret a vehicle to use for her errands. As she drove down Jackson Avenue towards the church, she sadly took in the many boarded-up shops of *Nihonmachi*. Some had reopened with new names and new owners. She noticed more Black people on the street than before, and she assumed that some of the new proprietors were from that community. Who could blame them? But she wondered how many of the Nikkei businesses still would be there when the war was over.

A boarded-up business was bad enough, but a boarded-up house of worship was heartbreaking. Even though she'd driven by St. Peter's several times since the evacuation, still she was taken aback by the sight of the church's red front door, nailed shut with a crossed pair of two-by-fours, on which had been painted the grim warning, "No Trespassing—Property of the WRA." Margaret reminded herself that this was for the church's protection; the last thing anyone wanted was for there to be vandalism.

The church's gymnasium, which once echoed with the sound of bouncing balls and shouting children, was eerily silent. In the place of a basketball court there was a checkerboard of five-foot squares into which were crammed chests and chairs, tools and musical instruments—the cherished belongings of parishioners. There were so many sewing machines that a special place for them had been reserved in the gymnasium balcony. Finally, after much packing and repacking of her car, Margaret managed to fit in all the items on her list. She hoped Reverend Andrews had left sufficient room in his Blue Box for all her things; if not, some would have to be mailed from Seattle.

Wearily, she returned to the Hustons', grateful that the Bishop and Reverend Andy would be loading up the Blue Box, not she. As the men worked, the canary Mrs. Kato had given Bishop Huston for safekeeping trilled continuously, as if dictating a long message it expected would be taken back to his owner in Idaho.

CHAPTER 53

November announced its arrival in Hunt, Idaho, with a light dusting of snow, which delighted the children but not their parents, who failed to be reassured by how quickly it melted. Already it had started to dip below freezing at night, and it would be weeks before there was enough coal for everyone's stoves. People had begun to venture beyond the confines of the camp, which was still unfenced, to collect greasewood for burning in outdoor campfires, or—more dangerously—indoors.

Though the dust had lessened with the changing season, the barracks offered as little protection from frigid air as blowing sand, since the gaps created by the green wood used in barrack construction allowed both to enter freely. Trudging outdoors to latrines in the middle of the night became an ordeal—though at least in the cold the offensive odors had diminished. Flush toilets were still several months away.

At least the wind calmed down as autumn advanced— except for the day when a gale snatched a wooden garage shed in the Administration area and deposited it, smashed, some 50 feet away. "It looked like a toy some kid had thrown away in a tantrum," Abe Hagiwara told Margaret. "I'm glad I wasn't driving the WRA truck then."

Abe was one of a small group of Minidokans hailing from southeast Alaska, though when the west coast Nikkei were sent to the camps, he had been a student at the University of Washington. Margaret hadn't known him before—he'd attended an Episcopal church closer to campus than St. Peter's—but he soon became one of her favorites. He was cheerful, hardworking, and possessed of a "can do" attitude—qualities which made him a valued employee of George Townsend, who oversaw the camp's recreation programs. Since many church functions were held in the rec halls, Abe could be a useful person to get to know, if you were a religious worker and had a specific need.

One evening in late November, at Margaret's request, Abe and his wife Esther hosted a meeting in their barrack to prepare for the upcoming visit by Bishop Reifsnider, who was going to conduct the first Episcopal Communion service held in camp as well as confirm several young people. A half-dozen Nisei, plus Margaret, were in attendance, crowding around a card table which had been retrieved on a recent Blue Box run to Seattle. Abe had borrowed a few folding chairs from the supplies at his disposal to accommodate his guests. A cheerful red and white checked tablecloth made the room seem warmer than the feeble heat coming from the pot-bellied stove, which Abe's wife Esther claimed jokingly was on a "coal diet."

"Did you say 'cold diet,' Esther?" Jerry Izumi teased in return. "If you did, I'd say it's a smashing success."

"Very funny," retorted Abe, leaping to his bride's defense. Abe and Esther had been the first of several couples to marry at Camp Harmony. Their friends enjoyed poking fun at one of the newlyweds, just to see the other react. Margaret looked on, her smile momentarily arrested as she realized, *Maybe Hallie and John used to tease like that. I'll never know.* The thought made the room feel suddenly colder.

"Mrs. Peppers hasn't all night," Abe's sister in-law Grace reminded them, after a few more jokes had been traded. "Let's get started." She turned toward the deaconess as the official church representative.

Vowing to write Hallie as soon as she got home, Margaret tried to corral her thoughts. "Let's see, we'll need an altar, a small table to hold the bread and wine and so on, and of course lots of chairs…"

"That's my department," Abe said with a grin. "How many do you think we'll need?" Only a week before two boxcars of chairs, as well as seventeen pianos, had arrived from Seattle churches through an arrangement they made with the WRA. Abe's job was to move these items around to the various recreation halls as needed.

"Maybe a hundred or so?" Margaret responded. "Everyone will want to be there—I just wish that bus the Administration got to take people around the camp hadn't broken down right away. It's too far to walk for some of the older folks."

"Yeah—the One Day Wonder," Mike Hagiwara said derisively, referring to the ill-fated transport. "Guess you camp mechanics have better things to do than fix a *passenger* vehicle, eh, brother?"

"I'm a driver, not a mechanic, and you know it," Abe answered, lightly punching his brother in the arm. "But you can pick up some of the older Issei in your car, can't you, Mrs. Peppers?"

"Yes, I can do that. And maybe I can get help from someone in the Federated Church, though they don't really approve of Episcopalians holding their own services."

"One thing I don't like about the Protestant Church is that they don't kneel," Esther commented. "My Catholic friend said that at Mass they kneel on newspapers on the floor. Could we do that when the bishop comes?"

"I don't know... it hardly seems like 'the beauty of holiness,'" Margaret said doubtfully, using a phrase from the *Book of Common Prayer*. "If only we could fetch the altar rail and kneelers from St. Peter's, but Reverend Andrews won't be making any more trips to Seattle before our service."

A smile crinkled Abe's face once again. "I think I have the solution to our problem. It's time for a midnight visit to the lumber pile!"

Margaret regarded him suspiciously. "You're not suggesting stealing from the construction site, are you? I couldn't approve that."

"Not stealing... borrowing. Mike and I can build what we

need, then take it apart again after church and return everything to the site. It won't even be missed."

Jesus could have had you in mind when he spoke about being 'wise as serpents and harmless as doves,' Margaret thought. She decided to pretend not to know about the provenance of the church furnishings if George Townsend should ask.

The War Relocation Authority was a civilian agency, and Minidoka Project Director Harry Stafford had insisted that the military presence be limited to the camp entrance, underscoring that the Nikkei were under the protection of the U.S. government. But "protection" soon morphed into "prison" in the minds of Minidokans confronted that fall with plans of the Army.

In late October, ominous columns by Stafford had appeared in the camp newspaper, the *Minidoka Irrigator*, citing military regulations concerning camp boundaries. Around the "relocation center," that is, the camp community with its barracks, halls, schools, and other facilities, a barbed wire fence was planned, along with eight watch towers that would serve as fire lookouts and "observation posts to curb trespassing of center limits between sunset and sunrise." Any other time during the day, the camp residents were free to venture to the limits of the larger "relocation area," which included the Northside Canal, a popular fishing spot. Already many Nikkei roamed the relocation area, the limits of which were marked with signs in English and Japanese, to gather wood, rocks, or even sagebrush to plant near the barracks to beautify their stark surroundings.

"It doesn't make sense," Mae Obata complained to Margaret, who was accompanying the young Sunday School teacher into Twin Falls one wet November day to buy supplies. "Why would they build a fence now, three months after we arrived? No one's ever tried to escape, have they?"

"No—the fence just sounds like an Army rule that has to be obeyed," Margaret admitted.

"I thought things were going to be different after they

moved us here. A colony with self-government and all that. Some things *are* better—we can have our Japanese books, no one opens our mail or our packages anymore, we can even go into town, but still…" Mae tactfully left unsaid that she was only free to visit town with an escort from the camp personnel.

"I wouldn't be surprised if Mr. Stafford is negotiating right now with Washington to make an exception here," Margaret said, conjecturing. "Let's see how things go before getting all worked up."

By and large, the Minidoka residents appeared to share Margaret's "wait and see" attitude. Some may have been buoyed by trust in the camp leadership, while others seemed resigned to accept the inevitable, whether good or ill. Finally, on November 6th, all speculation ended. A contractor arrived with his crew at nine o'clock in the morning and began erecting a five-strand, five-foot tall, barbed wire fence.

No one said anything to her directly, but at noon as Margaret walked between the Federated Church office and the staff dining room, she saw clusters of men, both Issei and Nisei, angrily eyeing the new fence posts which confronted them like hostile sentinels. She didn't need to understand Japanese to grasp the import of the mutterings, punctuated by an occasional raised voice, which reached her ears.

The first sabotage occurred west of Block 1. Someone severed two of the wires, restoring access to a ball field which the fence had blocked. The next day authorities questioned the children playing in the field, but none admitted knowledge. Another act of vandalism involved cutting the wires across the road between Blocks 5 and 7 that led to the camp dump. Not only were wires cut, but even some of the fence posts were uprooted.

One day Margaret found herself at lunch sitting next to Clarence Lee, head of Internal Security. He was a retired captain of detectives in the Berkeley Police Department, and Margaret mentioned having lived in Berkeley while training to become a deaconess nearly three decades ago.

"I don't remember you," he said, smiling. "I joined the

department in 1908, but I guess deaconesses didn't get into much trouble then."

"Nor do they now," she countered.

"I wish I could say the same about everyone at Hunt," he continued. "My experience in Berkeley was that the Japanese are a law-abiding people, but it only takes a couple of bad apples to ruin things for the rest. Just the other day, one of them said, 'If they want to play *shogi*, let 'em. They'll never beat us.'" The captain added as an aside, "*Shogi* is one of those games they bet on. We broke up a little gambling ring last week, you know."

Margaret did not know, but she didn't say that to her companion. Instead, she concentrated on finishing her lima bean soup so she could return to work. She was sure no one she knew in the church would be destructive in any way. After all, hadn't St. Paul written, "Let every soul be subject unto the higher powers"?

Friday, November 13th, dawned clear and calm, propitious weather for an unlucky day. Normally Margaret would have scoffed at taking special precautions on such an occasion—even if she did read the daily horoscope with more care than usual. Yet as she ate her bowl of cornflakes in her tiny duplex kitchen and prepared to go to camp, she couldn't shake the feeling that something would go awry today. She hoped it had nothing to do with Jane Chase, who was supposed to arrive from Portland and spend several days at the camp, visiting the Oregon Episcopalians. Somehow Jane had secured permission to stay in the barracks with the Anazawa family. Margaret had offered to sleep on the sofa so her friend could have her single bed, but Jane wanted to be able to tell her bishop exactly what the Portland Episcopalians were experiencing. *I wonder if Jane's bishop—or any—is so selfless*, Margaret thought. She wished she could be.

Her unease following her like one of the desert's prowling coyotes, Margaret hadn't been at work for long before she became aware of angry voices outside her office window. Looking up from her desk, she saw a group of young men and women go stomping by. "What the hell do they think they're doing?" she heard one Nisei say. Forsaking her lesson plans, Margaret decided to go outside to see what the commotion was about. *It can't be the fence,* she thought. *What now?*

Following the irate group across the road to the warehouse area, she saw a crowd gathering near the fence, pointing and talking loudly. It wasn't the barbed wire they were pointing at, but something she couldn't identify. When she drew closer and peered through a gap in the crowd, she saw a generator. The fence was now electrified.

"What's going on here?" Officer Virgil Barron of the Internal Security Section demanded, having suddenly appeared on the scene, accompanied by two Nikkei deputies.

A young Nisei man whom Margaret did not recognize detached himself from the crowd and faced the officer. Looking up at the policeman who, like so many of the white personnel, towered over the camp residents, the Nisei said, "That's what we'd like to know. We want Mr. Stafford to explain how this generator got here, and why."

"To remind us we're prisoners!" someone shouted.

"Obviously, the contractor put it here," Officer Barron replied, ignoring the interruption. "I can't say on whose authority. I suggest you take it up with your Block Manager."

"No, we want to meet with Mr. Stafford!" another voice called out from the crowd.

"Look, ladies and gentlemen, you're just wasting your time here. Move along now, please, and if you have a complaint, tell your Block Managers. That's all I have to say." Barron crossed his arms as if to emphasize the finality of his statement but made no attempt to disperse the group, many of whom remained to glare at the generator and the policeman.

Margaret had just turned away when she heard quick steps coming from behind. It was Philip Schafer, Assistant Project Director, accompanied by an Army officer she didn't recognize. After introducing the man in uniform as Captain Leehey of the Corps of Engineers, Schafer told the group that the generator had been installed by the contractor without prior approval from either the Army or the Project officials. "The electricity has been turned off and the generator will be removed," he said, prompting applause and cheers from the assembled Nikkei.

"What about the fence? Will it be removed too?" someone yelled.

"No, the fence is staying, and from now on, no more vandalism will be tolerated. I'm told that's why the contractor decided to electrify the fence—he was fed up with making repairs. I'll remind you that all the relocation camps are required to have fences; Minidoka is no different."

The grumbling abated, though it did not cease completely. If not completely satisfied, at least the Nikkei had seen their immediate objective achieved—the generator would go. Perhaps, as had become the case with minor thefts of lumber from the construction piles, the Administration would decide to look the other way when fence strands were forced apart or even snipped in places.

In the following spring two and a half miles of fencing were officially removed along the border of the farm plots, and access was also facilitated to the playground area. The watch towers were never equipped with searchlights and machine guns like those at Camp Harmony—owing, it was said, to war shortages. They remained unmanned for the duration of the war but stood as bitter symbols of residents' confinement, ready to be used if the need ever arose.

CHAPTER 54

When I think about what the meals for our Japanese friends are like, I feel almost guilty having dinner with you in your home," Jane said, as she sipped her coffee. "It's not so much the quality or quantity of food—what I had was fine, and the WRA is trying to have food the Japanese will like. It's the environment." She paused, then asked abruptly, "Do you ever get lonely, Margaret? I mean, Thanksgiving's just around the corner and all."

"What do you do on Thanksgiving?" Margaret asked, ignoring Jane's question. "Isn't your family in Wisconsin?"

"Yes, they are." Jane looked with mock sternness across Margaret's kitchen table. "You're changing the subject, my dear. I asked about *you*."

"Oh, I haven't decided what I'll do for Thanksgiving. Hallie is so far away and besides, I can't travel right now. Our new priest is being released from a Department of Justice camp and he'll be here sometime before the end of the month, but we're not sure when."

"That must be lonely for you—not being near your daughter," Jane said, persisting in her original inquiry.

"Well, I count my blessings and go on," Margaret responded quickly. "I also think what it must have been like to be an early settler here. Nothing but sand, sagebrush, and rattlesnakes. Now, *that's* lonely."

"Yes, I can't imagine being a pioneer. At least the people at Minidoka have plenty of company—too much, I think most adults there would say."

"The kids don't mind," Margaret observed. "They have lots of playmates and even get to sit with them at meals instead of with their own family. Not that it's good for families to be broken up like that. The mothers are always complaining to me."

"You know," Jane suggested, "if you don't have plans for Thanksgiving, maybe you should try to eat with some of your parishioners. Believe me, it's a different world than the staff dining room."

"Would they let me, though? We were told at our orientation that Caucasians were not allowed to eat in the evacuees' dining halls. I still don't know how you managed it."

"I think somehow my bishop arranged it—or maybe it was Bishop Reifsnider. At any rate, it would be worth asking." Jane glanced at the clock in the kitchen and quickly dabbed her lips with her napkin. "Goodness, it's already nine o'clock! I must be returning to camp. I'm sorry to make you drive all the way there and back—and leave you with the washup."

"It's really all right," Margaret said. She went to gather her coat and purse, making sure she had her pass to reenter Hunt.

The night gleamed with the light of numberless stars, unobscured by the clouds that would normally blanket Seattle this time of year. It was as if in compensation for its dreary land, God had ordained the Idaho sky to blaze with glory. Margaret wondered if any Nikkei who had been pining for their verdant Northwest homes had realized, as she did for the first time that evening, this unexpected reversal of beauty.

The next morning Margaret woke to the sound of rain drumming on the roof of her duplex. *Not the best weather for visiting farm labor camps with Jane, but it can't be helped,* she thought.

Azalia Peet had been right when she testified at the Tolan hearing in Oregon: locking up Japanese American farmers in wartime made no sense. If anything, their labor would become even more critical during a time of national mobilization. In the inland Northwest, the important crops were apples, potatoes, and onions, but especially sugar beets, which were used in munitions as well as to sweeten food and drink. As farms lost workers to the military or more lucrative wartime industry, migrant labor had to be recruited from elsewhere in the country and from Mexico and Jamaica, but it was not enough.

By spring, even the governor of Idaho, who had once opposed Japanese Americans moving to Idaho farms ("The Japs live like rats, breed like rats, and act like rats"), had changed his tune and began to support the use of Nikkei agricultural labor recruited from the assembly centers and eventually from Minidoka. The *Minidoka Irrigator* estimated that by fall, over two thousand Nikkei had left the camp to work in agriculture. It was a way to support the war effort, to earn some money—and to escape life behind barbed wire.

Some Minidokans, like Jane's parishioner Flo Anazawa, commuted to the fields each day via a camp bus and returned to the camp at night. Others lived on the farms where they worked, with housing provided by the farm owners. By far the largest group were those who lived at labor camps supervised by federal government agencies like the Farm Security Administration, or FSA. The Twin Falls and Rupert camps were the nearest ones to Minidoka.

The scene that greeted Margaret that morning when she got to Hunt reminded her of a Manila slum in monsoon season, the camp's tar paper barracks being surrounded by water, and lakes and ponds everywhere. If the lack of walkways was a problem in the dusty summertime, now people were having to wade in ankle-deep mud and slurry to get from one building to another, whether it be the dining hall, the schoolroom, or the latrine. Margaret had remembered to bring her overshoes with her, but she doubted Jane had come prepared.

Jane arrived promptly at 10 a.m. at the Federated Church Office wearing a pair of *geta* sandals, no doubt borrowed from the Anazawa family, and carrying her own shoes.

"Come in, before you catch your death of cold!" Margaret exclaimed, taking one look at her friend's dripping feet. "We don't have any towels here, but maybe I can use this Sunday school flannel to dry your feet." She started toward the supply cabinet while Esther McCullough, a Baptist worker, fetched an old *Irrigator* issue for Jane to stand on.

"Don't bother, Margaret," Jane said. "They'll just get wet again as soon as I leave. It was so stupid to leave my boots at home. With the rubber shortage, there's no chance I can find any overshoes, even if you were to drive me into Twin Falls."

"Maybe Mrs. Andrews has a pair you can borrow," Miss McCullough suggested. "They live in Twin Falls. Shall I phone her?"

"Yes, please do," Margaret answered. Mary Andrews was happy to lend a pair of boots, either her own or her teenage daughter's depending on the size needed, asking only that the shoes be returned by nightfall."

When Margaret knocked on the door of the two-story house where Reverend Andy and his family lived, a little blond-haired boy about five years old answered. Margaret remembered seeing him tag along with his father at Minidoka, but she couldn't recall his name. "Hello, I'm Mrs. Peppers," she said, crouching down to be on eye-level with the child. "And what is your name?"

"Brooksie," the lad responded, then turned abruptly and ran to fetch his mother. Margaret overheard a woman's voice in the kitchen, and a minute later "Brooksie" returned to say his mother would be coming.

"Who's the lady in the car?" he demanded suspiciously.

"My friend Miss Chase. Your mother is lending her a pair of boots." On the way over Jane decided it would make more sense if she stayed in the car and let Margaret bring her the possible pairs to try on, along with a wet rag to clean off her feet.

"I like your sailor suit," Margaret told the child, smiling. Just then a fair-haired woman about Margaret's age appeared, holding two pairs of boots.

"I guessed it was you," Mary Andrews said. "I think we've met before at the Federated Church."

Before Margaret had a chance to respond, the child asked his mother, "Is that mean man coming back?"

"No, Brooks, he's not coming back—today. You go and play now." Brooks left his mother and Margaret, whose curiosity had been aroused by the child's question.

"There's a cafe owner in Twin Falls who hates the Japanese and when he found out Emery is their pastor, he made him leave the restaurant—actually pushed him out the door. Somehow, he found out where we live and he's come by a couple of times since to yell at us, including this morning," Mary explained.

"Have you reported this to the police?"

"We have made a formal complaint, but nothing's been done. He doesn't threaten violence, only yells 'Jap lover' and so on."

Margaret knew what it was like to be on the receiving end of such abuse. Many of the white church staff, and some of the teachers, had been subjected to glares or muttered comments from a few shopkeepers or their customers, when it was discovered that the Minidoka workers were making purchases on behalf of the Nikkei. Margaret had never had the epithet "Jap lover" flung at her, but she'd never forget the day when an elderly woman who looked like Mary See herself refused to serve her at the candy counter after learning who would be consuming the sweet treats.

"Don't bother with the Jap brats!" the woman declared fiercely. "They and their parents should all be sent back to Japan. See if they get candy there!" Margaret turned on her heel without a word and stormed out. For several days afterwards she avoided Twin Falls and did her shopping in Jerome.

The first thing Margaret noticed as she and Jane pulled into the Twin Falls Farm Labor Camp was the absence of a guard tower and barbed wire enclosure. The smallness of the camp didn't surprise her—she expected it to be a fraction of the size of Minidoka—but the fact that the barracks, which she estimated might house some two hundred people, were finished with wooden siding, made the place seem more welcoming and less prison-like than Hunt.

They parked by the entrance, thankful for a pause in the rain, and noticed a small building with a sign that read, "Clinic." A freckle-faced redhead about six years old in a torn calico dress skipped by them while they stood outside the clinic, debating whether to go inside.

"Toki wrote me that there were people from Oklahoma and Arkansas at the camp, too—it's not just for the Japanese," Jane commented. "She said it reminded her of *The Grapes of Wrath*."

Margaret didn't respond, her mind still focused on finding Toki. "I think we'd have better luck if we went out to the field, rather than ask inside the clinic. Besides, I don't want to bother the nurse."

"Oh, I agree," Jane said. "Thank goodness you found some boots for me to wear." They started walking toward the field a few hundred yards away where dozens of men, women, and adolescents were bending over rows of beets. Farther away they could see a truck slowly approaching, into which other workers were tossing the harvested crop.

"Actually, it was Miss McCullough who found your boots," Margaret corrected her friend.

"Okay, if you insist, I'll give a Baptist credit where credit is due," Jane teased.

As they drew nearer, they witnessed what seemed to be an elaborately choreographed dance. Straddling a row, some workers bent down and pulled two large white beets at a time, knocking them together to remove the dirt before tossing them into a pile. As these workers moved ahead, others followed behind them with hooked knives which they used to trim the beet tops, leaving only enough to allow the beets to be grabbed and thrown into the truck.

Occasionally a laborer would straighten up and stretch, sometimes grimacing with pain. Margaret couldn't imagine being able to do such stoop work for long, yet there were men and women older than she in the field. And these Nikkei had mostly come from the city! It made their resilience even more impressive in her eyes.

"Let's ask this young woman," Jane said, gesturing toward an adolescent who had stopped to stretch. But neither she nor the next two Japanese Americans she asked knew Toki.

Margaret noticed the white farmer who was supervising the harvest regarding them suspiciously. Pulling at her friend's sleeve, she said, "We should leave, Jane. Surely, we can find someone to ask back at the camp."

"And what if they say, 'She's out topping beets'?" Jane responded. "Let's just try a couple more people. I know someone here will be able to point Toki out."

Finally, they got their answer. "Toki? She went into town to get her hair done," said an older teenage girl. "Maybe you can catch her walking back to camp."

Not long after they left camp, they saw a woman and her little boy walking towards town. Margaret pulled over and offered them a ride, explaining they were looking for a friend on the road.

The woman accepted gratefully. "If you don't mind my asking, how is it that you can go to town without a chaperone?" Margaret said, once they were on their way again. "That's not allowed at Hunt."

"As long as we carry our seasonal leave card and don't go beyond Twin Falls, there's no problem," the young mother—obviously a Nisei—responded. "It will be an adjustment to go back to Minidoka and its rules after the harvest is in."

They spotted Toki just outside the town limits, carrying a mesh string bag filled with purchases. When Toki saw Jane in the front seat, she waved excitedly. "Just let us off here," the Nisei mother insisted, thanking Margaret for the ride. Toki clambered in beside Jane in the back seat just as raindrops began to spatter the windshield.

"Oh drat!" Toki complained, after greetings had been

exchanged. "Wouldn't you know, the day I get my hair done it just had to rain."

"Got a hot date tonight?" Jane teased.

"Well… let's just say I'm going to the movies with a guy on my beet crew." Margaret could almost feel Toki blushing behind her. Then she added, her tone brightening, "I just remembered—it's a double date, and my friend's buddy has a car, so we won't have to walk."

"He was able to get someone to drive his car here from home?" Jane asked, as they started toward the barracks, Margaret having parked in the same spot as before.

"His friend lives on the family farm near Filer. They've been there since the '20s—one of the few Japanese in the area and because they're outside the restricted zone, they didn't have to relocate. Pretty strange that just because we lived on the west coast, we had to go to camps, but they didn't. What's the difference? We look and talk the same, eat the same kinds of food, read the same things. I just don't get it."

"The western states have a long history of race prejudice, especially against the peoples of Asia," Jane said. Margaret nodded, remembering the slurs she'd heard against the Filipinos when she was on missionary furlough in the '20s, giving talks to California churches and other groups about her work in the Philippines. "The seeds of this awful evacuation were sown many years ago. They've been watered and made to grow by ignorance, by selfishness–" Suddenly, Jane stopped and cast a glance over at Margaret. "I'm starting to sound like Azalia Peet, aren't I, Margaret? "

"Yes, you are," she agreed with a smile.

Toki looked relieved when they reached the barracks. *She didn't count on a sermon*, Margaret thought. *I'm sure she'd rather be thinking about her evening plans than about how unjustly she's been treated.*

"Here's my apartment," Toki said, when they reached one of the redwood-clad barracks located in the central section of the complex. Each barrack had six 14-by-16-foot rooms, and when they entered Toki's they saw it was furnished with two bunk beds, a metal utility table with two folding chairs, and a small woodburning stove. As at Minidoka, the barracks lacked indoor plumbing, but Toki explained there was running water and flush toilets in nearby restrooms, as well as separate laundry and shower facilities.

"I have two girls as roommates, but they're still working in the fields. They're better at this than I am, since they came from farms in California. Me, I get exhausted and sore after just a few hours." Toki groaned convincingly as she dragged a spare mattress onto the floor and sat down near her guests, after inviting them to sit at the adjacent table.

Margaret shivered and pulled her sweater around her more closely. "Don't bother to build a fire just for us," she said to Toki, when she saw the young woman glancing over at the small wood pile. "Save your fuel for tonight. Even though your barracks are more finished than at Minidoka, they don't have much insulation, do they?"

"No ma'am! That's why the barracks are just for seasonal workers. Most of us will be returning to Hunt or another camp in a few days—that is, we Japanese will. I don't know where the others will be going."

"What about the cottages?" Margaret asked. "They look as nice as some I've seen in town."

"Yes, they're even painted in pastel colors! To answer your question, these are for families who are here year-round. I was in one once. It had indoor plumbing, a kitchen, and two bedrooms. If you can take the back-breaking work, it's worth it to be at an FSA camp. I've heard some horror stories from guys who stay out at the farms during the harvest."

"What will you be doing next, Toki?" Jane asked.

"Oh, I suppose I'll get some sort of job in the camp. I'll go crazy if I just sit around. At least my younger sister has high school to keep her busy. It's starting next week, you know—they delayed it because many of the students have been working in the beet fields."

"Have you thought about college?" Jane suggested.

There was an embarrassed silence. "My family doesn't have the money, Miss Chase. I'd like to go if I could, but I don't see how."

"Listen, dear," Margaret interjected excitedly, "have you talked with Mr. Sandoz, the counselor? I was at a meeting last week and he told me about an organization called—what was it?—oh yes, the National Japanese American Student Relocation Council. They have scholarships to help girls like you with expenses for college. You should talk with him."

"Yes," Jane seconded. "And if you need any letters of reference, Mrs. Peppers and I would be happy to write them."

"You really think that might work?" Toki said, her face brightening.

"Well, talk with your parents and with Mr. Sandoz, and let Miss Chase and me know what they say," Margaret advised. Turning to Jane, she said, "We probably should return Mrs. Andrews' boots pretty soon, don't you think, Jane?"

"Yes, I'm afraid so," Jane responded reluctantly. "It's been grand spending time with you, Toki, and I wish I could stay longer, but I have a train to catch first thing in the morning. Besides, I promised Flo Anazawa I'd come to the Federated Church choir rehearsal tonight. Several Epiphany parishioners are members, as you probably know."

"That's one thing I won't be doing when I return to Hunt," Toki smiled. "I can't carry a tune in a bucket."

On their drive back, Margaret recalled something Jane had said earlier in the day. "Was there something you wanted to tell me about the Sunday School materials we use in the Federated Church?" She glanced at her passenger before adding, "I think I can guess."

"I bet you can," Jane said. "I looked the other day at the lesson from Genesis about the Creation. There was a question on the worksheet where the child was asked to explain why the serpent crawls on his belly. You know how the Bible says God cursed it because of having tempted Eve in the Garden of Eden, but we know the Old Testament is full of metaphors and stories that aren't meant to be taken as literal truth. But the Baptists take these literally, or at least the ones that wrote the Sunday School lessons you use. I don't like that our Episcopalian children are being taught such things."

"I don't either," Margaret agreed with a sigh. "I'm planning to start a church school class on Sunday afternoons for our children which will use the Episcopal Church curriculum. It may be a lot for the youngsters to sit through—two Sunday schools in one day—but I think it's important. Bishop Reifsnider agrees."

Margaret fell silent, her thoughts suddenly consumed with Sunday school concerns. She pulled up to the Minidoka gate and fished for her pass, waiting until the last possible minute to roll down the car window and let in the frigid night air. After the guard waved them in, Jane asked, "So you have no idea when the new priest is coming?"

"It's anyone's guess," Margaret admitted, driving toward the barrack where the choir rehearsal was taking place. "We hope and pray Father Joe will be here by Christmas. It's up to the hearing board in New Mexico, I suppose."

Jane regarded her friend with sympathetic eyes. "I think you mentioned his English is good. Can he relate to the younger generation, do you think? Father Shoji and Father Nakajo are fine with the Issei, but they don't really understand the Nisei. I've been told that even someone like Bishop Reifsnider, who spent so many years as a missionary in Japan, treats the Nisei like young Japanese folk."

"Which they resent because they consider themselves Americans first and foremost," Margaret added, remembering a similar complaint about ex-missionaries working with Nisei girls in the Federated Church. "Yes, I think Father Joe will do well with the Nisei, just like his brother did at St. Peter's. If only our Nisei haven't all become Baptists by then."

"Not if you have anything to do with it, I'm sure," Jane

said, smiling. Touching her friend lightly on the arm, she added, "I'm going to miss you, Deaconess Peppers. Can't you come for a visit right after Christmas?"

Suddenly, the night didn't seem cold at all. "I'd love to," Margaret said warmly, before she remembered her duty. She continued reluctantly, "But I probably shouldn't leave Father Joe to fend for himself so soon after he arrives, assuming he gets here by then. Thank you for asking, though."

"I understand," Jane answered. "There will be other times."

"Yes," Margaret said softly, "there will be other times." What right had she to feel sorry for herself when men were dying in war and her parishioners lived behind barbed wire?

CHAPTER 55

On Thanksgiving Day morning, Margaret awoke later than normal, her mood mirroring the gloomy weather outside. *Another holiday without Hallie,* she thought glumly. Instantly, she chided herself. *Count your blessings—Father Joe will be arriving soon!* Finally paroled from the Department of Justice camp, the priest was due to arrive in Minidoka tomorrow. Margaret tried to imagine what kind of Thanksgiving meal Father Joe would be served on the train. At Minidoka, it would be turkey and all the trimmings.

The thought of Father Joe, and the recollection that she was hosting a Thanksgiving dinner at her home, propelled her out of bed. She'd tried to get permission to join the Shigayas in their mess hall for the holiday meal, but the Administration had refused, citing WRA policy. Then she'd remembered Helen Amerman, the young 11th grade "core" teacher at the newly opened Hunt Junior/Senior High School. Helen had started to attend the Episcopal services conducted occasionally by Father Rolls from Twin Falls. Her family lived in New Jersey, so chances were she'd be alone this holiday.

Helen had accepted Margaret's invitation gratefully, but asked if a teacher colleague, Elma Tharp, might join them. "Tharpie," Helen explained, had once been a missionary in Japan, but since the Andrews family, her friends and fellow Baptists, would be in Seattle over the holiday, she had no Thanksgiving plans. "Plus, she has a car and I don't," Helen added—an important point, as the pair would be coming from Minidoka, where they lived in staff housing.

"The more the merrier," Margaret had responded, secretly disappointed that any discussion of church topics would have to be curtailed in deference to her Baptist guest. She was glad, though, when Helen suggested the two teachers bring the salad and dessert. Just fixing a turkey and all the trimmings would be challenge enough.

"I left the pie to Tharpie because I'm a terrible cook," announced Helen breezily as she stepped across Margaret's threshold at precisely three o'clock Thanksgiving afternoon, carrying a large picnic basket. "But I do know how to open a can of cranberries and make a Waldorf salad. I hope that meets with everyone's approval."

"Absolutely fine," Margaret said, relieving Helen of her burden. Tharpie, a gray-haired woman who looked to be thirty years older than her companion, followed Helen inside, after shaking the umbrella she must have used to shelter the two of them. Only a few minutes before the afternoon drizzle had changed into light snow showers.

"Did you know that the Japanese call snow 'winter blossoms?'" asked the former missionary, once they were settled down in Margaret's small living room. She'd invited Margaret to call her "Tharpie," too, saying she preferred that to her given name. "My twin is Eva, and since childhood I've wanted her name rather than Elma—it sounds so much more romantic," admitted the woman, whose plain appearance gave no evidence of a fanciful nature.

"I've never used my first name of Sarah either," said Margaret. "I was named after an aunt, but my mother must have preferred Margaret because that's the name she used."

"You never went by a nickname, Mrs. Peppers?" Helen asked.

"Oh, do call me Margaret, at least outside of camp. For a nickname, my family called me Maggie, but it's always made me think of magpies."

After they sat down to eat, the conversation shifted to school. Margaret had heard that textbooks and supplies were in short supply.

"Short supply? They don't exist!" replied Tharpie. "But I've been used to making do as a missionary, and I've made do here. I feel sorrier for the science teachers, who have no equipment. And one teacher told me they received health textbooks from the state of California, and they were published in the late 1800s!"

"I think everything's delayed because originally the junior/senior high was assigned half a barrack, but when the teachers arrived in September and looked it over, it became clear that wouldn't work. In the end, they had to remodel a whole block for our school. You'd think there might be time to get blackboards and desks and materials, but apparently not," Helen said.

Margaret said, "One of your students, Helen—it was Joyce Shibata—showed me an essay she was writing about herself for your class. She asked me if it was all right to say anything about her father being arrested and sent to a prison camp in Montana. Her family is trying to get him into Minidoka. She didn't want to do anything that might prevent that happening."

"Oh, she talked with me about that, too. I told her that no one besides myself will see these essays. It's a good way for me to get to know my students. I think Tharpie gave a similar assignment, didn't you?" Helen turned toward her fellow teacher.

"Yes, and besides acquainting me with the boys and girls, it also shows me what I need to emphasize in terms of spelling and grammar," Tharpie answered. "For the most part, they're really quite good. But you probably already know that the Nisei tend to excel at school," she added, addressing Margaret.

"Would you believe that once some parents at our local high school petitioned the school board to change the valedictorian requirements to include club activities in addition to scholarship?" Margaret sputtered. "They said 'the Japs' always had the highest grade point average, because they didn't participate in extracurricular activities." She shook her head at the memory. "I learned later that some of these clubs didn't take kindly to having Japanese members."

"You know, growing up in New Jersey and Michigan, I didn't realize the resentment and hatred that exists on the west coast toward Orientals. I first learned about it when I came to Stanford for my education degree," said Helen.

"I tell my students to ignore it—it's ignorance, pure and simple." Tharpie responded. "You know, Helen, for someone who professes not to know how to cook, this salad is really good."

Helen acknowledged the compliment with a smile and then became more sober. "I don't think I'll ever forget one boy's biographical essay, in which he said that it was as if on December 7th someone had lowered a basket over his head, and he's been in darkness ever since. For some reason, that really hit me."

"For the most part, my students didn't write much about what happened after Pearl Harbor," Tharpie said. "Though several did say how scared they felt when they learned that 'my country' had been attacked. That was their phrase—'my country.' They really do see themselves as Americans. It's ironic, isn't it, when you think about the way they've been treated."

Margaret and Helen both nodded. Helen continued, "When it became clear that I wouldn't have any textbooks to teach from, I decided to have a class debate on the justification for the evacuation. I planned to divide the class into teams, one side being pro-evacuation and the other anti-evacuation. Not a single student except one boy was willing to take the pro- side of the evacuation."

"You can't have been surprised at that," Margaret said. "Was that boy really in favor of the evacuation?" She wondered what Helen could have been thinking; under the circumstances, it seemed an insensitive topic for a debate.

"No, I don't believe he did favor the evacuation, but his brother had been collecting information, so he had a lot of resources. But when it came time for class discussion, he didn't speak up and no one else ventured anything in favor of evacuation. Most were pretty quiet, but I guess we were just getting under way at school and the students didn't know me very well. I hope they'll open up more later."

"Speaking of 'opening up,' I heard an amazing story the other day," Tharpie said. "Another Hunt High School teacher who shall remain nameless was extolling the virtues of democracy and the American Way before her class. Do you know, she was actually booed by the students!" She shook her head at the recollection, whether to underscore her amazement at the unprecedented behavior or her disapproval of it, Margaret was not sure.

"I heard that story, too," Helen said. "I think it shows how hurt the Nisei feel that their country has treated them this way. I don't approve of that class being disrespectful of its teacher, though I've always wondered how this woman managed to get hired. She doesn't belong."

Margaret thought about the Nisei youth she knew and couldn't imagine them booing a teacher, no matter how insensitive. But deep down, she felt they were right. "Even a gentle dog will snap if it gets poked enough with a stick," she heard herself say.

The room was suddenly quiet. Finally, Margaret broke the silence and said with a forced cheerfulness, "Maybe it's time for some of that delicious pumpkin pie. Who wants whipped cream?"

After her guests had departed, Margaret took off her pasted-on smile and put it away with the leftovers. Her mind swirled with thoughts and images that had been served up with dinner. Nisei booing their teacher. Forty-year-old science textbooks. A student who likened the days after the Pearl Harbor attack to being enveloped in perpetual darkness.

Soon, other things not mentioned over dinner began to elbow their way into her consciousness. Margaret decided she needed to unburden herself, but how? She had never kept a journal. Writing a letter might help, but to whom? Not to Hallie. Her daughter needed to perceive her as strong, not seething with doubts and perplexities. Once, she might have written to Myrtle and Julia, but they had both passed on to their heavenly reward. Lizzie Whitcombe? Scarcely a month ago she'd finally learned that the Japanese were holding the Bontoc missionaries in Camp Holmes, a former Philippine Constabulary site near Baguio. Margaret still didn't know how to contact her friend, and even if she did, the kinds of things she wanted to write about she was sure the censors would expunge.

That left Jane Chase.

Dear Jane,

I hope you had a pleasant Thanksgiving holiday with your friends. I'm finally taking a load off my feet after having cooked my first Thanksgiving turkey in years. (When I'd asked about eating in camp, the WRA said no.) I invited two Minidoka teachers over to my duplex. They are quite congenial, but the conversation was rather disturbing as they shared the challenges they face—old books, few supplies, upset students. I know this isn't the whole picture. I like to think that the Nisei children we work with in the Church have a brighter point of view because of the "hope we have as anchor of the soul, both sure and steadfast" (Hebrews 6:19). The hope of the Gospel is an everlasting consolation. Without it, even my life, as easy as it is in comparison to so many others', would be dismal indeed.

Still, I find that some days, hope seems far away. When I think of the Philippines my heart breaks; then, of course, there's Europe and Hitler. I can only pray that the latest Allied victories are the beginning of the end for the Axis. I tell myself it is just a matter of time.

Speaking of far away—here's something that happened here recently. Two Issei men went out looking for greasewood, either to burn or to carve. You remember *when you were here and saw that exhibit of Nikkei handiwork in the rec hall, what amazing things they make with greasewood and bitterbrush—birds and animals and whatnot. Anyway, they were allowed to go, as long as they returned by nightfall, but they didn't show up. When they were finally found the next day, they were <u>17 miles</u> from camp! It's a wonder they were even alive, since it's been getting down into the teens at night. No one suspects they were trying to run away, they just got disoriented in the sagebrush, poor men.*

It's funny, but more and more when I am among the Issei here, I think of the Igorots. I spend most of my time with the Nisei women and youth, and they seem so American (as they are), but it's the Issei that make me remember Bontoc. They cling to the old ways but want their children to advance in this society, so they push them to get an education and become like the rest of us. I never really appreciated when I was in Bontoc how it must have felt for the old ones to see their children develop into something different from themselves. I just assumed that I was bringing the Christian gospel and with it, progress. Don't get me wrong—I still believe that Jesus is everyone's Savior—but I guess I'm more aware that even people I've considered as heathens have goodness and love in them, and that allowing your children to grow up different from you is a way of showing that love.

Well, I'd better finish this and get to bed. I need to be fresh in the morning to meet our new priest. I haven't forgotten your invitation to come visit you in Portland, and I hope to do so sometime in the new year.

Faithfully,
Margaret

Chapter 56

We look to you, ministers, to help us build a spirit of unity here at Hunt. We have been spared any unfortunate incident of the magnitude of last month's riot at Manzanar, which was due to extreme and violent factionalism. Nevertheless, certain acts of petty vandalism have marred the cooperative spirit which has generally characterized our colony, and it is safe to say that a minority of dissatisfied and cynical adolescents are responsible. You have the authority and, if I may say so, the responsibility, to uphold the highest standards of conduct and to impress on those within your purview that it is the individual whose actions ultimate make or break a community." As if to emphasize his point, Assistant Project Director Philip Schafer glowered at his audience who had congregated that frigid January morning in the Caucasian Social Room.

It was two and a half hours into the first meeting of the religious workers convened by the Administration. Sitting at the crowded table, Margaret had by now heard lengthy reports on the overall health conditions of the project ("contrary to rumor, gonorrhea is *not* running rampant") and the creation of a Leaves and Furloughs section as a first step in a strategy of relocating college students and families away from the west coast. *If this is how long it's going to be each month, I'll have to find some excuse not to attend.* Immediately, she dismissed that thought as unworthy. In the Episcopal Church, deaconesses were not always allowed to deliberate with male clergy—in fact, women were even barred from serving on lay congregational governing bodies like vestries. Margaret was determined to hold up her end of the bargain, even if meant being lectured by a man at least ten years younger than she.

Stifling a yawn, she glanced toward Father Joe Kitagawa, sitting across from her at the table. *He hardly looks older than an adolescent himself, though he must be in his mid-twenties. And you wouldn't think he'd spent eight months in enemy alien camps in New Mexico,* Margaret added silently, noting the smoothness of his features, which were unmarred by any evidence of his prison experiences. In the six weeks since his arrival she'd learned that this carefree appearance could be deceiving, just as with some of the young Nisei she saw every day. Father Joe could be at turns playful, devout, absent-minded, incisive, idealistic, and wise beyond his years. He was "devilishly handsome," in the words of one smitten Nisei girl, and Margaret suspected he knew it. He'd even charmed Mrs. Ogawa into cooking Japanese meals for him, so he didn't have to eat mess hall food every day.

Where it had taken some time for his brother Daisuke and Margaret to settle into a congenial working relationship at St. Peter's and St. Paul's, the adjustment period with Father Joe had been much shorter. It was obvious he needed her. First, there was learning the ins and outs of working with the Federated Church while fostering a stronger Episcopal identity at the camp—a tricky business, calling for more diplomacy than Margaret could sometimes muster, impatient as she was to attend to the spiritual needs of those she saw as her own flock. She had been delighted to learn Bishop Reifsnider's plans to formalize the Episcopal presence by creating a new congregation in exile—the Church of the Holy Apostles, which would officially come into existence on Ash Wednesday.

Father Joe also trusted her to carry on the Christian education work which had been her specialty for so many years, without attempting to interfere. He had plenty enough to do as the chief pastor of the Episcopalian Nikkei—both Father Shoji and Father Nakajo being in poor health—and as a mediating force between Administration and the Hunt residents. As time went on, he developed a flair for politics, enlisting the support of sympathetic WRA employees to help improve life in the camp.

Finally, Father Joe did not drive, and even if he had, he would not have been allowed to do so by the authorities. Any trips he took out of the camp, to attend church meetings and whatnot, had to be with Margaret at the wheel. She was looking forward to getting out on the road occasionally, besides the periodic trips she still took to Seattle.

Once the flurry of Christmas festivities had ended—not only religious observances but a raft of organized secular activities aimed at boosting the spirits of Buddhist and Christian alike—life settled down to a predictable round of meals, classes (required for children, voluntary for adults), and keeping warm. Sagebrush—that versatile commodity which had provided heat before coal supplies improved and afterwards, holiday cheer as residents cast about for Christmas trees to decorate—was put to use in creating walkways through the ubiquitous mud. Children kept hoping for snow, but frankly it was too cold. On January 20th the thermometer registered twelve degrees below zero.

The winter brought other storms besides weather. On February 6th the *Minidoka Irrigator* blared the surprising news: "War Registration Ordered Here: All Males, Females, 17 and Older Are Affected." As she digested the article which reported that a four-man Army team would soon visit the camp to register all adults, except those who had applied for repatriation to Japan, Margaret felt annoyed that the Administration had said nothing about this to the religious workers. Nevertheless, the reasons given for the action made sense to her. The *Irrigator* article explained it was to facilitate leave clearances for employment as well as to allow men who wanted to serve their country to be inducted into a new, all-Nisei combat regiment.

"Look at this, Mrs. Peppers," said an exasperated Father Joe one morning soon afterwards, shoving a four-page questionnaire across her desk in the Federated Church office. "Even I am not sure how to answer all these questions. And I will have to translate for the Issei and give advice to everyone who comes to me. Another Army boon... boon..."

"I think you mean boondoggle, Father Joe," Margaret supplied, suppressing a smile. Though usually good-humored, her priest was clearly not in a laughing mood.

Scanning the first couple of pages, she could see no problem with the questions, except the length of time it would take to list schools attended, relatives in the United States and Japan, and the like. "What's the problem, Father?" she asked.

"Read the last question aloud, please, and tell me how I, as an Issei who cannot become an American citizen, should answer."

"*No. 28: Will you swear unqualified allegiance to the United States of America and faithfully defend the United States from any and all attack by foreign or domestic forces, and forswear any form of allegiance or obedience to the Japanese Emperor, or any other foreign government, power, or organization?*"

"You have to say 'yes,' don't you, or you'll be considered disloyal," Margaret interpreted.

"But I am a citizen of Japan. If I forswear allegiance to the Emperor, then I become a man with no country. Do you see the problem?"

"Oh." She turned over the page, hoping there would be a space to write an explanation for the examiner, but a simple "Yes" or "No" were the only options. "What are you going to do?"

"I don't know," he answered, running his hand through his thick hair. "I wish I could talk with my brother." Father Dai, obviously, was facing the same issue at Tule Lake.

The next few days there were a series of meetings sponsored by the Administration to answer questions about the registration process. Overhearing Esther Hagiwara talking at choir practice about a meeting the next night at Block 7, Margaret asked if she could attend. "Of course, Mrs. Peppers," came the gracious reply. "Abe and I know how we're going to answer the questionnaire, but you'll find that some people are still confused and upset."

The Block 7 dining hall was already crammed with people when Margaret arrived, and there was an agitated note to the murmuring in Japanese and English which she had not heard since the incident of the electrified fence. Earlier that day the guard towers had been equipped with searchlights, which doubtless affected the mood. Gone were the inventive Christmas festoons which had won commendation from the judges of the holiday decorating contest. Were it not for the size of the assembled mass—Margaret estimated more than a hundred men, women, and children—the room would have been frigid and bleak. She suspected that even if it had been freezing, the adults would not have noticed, so preoccupied were they with the matter at hand.

"We saved you a place," said Abe Hagiwara, who had been standing near the door, as he led Margaret to a bench near the back of the room. She smiled at several women she recognized from church, and they acknowledged her greeting with a small bow or a smile. Three-year-old Kiyoko Baba toddled over to her, clambering onto her lap, where she amused herself with Margaret's pen and notebook for several minutes before her older sister came over to claim her. Meanwhile, Project Director Stafford had entered the room, tall and affable looking, as usual, accompanied by a shorter man in Army uniform whose smile seemed forced in comparison to his escort's. Margaret assumed he must be Lieutenant Stanley Arnold, leader of the registration team. A Nikkei in his mid-thirties whom she did not recognize followed, and he and Stafford stood behind a table at the front, flanking Lieutenant Arnold who sat down in one of the three chairs provided.

"Ladies and Gentlemen, thank you for coming this evening to learn more about the registration process we are about to begin," said Stafford in a booming voice. He then introduced Frank Hattori, who would be serving as translator for the Issei.

"Lieutenant Arnold will first read a prepared statement, which is identical to what has already been published in the

Minidoka Irrigator," Stafford explained. "Following that, we will open the floor to any and all questions you may have." He paused for the translation and then invited the Army officer to the podium, seating himself at the table as Lieutenant Arnold stood to address the group.

His message, though familiar to anyone who had read the camp newspaper, was regarded attentively by most of the adults present. "Our mission is not an experiment," he began, "but marks the radical extension and broadening of a policy which has always intended that ways should be found to return you to a normal way of life. What is being done is being done with the authority of the United States government and the approval of the War Department. But whether it is to be successful will depend finally on the voluntary acts of free American citizens."

Several voices could be heard murmuring around the room as Frank Hattori translated. As if to forestall any protest, Arnold continued, "You may object that this—your life here—is not freedom. The circumstances were not of your own choosing, though it is true that the majority of you accepted the restrictions placed upon your life with little complaint and without deviating from loyalty to the United States."

Looking up from his paper, the Lieutenant briefly cast his eyes around the audience before resuming his remarks. Margaret decided he was trying to gauge the impact of his words before launching deeper into controversy. Then he continued more forcefully. "In any time of crisis, however, when national survival presents itself as the all-important issue, the best interests of the few must sometimes be temporarily sacrificed or disregarded for what seems the good of the many."

Where have I heard that argument before?, Margaret thought. *Somewhere in the Bible....* Meanwhile, Lieutenant Arnold was talking about how the questionnaire would weed out the disloyal while giving the loyal the opportunity to affirm their patriotism.

Bakani suruna, one old man called out. Abe Hagiwara whispered a translation, "Don't make fools of us." Then it was time for questions and answers. Margaret scribbled these down, intending to report on the proceedings to Father Joe the next day.

"When will the other branches besides the Army be opened to Japanese Americans?" [*For the foreseeable future, only the Army will accept Japanese volunteers."*]

"Will parents have any special privileges if their sons are serving in the armed forces?" [*"As with any American parent whose son is in the military, they will have the privilege of knowing their offspring is helping to win the war against the enemy. That is the greatest privilege of all."*]

"We want to know where the suggestion came from to have an all-Japanese combat unit. The government has said the Japanese congregate too much together and that is why there's been discrimination against us. Then why are we being segregated?" [*"As you are well aware, there are some elements who do not want anyone of Japanese blood to serve. By giving loyal Japanese Americans the chance to prove their valor in a combat unit dedicated exclusively to them, such voices of prejudice will be effectively silenced."*]

"Why should we trust what the government says?" a heavily accented voice demanded from the back of the room. Margaret couldn't see the questioner, but he sounded young—and angry.

Lieutenant Arnold stiffened almost imperceptibly before responding in a firm tone. "Throughout the evacuation and setting up of relocation camps, the government has always dealt honestly and in good faith with the west coast Japanese. Everything we have said is true. We have no 'hidden agenda.'"

The questions seemed to go on and on. Most were delivered respectfully, even if the answers that were given failed to satisfy the audience. She noticed a few young men clustered in one corner who seemed particularly agitated, muttering and shaking their heads. "Do you know them?" she asked Abe, inclining her head in their direction.

"Some," he whispered back. "They're Kibei, and you can be sure they're going to answer 'No—No' to the last two questions on the questionnaire, the ones about volunteering for the army and forswearing allegiance to the Emperor. They and a few others like them have been badmouthing America from Day One. They're making the rounds at camp, trying to convince anyone they can to see things their way."

Margaret remembered last month's lecture by the Assistant Director on motivating "cynical and dissatisfied" youth. She thought he'd been referring to a few Nisei with too much time on their hands, but now, hearing about the disgruntled Kibei, she wondered. What could she possibly do to help?

As the meeting broke up, Abe offered to walk Margaret to her car, which was parked near the Administration area. It was warmer than when she arrived, a sign that the gathering clouds meant snow was on its way. She was anxious to get home before it started and hurried alongside her companion.

"I hate that the Kibei are going around intimidating people," Abe said, picking up where he'd left off after the meeting. "They don't like ministers like Father Joe, because they see him as a traitor to the cause, since he's been helping the Administration."

"Do you think they would harm him?" Margaret asked.

"Nah, just call him names. Their favorite slur is *'inu'*— 'dog.' But they're all bark and no bite." Abe smiled at his little joke, but Margaret fretted all the way home. She resolved to talk to the priest in the morning and implore him to be careful.

The next day she raised her concerns with Father Joe, but he brushed them aside. "I am not living by myself, as Father Tibesar is in his rectory."

"That's not the same at all," Margaret objected. "Father Tibesar is not a Nikkei. People expect him to work with the Administration."

"Mrs. Peppers, I will take care. In my own little way, I have been of some use to the Issei and Kibei, even if they don't know it. Did you read that Question 28 has been reworded so that loyalty to the Emperor is no longer mentioned? Enough of us protested that this was changed. Now I can answer 'yes' to the question and advise others to do so."

"I doubt that will change any firebrand's mind," Margaret observed, but it was clear that as far as Father Joe was concerned, there was nothing to worry about.

The priest maintained his equanimity even after learning that the Nikkei Methodist minister at Tule Lake, a colleague and friend of Father Dai's, had been beaten in his own barracks for being a WRA "collaborator." Margaret, on hearing the news, pleaded with Father Joe to no avail to keep out of the registration controversy—just answer the questions for himself and be done with it.

"I have to help where I'm needed," Father Joe said. "Besides, I am not the only one involved—there are nine other Issei who volunteered to interpret and advise—even Dr. Shigaya. If I hide, they all should hide too."

He adopted a reassuring tone. "Tule Lake has a reputation for strife. There have been strikes and problems between the Administration and the people there from the beginning. Yet my brother is not worried. Minidoka is different. People are more willing to try to live together in peace and want to obey the government, even if it mistreated them. It will be okay."

Margaret remained unconvinced but held her tongue. Instead, she sent a note to Abe Hagiwara asking him to keep watch over Father Joe. "Just because both brothers are pigheaded doesn't mean they're right," she muttered as she penned her request but decided against putting that particular observation into writing.

CHAPTER 57

Within a week of the Block 7 meeting, the names of three brothers from St. Peter's—Bill, Kaun, and Satoru Onodera—had made the front page of the *Irrigator* for having volunteered for the Army. Ten days later they were edged out by four Sakura brothers for the honor of having the most enlistees in one family. The Sakuras' mother Mina had become known for standing up at recruitment sessions to urge enlistment, refusing to be silenced by the "Antis" who tried to shout her down.

"See?" Father Joe teased his worrywart deaconess. "Don't you think I am as capable of defending myself as Mrs. Sakura?" Likewise, both Reverend Andy and Abe Hagiwara had reassured Margaret that there was no need for a bodyguard because the mood of the camp, though it could hardly be described as 100 percent patriotic, was far from incendiary.

Accompanied by her mother Tamaki, nineteen-year-old Fumiko Onodera visited Margaret one afternoon soon after the announcement of her brothers' enlistment. "Just think, Deaconess Peppers," she babbled, "I'll have not one, but *three* men in my family in uniform! All my friends are jealous and are trying to get their boyfriends to sign up." Her face suddenly clouded. "Tak—he's not my boyfriend exactly, but a boy I like, or maybe *used* to like. Anyway, he says, 'Why do I have to prove my patriotism? America hasn't proven to me why I should be loyal to America.' If you ask me, I think the real reason he doesn't want to sign up is he's scared to fight. Not my brothers!"

Turning to Mrs. Onodera, Margaret said, "You must be

very proud of your sons."

"Yes," said the mother, smiling, "but it is a worry."

Fumiko said something to Mrs. Onodera in Japanese, who responded volubly. Margaret could have guessed what she was saying without Fumiko's explanation: "My mom said not knowing where they will be and what they will be doing bothers her."

Just like so many mothers across the country right now, Margaret thought, then said reassuringly, "God will be watching over them."

The Onoderas stayed for a few more minutes while Margaret told them about the Issei women's group she was organizing. Suddenly Fumiko, having looked at her watch, stopped translating and jumped up. "My shift at the hospital starts in a half-hour," she cried, taking her mother's hand. "I'm sorry to leave so fast. Thanks a bunch for listening, Mrs. Peppers."

As she stared out the window at the Onodera mother and daughter's retreating forms, Margaret reflected on the need to prove one's loyalty that seemed to be motivating many of the enlistments—and preventing a few, also. The pressure to sign up was great. No issue of the *Irrigator* was without its editorial urging enlistment, and lately it had reprinted positive opinions from the national press about allowing Nisei to join the Army. Even Margaret's former Sunday School student Eddie Sato had drawn a cartoon showing "Dokie," as his Nisei character representing Minidoka had been dubbed, dreaming of marching in uniform, while the sleeping youth's dog, bearing a scroll with the single word "Volunteer," prepared to jump on his master's bed. Yet sprinkled among the national kudos were reports of resolutions from organizations like California's Native Sons of the Golden West, which branded the government's decision as "dangerous." Such attitudes might stiffen some Niseis' resolve to enlist and prove the naysayers wrong, but it might cause others to decide that nothing, short of magically transforming into a *hakujin*—a white person—could cause them to be considered true

Americans. Margaret had heard that even a few Nisei were contemplating moving to Japan where, they hoped, they would finally find acceptance.

In a strange sort of way, she felt a kinship with these Nisei lads. Once, she had been a young woman poised on the brink of a decision that would change her life: to become a missionary, working among "savages" in the Philippines, an endeavor that at the time seemed as heroic to her as Dokie's dream of combat glory. With the hindsight of decades only now coming into focus, she realized what it all had been about. Yes, she had sincerely wanted to serve her Lord, just as the Nisei enlistees were sincere in their desire to serve their country. But there was more. Her naysayers hadn't harangued Congress, written letters to the editor, or refused to serve her at their places of business. But the Peppers clan had never accepted her, never thought she was "good enough" to be one of them, whether as the wife of Hal or the mother of the only grandchild in that generation. In their eyes it wouldn't have mattered what she decided to do with her life, only she didn't know that then. So she bravely went off to "war"—she would show *them!*—and prove herself worthy, by winning heathens to Christ. And in the process, lose her very own daughter.

Then another thought occurred to her. *Prove myself—or prove to myself?* Was it possible there was another naysayer in the chorus, one whose voice was equally as insidious as Martina's? A voice so familiar to her, it might have been her own?

It *was* her own. *Oh God, it's me. It's been me all along.* She looked down at her hands, which lay clenched on the desk, as if refusing to accept the understanding that had just been given her.

She, Sarah Margaret Guthrie Peppers, had labored as a deaconess for twenty-five years—for what? *Was it only to convince myself that I am worthy?*

No, not only. But, without a doubt, she knew that was part of the reason. How much, she didn't dare think.

Certain they had somehow been party to the revelation she had just received, Margaret glanced abruptly at her coworkers, snapping her head up so quickly that for days afterward, her neck would be sore. Nearby, Esther McCullough was unconcernedly pasting photos into the scrapbook she kept of all the Baptist doings. In another corner, Reverend Tom Fukayama was typing what Margaret assumed was the draft of a sermon, his open Bible on the desk beside him. Next to him, Reverend Everett Thompson talked animatedly on the telephone about plans for an upcoming concert by the Minidoka Mass Choir at a Twin Falls church.

Reassured by her fellow workers' preoccupation with their various pursuits, Margaret relaxed momentarily before another question intruded. Should she confess this to a priest? One-on-one confession was not something that was customary in the Episcopal Church, being only a feature of "high" or "Anglo-Catholic" parishes. Yet the seriousness of the discovery of mixed motives in her choice of vocations seemed to call for an equally serious response. Try as she might, she could not conceive of confiding in Father Joe or any Episcopal priest she knew, in or out of Minidoka. What would they think of her if she did? No, she would have to settle for confessing her duplicity to God and resolving to serve Him wholeheartedly in the future.

By the beginning of March the Army team had left, having registered nearly 7,000 Issei and Nisei over sixteen years of age. Ten days later the *Irrigator* reported there were 300 inductees, just shy of 20 percent of Hunt's eligible males—"far greater than any previously recorded volunteer response in the history of the United States," the paper bragged. It announced an upcoming series of seven-course, "sumptuous" banquets to honor the new enlistees and their families, and the next day Margaret received an invitation to one of them in the mail.

"I wonder how many Episcopalians besides the Onidera brothers volunteered," she commented to Father Joe, who had also been invited.

"Frank Shigemura talked to me about it, but I do not know what he decided. I am sure that Mike Hagiwara volunteered. He wants to join his brother Patrick."

"Patrick? I don't know him."

"He is the middle one, between Abe, the oldest and Mike, the youngest. He was in the Alaska National Guard when America went to war. I heard about him from his father when we were imprisoned together in Lordsburg."

Margaret remembered how, shortly after Mrs. Hagiwara and her children had been sent to Minidoka, Mike had written the governor of Alaska imploring him to use his influence to get the elder Hagiwara released from the Department of Justice camp and reunited with his family. It had apparently worked, because Mr. Hagiwara was now at Minidoka.

She hoped Abe would not decide to follow his brothers into the Army. His college education had been interrupted by the war, but it sounded as if he could attend a school away from the west coast come summer or fall. Both Mike and Abe were clever, charming, and talented, and Margaret hated to think of them risking their lives just to prove their patriotism. She suspected many mothers and wives felt the same about their young men, even if they didn't admit it publicly.

Nevertheless, the night of the banquet Margaret resolved to put aside her concerns, wanting to enter fully into the occasion and support the volunteers and their families. Ever since that day her eyes had been opened to her own youthful predicament, she had felt her own solidarity with the Nisei deepen. It didn't matter on which side of the enlistment question they stood. She felt compassion for them all: the idealistic and the bitter, the determined and the wavering, the brave and the fearful. Not only them, but the older generation as well: she was, after all, nearing fifty, far closer in age, if not in culture, to the Issei than to the Nisei. *These are my people,* she had begun to say to herself about the Nikkei, conscious of a new identification. *We will prevail.*

Dining Hall 7 had been transformed into a spectacle of red, white, and blue. American flags were everywhere: on the long, white cloth-covered tables; fluttering overhead, suspended on ropes which crisscrossed the hall; on a stand at the front of the room; and displayed prominently behind the speaker's podium. Hanging on the walls around the room were red and white service flags representing the various blocks, each bearing blue stars according to the number of enlistees in that block. Every volunteer wore on his coat sleeve a blue "V" insignia on a red and white background. The honorees stood in clusters about the room, surrounded by proud family and friends.

After marveling for a moment at the decorations, Margaret scanned the hall to find people she knew. She noticed Abe Hagiwara, deep in conversation with one of the musicians. Even if his brother hadn't been one of the honorees, as a member of the Community Activities Department, Abe was always in the thick of things. Nearby, Fumiko Onodera stood beaming between her brothers Kaun and Satoru. Then, with a sinking heart, Margaret spied newlyweds Cherry and Tad Fujioka receiving congratulations. She thought, *He didn't go and sign up, did he, after being married less than a month?*

Cherry Fujioka's smile broadened at the sight of the deaconess. "Mrs. Peppers, I'm so glad you could be here. Won't you join us for dinner? I'm afraid I'll have to jump up to play the piano part of the time, but you can keep Tad company." She turned and planted a kiss on the cheek of her husband, whom Margaret was relieved to see was not sporting an enlistee's "V" on his sleeve.

"I don't mean to intrude—" Margaret began, thinking the couple would prefer to sit with friends.

"Not at all," Tad gallantly replied, only slightly diminishing the effect by adding, "We really don't know many people here."

Cherry hastily covered for her husband. "What Tad means is he's delighted to sit with someone who's a friend. I managed to get him invited at the last minute because I'm performing."

The amplified voice of 75-year-old Kinya Okajima, Chairman of the Hunt Self-Government Planning Commission, rose above the murmur of conversations to invite people to be seated. For a change, the guests did not have to line up for their food, cafeteria style, but were served at their tables by a cadre of women, both Nisei and Issei. The first course was already at the table: sliced, pickled daikon radish, which Margaret enjoyed, unlike some of the other white staff members, who ventured only a bite or two. This was followed by a succession of foods, both American and Japanese, including Campbell's chicken soup, rice, stewed tomatoes, *tonkatsu* fried pork chops, and for dessert, slices of yellow sheet cake with white icing and red and blue piping. Albeit eclectic, it was a much better meal than the usual fare, Cherry and Tad assured her.

During dinner one of the several Hunt musical groups, the Minidoka String Quartet, serenaded the guests. While dessert was being served to the head table, and before she had finished her entrée, Cherry excused herself to accompany the male vocal quartet, two of whose members were Mike and Abe Hagiwara.

"It will be a great loss for us when Mike leaves for the Army," Margaret said to Tad, as the group prepared to sing. "But of course we have to consider the bigger picture."

"They're both swell guys," Tad responded. "I haven't been a member of your church for long, so I haven't gotten to really know them, but I hope to, before Mike leaves and maybe I–" He paused, flashing a look toward the piano where his wife had positioned herself.

"Join up yourself?" Margaret supplied, guessing what her companion had left unsaid. The start of "Chatanooga Choo Choo" spared Tad the need to reply.

After another much-applauded number, "Boogie Woogie Bugle Boy," the group finished its performance on a quieter note, with the latest hit by Dinah Shore, "You'd Be So Nice to Come Home To."

> *You'd be so nice, you'd be paradise*
> *To come home to and love.*

"That's what I'll be singing someday to Cherry," Tad whispered, leaving Margaret no doubt as to his enlistment intentions.

Director Stafford signaled the start of spoken program by inviting everyone to stand and say the Pledge of Allegiance. First of the speakers who followed, he lauded Minidoka as the leader in enlistments among all the relocation camps. "Winston Churchill praised the Hurricane fighter pilots who defended London during the Blitz with a tribute that has now become famous: 'Never in history did so many owe so much to so few.'" He paused to allow his interpreter to catch up. "I contend," he continued, looking around the room which he held in rapt attention, "that when America and her allies have triumphed over the forces of evil that threaten the very foundations of our civilization, history will judge the contribution of the Japanese American military unit in similar terms. You, the volunteers of Minidoka, have shown that you have the 'right stuff' and are ready to take your place with the heroes of our society, indeed of our world!"

The audience erupted in thunderous applause, cheers, and table pounding as Stafford took his seat. At that point Dyke Miyakawa pre-empted the next speaker to offer the toast he was scheduled to make later in the program. "To the heroes!" he cried, raising his glass of 7-Up (which, though hardly champagne, was an unaccustomed treat in the dining hall.)

"To the heroes!" Margaret responded, swept up in the emotion of the moment. Around the room some of the more fervent Issei shouted, *"Banzai!"*

After this rousing beginning, the speech by Assistant Director Schafer was anti-climactic. Margaret found her mind wandering, but when the Nisei volunteers began to speak, she listened attentively. Finally, it was Mike Hagiwara's turn. Like the Nisei speakers before him, he seemed bemused by all the fuss. Still, when he began to address the crowd, his voice echoed as confidently as earlier when he was crooning hit songs.

"At this time, I would like to pay tribute to a few

individuals, groups of individuals and others who have been able to help us keep our faith in America. I believe the schools and the culture of America gave us a defense against the trying times which we faced directly following evacuation. For it was the American ideals and culture upon which such men as our project director Mr. Stafford, his appointed staff and many such men have based their convictions concerning we American Japanese as true loyal citizens. It was hard work against tremendous odds which enabled our friends on the outside to sway the public opinion and influence the Army in such a way as to make possible the volunteer induction program."

Turning from the podium to the head table, Mike concluded in a voice full of emotion, "Mr. Stafford, Mr. Schafer, Mr. Townsend, you and many honest Americans have been working untiringly for us. The time has now come when we Americans of Japanese ancestry must do some ball carrying for ourselves. On behalf of the volunteers and their families and friends, I wish to give this last word of assurance. We now have our chance to prove our loyalty, and we won't let you down."

Again, the room erupted in applause. As Mike resumed his place, Margaret, still applauding, glanced at Mr. and Mrs. Hagiwara, who were seated at a nearby table. Mrs. Hagiwara was dabbing her eyes. *Tears of pride*, Margaret said to herself, *but also tears of sorrow? What mother would not feel worry if two of her three sons had joined the military?*

It was this way for thousands of other mothers in a similar situation right now. And yet it was different. For unless they were Japanese hailing from the west coast, these other military parents were not listening to patriotic speeches behind barbed wire.

Chapter 58

March 1943 at Minidoka had its fill of rain, though spring in the Idaho desert was generally not as wet as autumn. Still, the first storm had left behind its calling card of ubiquitous mud, which caused some Issei to return to wearing *geta* sandals outdoors, despite the forty-degree temperatures.

Yet there were rainbows—both literal and symbolic—to be appreciated during the month. If someone had asked the Episcopalians of Minidoka that March, they would likely have said that the grandest "rainbow" appeared on one of the most solemn days of the church year, Ash Wednesday, when a service was held not only to mark the beginning of Lent but also the birth of the Church of the Holy Apostles, the Minidoka Episcopal mission. More than 150 men, women and children crowded into Rec Hall 28 to witness the Bishop of Idaho install Father Joe as the mission's Vicar. To add to the delight of the St. Peter's folk, Bishop Huston had come from Seattle to preach and visit the faithful. The only disappointment was that in keeping with the penitential nature of Lent, the altar had to be kept bare of any decoration, particularly flowers.

Before she had come to work among the Nikkei, Margaret had always considered ornamental gardening to be an exclusively feminine preoccupation, though one she did not happen to share. This was not true of the Japanese. Except for apartments—and even these were usually graced by window boxes and potted plants—nearly every Issei home of Margaret's acquaintance had its ornamental garden, with those most typically Japanese in style having usually been crafted by men.

Now, with time to kill and a desolate environment to overcome, the challenge of creating beauty and tranquility outside the barracks was one that many Issei men took to heart.

Margaret was reminded of this one day at the end of March, when she decided to take a break from writing her various quarterly reports and instead visit a few parishioners living west of the church office. It had not rained for several days, making the mile and a half round trip feasible on foot, even with her increasingly troublesome rheumatism. At least now there were wooden boardwalks linking many of the barracks, thanks to the enterprising Nikkei's use of scrap lumber.

Spring was in the air, and it seemed like everyone was outside, except for the school-age children, who were for the moment confined indoors in one of the barracks that functioned as classrooms. The fierce wind that so often barreled through the camp had gentled today to a light breeze, carrying with it the scents of the desert awakening to life. Margaret headed due north. It was slightly out of her way, but she preferred the bitter-spicy fragrance of sagebrush to the fumes of the sewage plant located on the most direct path to the barracks. She passed a large, recently graded expanse destined to become athletic fields for the schools. Next week, the Administration promised, two baseball diamonds would finally be laid out. The high schoolers—at least the boys—seemed to talk of nothing else these days.

As she glanced to her right, Margaret could see another project just beginning to take shape. Last fall Nikkei crews had built a five-mile ditch intended to irrigate victory gardens which would supply fresh vegetables not only to Hunt but also to the other nine WRA camps. Now, as she listened to its engine droning in the distance, Margaret noticed a drab green Army tractor moving up and down the nearby field like a munching grasshopper. Soon some Minidokans would have the chance to do their own farming rather than merely hire out to local beet growers. *But on the outside the government insists they get prevailing wages,* Margaret remembered. *That's a lot more than the $12 a* *month they'd get paid here.* She wondered if the Administration would have trouble getting enough people to work the Minidoka fields.

As she reached the first block of barracks, Margaret was reminded of something that Father Joe had said recently: "Every prisoner who can look through bars of a cell and see mountains beyond has reason to live." She'd asked, "Are you talking about the reasons people go out of camp and into the desert?" The mountains around Minidoka were not much to look at, she thought, compared with the Cascades back home.

"That is part of it," Father Joe replied. "But people find beauty in many ways. In church, out of church—it is all part of God's beauty. We are here to help others find it, you and I, and to let them share with us what they have found."

Now, on this early spring day, as fleecy white clouds scurried across the sky like lambs trotting after their mother, the Nikkei quest for beauty and harmony in a harsh and dehumanizing environment was everywhere in evidence. Nearly every barrack had some sort of doorstep garden. Many of these were an amalgam of features from the desert surroundings, such as basalt rocks and carefully bonsaied sagebrush, among which nestled potted plants and transplanted saplings that, against all odds, had been transported from home, either by the internees themselves or by sympathetic friends. Margaret herself had once helped Reverend Andy dig up a small pine tree in the yard of one of his Seattle congregants and maneuver it into the Blue Box to take back to Hunt.

It was amazing, really, what the Minidokans had already been able to achieve, through a combination of ingenuity, hard work, patience, and fortitude. Margaret paused before the garden she recognized as the creation of Tomota Akiyama, having recently seen a sketch of it by Eddie Sato. She remembered Eddie telling her how last fall, Mr. Akiyama and his eighteen-year-old son Tak had carried rocks from beyond the camp confines, using an improvised sling which allowed them to manage some too heavy to carry by hand. While Tak was away working in the beet fields, Mr. Akiyama had created a steep mound representing a mountain, which he covered in moss and rock, adding sagebrush which he transplanted to strategic places and bonsaied. He had leveled the top of the mound into a rock-rimmed pond to suggest a lake. Around this water feature he had planted willow slips, swamp grass, and a variety of little plants. There was even a pagoda made of carefully piled flat stones. "Tak said his dad did it for himself and for his family, but also for the neighbors," Eddie had explained, going on to describe his friend's puzzlement at investing so much time and energy towards a temporary living arrangement. It was a sentiment he obviously shared.

So many Nisei are in a hurry to get out and be doing things, Margaret reflected as she recalled her conversation with Eddie. She understood that youthful desire, yet more and more she found herself admiring the older generation's embracing of *gaman*—endurance—which had served the Issei well during their difficult sojourn in America.

She found thirty-year-old Shea Aoki in front of her barrack, installing a short white picket fence around the perimeter of what promised to be a lovely flower garden in a couple of months. Already pale green iris leaves were poking up from the tan rhizomes half-buried in the soil. Margaret had been hoping to find Shea at home, since her job as a nursery school teacher ended each day at noon. It had been a while since they had had a good chat.

"Mrs. Peppers!" Shea said, greeting the deaconess with a smile as she brushed off the dirt from her hands. "Isn't it a lovely day? For a moment, you can almost forget that next week it might snow, or that in a few weeks, it'll be sun, heat, and dust storms." Margaret agreed as she admired the woman's work.

"Won't you come inside?" Shea asked, motioning toward the set of wooden steps leading to a white front door which contrasted sharply with the tarpaper wall surrounding it.

Shea and her husband Jiro had been among her favorite couples at St. Peter's. Shea had grown up in Portland and met

Jiro at a Japanese American Citizens League convention in Auburn. Though raised a Buddhist, she had joined Jiro's church when she married him, becoming an active member like her husband. Before the war, the couple had been involved in managing the two hotels owned by the Aoki family, both of which had to be sold for a pittance when the Nikkei were forced to leave Seattle.

"Your curtains turned out so pretty and set off everything in your apartment," Margaret said, admiring the blue and green calico fabric which coordinated with the aqua chenille bedspread and the blue oilcloth on the table. Like Mabel Shigaya, Shea was a talented seamstress. Margaret couldn't imagine her ever buying curtains from a catalog.

"Thank you. Mrs. Howard at the fabric store in Twin Falls was kind enough to give me a few swatches so I could match what I already have. I didn't care for what they had at the Co-op." The popular Nikkei-run Minidoka Consumers' Cooperative, incorporated in December, operated camp businesses such as a general store, a fish market, clothing stores, barber and beauty shops, a dry cleaning business, canteens, and other enterprises. "Do take a seat, Mrs. Peppers," Shea said, motioning to the navy-blue loveseat which was the only piece of upholstered furniture in the room. She added, "Won't you join me in a cup of tea?"

Smiling her assent, Margaret commented on the change of heart on the part of Twin Falls and Jerome townspeople toward the Nikkei since they had stepped in to harvest the beet crop last fall. "Even Governor Chase Clark said the Japanese Americans had saved the crop," she remarked.

"That certainly helped," Shea agreed, taking the whistling kettle off the pot-bellied stove. "But I think the shopkeepers also found we have money to spend—at least some of us do. What's the saying—'Money talks'?"

"That's it. Though to be fair, not everyone around here was prejudiced from the start. And the more they get to know real people from Minidoka, the more they'll see there's a difference between the Japanese overseas who are our enemies and the Japanese who've lived in the U.S. for years. I just heard that local churches and service organizations are going to be donating trees and shrubs for the Hunt beautification project."

"That's great. I wonder if our block will get any. I hope it won't just be on Admin Hill."

Margaret helped herself to a couple of vanilla wafers which Shea offered her. They conversed some more about Hunt affairs, church activities, and the nursery school, before Margaret brought up the topic of Jiro's parents, Seita and Sei, whom she hoped to visit next door, along with Jiro's sister Hannah Maekawa and her four-year-old daughter Linda. Hannah's husband Roger had a camp job during the day.

"I'll take you over to see them. Jiro's mom's doing fine but his dad's still pretty depressed. He felt so betrayed by our country when he was sent to Missoula as an enemy alien. They say it's because he was active in the Japanese Chamber of Commerce. In Seattle he was an important businessman, a community leader, and now… He's 65 years old and has nothing but time on his hands. He drives Jiro's mother crazy."

As Shea knocked on her in-laws' door, Margaret thought, *Too bad Mr. Aoki can't take up gardening like Mr. Akiyama did—or even fishing*. Now that the weather had improved, scores of Issei and Nisei men lined the banks of the Northside Canal, hoping to catch trout. Many succeeded.

Sei Aoki, an energetic woman in her mid-fifties, greeted them at the door and immediately bowed to Margaret. She invited the pair inside, pulling out two chairs from a table. Margaret, who knew enough of Issei ways not to wear her shoes indoors, produced a pair of soft-soled slippers from a canvas bag she had carried from her office. Recognizing her intent, Mrs. Aoki immediately brought one of the chairs near the threshold to allow the deaconess to sit down as she swapped her foot attire.

While Jiro and Shea's apartment, which measured 16 by 20 feet, was even smaller than Margaret's own duplex, the unit shared by the remaining five members of the Aoki family was only 20 by 20 feet and had to accommodate more people. Like many Nikkei families, the elder Aokis and the Maekawas separated their sleeping spaces with blankets, which afforded minimal privacy. Otherwise, it was a communal existence.

Shea's mother-in-law was cooking something on the coal burning stove, which turned out to be a perch from the Co-op. The fish had been broiling in what usually served as the stove's ash receptacle. Mrs. Aoki offered a piece to Margaret, who politely declined, knowing it was intended for Mr. Aoki, who after greeting Margaret and Shea with a bow, had returned to whittling something as he sat on one of the two cots, which were arrayed at right angles. Margaret, in turn, reached into the canvas bag she'd been carrying and took out several apples from the Jerome grocery. She knew the Nikkei craved fresh produce, and the gift was received with delight.

Meanwhile, on the other side of the blanket which separated the Aoki and Maekawa quarters, they could hear Hannah trying to soothe her child to sleep.

"I'm sorry—did I wake Linda from her nap?" Margaret asked in a low voice. "I can come back another time."

"No, please stay," said Mrs. Aoki. Having run a hotel, her command of English was better than that of many Issei. "Linda has fever and must stay in bed. Hannah tries to cheer her up." Excusing herself, she said something to her husband in Japanese, who put down his whittling and joined the visitors at the table to eat a small plateful of fish and rice. Taking up a kettle from the stove, Mrs. Aoki poured everyone a cup of tea, making sure to serve Margaret first as hospitality required. Then, from one of the orange crates that served as shelving, she extracted several paper-wrapped mandarins which she quickly peeled, arranging the segments artistically on small dishes which bore the name "The Alps Hotel."

Because they were Buddhists, the elder Aokis had not been members of St. Peter's, and Margaret didn't know them very well. She tried not to glance too often at the small, gilded Buddha in the corner of the room, which both repelled and fascinated her. She wondered if it had belonged to the Aoki family for generations. Rather than fuel her inner conflict, she decided to ask instead about Seita Aoki's whittling.

"Mr. Aoki, I am curious about what you are carving. Would you please tell me about it?" Margaret knew enough about Issei ways to avoid abrupt questions.

"It is a little nothing, Mrs. Peppers. I will show you." Having finished his light meal, Seita Aoki rose from the table and returned with the half-finished carving. "It is a small horse for my granddaughter."

"*Otousan*, please show Mrs. Peppers some of your other carvings," Shea said, as Margaret admired the finely executed head and mane of the diminutive horse. "He's made a rabbit, a bird, and a cat, too, but Linda has them now," the younger Aoki explained.

This time, when Mr. Aoki returned to the table, he carried a cane and a vase. Like the animal figure, they were made of greasewood, except as finished items they had been polished to a smoothness that Margaret's fingers itched to feel.

"Oh, how lovely!" she exclaimed, instinctively reaching to touch the vase until she realized her rudeness and hastily withdrew her hand. Seita Aoki seemed not to mind and passed first the vase, and then the cane, for her to hold. "These deserve a place in Hunt's next arts and crafts exhibit," she added, and was dismayed to see the elder Aoki shake his head no.

"He thinks he is too much of an amateur," Shea murmured to Margaret. "That, or he says these exhibits are for women. We've tried to convince him otherwise but haven't succeeded yet."

Margaret decided against urging him to change his mind. She supposed he'd listen more to a man than a woman and resolved to ask Father Joe to try. Or maybe Father Shoji.

Silence reigned on the other side of the hung blanket, indicating that Linda had at last fallen asleep. Perhaps the child's mother had, too, because Hannah had still not emerged.

"I think I'll take a peek and see what's happening," Shea

said. "We could hear Linda moaning in the night—sounds carry in the barracks, you know. I think Hannah was up a lot." Pulling aside the blanket, she pointed to Hannah and Linda cuddled together on the cot, asleep.

"Poor things!" Margaret murmured. "I hope Linda recovers soon, and that Hannah doesn't get sick. Please tell them I'll visit another time when they're feeling better." Reaching into her pocketbook, she pulled out a carefully rolled piece of paper and left it on the table. "It's a picture of Jesus the Good Shepherd for Linda to color," she explained. Then, thanking her hostess for the hospitality and remarking once more on Mr. Aoki's carvings, she took her leave.

Margaret's steps slowed as she approached the Shojis' barrack, but not on account of her rheumatism. Visiting the family gave her the same feeling she had whenever she was in Seattle and glimpsed St. Peter's, boarded up and with weeds growing all around. *It's not right that a house of God be treated this way,* she thought whenever she saw the forlorn site. *Neither is it right,* she now reflected, *that the Shojis, of all people, have to suffer as they are now suffering.*

Culture and language had always been a barrier between the first vicar of St. Peter's Japanese mission and his deaconess, despite their common commitment to the welfare of the congregation. That was as true before the war began as since, so any insight into how Father Shoji felt about his and his family's incarceration at Minidoka had to come through Father Joe. From him Margaret had learned that, as was true also for Seita Aoki and so many other Issei, in the aftermath of Executive Order 9066 Father Shoji was left feeling betrayed by the country he had adopted as his own. Not that he chose to dwell on this injustice, focusing instead on his priestly and pastoral duties, especially among his fellow incarcerated Issei. But his spirit had been dealt a blow every bit as harsh as the hammer-blows securing the "No Trespassing" sign to the front door of his beloved church.

As much as Margaret felt for Father Shoji, it was Mrs. Shoji and her daughter Florence to whom her heart went out most. Kane Shoji had come to America in 1921 as a "Bible woman" to work among the female Issei, marrying Gennosuke Shoji the following year. Their four children were now teenagers, but only the oldest three had been in Margaret's confirmation classes. Fourteen-year-old Florence was so profoundly handicapped she could neither speak nor walk.

Mrs. Shoji was an accomplished woman, having earned the honor of being declared "Head Master" of the Senke School of Japanese Flower Arrangement and establishing her own school in Seattle before the war. Executive Order 9066 killed that dream and now Mrs. Shoji spent her days caring for her daughter. Years of patient nurture had brought Florence to the point where she could move by dragging her semi-paralyzed body and communicate to family members by various grunts. Now, under the conditions at Minidoka, she was regressing.

Margaret tapped on the door of the Shoji barrack after admiring the nascent flower garden which, she knew, had been planted by some of Mrs. Shoji's grateful former pupils. The rhythmic whick-whick of a knife chopping vegetables suddenly ceased, and the ensuing shuffling sound told Margaret that it was Mrs. Shoji, rather than nineteen-year-old Elizabeth, who would be answering the knock.

"Mrs. Peppers, please to come in," said Mrs. Shoji, bowing. Anticipating Margaret's need to take off her shoes, she fetched a chair as Mrs. Aoki had done. Margaret bowed in turn and presented her hostess several more apples from her capacious bag before sitting down. This time she put on the proffered *geta* sandals that must have belonged to Father Shoji, for his wife's feet were much smaller than Margaret's.

The room was like the Aokis' and Maekawas' in size and basic layout. The Shoji sons had put up wallboard which masked the wood and tar paper, and on one wall several lengths of blue and white checked cloth had been tacked for decoration, presumably by Elizabeth, who had once asked Margaret's opinion on the scheme. Suspended blue blankets separated the sleeping areas from the living/dining area. There was no sofa and only one upholstered chair.

Instead of a Buddha, the Shojis displayed a simple wooden cross, about a foot high, on the wall facing the door. Underneath it a Bible lay open on a small shelf, along with a *Book of Common Prayer*, both in Japanese. On one of the other unadorned walls, there was a large, framed picture of Jesus praying in the garden of Gethsemane.

Before sitting down at the table to drink her obligatory cup of tea, Margaret walked over to the corner where Florence sat propped up with a pillow on her right side. Reaching into her canvas bag, her fingers touched the last treasure she wanted to give this day. It wasn't an apple or a picture to color. It was a Raggedy Ann doll— Hallie's.

"Florence, dear, here's a little dolly for you," Margaret said, her voice catching as she remembered how she had given it to her daughter before leaving for the Philippines. It bore the evidence of having been played with, but she knew Florence wouldn't mind. *I'm glad this doll has dark hair, like Florence's, rather than the garish red hair of today's "patriotic" Raggedy Anns.*

"Mrs. Peppers, this too good!" Mrs. Shoji began, before Margaret cut short her protest.

"This belonged to my daughter. She was going to keep it for her daughter, but when her baby died, she wanted to throw the doll away. I took it back and knew someday there would be a child who would love it. I want Florence to have it."

"Thank you so much!" exclaimed Mrs. Shoji, bowing in gratitude before she turned, smiling, towards her child, who was making noises Margaret interpreted as expressing pleasure.

Suddenly Florence cried out and stiffened, losing consciousness. Her mother rushed to get a belt from a nearby orange crate and place it between her daughter's teeth. Then the convulsions began—horrible jerking which made Margaret think of a puppet being yanked on a string. Immobilized, Margaret stood looking on, as if all capacity for movement had been transferred to the writhing child. Mrs. Shoji did not try to restrain her daughter but merely held her head securely between her capable hands, while ensuring that the belt remained in place for Florence to bite.

Finally, after what seemed like hours but was only a matter of minutes, Florence lay slumped and quiet in the chair, her eyes closed as if sleeping. The stench of urine and feces permeated the room. Overcoming her paralysis, Margaret jumped to assist Mrs. Shoji in standing the groggy girl up, then supported Florence while her mother stripped off the soiled diaper, dropping it into an empty bucket which she immediately took outside. "Please hold her," Mrs. Shoji implored, a request Margaret struggled to comply with, as supporting Florence felt like keeping a four-and-a-half-foot sack of flour upright. "So sorry, so sorry," the priest's wife kept repeating, as she mixed the remaining water from the kettle on the stove with cold water held by yet another bucket in the kitchen. Soaping a cloth, she used part of this lukewarm mixture to wash her daughter, then rinsed the affected area clean. Tenderly she patted Florence dry, and together she and Margaret pulled the girl to the nearest cot and laid her down. Florence immediately fell asleep.

Mrs. Shoji was clearly embarrassed by what had happened, even though Margaret assured her there was no need to apologize. "Thank you, thank you," the woman murmured, after hastening to put all evidence of the incident outdoors. Margaret watched Mrs. Shoji meticulously wash her hands with soap and water before going to a suitcase stored under another cot, from which she extracted a small white piece of cloth. "Please take," she said, presenting a handkerchief embroidered with plum blossoms to her guest.

"There's no need," Margaret started to say, but at Mrs. Shoji's insistence, she accepted the gift. She wished she had something to offer in exchange, but except for her slippers, her canvas bag was empty. For now, Margaret would have to content herself with offering a prayer for Florence and the whole Shoji family. No matter if it was in English—she was confident the priest's wife would know what she intended.

Chapter 59

"Mrs. Peppers, please to sew knot in *senninbari*?" Mrs. Ito held up a white sash, adorned with red knots stitched in orderly rows like parading soldiers, in the center of which appeared a red-outlined tiger's head with black features. To the left of the tiger's face the sash seemed complete, but on its right a few knots were lacking.

It was nine in the morning on a Sunday in early April, and Margaret and Mrs. Ito had just finished preparing the simple altar for the 9:30 service, which served the Episcopalians on the east side of the camp. During the week this block housed the elementary school, and it worked well for the Sunday school classes held after worship. For the service itself, though, adult-sized chairs had to be brought in, as well as a lectern for Father Joe. Fortunately, Abe Hagiwara could be counted on to take care of these arrangements.

"Certainly, Mrs. Ito, but what is this?" Margaret wondered if she should be seeking a Nisei to translate, given Mrs. Ito's shaky English.

"*Senninbari* protect soldiers," the Issei woman responded. Margaret's puzzled expression must have also prompted Mrs. Ito to think of translation, for she immediately appealed to Father Joe, who happened to have entered the room, vestments in hand.

Hurriedly he explained. "Women believe if a soldier wears a *senninbari*, he will be kept from harm. Shintoists, Buddhists, even Christians sew them. My mother made one when I served in the army. The belt is supposed to have one thousand stitches by many different women, and each stitch carries a prayer."

"Why the tiger?" Margaret asked.

"People believe tigers can travel far from home and return safely," Father Joe said. "Not every belt has a tiger, though. Mine had a Bible verse." Just then Paul Shigaya entered the room and Father Joe excused himself, saying he needed to talk with the doctor.

Margaret turned back to Mrs. Ito. "Yes, I will be happy to sew a knot. After church?" The Issei woman smiled and bowed, making Margaret feel as if she had done her the greatest honor.

Later that evening, as she was glancing over yesterday's *North Side News*—and if her eyes strayed to the horoscope, how could she help it, since it appeared right beside the religious reporting?—an idea popped into her head. The Protestant Issei women's sewing circle had been making teddy bears for the children in the pediatric ward at St. Luke's Hospital in Boise. Why not expand their focus to include *senninberi* for Christian soldiers belonging to the Federated Church? She would talk with Reverend Thompson about it in the morning. *He should be pleased—he's always after me to devote more time to the Federated Church and less to Holy Apostles.*

Smiling at the prospect of pleasantly surprising the Methodist pastor for a change, Margaret returned to her newspaper. "The stars encourage the writing of letters to absent sons and daughters and husbands and fathers, from whom good news is indicated," she read.

She did some quick math to figure how long it had been since she'd heard from Hallie. Only her last letter would give her the true answer, so she shuffled to her bedroom, riffled through several drawers, and at last, found Hallie's letter in the pocket of a sweater that had been languishing on her mending pile. It was several weeks old. Now, as she scanned her daughter's crabbed handwriting, Margaret remembered why she'd been in no hurry to respond.

No epistle of Hallie's was complete without some dig at the "Japs in America," as she persisted in calling the Nikkei when her mother wasn't physically present to correct her. Often it took the form of a clipping from the Los Angeles *Examiner*, the Hearst-owned paper which never missed an opportunity to portray Japanese Americans in a negative light. In her last letter, Hallie had repeated rumors that the inmates of relocation centers were feasting on meat, eggs, butter, and other foods that the average American was denied. In a similar vein, she had enclosed a clipping with the headline, "Quit Coddling the Japs," referring to the move to form an all-Japanese American Army unit. The legislator who claimed to be "shocked beyond words" at the decision did not explain how sending men into combat could be considered "coddling," and Hallie had chosen not to comment.

If she could visit Minidoka and see that children are lucky to get two cups of milk a day, the bare minimum doctors recommend, she might think differently about "coddling."

There really wasn't much to write about that didn't involve her work with the Nikkei. Maybe the horoscope was wrong this time. She stuffed the letter back into the sweater pocket and went to bed.

To her great surprise, Margaret met staunch resistance from Reverend Thompson when she mentioned, causally, where she was going after services. "Mrs. Peppers, I commend your initiative, but we can't be encouraging a superstition like this. "

"I know that *senninbari* began among the Shintoists in Japan," she shot back, "but the Church has taken over other pagan practices for the greater good. What about Christmas trees? The pagans worshipped them, but we put a star on top and say it's the star of Bethlehem. Why can't we do the same with *senninbari?*"

"Have you been reading the papers? Representative Dies's Un-American Activities Committee is going to have hearings about the WRA camps and how they're run. The last thing we need is someone snooping around and finding the Federated Church is sponsoring a Shinto ceremony."

"It's not a ceremony. It's—"

"If the *Episcopalians* want to do this, go right ahead. But if I were you, I wouldn't mention it to the Administration and I wouldn't put any announcements in anything the Administration reads. That includes the Federated Church newsletter."

Swallowing the protest rising in her throat, Margaret made her way back to her desk. From the adjoining desk Esther McCullough leaned toward her to offer her own piece of advice. "Why don't you teach the women to knit? Twice a week the Baptist women come to my house to knit booties for the unfortunate inmates of the Idaho State Hospital. I'd be happy to share my pattern with you."

"Um, let me think about that, Esther—thanks. It's been a long time since I knit anything."

"You don't really need to knit. You're the hostess. I don't knit that well myself," she added modestly.

Esther's well-meaning suggestion took some of the sting out of Reverend Thompson's rejection of her idea, even though Margaret had no intention of following it. And yet–

"What days do you host the knitting circle, Esther?"

"Wednesdays and Fridays. The ladies take the bus into town and walk to my place. They enjoy the fellowship and, I have to admit, also having access to my bathroom. The merchants are so much nicer towards the Japanese than at first, but the ladies still don't feel very welcome to use the sanitary facilities in town."

Esther lives in Twin Falls and I live in Jerome, Margaret thought. *If I picked a different day of the week I wouldn't be competing.*

It just might work.

Chapter 60

peso Sho 6:11—in English, Ephesians 6:11—had its inaugural meeting a week later. Margaret had picked the name because the Bible verse it referenced spoke about heavenly protection, and wasn't that the purpose of *seninbari?* That verse, with its military overtones—"Put on the whole armor of God, that ye may be able to stand against the wiles of the devil"—had never really spoken to her, though it was one her Sunday school boys over the years had relished as they colored pictures of helmeted crusaders. Suddenly she found herself humming another martial favorite from her Baptist childhood, "Stand Up, Stand Up for Jesus, Ye Soldiers of the Cross," on her way to work as she turned over in her mind how to execute her plan.

One morning after church, Margaret quietly approached Mabel Shigaya, hoping to enlist her help in translating an invitation she wanted to give Mrs. Ito to pass along to other interested Christian women. "Father Vicar gave his blessing, even though it's not an official activity of our church," Margaret had assured her, trusting that Father Joe's preoccupied "mm-hmm" counted as a blessing.

Mabel was enthusiastic, and together they crafted a simple invitation to come to Margaret's duplex Tuesday afternoons to work on, and pray over, *senninbari* for any Christian Nisei soldier in the camp whose womenfolk—mother, sister, wife—wished to participate. They took a dozen three-by-five index cards, with Margaret writing the information in English on one side and Mabel copying it out into Japanese on the other. Then they approached Mrs. Ito about passing the word to families of Nisei volunteers.

Mrs. Ito had several friends in camp from other denominations, some of whom had agreed to sew knots for her own *senninbari*. She also knew which Federated Church ladies had refused to participate because they considered the practice unchristian. Slowly the word spread, and when it came time for the first meeting of *Epeso Sho 6:11,* there were barely enough chairs in Margaret's living and dining rooms to accommodate all the women who showed up.

Several Issei ladies had come with their daughters or daughters-in-law, reassuring Margaret that language would not be a barrier to communication. She recognized one of the Nisei women as a newcomer to her weekly Bible study—was her name Janet?—and decided to ask if she would be willing to act as interpreter, since Mable was working that day and couldn't attend.

"Yes, of course," Janet answered, even as she shot an anxious glance in the direction of her older companion, whom Margaret didn't know. "Let me just tell my mother-in-law Mrs. Miyauchi that I will need to sit next to you." She turned to the woman beside her and began speaking to her quietly in Japanese.

For a moment Mrs. Miyauchi looked slightly alarmed, as if she herself were being asked to translate. Margaret gave what she hoped was a reassuring smile, which was met by a smile in return. "If you'd rather not, I can ask someone else," she said, turning to address Janet once again.

"No, it's fine, Mrs. Peppers. My mother-in-law is shy, and I came along to give moral support as much as anything. She's a Buddhist and hasn't been among many Christians."

"And your husband?" *What am I going to do if he's a Buddhist?* Margaret thought. *It's bad enough that we're sewing Christian* senninbari, *but if word gets out that we're making Buddhist ones, there'll be heck to pay.*

"Oh, he joined the Presbyterian Church when he married me," Janet answered. He doesn't go to church services that often. He believes in God, though, and both my mother-in-law and I want him to have this reminder that he is loved and protected."

"That's good," Margaret responded, relieved that a potentially sticky issue had been avoided—at least this time. *Maybe it's not a bad thing that a Buddhist came today. Who knows what might happen if she spends time with Christians—she may become one herself.*

"I suppose we'd better begin," Margaret told her new assistant, and clapped her hands twice to get people's attention. After the chattering subsided, she welcomed the group with a bow.

"Thank you for coming here this afternoon to the first meeting of *Epeso Sho 6:11,*" she began, pausing for Janet's translation. "We are here to make *senninbari* for our churchmen who have volunteered to serve this country in combat against the enemy. As long as we remember that *senninbari* are not some kind of magical protection but a way of reminding the ones who will wear them of God's love and care, we will be approaching this in the right spirit."

"I see some of you have come prepared to sew today," Margaret continued, after allowing Janet to catch up. "If any of you are just starting and want to include a Bible verse in your *senninbari*, I've written a couple in English you may wish to use." She held up a large sheet of paper on which she'd written, "Fear not" and "He will keep thee in perfect peace." Then she asked, "Does anyone have another suggestion?" She had worked with the Nikkei long enough not to expect someone to volunteer and thus appear to be upstaging a religious worker, so after only a brief pause, she began talking about how the women were welcome to bring flour or rice sacks to cut up next time, if they hadn't already begun their *senninbari*.

Doris Furuya, a twenty-year-old Nisei who hoped to resume college in the fall somewhere back east, raised her hand. "It occurred to me," she said hesitantly, "that if we left our sewing of Bible verses, or tigers, or whatever else to do at home, then we could concentrate on sewing knots here. We could pass along the *senninbari* from person to person, like an assembly line, and finish sooner."

Several other Nisei women nodded their heads while Janet translated. But not all the elders were so enamored of efficiency, Margaret guessed. Probably many had been looking forward to sketching and embroidering embellishments with their friends. One of the few bright spots in the bleak internment experience was that for the first time, Issei women had the leisure to pursue activities and friendships outside the family circle.

In the end the matter of how to complete each *senninbari's* "thousand knots" was left to the family whose relative was destined to receive the gift. No one brought up the question of who was invited to the group, and Margaret, throwing her usual caution to the winds, decided to say nothing. *Let the women decide instead of assuming what they need.* With that unaccustomed thought, something inside her seemed to loosen, almost like giving play to a too-tight rope.

Soon the women set to work, talking and laughing. Margaret knew, though, that none was oblivious to the fact that the loved one who would leave the camp with his *seninbari* might never return, no matter how many prayers had been stitched into its fabric.

The bus was already an hour late. For the assembled crowd of several thousand well-wishers, the initial excitement of seeing off the first contingent of army volunteers had started to wear thin. To Margaret's ears, the banter among the young Nisei had begun to sputter like the '33 Chevy she used to drive. On the fringes of the group stood the Issei, grim-faced and mostly silent. She could tell the parents of the volunteers because they were the ones dressed in their Sunday best.

Father Joe had gone near the front, to be with Mike Hagiwara and the Onodera boys in their last hours of civilian life. Margaret had already said her goodbyes to them, personally giving each a copy of the New Testament, courtesy of the Federated Church. She wanted to stand with the Issei.

Standing beside her in the now-dimming light were two

mothers she'd come to know through *Epeso Sho 6:11,* Mrs. Abe and Mrs. Murakami. An hour before she'd seen Mrs. Abe tearfully give her son his *senninbari* before he joined his cohort in the center of the milling group. Her husband had shaken the young man's hand, murmuring *Shikkari se yo* — "Do a good job, like a man" — according to Father Joe, who at the time had been standing with Margaret.

Another woman stole up beside them. Margaret recognized Hideko Yasutake from some Federated Church affairs and greeted her, wondering if she too had a son who was leaving for the army. Then she remembered: Tosh had just volunteered, according to Father Joe, who had been counseling the young man. It would be a while before he would be inducted, but perhaps Mrs. Yasutake was trying to accustom herself to her fate as a military mother. Tosh had asked Father Joe to deliver the news, hoping his acquaintance with Mr. Yasutake when both were confined at Lordsburg might somehow soften the blow. She had not been happy with her son's choice until the priest pointed out it might hasten Mr. Yasutake's release back to the family in Minidoka, since he was still being held in New Mexico.

"Soon my son go," Mrs. Yasutake commented unsmilingly to Margaret. "Mitsuye make."

"Your daughter made him enlist?" Margaret had once met Mrs. Yasutake's twenty-year-old daughter and thought her unusually outspoken for a Japanese American girl, but it was hard to imagine her "making" her brother do anything he didn't want to do.

Mrs. Yasutake nodded her head. Margaret was spared having to respond by the crunch of tires on the gravel road ahead, signaling the appearance of the bus that would take the volunteers to Fort Douglas, Utah. Suddenly the crowd sparked once more with energy — all except the circle of Issei on the fringes, who somberly regarded the smiling enlistees as they said their final goodbyes and made their way to the front of the crowd.

The Boy Scout Drum and Bugle Corps, who after an

initial musical foray had been fidgeting for a half-hour on the sidelines, sprang into action, reprising their renditions of patriotic favorites such as "Grand Old Flag" and "Stars and Stripes Forever." Margaret, her eyes moist, forgot for a moment that young men like Tosh Yasutake might enlist to free their fathers, forgot that many Nisei just wanted to prove they were "real" Americans, willing to die for their country. When the Boy Scouts struck up "The Star Spangled Banner," she sang, hand over her heart, as loudly as anyone.

CHAPTER 61

As spring gave way to summer the choking dust-storms returned, though the presence of established gardens and newly planted trees throughout the camp, along with acres of crops around its perimeter, moderated the wind's impact. Little could be done about the scorching heat, however. The elders accepted it with their usual precept—*Shikata ga nai*—and tried to stay out of the sun, while the youngsters saw it as an opportunity to frolic in the North Side Canal.

A few bolder Nisei had tried to use the public pool in Twin Falls, but after a few days a "For City Residents Only" sign was posted, putting an end to that experiment in integration. Then, on June 21st, Noburu Roy Tada, an eleven-year-old playing with his friends in the North Side Canal, drowned. Once again, the *Irrigator* issued warnings about wading in the rapidly flowing water. Father Joe and others urged the Administration to give the Nikkei an alternative, and finally in August a six-foot-deep swimming hole was dug south of the warehouse area.

Roy Tada's death saddened everyone in camp, but another event that June struck particularly hard at the band of Episcopalians. Florence Shoji, whose condition had continued to deteriorate, was moved to the Idaho State Hospital in Blackfoot, a two-hour drive from Hunt. Its patients included everyone from violent criminals to persons existing in a vegetative state. Despite periodic legislative investigations, the hospital had neither the funding nor staffing it needed. If the food allotment for Minidoka residents was capped at a measly $.50 a day, the State Hospital allocation was worse—only $.17 a day.

For Florence, that allocation was probably sufficient. During the spring she had withdrawn more and more, and neither food nor her family's attempts to entertain her were of any interest. Margaret, who had continued her regular visits right up to Florence's leaving, resigned herself to sitting with the girl and stroking her hand during those times when she was not suffering a seizure. Toward the end, Florence didn't even recognize her, though she still clutched the doll that once belonged to Hallie.

At Evening Prayer the night before Florence left, Margaret listened to the Bible story of how St. Peter had healed a crippled man. "

In late September, Minidoka put out the welcome mat for more than 1,500 "loyal" Nikkei being relocated from Tule Lake, after the California camp had been designated a "segregation center" for the "disloyal," which included anyone who had given "wrong" answers to the registration questions. Suddenly, housing was in short supply again, just as it had been in the early days of the camp.

Once the final convoy of trucks bringing Tuleans from the train station had unloaded its passengers and their belongings, it was time for the couple hundred "disloyals" from Minidoka to reverse the journey. For most, their eventual destination would be Japan. No one from the Church of the Holy Apostles was among that group, but Margaret went anyway to see off the departing contingent. Several children she had taught in the Federated Church Sunday school were moving with their families to a country that would, in a way, be far stranger to them than this Idaho desert.

It didn't take long for tensions to develop between the citified Minidoka Issei and the newcomers, most of whom were farmers. "*Inaka mono*"—country bumpkins—became a commonly heard epithet. For their part, many new residents of Hunt resented the former city dwellers' superior ways and comparative affluence.

The congregation of Holy Apostles swelled with the arrival of many former White River Valley Episcopalians, but if there was ill-feeling between the new group and the old, Margaret wasn't aware of it. She'd hoped that Father Dai would be among the Tule Lake arrivals, but he had been persuaded to stay in California during the inauguration of the segregation center. In October he wrote to his brother of his decision to relocate to Cincinnati that fall. "But first he plans to visit Hunt," Father Joe told Margaret, who tried to mask her disappointment that her former priest would not be joining them for the long run.

There's nothing wrong with Father Joe, but I feel more comfortable with Father Dai, she thought. Father Joe was a puzzle to her. Fun-loving and gregarious, he was very popular with the young people. He smoked like a chimney and enjoyed an occasional beer when he was away from camp. The Administration trusted him. At the same time, he could be almost otherworldly. He'd never bothered to learn to drive, and if something mechanical had to be fixed, he would be the last one to ask. The more intellectual the discussion, the happier he was. Margaret could envision him in a seminary debating the nature of the Resurrection with his fellow theologians.

Yes, he was devout, and he cared about his flock. *But Father Dai was my kind of pastor. Steady. Down-to-earth. No task was too small, no person too insignificant to merit his attention.* Margaret could see herself—almost—bringing up with him those doubts about God's mercy that had plagued her all summer. Maybe there would be time to talk when he came in November.

Chapter 62

October 1943

You know, Mrs. Peppers, I feel sorry for these Californians," Mitsuye Yasutake said one day, as she waited for Father Joe to arrive in the office. Though raised a Methodist, she and her oldest brother Seichi were preparing to be confirmed in the Episcopal Church. "You should hear people like my mom make fun of the Tule Lakers' clothes and how they talk. Of course, my mom looks down on anyone who wasn't brought up genteel in Japan. Do you want to hear a funny story?"

Margaret felt she could use a good laugh and said yes.

"Well, this part isn't exactly funny, but my story doesn't make sense otherwise. I was born in Japan but didn't live with my mom and dad until I was almost four years old. My mom had gone back to Japan for a while with Seichi and Tosh because, according to her, she knew it would be too much to have a baby and take care of two little boys at the same time, my father being so busy with his work and all. She figured my dad's parents would be happy to help with my brothers while she took care of me. But Tosh got very sick right after I was born and the best doctors were back home in Seattle, so she returned there with him.

"So you and Seichi stayed with your grandparents?"

"Seichi did, but she hired someone in the village to care for me. A wet nurse."

"I see." *I wonder what the funny part is,* Margaret thought.

"Tosh was sick for three years," Mitsuye continued.

"Then my parents offered to pay for a couple to sail to Japan on their honeymoon if they would get Seichi and me and bring us home."

"Tosh seems robust enough now. Your mother must have done a good job nursing him."

"Yeah, it's Seichi who came down with TB, but that's another story. Anyway, our *Baba* didn't want to give Seichi up right then, so I came back to Seattle by myself—that is, with that couple. By then I was a little girl. When I arrived Mother couldn't believe I was her daughter because I was so brown and ugly, not like the pretty, white-skinned baby she remembered. The first thing she did was look for my birthmark on my shoulder, and when she found it, she had to accept I was her daughter."

"But I'm sure—"

"Then she was afraid I was deaf and dumb because I didn't say a word. She decided that I needed to come home in something nicer than the kimono and sandals I wore on the ship, so we stopped at a shop in Japantown. When we were in the shoe department, all of a sudden I shouted, '

Margaret had spent many years justifying the behavior of Issei mothers to their adolescent daughters, but now she was at a loss for words. Did Mitsuye expect her to laugh?

At that moment Father Joe breezed into the office, saving Margaret the trouble of figuring out an appropriate response. "Hello, Mrs. Peppers. Hello, Mitsuye. I apologize—my meeting with the Administration ran late. How to get people who have been here all along to want to share barracks with new people they have never met, and so on. Well, Mitsuye, I want to hear what you think about whether there are two sacraments or seven sacraments. Shall we go into the chapel and discuss this?" He gestured to the younger woman to accompany him to the rear of the office building.

Margaret knew Mitsuye's and her brothers' days at Minidoka were numbered. Tosh was due to leave for Fort Douglas in the next few weeks, while Seichi had been accepted at the University of Cincinnati. "It's a miracle he wasn't sent to Tule

Lake, because he's a 'no-no' boy," Mitsuye had whispered to Margaret when Seichi's acceptance was announced. "Somehow the Powers That Be overlooked that." Mitsuye was also going to Cincinnati.

I'll miss Mitsuye, even if she is a cutup, Margaret thought. She smiled as she remembered the day Mitsuye had regaled the *senninbari* group with tales of *hinotama* supposedly having been seen behind the hospital where she worked. According to Japanese folk tradition, *hinotama* were fireballs that floated through the air several feet about the ground, embodying the souls of the recently dead. "We never used to hear these stories until the farmers from California came," one Nisei embroiderer had responded scoffingly, but the ensuing conversation among the Issei became so excited that Margaret suspected other corroborating evidence was being offered and weighed. It was a while before she had been able to steer the conversation to a topic more worthy of a Christian gathering.

When Margaret was younger and new to St. Peter's, occasionally a teenage girl would confide about her latest "crush," but these confessions had become a thing of the past. *Now that I'm nearing fifty, they think I'm too old to remember what it's like*, she reflected one day, as she regarded her graying hair in the mirror. *I could at least try a different hair style*, she thought. For years she had settled for winding her shoulder-length hair into a loose bun. It was easy and practical, especially since her hair tended to fly every whichway.

Margaret was not trying to look younger so much as seek some kind of change in her life, however small. She could not shake a gnawing sense of restlessness which had only seemed to grow in the last few months. Maybe it was seeing young people like Mitsuye and Seichi getting ready to leave Hunt for college, never to return. Or maybe it was something else.

One day, when she was visiting Mrs. Yasutake, she overheard Mitsuye and her friend Nora talking and giggling behind the suspended blanket which served as a room divider.

Nora, she knew, was seeing a young man who, like Tosh, had volunteered for the army and was awaiting induction. She wondered if the boyfriend had proposed. Dating and courtship were a challenge behind barbed wire, with so little privacy possible for young couples. The formality of using *baishakunin*, or go-betweens, was still frequently observed in camp, though even before the war only the most traditional Issei still arranged marriages for their children. Instead, most Nisei made their own choices, and so-called *baishakunin* were often friends or family members who arranged matters after the fact.

"They do hair," Mrs. Yasutake observed dryly, nodding toward the girls. "Mitsuye, greet our guest!" she reprimanded her daughter.

"Sorry, Mrs. Peppers!" The girl hastily emerged, clutching a green booklet, *How to Dress Your Own Hair*. "I can't decide between this one"—Mitsuye stabbed a page depicting 'The Back Sweep Pompadour Curl'—"or maybe this one. What do you think?" She flipped ahead to display 'The Wave Curl.'

"Honestly, I think the first one suits you better," Margaret said. "The other one looks a little mature for you."

"That's what I thought," interrupted Nora, who had moved into the barracks "living room" to chat.

"When you are done with the book, do you mind if I have a look at it? I'm thinking of trying a different hairstyle myself," Margaret said.

"Sure, Mrs. Peppers. Say—would you like me to fix it for you?" Mitsuye responded. "I could use the practice. It may come in handy when I'm in Cincinnati, who knows?"

With Mrs. Yasutake's permission, it was agreed that tomorrow after work, Margaret would pick Mitsuye up and take her home to spend the night. That would give plenty of time for hairstyling—and conversation. There was one question in particular that Margaret was burning to ask.

The pockmark-faced military police officer checked his list of approved overnight leaves, waving Margaret and Mitsuye through the gate as dusk began to fall. "I hope you don't mind eating at Wood Cafe—my treat. I didn't have time to shop or fix anything for tonight, but we'll have a good breakfast in the morning," Margaret said.

"Anything besides camp food would be wonderful! Though I may have more sympathy for cafeteria workers after I start my food service job at the University."

"Did they tell you that you couldn't be a student because you were born in Japan?"

"No, I didn't ask. It would be too humiliating."

"I think you should find out, once you're there. I'll bet once they get to know you, they will be happy to have you as a student."

"Seichi and Father Joe say the same thing. In fact, Father Joe has offered to write a letter of reference I can bring along with me. I guess it won't hurt."

Wood Cafe did not advertise in the *Irrigator* like the No Delay Cafe or Campbell's in Twin Falls, restaurants that clearly signaled by their ads their welcome of people of Japanese descent. But Margaret knew that Father Tibesar and the Holy Name Society of Hunt had eaten there without incident. She expected no trouble, and they experienced none.

By the time they finally sat down in her kitchen for the task at hand, Margaret was having second thoughts about sporting one of the hairdos in Mitsuye's book. They all looked too glamorous for a middle-aged church worker. Finally, she picked a "plain wave with curly ends," which, when dried, didn't look overly fussy. She didn't know if Mitsuye would be able to handle it, though—the directions seemed rather complicated.

"What about this?" Margaret asked, pointing to the hairstyle's two pages of instructions and drawings. She expected a confident response from Mitsuye and got it.

"Oh, sure," the girl said, after quickly glancing at the directions. "Let's get your hair wet and then we can begin."

After several attempts at twisting, holding, and shaping

bunches of Margaret's hair into curls, Mitsuye admitted that the book's instructions were easier to execute on one's own hair than on another's. Still, she persevered, her "client" offering an encouraging word from time to time until the desired outcome, or at least an approximation of it, had been achieved.

Margaret was patient. She sat musing what it might have been like to have a daughter to share such mundane, yet intimate moments. *How much I've missed!* She tried to push the thought away, but suddenly, as if she were about to be engulfed by an unstoppable wave, she took a sharp breath, startling Mitsuye.

"Are you all right, Mrs. Peppers?"

"Yes—yes. I was just thinking I should have put a little Brilliantine on my hair after I washed it," she lied.

"Oh… I should have thought of that. I guess I should've practiced on my friend Nora before offering to do your hair," Mitsuye lamented. "My mother always tells me, *Mi no hodo wo shire*. It means, 'Know your limits.'" She made a face of mock despair before breaking out in a smile. "I like what my dad says better: *Ki ni mochi ga naru*. Basically, it means there are happy outcomes when you least expect them. Let's say a prayer tonight that your hair will be beautiful in the morning."

Margaret wasn't worried—she knew she could always tame her hair in the morning with a hair net, or resort to her standard bun, if she had to. For now, she needed to tame her emotions. The regrets of her private life should stay that way: private.

"You miss your father a lot, don't you?" Margaret ventured later, as she and Mitsuye sipped bedtime cups of cocoa.

"Yes." Mitsuye paused, and for a moment Margaret wondered if she had probed too deeply. Then the girl blurted out, "I don't understand why they have to keep him in that detention camp. Look at Father Joe—he was in the Japanese Army, and even he's been released. Meanwhile, my father was a translator for the Immigration and Naturalization Service and look where it got him!"

It seemed to make no sense. But what did, these days?

"You know what I miss the most, Mrs. Peppers? It's the talks my dad and I used to have when he came home late at night from a Senryu Kai meeting. When he drove into the garage his headlights would always shine right in my bedroom window and wake me up. He'd come in to talk and he'd always ask me what I was reading. When I got older, my dad let me read books in his library. They were a lot of poetry books—he writes poetry, you know—and we'd talk about them." Mitsuye's face grew somber, and her eyes misted. "The FBI took most of those books away when they came for my dad. They probably burned them.

"And then my mom would come in and make us stop," Mitsuye continued, her voice becoming more agitated. "She'd say, 'What are you doing? It's two in the morning! You've got school!' and hiss at my dad. So, in answer to your question, Mrs. Peppers, I miss my father, but I don't miss the fights he and my mom used to have."

Margaret opened her mouth to say something, but Mitsuye went on. "My mom can't figure me out—or maybe she can, and she doesn't like who I am. When I was a girl, I had to go to *odori*—Japanese dance—and do all that other stuff I'm not interested in. My brothers got to do judo, Boy Scouts, and Drum and Bugle Corps, but I had to become a quiet little Japanese lady. It's not fair!"

"It's hard sometimes for people of your mother's generation to accept that their children—daughters, especially— are Americans and not Japanese. She does these things because she loves you, even though you may not understand it now." Margaret had offered this explanation so often to Nisei girls that she hoped it didn't sound like a rote recitation.

"I suppose so," Mitsuye sighed. She put her cup and saucer on the coffee table and started to rise from her seat, but Margaret stopped her.

"Mitsuye—If you don't mind, I'd like to ask you something. Have you and your mother ever talked about your being raised as a little girl by a foster mother?"

"Well, sometimes I've told her how I don't understand

how a mother could leave her baby with strangers for three and a half years."

"What does she say to that?"

"You mean, after she stops crying? Then she says, 'It was the only thing we could do'—because Tosh had encephalitis, you know. But it seems to me she could've found another way if she'd really wanted to. She didn't have to abandon me."

Abandon. The word throbbed in Margaret's mind like a punishing headache. What could she say to this young woman to justify her mother's actions? Even as she struggled to give a response, she remembered another time, in a garden near Portland, when she had tried—and failed—to explain to her own daughter the terrible choices a mother must sometimes make.

After a beat, she composed herself and looked Mitsuye right in the eyes, staring at her as if Hallie was inside and staring back at her. "You shouldn't be too hard on your mother," she offered in as gentle a voice as she could. "Don't make her feel guilty by bringing this up all the time. It won't make things better for either of you. Someday, when you're a mother, you'll understand."

"I'm not sure I will," Mitsuye said, sounding doubtful.

"Oh, you will," Margaret responded, softly. *Someday, Hallie, you will.*

CHAPTER 63

The stars had not yet disappeared when Margaret's "Big Ben" alarm clock jolted her awake. *Six-fifteen*, her bleary eyes read. Sunrise was still two hours away. But there was no lingering in bed this November morning; today she was going to drive Father Joe and Lay Reader Frank Watanabe on a tour of farms in southern Idaho and eastern Oregon, to meet with and encourage Nikkei Episcopalians living outside the confines of Minidoka. And in the evening, she'd be staying with Azalia Peet, the Methodist missionary who had followed some of her Gresham, Oregon, Nikkei farmers to an agricultural camp in the eastern part of that state.

This was not Margaret's first visit to the agricultural country along the Snake River. During the summer she and the Shigayas had visited the scattered settlements of former White River Valley Nikkei who had been given early release from Tule Lake. For Margaret, it had been a bittersweet reunion. The joy of seeing so many she had known at St. Paul's was tempered with the knowledge that these people, though free from WRA camp restrictions, were not free to return to the valley they had once called home.

Margaret and her companions had many miles to cover, and they needed an early start. By seven o'clock Father Joe was waiting at the gate house, smoking a cigarette and chatting with one of the guards. Frank Watanabe would join them later in Emmett, northwest of Boise: he was one of the St. Paul's folk who had found a farm where he, his wife, and four sons could live and work year-round.

"Did you get something to eat, Father?" Margaret asked, hoping they wouldn't need to stop at a diner along the way.

"Yep," answered Father Joe, whose grasp of colloquial English was becoming better each day. "I ate something in my room rather than stand in line for another greasy breakfast. How about you?"

"Oh, toast and coffee, as usual." After waiting for the military police to raise the guard rail and allow them to exit the camp, she turned from Hunt Road onto the highway. "I'm really looking forward to seeing all the St. Paul's families. They seem so neglected in comparison with the St. Peter's congregation. I mean," she quickly added, "since they moved out of Tule Lake. I know Father Dai did his best by them."

"It's too bad my brother couldn't have come on this visit," Father Joe said. Earlier in the month Daisuke Kitagawa had spent a few days at Minidoka on his way to Cincinnati, where he hoped to begin new pastoral work among relocated Nikkei. Father Dai's former Seattle and White River parishioners had greeted him fondly and sponsored several parties in his honor. People came who were not Episcopalians, or even Christian, for the priest had helped many during his time at Tule Lake.

"When I think how Father Dai managed to get out of Tule Lake just before the riot—"

"I think 'riot' is overstating it. You heard Stafford say the papers were blowing it all out of proportion. But it's true that my brother was seen as a collaborator by some Kibei. Who knows what they might have done in time. All in all—is that the expression?—I'm thankful that God took care of him and made it possible for him to leave when he did."

Margaret still didn't understand why God seemed to take care of some, like Father Dai, and not others, like Florence Shoji, but she nevertheless agreed with Father Joe. It must have been Divine Providence that paved the way for the priest to leave that troubled WRA camp before violence erupted.

"I got to know Watanabe-*san* when we were together at

Santa Fe," Father Joe recalled after a while. "I never understood why he was sent to a Department of Justice camp, but I could say that for most people imprisoned there. He used to come to my Bible study class, and we would talk afterwards. He missed his family very much. I am glad they are together again."

Descending into the Emmett Valley along a steep, winding drive, Margaret was reminded that without water, virtually all of southern Idaho would be like the sere hills that nudged the road. Here, a series of irrigation projects, culminating in the Black Canyon Dam on the Payette River, had done its transforming work, making the valley Idaho's most important cherry growing region. The orchards, their dead leaves scattered like feathers from a flock of plucked chickens, stood on a bench above the town. They'd arranged to meet by the county courthouse, a two-and-a-half story Art Deco concrete building that was a legacy of the New Deal. From there, Frank Watanabe would guide them to his farm.

Margaret remembered Frank—or Fred, as he was sometimes called, though his given name was Tokuzo—mostly as the father of four rambunctious boys who had fidgeted, jiggled, and squirmed their way through Sunday School classes at St. Paul's. At the rendezvous point he greeted the visitors with a bow and a smile. With sadness Margaret noted how the ordeal of imprisonment and separation from his family had left its mark on the forty-year-old, in hair turned prematurely gray and a forehead creased with worry-lines.

Nevertheless, for Nikkei living in the West, Mr. Watanabe and his family were fortunate. The leased white farmhouse he led them to was in good repair, with two bedrooms and indoor plumbing. Its owner had been drafted into the army, and his wife and child were living somewhere else with her parents. Other Nikkei farmers they would visit lived in less commodious quarters and worked under the supervision of white overseers.

"I am honored you are my guests," Mr. Watanabe said, as he opened the front door, inviting Father Joe and Margaret inside. Mary Jane Watanabe hurried out of the kitchen to greet them before disappearing once more while her husband carried on a conversation in an amalgam of English and Japanese. "My wife—she is Nisei and speaks English better," he apologized.

During a lunch of tofu and vegetable *okazu* and rice, the two women conversed in English at one end of the table, while the men spoke in Japanese at the other. Since Mrs. Watanabe and her sons had been sent to Tule Lake rather than Minidoka, there was news of the children to catch up on; Margaret sensed that the past difficulties of family separation was a topic to be avoided.

"The children all go to school in Emmett?" Margaret asked.

"Oh yes, and they're better schools than the ones at camp," Mrs. Watanabe responded. "I'm sorry you've missed seeing the boys because it's a school day. They'll be so disappointed."

"I'm sorry, too; next time we'll have to arrange to come on a Saturday." Margaret paused, before asking gently, "Do the other school children accept them?"

"Well," Mrs. Watanabe admitted, "for most children, it's their first experience of Japanese Americans. A couple of times one of the boys has come home with a black eye, but then there were fights even among the kids at Tule Lake, so I don't know for sure what really happened. I don't get a straight answer when I ask. Richard—he's fifteen—is watching out for his younger brothers, and I think by now all the kids in town know it. It will be all right." Before Margaret could respond, the hostess excused herself to get a jar of home-canned cherries from the pantry for dessert.

"Are these from your orchard, Mrs. Watanabe?" Father Joe asked.

"Yes," she replied. "We are very fortunate. And Father, speaking of good fortune: I wish you could see our new church. Maybe you passed it in town—it's St. Mary's. The rector has made us feel very welcome, and he's invited Henry, James, and Arthur to become altar boys. We can hardly believe we're able to worship in a real Episcopal church, with stained glass windows and everything. So different from worshipping in a barrack!"

"But we do miss Father Dai," added her husband.

"We all do," agreed Father Joe and Margaret, in unison.

Twenty minutes later, with Father Joe beside her and Frank Watanabe in the back seat, Margaret pulled away from the clapboard farmhouse, her automobile tires crunching the gravel like a child devouring peanut brittle.

"Dai wanted us to be sure to check on Kanata-*san*," Father Joe reminded her. "He fell and broke his leg last month. The Mormons who own the farm have felt sorry for him and have taken care of him, so that is good."

While Margaret paid attention to driving, the two Issei men chatted in Japanese. Father Joe occasionally called out directions using a county atlas on which the approximate locations of the farm destinations had been marked, thanks to Margaret's careful notations from her summer visit to the area. It was surprising how the habits she'd acquired as a rural worker in Washington still stood her in good stead.

The places they visited ranged from the tidy leased farms of families like the Watanabes', down to glorified sheds which were little better than the Minidoka barracks, except they had greater privacy. Single men such as young Sus Kanata tended to live in these sheds, though in Sus's case his broken leg had earned him an invitation to recuperate in his employer's home. Some of the men even lived on property owned by the small number of Japanese who had farmed the area for almost a generation.

As night fell they crossed the Snake River near the town of Ontario, Oregon, which had become home to the largest concentration of Nikkei in the state since the wartime exclusion took effect. They ate at a Chinese restaurant—operated by an Issei couple—before going to a bungalow on the outskirts of town, where for the next two nights, Father Joe and Mr. Watanabe would be staying with the local Episcopal priest and his wife. Margaret still had an hour's drive ahead of her before she would reach the converted Civilian Conservation Corps camp that was now home to Azalia Peet and dozens of Nikkei families.

Cow Hollow, here I come, muttered Margaret wearily as she started her car, after saying goodbye to her Episcopal comrades. She checked the driving directions she'd received in the mail from Miss Peet. "It's located near the Old Oregon Trail—so romantic!" the woman had gushed, as if that compensated for the site's prosaic name. "Just take the main road south out of Nyssa and then head west. You can't miss it." *She might as well have said, 'Just watch for the covered wagons,'* thought Margaret with annoyance, as she flipped open the county atlas for more precise information.

At precisely nine o'clock her headlights shone on the cluster of wooden buildings that comprised the old CCC camp. With the aid of a flashlight, Margaret walked to Azalia Peet's apartment, located at one end of the nearest barrack. Light gleamed through an ivory curtain drawn across glass in the upper part of the door. Margaret read the words "Azalia Peet, Missionary" carefully painted on a small wooden sign nailed to the door and knocked twice.

"Mrs. Peppers, do come in! I was beginning to worry that you might have missed our little enclave. I don't drive around here, so I may not have given the best of directions." Miss Peet stepped back from the threshold revealing a simple interior lit by a single electric light, with a table, several wooden folding chairs, a small sofa, a cot and a dresser. Packing crates served as end tables and bookcases. In one of the corners a wood stove burned cheerfully. In its dimensions the room resembled a small Minidoka apartment, but the barracks were shorter here than at Minidoka, with fewer apartments per barrack, and the buildings were clad in wood rather than tar paper. Margaret decided that, at least physically, it would be a more comfortable environment than at Hunt.

"If you don't mind, I'll put your overnight bag on the cot for now," Azalia Peet continued, taking Margaret's little suitcase and placing it on the bed, which was covered with a green and brown patterned spread. "And if you give me your coat, I'll put it in my 'closet' right here." She pulled aside a curtain made of the same fabric as the bedspread, revealing a wooden rod suspended from ropes slung around hooks in the rafter. Margaret's gray trench coat soon took its place alongside a red plaid bathrobe, a few dark-colored dresses, and a navy-blue overcoat.

"Thank you, Miss Peet. You've made this very homey," Margaret said, spying a small cornucopia basket on the table which held an ear of dried corn, a couple of apples, and a few walnuts.

"Please call me Azalia, won't you? And may I call you Margaret? It seems as if we might dispense with the formalities if we're going to be roommates now." Margaret nodded. "My neighbor Mr. Mizote helped me fix things up," the Methodist missionary continued. He and his wife live on the other side of the partition." Azalia pointed her head towards the tent canvas that separated her apartment from the Mizotes'. For the first time Margaret noticed muffled talking coming from beyond the partition.

"I do love the kiddies, but I must say I'm glad there's not a family with a newborn next to me," Azalia said. "There was one when I stayed in the tent camp at Nyssa. The poor wee one had colic and seemed to cry most of the night. How the mother managed to do any work in the fields is beyond me, but the Japanese are a strong lot."

"*Gaman*," murmured Margaret.

"You're right: endurance. It's more than simply physical strength; it's bearing the unbearable. I'd like to see some of these politicians who want to send all 'Japs' back to Japan do a real day's work like the people here!" Azalia's eyes flashed with the same fire Margaret had witnessed when the missionary testified at the Portland hearings. Then she added, "But where are my manners? I get so upset when I think about people like Senator Mahoney that I forget simple courtesy. Would you like a cup of tea?"

Margaret declined politely, hoping to avoid a midnight visit to the latrine. There was no indoor plumbing in the barracks. "Isn't Mahoney the Oregon legislator who wants Congress to cancel the citizenship of the Nisei and deport them and the Issei back to Japan at the end of the war? I read something about that in an Episcopal magazine. I know our denomination has gone on record against him."

"You're right—and the Methodists have opposed him, too. But the forces of racial prejudice are strong. That's what keeps my pen busy—writing to the newspaper, the Governor, even Mrs. Roosevelt."

"Mrs. Roosevelt?"

"Well, you know she visited the Gila River camp in April and wrote about the loyalty and industry of the Nikkei interned there."

"Yes, I read about it in the *Minidoka Irrigator*."

"Well, I was hoping she might visit us here in the Northwest. You know, see how this CCC camp is being put to a new use. How much the Nikkei here are doing for the war effort—helping to feed the nation, raise and harvest a crop like sugar beets that will be used in munitions, and so on. I sent her a letter and suggested she might come to dedicate the Minidoka Honor Roll in October, but she wrote back and said that unfortunately she had other commitments."

"She wrote you?" This was more surprising news to Margaret than Azalia's knowing that a display panel had been erected near the Minidoka camp entrance to honor Hunt's Nisei serving in the military.

"Yes—would you like to see the letter? I have it here somewhere."

Margaret wearily considered her answer. All she wanted to do was to go to bed, even if it meant she'd be lying in a semi-illumined room, should her hostess not be ready to retire. It was nearing eleven p.m., but Azalia still seemed full of energy. "Thank you, but if you don't mind, I think I'll get ready for bed.

Do you mind pointing me to the latrine building?"

"I'll do better than that—I'll go with you. I should be going to sleep myself. Tomorrow, I have a mothers' crafts group meeting here and I still must do a few things in the morning to get ready."

Azalia was already bustling about the room when Margaret's alarm clock jangled her awake at six a.m. After dressing quickly, she hurried to the latrine, noticing that a line was already forming outside the mess hall for breakfast. She wondered if she was going to eat there or in Azalia's apartment.

"Even though I'd like you to meet some of my Japanese friends, I thought you might want to eat here," Azalia said after Margaret returned, answering the deaconess's unspoken question. "I know you need to leave in good time to pick up your companions. I like to have toast and Postum for breakfast, and I have a jar of peaches Reverend Shaver, the Methodist minister, gave me. But if you'd prefer coffee and something else hot to eat, we'll trot over to the mess hall."

"I'm happy to eat here, if it's not too much trouble." Margaret imagined the sight of two ladies on the far side of middle age "trotting" and had to squelch a giggle.

"Jane Chase wrote me about the nursery school you ran to help the mothers working in the fields," Margaret said later, sipping her second cup of tea. She had never learned to like the molasses-flavored coffee substitute that Azalia drank for breakfast.

"Yes, it was something I knew how to do—I ran kindergartens in Japan, you know. It was great fun. See this curtain? I used to pin pictures of children at school, at play, and at prayer onto it, and one picture of Jesus with little children around him. We had toys and games, but the favorite activity was when I would bring out my tiny folding organ—there it is, in the corner—and we'd sing songs. Then we'd end with a simple prayer. Some of the children were Christian, but many came from Buddhist families. I didn't proselytize—in fact, some of the most grateful mothers and grandmothers were Buddhists."

"Why don't you have a nursery now?"

"So many of the families have left to live on farms that there aren't enough children. There are a few kiddies still here that I care for from time to time so their mothers can have a break. Of course, on Sundays I teach Sunday school, which I love. But now I have more to do with high school youth and young married women. And college-aged youth; I've been writing a lot of recommendations for Nisei who want to continue their education."

"I do that, too, for some of our girls. Father Joe spends hours at it."

"Well," said Azalia with a smile, "with you Episcopalians it's the priest who really counts, isn't it?"

"I wouldn't say that–" bristled Margaret.

"And the priest is *always* a man."

"So are your ministers!"

"All right, all right!" laughed Azalia. "I think we can agree that both our denominations have a way to go to recognize that women can and should be leaders. But then I speak as a graduate of a women's college, where we were indoctrinated as to our rights and responsibilities as leaders of the next generation. And by the way," she added with a twinkle. "I did attend an Episcopal church now and then when I was at Smith. It seemed more interesting than the Methodist Church in town—maybe because I had a crush on the curate."

"Father, may I ask you something?" The Nikkei farm tour completed, Margaret and Joe Kitagawa were headed back to Minidoka.

"Sure—fire away."

Margaret kept her eyes on the road as she considered how to phrase her question. "How can you forgive the people—that is, us Americans—who said you were our enemy? Who made you leave seminary and go to a prison camp in New Mexico? Who sent you to a place like Minidoka?"

Father Joe was quiet for several minutes before he spoke. "Mrs. Peppers, I hope I won't disillusion you when I say that I try to forgive America for what has happened to me and to the Nikkei, and if I keep it on an impersonal basis—'the American people,' rather than specific individuals, I can convince myself I am living as our Lord would want me to. But it's harder when I encounter out-and-out racists personally, or even read what they've said or done. And harder still when I witness the suffering of my fellow Nikkei that has been caused by such hate-mongers. Sometimes I think that Jesus, knowing how his dear friends would be tortured and killed, must have had struggled more to forgive those perpetrators than to forgive his own killers. It's harder to watch people we care for suffer than to suffer ourselves.

Like me witnessing the Shojis suffer, Margaret thought.

"Did I ever tell you what happened to me when I was in the Japanese Army?" Without waiting for Margaret's answer, he continued. "I had intended to go to seminary in the United States, but my departure was delayed because of my father's illness. Before I was able to leave the country, I got drafted. Suddenly I found myself in China, part of the invasion force. I was the only Christian in my platoon. One day—it was sunny, though bitterly cold—I came upon a badly wounded Chinese soldier."

Father Joe paused, brushing the back of his hand over his eyes. The movement was so quick that Margaret wasn't sure that she hadn't imagined it. "He thought I was going to kill him, so he made the sign of the cross. When I saw that, I made the same sign to show him that I, too, was a Christian. Then I knelt and gave the man a drink from my canteen."

Margaret gripped the steering wheel and held her breath.

"The Chinese soldier began to pray the Lord's Prayer. My parents had been missionaries in Formosa, and I knew Chinese, so I prayed with him. When we reached the phrase, 'Thy will be done' he died. I finished the prayer alone."

She exhaled slowly, then inhaled again and held her

breath, sensing more to the story.

"It wasn't until then that I really understood the doctrine of the Incarnation. It isn't just that Jesus was born as a human being two thousand years ago. Jesus looked at me through the eyes of my enemy that day in China, and he looks at me in the eyes of those I'm tempted to call my enemies today. If I hate them, then I hate my Lord and Savior."

"What did you do after that? Did you stay in the army?"

"I thought of deserting, but if they caught me, I knew I'd be killed. No, I prayed to God to find me a way out. And He did—I caught malaria."

The priest turned to regard Margaret who, sensing his movement, turned to look at him. Then he said quietly, "Miracles do happen, Margaret. I know they do."

Chapter 64

She was in New York City when the news broke near the end of January 1944. "5,200 Americans, Many More Filipinos Die of Starvation, Torture, After Bataan," the *New York Times* headline bellowed. Her scrambled eggs and bacon sat half-eaten as the words "buried alive," "murdered," and "March of Death" swam before her eyes. When she'd finished reading the joint Army-Navy report of atrocities, she stumbled out of the Chelsea Hotel restaurant and fled to her room, a futile attempt to escape the images of horror swirling in her mind. For the victims, she began to recite the ancient committal prayer: *Rest eternal, and may light perpetual shine upon them.* For the perpetrators, she could not yet pray.

Scarcely had her brass key clicked in the lock when the thought gripped her: *What about Lizzie Whitcombe and the other Bontoc missionaries?* Last week *The Living Church* reported on the Episcopal and other western internees at Camp Holmes near Baguio. According to the article, food was adequate, and there was even a hospital and school of sorts. Margaret had not heard from her friend Lizzie for two years but had been reassured by what she'd read. Now, she wondered if it was all a lie.

The article had made Camp Holmes sound like a WRA relocation center. To calm her fears, Margaret tried to picture the Philippine location and superimpose on it certain familiar elements of Minidoka, when suddenly another ghastly thought arose: *What will happen to the American Nikkei?* It was easy to imagine a bloodthirsty mob descending on camps like Hunt, intent on retribution. Could the military police offer enough protection?

Settle down, she told herself. *You're letting your imagination get out of hand—the Issei and Nisei at Minidoka will be kept safe, no matter what.* But there were also the thousands of Nikkei who were now living outside the camps, men and women like the ones she was going to be visiting on her five-week trip to the east coast. How would they fare?

She offered a desperate prayer for the people of Bontoc and for all the Nikkei, then hurried to catch a taxi to General Theological Seminary, where she was registered to attend—and speak at—an institute on "The Rural Church and Christian Community Service." If she had to endure such uncertainty, at least there would be comfort in being with like-minded Christian people.

Margaret managed to slip away from the conference long enough that day to send a telegram to Father Joe asking him to write her with news of the camp. In the meantime, she scanned the newspaper anxiously for any reports of violence against the Japanese Americans. The only report she found concerned the arrest of a pair of "vigilantes" who had set fire to a Nikkei farm in California.

Father Joe's letter reached her on her last day in New York. "The camp was shut down for three days," he reported, "and we were all anxious about possible retaliations, but everything is fine. Afterwards, Reverend Andy and I went into Twin Falls to test the waters, and people greeted us as normal. They understand there's a difference between the sadists of Bataan and the people here who saved the sugar beet crop or whose sons are now fighting in the 447th in Europe."

Later that night, over a *sukiyaki* dinner at the Toyo-Kwan restaurant a few blocks from her hotel, Margaret shared the news with Mary and Lily Otana, twin sisters who were studying journalism and education at Columbia. They'd left Minidoka after a few months to finish their education, but their parents were still at the camp, and the sisters were worried.

"We've tried to get Mom and Dad to join us," Lily said,

laying down her chopsticks to concentrate on the conversation. "They say they're too old to uproot. All they know is farming—what are they going to do in a huge city like New York? So, they wait until they can go back to the White River Valley."

"I can't say as I blame them," Margaret said. "But they'll need help when they return. What are your plans?"

Mary chimed in. "Oh, we don't want to go back—at least not to Kent. We've had enough of farming. Even Seattle seems pokey compared to here."

"What about Howard?" Margaret asked, referring to the girls' older brother, now fighting somewhere overseas.

"Oh, he'll go back—after all, the farm is in his name," Mary responded. "And his girlfriend Jenny would make a perfect farm wife. She likes all the homemaking stuff. Howard told me once how she'd done such a good job decorating her family's apartment at Minidoka that the WRA came and took pictures of it for their publicity."

"Better hope you're not stuck writing the women's page when you graduate and get a newspaper job," Lily teased. "I can just see it now: 'Ten Ways to Use Curdled Milk, by Mary Otana.'"

Mary rewarded her sister with a scowl. *It's good to hear people joke for a change*, Margaret thought. *My meetings have all been so serious.* In her mind she was already composing the positive report she'd write to Father Joe about the New York Nisei.

If she were honest, not everything was upbeat. Housing was a problem, especially for families who sometimes had to cram into quarters not much larger than a Minidoka barrack. Interdenominational resettlement committees worked overtime to find suitable jobs and places to live for Nikkei leaving the camps. The WRA discouraged them from congregating in groups, emphasizing the importance of integrating into their new communities and avoiding the "ghetto mentality" that had made them the target of hatred on the west coast. But even in the more cosmopolitan cities of the east, not everyone received these new arrivals with open arms. If the Nikkei took refuge in one another's company, who could blame them?

After five weeks, twenty-two speeches across three states, and many conversations with former parishioners like the Otani sisters, Margaret was ready to rest her city-weary eyes on the sagebrush of southern Idaho. When she finally arrived home, she found a letter from Hallie waiting for her, with a return address of San Bernardino, California. Weeks before Margaret had received Christmas cards from both Hallie and Martina, but neither had mentioned a move. Could Martina have suddenly fallen ill? San Bernardino wasn't very far from the town where her sister-in-law lived. Margaret tore open the envelope and scanned the contents.

> *Dear Mama,*
>
> *You might be surprised to see I moved, but maybe Aunt Martina explained that Uncle Charles has decided to retire in Palm Springs. He's going to raise Arabian horses in Indio! Anyhow, it was time for me to move on and I started to apply for jobs here and there. I wanted to try something different besides working in a doctor's office, and I found a clerical position with San Bernardino County in the Health Department. I started January 10. The pay is not bad and I'm about a half-hour's drive from Aunt Martina in Redlands. I've rented a nice little bungalow which has a view of the mountains. I hope you can come for a visit sometime this year.*

I hope so, too, Margaret thought. How long had it been since she had seen Hallie in her own home? Before the war, before her marriage to John Bauer. It seemed like a lifetime away. *As soon as this war is over, then I'll visit.* But the news didn't suggest it would be over anytime soon. The Japanese army was advancing in Burma, and the Germans had just pummeled London in a devastating night raid reminiscent of the Blitz. She knew that if she was going to see Hallie before the year was out, she would just have to get on the train and go down there herself—no excuses. But for one reason or another, she still put it off.

Years before, at the urging of her movie-mad daughter, Margaret had gone to see Walt Disney's "Silly Symphonies," with its comic-macabre "Dance of the Skeletons." She hadn't thought about the cartoon in years, but one late spring day, as Margaret was sitting through yet another interminable administrative meeting, the image of prancing bones suddenly came to mind.

Is that what we've become—a bunch of dancing skeletons? The camp, its population diminishing steadily due to resettlement and a new order to draft Japanese Americans, was a shadow of its former self. Morale had plummeted, and there had been several worker strikes. Yet the Community Council elections, the arts and crafts exhibits, the baseball tournaments, and the community sing-alongs continued, giving the impression of normalcy.

That night, Margaret vented a little in her weekly report to Bishop Huston.

> *It is so hard trying to find the best way out for so many different types of people, each with different problems. I cannot help but wonder what the future will bring. With all the mental upsets and everything, combined with the uncertainty of what has happened to their relatives in Japan—and not knowing how they would be welcomed back home, judging from the somewhat uncertain welcome they received before Pearl Harbor. Taken all in all, life is a mess for them.*

Putting down her pen, she thought, *I wish I could write these things to Hallie.* But she knew any worries she voiced about the Nikkei would be met with silence, or scorn.

There had always been an undercurrent of grief flowing beneath outward activities of Minidoka, but when the first notices of

Hunt war casualties arrived in July, that grief broke to the surface, though its public expression was muted in accordance with Japanese norms. On July 22nd, the *Minidoka Irrigator* announced the first three Nisei killed in combat; a week later there were five more listed dead. One of them was Satoru Onodera, the St. Peter's lad who had enlisted with his two older brothers early in 1943.

Father Shoji was the first to hear the news from Satoru's parents, as Father Joe was visiting Nikkei in the Midwest. Before the elder priest could tell Margaret, Fumiko Onidera sought her out in the Federated Church office. One look at the young woman's grief-stricken face told Margaret the news was bad.

"Let's sit in the chapel, dear, and you can tell me all about it," Margaret said, drawing her toward the rear of the building where they could be alone. Fumiko sobbed out the story of how her brother had been killed as his company captured the town of Castellina.

"They said he'd be buried at the military cemetery in Italy with full honors, and they're sending us his Bronze star and Purple Heart," Fumiko said, wiping her eyes with the handkerchief Margaret had given her. "I don't want his medals. I want *him*—if not alive, then what's left of him on this earth. I know I shouldn't think this way, but it seems he must be lonely, lying in a country so far away. Bury his medals wherever they want, but bring my *onii-chan* home."

Margaret reached to take Fumiko's hands but instead found herself embracing the distraught woman. She said nothing, letting her own tears offer silent acknowledgement of Fumiko's loss. For the moment, that was enough.

On August 11th, almost two years to the day since the first Nikkei arrived at camp, an interfaith service was held to honor the first nine men from Minidoka to have given their lives for their country. Over the next year, there would be three more such memorials held at Hunt, and another young man from St. Peter's, Frank Masao Shigemura, would be remembered for dying on the battlefield in France. The Church of the Holy

Apostles grieved for their dead and prayed protection for their sons fighting overseas. Meanwhile, more and more gold stars began to appear on service banners throughout the camp.

In December, the Roosevelt administration, having been advised that the Supreme Court would rule against detaining loyal Japanese American citizens, announced that the Nikkei could begin returning to the west coast in January 1945. "That's the end of WRA camps," Father Joe declared to Margaret when he heard the news.

Back home, church groups, social service organizations, and local governments began to prepare for the Nikkei's return. When Minidoka finally closed, Margaret knew she wanted to join the effort.

Chapter 65

Relaxing on the worn maroon armchair she'd brought all the way from Seattle, Margaret flipped idly through the *Time* magazine which had arrived in the day's mail, accompanied by the latest issue of *The Living Church*. A half-page picture of something that looked like a set of tickets, topped by what appeared to be a Japanese yen banknote, caught her eye. "Ever See a Japanese War Bond?" barked the headline below the image.

> *This one belonged to a Japanese soldier who has gone to join his ancestors. But back in his homeland, Japanese civilians are buying other bonds by the millions. One of those Japs is your counterpart—and your fanatical enemy. He hates you and all you stand for.*

It was an advertisement for the latest war bond drive. Margaret, having just come home from donating blood at the Twin Falls hospital, felt she had done her patriotic duty for the day and stopped reading. She had no doubt that many Japanese soldiers did, indeed, bear a virulent hatred toward America. *But I'll bet just as many have no choice but to follow orders and really don't care about us one way or the other. They just want to stay alive.*

She put the magazine aside and opened *The Living Church*. All at once, the words began to ripple before her eyes.

Miss Eliza Whitcombe Dead

> *A letter from Bishop Binstead in the Overseas Department dated May 12th contains the following passage:*
>
> *"I have just received a report from Dr. Manalo, the director of Notre Dame hospital, Baguio, in which Miss Eliza Whitcombe was a patient. He tells me that during the late fall of 1944 Miss Whitcombe failed to respond to treatments and gradually grew weaker day by day until she died a few days before Christmas of 1944. Before she died, she was paralyzed in both legs. I am thankful that she was taken before the hospital was destroyed in the bombing. She was buried in the garden at the rear of the hospital in Baguio."*

"Oh, Lizzie, Lizzie!" Margaret felt suddenly weak, like she had given a quart of blood rather than only a pint. She slumped in the chair, as incapable of movement as her stricken friend, while the mantle clock ticked heartlessly on. Thoughts came in spasms. *The Japs did this to her. She didn't deserve this. Did she die alone? Please God, no.*

The Japs. Had that word really entered her thoughts? It was a term she abhorred, would never use for the Nikkei, and refused to apply to her country's enemy overseas. Until now. Suddenly, all her fine distinctions between the sadistic perpetrators of atrocities and the hapless Japanese foot soldier dissolved, like the salty tears falling on the magazine which lay open on her lap. She remembered Hallie's friend Louise Stanley and how the death of her husband unleashed a hatred toward anyone of Japanese ancestry. Margaret finally understood firsthand the way certain moral distinctions withered under the blast of grief.

Margaret didn't know how long she sat stunned by the news of her friend's death before the habit of decades took over. Struggling to her feet, she went to her bedroom, where the *Book of Common Prayer* lay on a nightstand. For a moment she thought of reading aloud the service for Burial of the Dead. But instead, she turned a few pages before, to the Prayer of Commendation for a dying person, for what Margaret regretted most at this moment was not having been at Lizzie's bedside in her final illness. With a trembling voice she read,

> *Depart, O Christian soul, out of this world,*
> *In the Name of God the Father Almighty who created thee.*
> *In the Name of Jesus Christ who redeemed thee.*
> *In the Name of the Holy Ghost who sanctifieth thee.*
> *May thy rest be this day in peace,*
> *and thy dwelling place in the Paradise of God.*

When she put down the book, she seemed to see Lizzie's face, and then—miracle of miracles!—her own Hal's, somehow superposed upon it. And each of them was smiling.

Chapter 66

November 1945, Portland

When Minidoka finally closed in October, Father Joe boarded the last train out of camp, and Margaret was left to drive herself and her belongings, as well as various church supplies, back to Seattle. She spent a few weeks in town, helping herself and her parishioners get settled, but now it was Hallie's turn. The four years since Margaret had seen her daughter seemed like a lifetime.

"Come for Thanksgiving," Jane Chase had kept urging her, and this year she would. Visiting Jane felt like a reward—even considering her friend's less than superlative cooking. She was as close to family as she had at this point.

By prearrangement, Margaret had brought a basket with rolls, canned cranberry sauce, and an apple pie, to supplement Jane's boiled chicken and vegetables. It was a mildly unconventional Thanksgiving menu, but that didn't seem to matter. It was just good to be together again.

Rain drummed on the windowpanes of Jane's apartment as the two friends faced one another across the mahogany dining table that night. A pair of white tapers cast a convivial light, glinting off the small golden cross Jane wore at her neck. It was the only adornment to her simple green woolen dress. Margaret, dressed in a lightweight navy sweater and matching skirt suitable for a California climate, wore a string of pearls, a long-ago gift from Myrtle and Julia. Each time she wore them, she remembered her Fairy Godmothers with affection.

Margaret rested her fork on her now-empty dinner plate and said, "It's hard to believe it's all over, Jane. Even after several weeks in Seattle, when I wake up and hear the rain, I still think, 'I'd better put on my galoshes because otherwise I'll be mired in Minidoka mud.' You remember how it was when you visited." She added a scant half teaspoon of sugar to her cup of coffee before taking a sip. Even though V-J Day had put an end to many restrictions, sugar was still subject to rationing.

"I'll never forget it," Jane responded. "The Nikkei who've returned to Portland still talk about the mud—and the dust."

"How do you feel about Bishop Dagwell's decision not to reopen the Epiphany Japanese mission?"

"You really want to know? Well, I think he's wrong. The church leadership seems to feel that the day of immigrant missions has passed—that everything needs to be integrated— because otherwise we'll just recreate the ghettos and ghetto mentality that we had before the war, and Caucasian hostility and prejudice will continue."

"That was the WRA view," Margaret interrupted. "They told the people that were relocating back east, 'Spread wide and thin,' hoping that Caucasians would be more likely to accept Japanese Americans if they were only a small minority. But when you've been through what the Nikkei have been through, your community is what sustains you. To destroy that community is wrong."

"As wrong as breaking apart the community in the first place, when the Japanese Americans were forced to leave their homes for the camps," agreed Jane.

"I'm glad that our Bishop Huston decided not to close St. Peter's, even though we don't have a permanent vicar right now. I wish Father Dai would agree to come back, but he and his wife have settled down in Minneapolis, and he's busy helping the Nikkei there get resettled, as well as ministering to a Japanese American congregation."

"And his brother?" Jane asked.

"Father Joe is here only until he's allowed by the

government to move back to Chicago. He's helping a Caucasian priest, Father Andrew Krone, who is temporarily in charge, but Father Krone also has another mission to attend to—a Negro one, located a couple miles away. Father Shoji is seeing to the Issei, just like old times." Margaret thought, *Not quite like old times, for the Shojis had to leave their daughter at the hospital in Idaho.*

"And you're at St. Peter's, too." Jane pointed out.

"Yes, I'm there, though what I'd really like to do is to get something going again in the White River Valley. After living so long in the sticks, it's hard to be back in a city like Seattle, especially the way it's grown and changed. I tried to talk the Bishop into letting me live at Father Dai's old cottage at St. Paul's mission, but he says no, it's a wreck. And so few Nikkei families have dared return to the Valley—the prejudice against them is something ferocious."

"What was it like at Minidoka at the end?" Jane asked, after placing a generous slice of apple pie before her guest.

Margaret grew somber. "It was awful. The Administration did everything in its power to get people to leave. Don't get me wrong—I understand that they had a deadline to meet, but the tactics they used toward the end were almost inhumane. On October 1st, laundry rooms and latrines started to be closed, even though people still lived in nearby quarters. A bunch of mess halls had already been closed, so that in the final weeks, there were only four open for the entire project. People who hadn't yet made relocation plans got moved from barrack to barrack. Each time a barrack was emptied, the electricity was shut off, so the camp got darker and darker."

"I read that some Issei and Kibei in the camps refused to believe that Japan lost the war," Jane said.

"Yes, there were people who thought it was all American propaganda, that *Life* magazine had faked the photos and such. They didn't want to leave because they expected the Japanese Army would be marching up to the gate any day to liberate them. It was pitiful."

Margaret shook her head, remembering how it was. "You

know what I think the most pitiful thing was? The people who were so afraid to leave that when they were put on the train— you know everyone was given $25 and a train ticket to a destination of their choice—they immediately got off on the opposite side. The authorities soon caught on to that stunt. I heard that one old woman tried it so many times they actually handcuffed her to her seat."

"But you and Father Joe stayed to the very end," Jane said, reaching across the table to touch her friend's arm.

"Yes, we did. It was the right thing to do."

Jane seemed to sense that Margaret had said all she cared to about the final days at Minidoka. She got up to clear the dishes, refusing her friend's help. Alone with her thoughts, Margaret remembered the last time she had stepped inside a Minidoka barrack.

It had been one of the last to be abandoned, and there was a strange mix of life and death. The doors to the building were all open, and they swayed noisily on their hinges as the wind blew. Many of the windows were open, too. When one suddenly slammed shut because of the draft, she'd jumped, her heart pounding. Beside one of the stoves there was a neat stack of kindling, as if the occupants had been forced to leave just as they were building a fire.

In her mind's eye, Margaret saw again the apartment where the wood had been ripped from the walls, ceilings, and even the floor, probably to build crates for shipping belongings. But to her the most forlorn apartment was the one which had been occupied by a family with small children. She could still see the foresaken ragdoll and the toy wagon made from a rusty Folger's coffee can and scraps of lumber.

Wherever did that can come from? There weren't any metal coffee cans during the war. And the child, or children, who'd played with these things—where are they now? Are they laughing and running free? Do they miss Minidoka sometimes, because until a few weeks ago, this place was their first and only home?

As Margaret gazed out the darkened window, her wonderings swirled like the night mist. She took no notice of her friend, who had slipped silently beside her. Outside, a lone car was making its way cautiously down the rain-soaked street. Like the vehicle's receding lights, her questions disappeared, unanswered, into the gloom.

"You said Father Joe is back in Seattle for a while?" Jane asked the next morning, over a breakfast of Cream of Wheat and coffee.

"Yes, but we don't really know for how long. There's some red tape involved in getting permanent residency in the U.S., and until then, Father Joe has to stay here. Right now, he's busy getting a community center set up at St. Peter's, with a real gym, where there can be basketball tournaments, boys' and girls' drill teams, that sort of thing."

"Did the high school gym at Minidoka ever get finished?" Jane asked. "Seems like it was taking a long time."

"No, it didn't, and that was too bad. I think that contributed to some of the problems we had with teenagers, especially in the last two years. Kids that age have to let off steam." Margaret took a couple of bites of cereal before laying down her spoon. Jane could see she wanted to say something more and waited quietly.

Margaret sighed and began, "I just wish… " Her voice trailed off as she fingered the words in her mind like a hat she wasn't sure she wanted to wear.

"What do you wish, my friend?" Jane prompted.

Another pause. "I—I wish I were more like Father Joe." She was shocked to hear herself speaking these words. "I wish I could bridge two worlds, like he can. It's more than being able to speak the language—he understands Japanese culture, because he comes from it, but he's also young, and clever, and has spent enough time in America that he can be part of that, too."

Jane's response was emphatic. "But Margaret, you've helped so many young Nisei girls grow into women—American women. Didn't you tell me once that Bishop Huston called you their 'second mother,' who understood them better than their own mothers?"

"Yes, but—" Margaret paused, gazing momentarily out the window as she remembered how that once felt like a badge of honor. Then she said, "It's just that these days I feel more kinship with the Issei mothers, somehow. I'd like to tell them not to worry, that their daughters may dance to Glenn Miller and swoon to Frank Sinatra, but in the long run, it's their family that matters, and they'll love and respect their own *okaasan*—their own mothers—long after they've forgotten someone like me."

Jane looked intently at her friend, her eyes softening. "Let's say you *were* miraculously given the power to reassure the Issei mothers in Japanese, do you think they'd believe you?"

"Oh, yes," Margaret answered without a moment's hesitation, "if the Lord gave me the power to speak just the right words—"

"Would you believe *me* if I said that *your* daughter will always love and respect you, her birth mother, no matter what?" Jane persisted quietly.

Margaret replied, even more quietly, "How I wish that were true."

"It *is* true, and if you would just listen to that voice of hope you carry in your heart, you would know it yourself." Margaret heard the note of exasperation in Jane's voice but to her surprise, did not bristle at it. "Don't you see, people like you and Father Joe and Azalia Peet are the acolytes who each carry a lighted candle into the dark church at Christmas midnight Mass. You pause at the end of every row while the person closest to you lights his candle from yours, and he in turn lights his neighbor's candle, until the whole building is aglow with light. There's enough light for everyone—there's enough hope for everyone. Even you."

Even me?

Suddenly, Margaret realized that what she really wanted to be able to say to an Issei mother had nothing to do with an Americanized daughter's loyalty and love. Not even to offer an apology for wanting to cling to the honor of being regarded as the mother of many girls, temporary though that honor might be. No, what she wanted to speak about went deeper than that.

It had to do with shame.

She had seen the shame seared into the faces of so many men and women who'd found themselves behind the barbed wire of Hunt, and it was that, more than anything, which formed the bond she now realized she shared with the Issei. It had taken the emptying of Minidoka, the ebbing away of its tenacious if unnatural life, to reveal what had been there all along, hiding beneath layers of people and activities. In her mind she was addressing the brave, battered Issei. *You are ashamed because of what has happened to you, and you are afraid your children will be ashamed of you, too. What I most want to say is, it's not your fault. You couldn't have known that the country you chose to live and raise your family in would turn against you. You've done your best. You should be proud, not ashamed. For the sake of the children—or as you say,* Kodomo No Tame Ni—*be proud.*

Even as she uttered these silent words, she realized the unlikelihood that shame could be so quickly discarded, like an unwanted coat. After all, she had her own secret garment beneath all the outward trappings of piety and dedication, and she'd worn it so long it was as much a part of her as her own skin. How could she urge another to be done with shame when she could not imagine doing the same herself?

When had her own intricate garment of shame begun to take form? She thought back to her childhood, to the schoolboys who mocked her and her family relentlessly. But there were other reasons for her shame: the shotgun marriage, the withering of her love for Hal, her failure as a mother.

"Margaret, are you all right?" Jane's voice sounded like a distant bell pealing.

She looked up, suddenly aware of her friend. At the same time, she relaxed her clenched hands, releasing the napkin she had twisted so much that it resembled a white croissant fallen into her lap.

"I'm sorry—I don't know what came over me," Margaret apologized, holding up the mutilated linen. "I realized I believe in hope for others, but not so much for myself. Maybe that can—*I* can—change." She hesitated, weighing how much to reveal to this dear woman, but the habits of a lifetime of reticence are not easily overcome. It seemed to Margaret that before she could talk about the ridding of shame, there was something she needed to do first.

CHAPTER 67

November 1945, Southern California

At ten o'clock on a balmy, sky-blue morning, Margaret was making her way toward Redlands in her daughter's borrowed car. She had spent a poor night, the resolution she'd felt when she was with Jane having evaporated as she imagined countless ways this encounter might turn out badly. All she told Hallie was that she wanted to catch up with her sister-in-law.

The house was in the older part of town, down the street from the Mission Revival public library building named after one A. K. Smiley, presumably a benefactor. Prompted by the comical name, Margaret composed a little jingle to give herself courage: *Take a cue from him—don't be so grim!* She repeated it to herself as she walked up to the front door of a white, one-story clapboard house dating from the turn of the century. Pasting a smile on her face, she pushed the doorbell button, and before the abbreviated Westminster chime had finished sounding, the door opened, revealing a tall woman in her late sixties.

"Margaret, how good to see you!" Martina declared. "I'm glad you called me—it's been far too long." She extended her hand in welcome and seemed surprised when Margaret clasped it for a moment in both of her own. "Won't you come in?" As she stepped to one side, a ray of sunlight glinted off the gold-framed glasses framing her pale blue eyes.

The living room was furnished in the Colonial Revival style which had been popular two decades ago. At her sister-in-law's invitation she sat down on the blue and white floral-patterned davenport, while Martina excused herself to fetch some refreshments.

"I'm afraid I can't drink coffee any longer—it keeps me up at night no matter how early I have it—so what I have to offer is either tea or Sanka. Which do you prefer?" she called from the kitchen.

"I'll have a cup of tea, please," Margaret responded.

"Wonderful. I'll get the kettle going and then come join you."

When she returned Martina was carrying a tray with cups and saucers and a plate of vanilla creme sugar wafers. "I do love these," she said. "I always give them up during Lent, but as soon as Easter arrives, I start in with them again. Although I did cut back during the war, out of patriotism." She passed a cup and saucer and the cookies to Margaret, who helped herself to one. Excusing herself once more, Martina returned with the teapot and began to pour. Her hostess duties accomplished, she sat down in a nearby rocking chair and resumed her chatter.

Martina never seemed very talkative before, Margaret thought. Her eyes took in the room, where every pillow, every knick-knack was placed just so. A framed photograph of Hallie in her high school cap and gown hung to the left of the china cabinet, while another large picture of Hallie as a child shared the fireplace mantel with a pair of Staffordshire dogs. Margaret's fingers itched to pick up the image of her young daughter, but she remained resolutely in her seat.

"… It was difficult when I moved to San Bernardino to help my brother, and Ruth stayed in Los Angeles. Now that she lives in Redlands, we're just a few minutes' drive from each other. But you found that out for yourself this morning, didn't you?" Martina didn't seem to expect an answer, for she continued talking about how she preferred not to drive at night anymore because of how poorly lit everything was. "My doctor says I'm getting cataracts. I hope I won't go blind—I do so love to read."

Margaret took another sip of her tea while she studied

her sister-in-law. Despite her professed love of wafer cookies, Martina had not grown plump over the years, only a bit less angular. Her hair, medium-brown when Margaret first came to know her, was now the color of a weathered Iowa barn.

"Martina," Margaret found herself saying, "do you happen to have any photos of Ruth Hal when she was younger? I noticed a couple on your mantel I'd like to see." She began to rise, intending to walk over to the pictures, but Martina motioned to her to stay and said, "I'll get them. Just sit and relax."

Relax? We're both wound tighter than a drum, thought Margaret, who shifted uncomfortably in her seat, wishing she could at least move around a little. The room had begun to feel like a prison cell.

"Here we are," Martina said, returning with a leather photo album featuring a painted cover image of an Indian in a feather headdress. She sat down next to her sister-in-law and opened the album carefully.

The first photo was taken in 1918, a month after Margaret had left for the Philippines, and it showed an apprehensive-looking seven-year-old standing in front of her new school. The last photo was a bridal portrait. Margaret had a copy of that one, but Martina had shared only a few of the rest with her over the years. Each image was captioned in her sister-in-law's precise lettering: "RH dressed for Halloween," "First Communion," "Santa Monica pier," "Off to camp!"

She gazed at each photo hungrily, like a child with her nose pressed against a bakery shop window. Sometimes she felt a stab of recognition, when she saw a photo, or one similar, that Martina had enclosed in a Christmas card. Just as often it was a stab of pain. She had missed so much! She knew just how returning soldiers must have felt when they came home to lay eyes for the first time on a son or daughter they'd never met. Only she was a mother—*Hallie's first mother*—and the time she'd missed had been far longer, the experiences she'd been robbed of vastly greater in number. Really, there was no comparison.

It's now or never. "Martina—" Margaret spoke the name slowly, as if uttering it for the first time. "There's something I need to say to you." She turned to face her sister-in-law. Martina looked back warily, her thin lips clamping together as she abruptly shut the photo album. Somewhere, the *flit-flit* of a lawn sprinkler began a slow counterpoint to the rapid beating of Margaret's heart.

"Martina," she repeated, "I want to say that I'm sorry."

Hurry, before I lose my nerve. "I'm sorry for resenting you all these years because you got to be the one to bring up my daughter. And I'm sorry for not seeing that you really did love Hallie, and that you didn't keep her just because you hated me."

"Of course I–" Martina began to protest, but Margaret continued, her voice gaining strength. "I understand myself better now. I didn't want to be her second mother, but her first and only one. I wanted to be the most important person in her life." She paused a moment, then added, softly and deliberately, "And I blamed you for my inability to do that."

For a long time, Martina said nothing. It seemed as if her gushing well of words had suddenly run dry.

"I forgive you, if that's what you want," the older woman said at last, squeezing out the sentence like toothpaste from a nearly empty tube.

Margaret took a breath, as if preparing for the deepest plunge of her life. She breathed out her words like a benediction: "And I forgive you, too, Martina, for keeping Hallie for yourself."

In the silence which followed, Margaret got up and walked to the fireplace. Cradling the framed photo of her daughter, she brushed her thumb gently across the little girl's cheek before returning the picture to its place. Then she turned to go back to the Hallie that awaited her.

CHAPTER 68

They'd been sitting at Hallie's kitchen table, lingering over morning coffee. When Hallie got up to show her mother the new skirt she'd made, Margaret decided to follow. Too much sitting didn't help her arthritis.

Intent on retrieving the garment, Hallie seemed unaware that Margaret was with her in the bedroom. When she scooted a few clothes to one side of the closet rod, suddenly there appeared an infant's white dress trimmed in lace. At the sound of her mother's exclamation Hallie whirled around in surprise. Coloring, she stammered, "I—I just couldn't keep any wedding presents after John died. I gave them all away, but I saved the Bontoc lace from your pillowcases. I'm sorry I ruined your gift. Don't be mad."

"No, dear, I'm not mad—I just didn't expect to see the lace at all. And I do understand why you might not want to keep things around to remind you of your wedding." Stretching out her hands toward her daughter, Margaret said quietly, "I'd love to see the dress, dear. You made it for your little girl?"

"Yes, I did," Hallie answered, carefully removing the garment from its hanger and placing it in her mother's hands. Together, they sat down on the bed, as Margaret admired how well Hallie had embellished the puffed sleeves, collar, and yoke with the fine Bontoc lace.

Hallie turned her gaze to the window before them and began to speak in a voice that sounded as if were coming from far away. Her eyes were rimmed with tears. "I made this before Patsy was born—I wanted her to be christened in it. Then, when

Patsy was—taken to Heaven—I was going to bury her in the dress, but it was too big, and Aunt Martina wanted me to use a dress she'd bought. So I did, but I couldn't let this one go. Every once in a while I take it out and look at it and think of my little girl."

"Oh, Hallie–" Margaret drew her daughter into a tight embrace. "I'm so, so sorry," she murmured, stroking her hair.

In a little while Hallie pulled gently away, dabbed at her eyes, and continued. "As Patsy's first birthday got closer, I was having a tough time. Didn't want to get out of bed and go to work, didn't feel like seeing anybody or doing anything but sleep. I used to make myself go to Uncle Charles's office each day. Then I thought, 'Why not make Patsy a dress for her first birthday?' When I was pregnant, I dreamed about how I'd dress her, what colors she liked—pink and yellow, my favorites, of course—how I'd fix her hair, that sort of stuff. So, I got some pretty fabric and a pattern and sewed. Do you want to see it?"

"Of course I do!"

The pink and white seersucker dress was in a similar style, but slightly larger, with a white piqué collar and sleeves. "I told my friends I was making it for a cousin. I didn't want them to think I'm looney," Hallie explained. "It really did help me at the time, but I don't need to keep it—not like the christening dress. Maybe you want to give it to one of your girls?" She picked up the dress and started to hand it to Margaret.

"*You* are my girl, Hallie. Always and forever." Margaret wanted to shout it from the housetop but kept her voice low.

Hallie started as if her mother had indeed cried aloud. "But you had so many children," she half-whispered. "I felt I didn't count. Otherwise–"

"Otherwise I wouldn't have left you?" Saying those words tore at Margaret's heart, but they needed to be said.

This time, Margaret didn't try to explain. Just listen.

"I was so jealous, for so long. You and your savages. People took it for granted that Martina was my mother, and sometimes I didn't bother to correct them. Do you remember that time we went to that park in Portland?" The words were pouring out of Hallie like hot oil. "I was so angry and sad that *I* couldn't be a mother that I took it out on you. You and the Japanese..."

Margaret willed herself not to interrupt. She understood the jealousy, the grief...

"On December 7, 1941, my little girl was born. DEAD. The day I became a mother was the most important day of my life, and then that bastard Tojo gave the command to bomb Pearl Harbor, and suddenly even my daughter's life—and death—were snatched away from me. The only thing that mattered to everyone was the war. So why should I care about what was happening to the Japanese here, in this country? I guess I felt they should be punished too, because I was suffering. I know it's not very Christian, but that's how I felt."

There was no need for Margaret to say anything. Only to embrace Hallie and let her own tears flow freely, released as from a long imprisonment, joining her daughter's in common tributary to one mighty river of sorrow.

She wept for Hallie, and for all the mothers deprived of their children. She wept for Mrs. Shoji and Mrs. Onodera and Mrs. Shigemura. She wept for the young Nikkei mother back home whose name she did not know, who had hemorrhaged to death because she was afraid to go to the hospital and violate the wartime curfew.

And last of all, she wept for herself.

Finally, after the flood of tears had subsided, Margaret took her handkerchief and tenderly wiped her daughter's face. Later, perhaps, she would tell Hallie that she herself had been jealous all these years, but that she was now free. She would not reveal the ultimatum Hal's family had given her so long ago. But she would tell Hallie that being a mother means wanting the best for her child, though it may bring suffering to herself and even to the child.

And having at last forgiven herself, Margaret would ask Hallie's forgiveness.

CHAPTER 69

January 1947, Redlands, California

Everything was ready. Margaret tucked the farewell letter from Bishop Huston back into her handbag—she had read and reread it several times already, savoring its words of affection and commendation—and dabbed at her eyes, which still teared up whenever she thought of leaving him, his diocese, and the people of St. Peter's and St. Paul's. She had done her work well: the Nisei boys and girls whom she had taught in Sunday school, prepared for confirmation, and advised in youth groups, were ready to be fully in charge. When she'd prayed about her future, God seemed to be saying, *It is time to go to a new land, and a new people.* The Good Shepherd Mission in Fort Defiance, Arizona, had appealed for a deaconess, and she had answered the call.

She would not be working at the main mission but at an outstation in the tiny community of Sawmill, fifteen miles away. How many years ago had she staffed that outstation at Tukukan? At least twenty-five, she calculated. There was something fitting in beginning and ending her ministry as a deaconess by working among indigenous people. For in her bones—which she hoped would ache less in the Arizona climate—she knew that this would be her final posting. She was only fifty-three, and she planned—God willing!—to work among the Navajo as long as she had ministered to the Nikkei.

She smiled to see Hallie deep in concentration as she studied the Texaco map splayed across the hood of her car.

Margaret had been surprised, and inordinately pleased, when her daughter had volunteered to accompany her to Arizona. Hallie would have a long drive back to California, but she was meeting her friend Louise at the Grand Canyon, and they would go back together in Louise's car.

That wasn't the only surprise. The other one was standing next to her, holding a camera.

Margaret hadn't seen Martina since their memorable meeting two years ago. They continued to exchange Christmas cards, always with a brief note, neither woman alluding to what had been said during that visit. Margaret did notice that her sister-in-law had begun sending her birthday greetings, and she had started to do the same. Martina's birthday had been earlier in the month; maybe it was the card mentioning the move to Arizona that had brought her here today. *Has she come to say goodbye to me, or is it really Hallie she is seeing off?* Margaret thought. She realized it didn't matter that much anymore. It was just good to have someone wave you farewell.

Margaret glanced at her watch. *Time to be on the road—we have a long day's drive ahead.* She moved to embrace her sister-in-law, until Hallie suddenly grabbed her hand.

"Aunt Martina, will you take a picture of Mama and me?" Hallie led her mother to the front step of her bungalow, positioning her beside the poinsettia shrub. She slid her hand around Margaret's waist and gave her an affectionate pat.

"Sure," Martina said, "I'm starting a new album, and this will be perfect."

Head held high, Margaret looked directly at the camera and smiled.

Author's Note

…[H]istory writing is always the chance to change the terms in which some are remembered and others forgotten. — Alison Light

I first encountered Sarah Margaret Guthrie Peppers nearly forty years ago as I was researching a book chapter I'd been commissioned to write for the centennial of the Episcopal Church in western Washington. On the alert for evidence of women's contributions to balance what was sure to be a male-focused chronicle of bishops and priests, I was delighted to discover some files in the Diocese of Olympia archives pertaining to deaconesses. Beginning in the late 19th century, this was an officially recognized ministry whereby women who felt a calling to fulltime, paid church work could exercise their gifts in Christian education, social welfare, foreign missions and other "womanly" functions. Deaconesses were often in the vanguard of work in places and among people where the Church had previously little or no presence. Their contributions, however, were frequently overlooked or minimized in official historical chronicles, succumbing to the bias, both in church circles and in society at large, that regarded men as the achievers and women as the helpmates.

A yellowed newspaper clipping from 1942 set me on the trail which has resulted in this book. Entitled "Deaconess Margaret Peppers Hopes to Follow Evacuees," it described the desire of a middle-aged white woman to accompany, into the unknown, a Japanese American, or Nikkei, Christian community with which she had been intimately associated for years. Petitioning the authorities, she was eventually allowed to spend the wartime years working in the Japanese American incarceration camp of Minidoka, also known as Hunt, in the Idaho desert, one of ten War Relocation

Authority (WRA) camps to which some 120,000 west coast Nikkei were unjustly confined. She was the only white woman from the Episcopal Church to work among the incarcerated Japanese Americans as a minister (though at the time, that term would have been limited to ordained men in her denomination.)

Because of space considerations, I only was able to give Margaret Peppers a couple of sentences in my book chapter, but I was determined to learn more, and in the ensuing years I have visited libraries and archives in several states and talked with people from coast to coast. Their names appear among the acknowledgements at the end of this book. What I want to do now is to discuss briefly how much of Margaret's story is factually true and how much is imagined.

I have been faithful to the basic outline of Margaret's life, which began with her birth in Bloomfield, Iowa, in 1894, and ended with her early death in Los Angeles in 1952. By then she was living with her daughter Ruth Hal Peppers Slocum, a fact which, though outside the timeframe of this novel, played a significant role in how I chose to frame Margaret's relationship with her only child.

Behind and beyond the story of Margaret the deaconess—which encompassed missionary service in three settings in the Philippines; several years as the first paid Episcopal "rural worker" in western Washington; more than a decade serving the urban Japanese mission of St. Peter's and its rural counterpart, St. Paul's; four years at Minidoka; and, finally, eighteen months at Good Shepherd Navajo mission in Arizona—there is the story of Margaret's personal and family life. If there were challenges in fulfilling her religious vocation—the story of conflicts with superiors such as the mentally unstable Father Henningsen or the unsympathetic Bishop Mosher in the Philippines can be read in the Episcopal Church's archives—the personal challenges this remarkable woman faced were legion. Raised in a family of precarious economic and social status because of her father's mental illness, Margaret Guthrie's personal fortunes may have temporarily improved with her marriage to Hal Peppers, only to plummet once more when tuberculosis made her a penniless widow at age nineteen, with sole responsibility for a two-year-old daughter, Ruth Hal. If she had been a victim of circumstances before, she was determined now to secure a future for herself and Hallie (a nickname of my own invention) that nothing and no one could jeopardize.

Margaret's choices, however, were limited. In one of her rare surviving letters, written a few years after this critical period in her life, she describes her younger self as lacking any skills to earn a decent living. She was unable—or unwilling—to move home and rely on her mother to help with childrearing. How she came to seek entry to St. Margaret's House in Berkeley, California, and train to become a deaconess can only be conjectured. She had by then transferred her denominational allegiance from the Baptist to the Episcopal Church, perhaps under the influence of her husband's family, as newspaper research reveals Margaret's sister-in-law Martina Jury was an active Episcopalian, at least in later years. What we know for certain is that by 1915 she was enrolled as a scholarship student and living on the Berkeley campus, as required, and that Martina was the one caring for Hallie. Never again would mother and daughter live together—until the final years of Margaret's life.

The relationship between Margaret and Hallie is central to this story, yet the tantalizingly few existing documentary clues require that it be a largely imagined relationship on my part. In another rare surviving letter, written to a missions board executive uncomfortable with the idea of a mother and her child living apart, Margaret explains that her husband's family agreed to educate and support Hallie, but only if the child remained with them. I have recast these words and put them into a letter that I imagine Charles Peppers, who was in real life the eldest of the clan and a financially successful physician, to have written to Margaret, possibly at Martina's behest. We also know from Margaret's correspondence to the missions board that at the end of her first furlough in America she had asked her daughter about returning with her to the Philippines, but Hallie had refused. It's not difficult to imagine Margaret believing Martina had poisoned Hallie's mind against her. The question remains, why?

I have tried to suggest some reasons the Peppers clan might

have looked askance at Margaret marrying into the family and ultimately having sole responsibility for raising the first of the Peppers grandchildren. The roots of the conflict are likely socioeconomic—for instance, Margaret's father John Guthrie did indeed die in disgrace in the Davis County Poorhouse—as well as intensely personal, involving competition between Margaret and her divorced, childless sister-in-law. It may also have been a "shotgun marriage" which united the Guthrie and Peppers families, but that cannot be proven.

Then there is the still greater mystery of Ruth Hal Peppers herself, a mystery likely to persist because of the absence of any living relatives able to speak from personal knowledge. The documented facts of Hallie's life reveal an undercurrent of tragedy that sometimes bears an eerie resemblance to her mother's biography. For instance, both women were widowed very early in their respective marriages, Hallie after less than a year. Hallie's first husband—she remarried sometime in the late 1940s—was a lay evangelistic worker, and while he was alive, it is likely that Hallie may have been involved in his church activities. There is an added tragedy in Hallie's story, in that her only child, a daughter, died as a result of a miscarriage or stillbirth. Lastly, Hallie succumbed to an early death at age 51, Margaret at age 58. The fact that Margaret spent her final days at the home of her daughter suggests that whatever the physical and emotional distance that had developed between them over the years, it had been bridged later in life.

One of my hopes in writing this book has been to shine a light on women, like Margaret Peppers, who deserve recognition but have been relegated to the shadows of history. Anita Hodgkin, Mootie Brookman, Eliza Whitcombe, Jane Chase, Azalia Peet, Helen Ammerman—these were all real people, and I have tried to accurately portray their roles and accomplishments. Of this group, Anita Hodgkin, Eliza Whitcombe and Helen Ammerman can be documented to have known Margaret, but the likelihood the others also knew her is high.

There is one element in Margaret's life where I have taken special care to adhere to documented facts, and that pertains to the experience of persons of Japanese descent in America, especially on the west coast, where anti-Asian racism was the most virulent. Here I have been aided by a wealth of primary sources, in the form of government reports, newspaper coverage, and first-person narratives of Nikkei, especially those living in the Seattle area. Certain incidents which may seem unlikely or exaggerated, such as the violent response to a few Japanese American students trying to attend the University of Idaho, or the proposed scheme whereby white people might informally adopt Nisei children for the duration of World War II, actually happened as described. Similarly, the story of Florence Shoji, whose fragile progress as a severely disabled person was tragically reversed by her incarceration in Puyallup and Minidoka, resulting in her early death, is regrettably true.

But to portray the history of the Nikkei in America, even during the dark times of World War II, primarily in terms of victimhood is to do a disservice to a vibrant and resilient community. Recent scholarship has highlighted many examples of agency and resistance to injustice within the WRA camps, some of which I've chosen to include in this book. Men such as Daisuke and Joseph Kitagawa (real colleagues of Margaret's) worked tirelessly to improve the lives of the Nikkei who, like them, were unjustly confined behind barbed wire, or struggling to begin life anew in a strange environment away from their homes on the west coast. They were aided by many others, including white people like Reverend Emory Andrews (also real), whose commitment to Jesus inspired them to care for the stranger, the poor, and the dispossessed in their society. Readers desiring deeper insight into the lives and stories of the west coast Nikkei and their allies will find a treasure trove in the online resources of the Denshō Project (densho.org).

For Margaret Peppers, what I see as a sense of personal exile from her deepest family bonds intensified her dedication to a vocation to help others in need, especially women and children. As she wrote in one poignant passage explaining her desire to return to the Manila orphanage after her daughter's refusal to accompany her, "It has never been easy nor will it be—but I know that though I may have failed with what is my own I am thereby able to do perhaps far more for those less fortunate ones over there." I believe Margaret's journey of exile, when it intersected with the journey of exile of the Pacific Northwest Nikkei, was transformed into a journey of healing. For the Japanese American community, the healing journey continues, as generations not directly experiencing the trauma of wartime incarceration are nevertheless confronted with its lingering impact. My hope (vain though it may seem in these days of politically incited fear and hatred of the "other") is that never again will the forces that made places like Camp Harmony and Minidoka possible be allowed to prevail, and that America will finally realize its cherished ideals of liberty and justice for all.

> *Teach us to listen,*
> *Teach us to remember,*
> *Save us from forgetting.*

—The Reverend Polly Shigaki
St. Peter's Episcopal Church 110th Anniversary Service, 2018

Acknowledgements

From that long-ago day when I first opened the folder entitled "Japanese Internment" in the Bishop S. Arthur Huston papers at the Episcopal Diocese of Olympia Archives until now, I have been helped by a throng of librarians, archivists, readers, and cheerleaders. Many I am privileged to call friends, and one holds a place in my heart that no words of mine can adequately convey.

As a retired librarian and archivist, I am particularly indebted to those institutions and people who made my historical research possible: the Archives of the Episcopal Church; the Boise State University Libraries; the Episcopal Diocese of Olympia; the Idaho State Archives; the Immigration History Research Archives at the University of Minnesota; the Smith College Libraries; and, last alphabetically but by no means least, the University of Washington Libraries (especially archivist John Bolcer and librarian Theresa Mudrock.) The oral histories conducted by the Denshō organization of Seattle were an important source of first-hand accounts of the Nikkei experience during World War II.

While the St. Paul's mission in the White River Valley is no more, St. Peter's Episcopal Church in Seattle continues its proud tradition of spiritual nurture and service. Insight into the remarkable story of St. Peter's came from many sources, but especially from Jay Shoji, grandson of the Reverend Gennosuke Shoji, and the Reverend Polly Shigaki, who cheerfully made available to me a wide range of primary sources.

I was privileged to interview the surviving children of the Kitagawa brothers: Anne Rose Kitagawa, daughter of the Reverend Mitsuo Joseph Kitagawa, and the Reverend John Kitagawa, son of the Reverend Daisuke Kitagawa. They gave unstintingly of their time, and I am grateful for the insights they provided into the life and character of their distinguished fathers. *Sicut pater sicut filii.*

Fortunate is she to have such a wise and committed group of midwives as I have had attending the birth of this book. My readers Jillian Hershberger, John Kitagawa, Mary Ann Laun, Joyce Ogburn, and Debby Schauffler provided many helpful comments, suggestions, and corrections. Jennifer Kurdyla offered a keen editorial eye at two critical junctures, and Brianne DiMarco at Blue Forge Press has skillfully overseen the final stages of labor. Besides these folk, my cheerleaders have included Stephanie Beaudin, Steve Best, Jenny Cleveland, Diana Di Biase, Evelyn Wemhoff, and members of my community at St. Augustine's-in-the-Woods Episcopal Church in Freeland, Washington. Thank you for never failing to ask, "How is Margaret doing?" and for being genuinely interested in my response.

The generation who personally experienced the trauma of incarceration in World War II Japanese American camps has almost completely passed, and I consider myself supremely fortunate to have known the Reverend David Nakagawa before he departed this life for the next. Never bitter, he was able to transmute his experiences of racial injustice into a lifelong dedication to serving the marginalized. Amid his painful World War II memories of living behind barbed wire in Gila, Arizona, were some brighter ones he shared with me. Among these were his introduction to the Christian ideal of universal love, when as a Buddhist boy he was overjoyed to be included in the distribution of Christmas presents contributed by Christian churches from around the nation. This ideal became the lodestar of his subsequent years of ministry in the Presbyterian church. I like to imagine David and Margaret Peppers trading tales around the heavenly banquet table.

To say this book would never have been completed without the unwavering faith and encouragement of my husband Frank Shirbroun cannot begin to capture the breadth and depth of his contribution. With every step on this journey, he has been my truest companion and my deepest joy.

9 798894 390673